TRAIL TO TIN TOWN

COLTON BROTHERS SAGA

MELODY GROVES

WOLFPACK
PUBLISHING
— EST 2013 —

Trail to Tin Town
Paperback Edition
Copyright © 2023 Melody Groves

Wolfpack Publishing
9850 S. Maryland Parkway, Suite A-5 #323
Las Vegas, Nevada 89183

wolfpackpublishing.com

Paperback ISBN 978-1-63977-749-5
eBook ISBN 978-1-63977-750-1
LCCN 2023931115

TRAIL TO TIN TOWN

CHAPTER ONE

MARCH 1864 — *MESILLA, NEW MEXICO TERRITORY*

James Colton leaned back in the wooden saloon chair, tapped the table and eyed his three brothers. What would they think when he plopped down his three eights and two kings? Lucky again, is what they'd think. In fact, despite some bad times, the entire family had been lucky. But tonight, this poker game, his incessant winning... luck had nothing to do with his success. Skill, pure and simple. James knew how to play poker and tonight was his night. Inside he smiled. Who was he kidding? Skilled he wasn't. Tonight, he was pure-out lucky.

On his left, youngest brother Andy grunted and folded his hand, the cards stacked under his drumming finger. On his right, Luke. This brother, less than two years behind James in the family lineage, was a careful, crafty player. His poker face, which admittedly looked like the others, was in place tonight.

"You gonna play or sleep?" Trace elbowed Luke

sitting on his left. "I'm sprouting cobwebs here." He polished off the two fingers of beer left in his mug.

"Give him time, older brother." James calculated his cards for the millionth time in the last three minutes. "Thinking comes slow for Luke. We gotta be patient."

"Hell, he can't help himself." Andy shrugged. "Ma said he was a slippery little devil as a

baby. Dropped on his head too many times." That family grin, the one their pa passed on to all four boys, stretched his cheeks.

All but Luke snickered. James tilted his head and leaned closer to his brother. What was Luke waiting for? James had the upper hand. No way his brother could beat him. Or could he? James calculated the pot. Twenty-five dollars, maybe a bit more, sat in the middle of the table. His brothers could afford to gamble. The past few months had been profitable for the family.

James considered. Maybe tonight would be the time to mention an idea rattling in his head. But what if they said no? He'd done research, talked to men, ranchers. His brothers couldn't turn down such a chance to get rich. Maybe not rich, exactly, but rich-*er* than now. Yeah, tonight would be right.

Luke fingered two silver coins and dropped them onto the pile of money. "I'll see your raise and call."

More coins spun into the middle. Trace spread his hand. "Two pair." Two queens, a ten, two threes. Not enough to beat James. Next, Luke fanned his cards.

"Read 'em and weep, brothers. Two pairs, kings over jacks." Luke pulled in a drag on his

cigar. A smoky *o* spiraled from his mustache-draped lips. Lines around his eyes crinkled as

he grinned through the smoke. His arms stretched for the money.

"Hold it right there, partner." James reached across the table and smacked Luke's hand.

"*You* read 'em and weep. Full house. King high."

"Looks like you done been taken!" Andy's high cackle cut the tension. "Yep, taken all

your money, Luke. Everything you come in here with. Looks like James learned a thing or two

about card playing."

Money scooped together, James held up the bills. "Can you believe we're playing like

this? Seems hardly likely considering last year we had mostly dust in our pockets."

"And one angry moth." Trace sorted the deck, evening up the edges and turning them all the same way. "One more?"

Heads shook, a mumbled oath from Luke. Andy pushed back from the table bringing his lanky body to its fullest height. James waved the money. "Wait. I have something to talk to you about. An idea." Three pairs of brown eyes turned to him. "Kind of a family business venture, so to speak."

"Only venture this family's taking is home to bed." Trace stood and stretched, his back arching like a cat's. "I still need to walk my rounds, Andy needs to close up here, and—"

"Wait. Hear me out." He would have to voice his idea. It was now or never. James had done a lot of thinking, planning, more thinking, and his plan made sense. Andy, the part-time bartender, could lock up Sam Bean's Saloon as well ten minutes later, and Trace could perform his sheriffing rounds ten minutes later too.

Luke stood, glass in hand. His straight body, shoulders thrown back, reminded James of their pa when he was angry. Losing didn't set well on Luke, and James knew he had beat

him into the ground tonight.

"All right, little brother." Trace grabbed glasses and headed toward the bar. He tossed a glance over his shoulder. "Shoot. What's so all-fire important?"

"Cattle."

If he hadn't been so serious, James would've laughed at his brothers. All three froze.

Heads swiveled toward him. Eyebrows arched.

Easing to his feet, he pointed west. "Cattle. Now that the war's about over, those soldiers and goldfield people in California are hungry. For beef." He sucked in a breath. "And we're in a

position to give them steaks."

Luke pushed in his chair, the wooden legs screeching against the sawdust-strewn floor. "Ah hell, James. I thought you were serious." He glanced at the other brothers. "He look serious to you?"

Heads wagged.

Andy frowned at James. "Hell, we don't know nothing about cattle."

"Not yet." James smacked his hand on the table, hoping his brothers would see his point. They froze at the slap. If he couldn't convince them now, this proposal would be nothing but a shattered dream. He certainly couldn't manage a drive alone. He pulled out all the stops. "But we have money. Enough anyway. And we don't have to understand a lot about cattle. We'll hire men who do." His words spurted out quick, concise. "We'll buy a herd, hire some drovers, cowhands, a trail boss, and wait for our investment to walk to market."

"A cattle drive?" Andy cocked his head, a lopsided smile riding up his face.

"Easiest money we'll ever earn." James pushed in his chair. His gaze travelled from Trace to Andy and rested on Luke. If he could convince this brother, the hot-headed naysayer of the group, then he'd have a fighting chance of seeing his dream. His dream for Morningstar to be happy.

"Where the hell you gonna get cattle?" Luke wedged a cigarette between his lips and spoke over it. "And even if we had the money, where you gonna get an outfit? Wagon for food, extra horses? You're for sure gonna need somebody to cook. Hell, James, somebody to ride along-side those doggies, for weeks on end. And where you sending them, anyway? Got a

contract? How about—"

"Long as we got the money, we can get cattle driven to California." James moved in

closer to Luke. How far would Luke let him push? He'd have to try. "And I'm sure you're wanting to bring Sally and the kids here. I bet you miss your youngsters. You'll be needing a house... with a yard... chickens... a garden. Maybe Sally would move from Kansas if you had all that here."

Silence enveloped the room. Three kerosene lamps hanging on the walls spread yellow glows across the floor, lighting the brothers' faces. James strode toward Trace. "And with you being sheriff and all, your salary is nearly nothing. The bounty from catching those wanted men and collecting taxes doesn't amount to much. Besides, the work could be dangerous. Always a chance you'll get yourself killed. The strain on Teresa must be hard."

More silence. Pairs of brown eyes flitted from person to person.

Trace sighed, stood straight, glanced behind him at

Andy. "All right. If we're dreaming here, I've been thinking about opening a saloon. Me and Andy. He already knows how to pour, and I know how to keep the peace."

Andy tossed the towel on the bar. "You weren't supposed to tell anyone, Trace. Now you've gone and ruined the surprise."

Shrugging, Trace held up a hand. "I know. Sorry. But it seemed—"

"The right time!" James displayed the wide Colton family smile. "See? You'll make enough to open a saloon. Perfect!" He hung an arm around Luke's shoulders. "I've looked into this project. Trust me. We can make it work."

CHAPTER TWO

James pulled the curtain back and stared out the living room window into the darkening world.

Would they ever show up? How long did it take to get your wife and toddler out the door? And how about Andy and Luke? Maybe they changed their minds, weren't coming. James checked his watch, shoved it back into his vest pocket, released the curtain and sighed. They were all a full minute late.

Morningstar, her dark eyes gleaming, set a tray of sandwiches onto a living room side table. "They'll be here." She slid her arms around him and nestled into his chest. "Things'll be all right. I think running cattle is a great opportunity and now that they've had time to think, I'm sure they'll agree." She stretched up and kissed his cheek. "You'll see."

A light rap on the door and then it pushed open. "You in here?" Luke stepped in, shutting the door hard. He hugged Morningstar and shook hands with James.

"I've got a pie ready to come out of the oven." She pointed over her shoulder. "Excuse me."

Luke raised his nose and sniffed. "Smells good." He turned to James. "Forgot what home cooking smells like."

James let a comfortable silence settle.

Luke pried off his hat, ran fingers through his hair. "This cattle idea. Ain't gonna work." Luke paced the length of James' front room. "Don't get why you keep saying it will. Clearly, it flat ain't gonna work. I thought about your little plan. And I sure as hell ain't gonna give you any money to see my dollars blown away in some spring dust storm." Luke pointed his cigar at James' face. "Cattle drive my ass. What the hell're you thinking?"

"I'm thinking this drive's a money-making deal. And the timing's perfect." James fought to keep his anger under control. Of the four brothers, this one, Luke Jeremiah Colton, didn't fit in as well as the others and knew it. They all knew. Yet, there was a charm, an intelligence, and at times, a willingness to work with the family that made him a Colton.

"Right timing? Yeah, I'll give you that." Luke stopped and gazed out the window. Long

silence. His shoulders slumped as he turned around. His narrowed eyes studied James. "I'm not sure even if I had a house, Sally would come. She hardly never writes."

What could James say? He knew Sally and there was a good chance Luke was right. He'd hurt her beyond reason when he'd lied about riding with Quantrill and the Raiders last August. He certainly hadn't been the husband and father he should have been. Family gossip was she'd thrown him out of the house. In many ways, James couldn't blame her. But those children...

Luke eyed a sandwich. "You mind?"

James waved an arm that way.

Mouth full, Luke spoke over the food. "Honestly, you think there's money in this?"

James nodded.

"What do Andy and Trace think?"

"Have to ask them." James knew what they'd said this morning. Each had confidence in him, and he wouldn't let them down. Couldn't let them down. With all they'd been through together and separately, the bond was strong, and the brothers would back his play, whichever way he went. "They've already put money in the bank under our business name."

"Which is?" Frowns and lines of doubt raced across Luke's face.

"Four C Square."

More frowning.

"Four Coltons. Square sounded right." James produced what he knew was a contagious

smile. Luke possessed one, too, but used mostly around women.

Finishing his sandwich, Luke muffled a light belch while easing down to the sofa. More

gazing into space. More breaths. James refilled his brother's coffee cup on the end table, then his

own, and waited. Luke stared at the steaming cup as if the black grounds held answers.

"Maybe I'm as thick-headed as an adobe fence, so tell me again." Luke played with the end of his mustache. "How does all this work?"

"Simple." James knew he had him. "We buy the cattle from different ranches, bring them in as a bunch, a herd, drive them to market. We sell, collect our money."

"And we hire men to do this?"

"Uh huh. The boss, his ramrod, drovers, wagon and supplies, the cook. The whole kettle. When the drive's done, the cattle move on to somebody else's herd or supper table." James shrugged. "Easy."

Luke held his cup and blew on the coffee. "So, what's the catch?"

"Always a chance the Indians run them off. Steal 'em, maybe."

"Or stampede and all die." Luke cut his eyes sideways at James. "Look. My little freighting business is barely off the ground. I'm making money, that's true, but not much and I'd sure as hell hate to see my profits run off by Indians or over a cliff."

He was right. There was a risk, a gamble. Again, James knew all about risking everything. He'd risked his life before and soon he would be risking his family's money. But he had talked and thought and thought some more, and currently, luck seemed to be in his corner—for a change. This would work.

* * *

"Anybody home?" Andy held the door while Trace, his wife Teresa, baby in her arms stepped in. Trace's other daughter scooted in between legs and screeched "Hi!"

Andy pushed the door closed.

Morningstar greeted them halfway across the living room. "Welcome. Good to see you all." She bent down to Trace's toddler now hugging her leg. "Look at you, Faith. So big!" She swept her up into her arms, a smile filling the room.

None of this was lost on James. His heart ached for his precious wife. How could he give her children when he couldn't... couldn't perform like a man? *Be* a man? That familiar knot throbbed in his chest. She deserved more. So much more. He vowed for the hundredth time he'd at least make enough money to buy a bigger house. Then maybe they'd find a couple of children who needed a home. Star would be the perfect mother.

"Help yourself to sandwiches, please."

Morningstar's sweet voice brought James back to his living room now crammed full of Coltons. The room glowed like sunrise thanks to the oil lamps and candles his wife had set on tables. Luke and Teresa took opposite ends of the sofa. Trace leaned against the front door while Andy slipped into the rocking chair and held cherub-faced Maddie, Trace's two-month-old daughter. Wiggling out of Morningstar's arms, Faith scampered around the adults. Between her high-pitched squeals, Maddie's gurgling, the brothers' bass tones, and the women's soprano voices, James knew his ears would start bleeding if he didn't take control of this meeting.

He stood in the middle and held up his hands. "Let me have your attention." His words

bounced off the plank ceiling. He waited until most eyes locked on his. "This meeting of the

Colton clan will come to order."

James glanced at the kitchen doorway where his half-Apache wife stood, porcelain coffee cup in hand. She'd produced the same smile when he'd first met her three years ago in Tucson. The same smile when she'd agreed to marry him. The same smile that always made his heart melt. A nod from her. James stood straight and breathed as deeply as the room allowed.

"As you all realize, this family's about to embark on a new adventure." James' gaze

roved over his brothers, across the women's faces, down to the children. "I've done a lot of

thinking and talking to people and I'm convinced this

will work. Californians are hungry. They spent the past few years either digging in the dirt or fighting. They're hungry for steak and nobody's bothered to raise cattle."

James looked from face to face. Confusion, thinking, agreeing and doubt. He pulled a folded piece of paper from his pocket. Holding it up, he cocked his head toward it. "Listen to this." He unfolded the single page.

"This a long speech?" Luke uncrossed his legs and leaned forward. He glanced at the others. "I thought old Mister Lincoln was the windbag. Looks like we have us our own—"

"Hear him out, Luke." Trace rapped the top of Luke's head. "Quit giving him a hard

time." He nodded at Luke then at James. "Continue." He returned to his spot leaning against the front door.

"This is a letter from the California town of Tin Town. The mayor no less. Here's what he says." James cleared his throat. "Thank you for your recent correspondence. This letter is to certify you are to deliver two thousand head of cattle to Tin Town, California no later than July first, eighteen sixty-four. We will pay thirty-five dollars a head if you deliver on time and in good condition. Best regards, Carter Samuels, Mayor."

Trace whistled through his teeth, Luke squirmed on the sofa, Andy grinned. James

gripped the paper and waited.

"Looks like it's official." Andy rocked forward. "I think it's a great idea. Can't wait! Never been to California. Exactly." His gaze swept the room as if telling a story no one had heard before. "James and me rode as far as the border, had us what they call oranges. Boy, were they juicy and sweet! But we never made it all the way across that Colorado River."

Memories. James cringed. He and Andy, both Union soldiers, had been wounded at

Yuma during a skirmish with Rebels. He pushed images aside and clenched his shaking hands into fists. A deep breath. Another one. Those days were past. Long past.

Trace pointed a finger at Andy. "You can't be leaving, little brother."

"Why not?"

"Somebody has to pour drinks at Sam's. There's some mighty thirsty *hombres* around here and there's nobody better at... how do I put this?" Trace pursed his lips. "At

procuring the best rot-gut whiskey around. To lose you to stinky cattle would be pure sin."

Goading Andy was too easy. So gullible at age nineteen. Teasing never grew into anything more than good-natured ribbing, and this would be fun.

Andy's head swiveled from brother to brother. "But—"

"A real tragedy." Luke wagged his head.

"Besides," Trace said. "Who'd take your place? Be my second deputy? You're the best there is... at fetching my coffee."

The brothers laughed, shoulders shaking.

"You boys sound like if he leaves, he'll never be back." Teresa adjusted her dark blue skirt, pulling the hem out from under her shoe.

"If he does go, I'll wager he gets back as soon as he can." Morningstar scooped up Maddie from Andy and squeezed between Teresa and Luke on the couch. "That new mercantile in town?" Her almond-brown eyes glowed as she looked first at the baby then at Teresa. "Well, the owner's daughter works there."

"You don't say?" Teresa leaned away from Morningstar in mock surprise.

"Pretty thing, too." Morningstar's mouth curled up at both ends. "I hear Andy's over

there all the time."

"That's not true!" Andy held up both hands. "Once... maybe twice." His cheeks pinked. He ducked his head. "All right. She's not hard on the eyes."

James held one hand palm up. "Idea is for all of us to stay here and let men who know what they're doing, drive the cattle." He waited for nods. "We're in this together, so we all need to have the same information. We'll split the costs four ways—"

"And profit four ways." Trace's baritone words rolled across the room.

"Right." James nodded. "We'll have supplies bought and the men signed on in a month or two." He searched the room for signs of discontent. "I have a lead on a trail boss and he'll hire men."

"Don't we need cattle?" Luke folded his arms against his chest. "Unless you plan to feed the *drovers* to the Californians."

James fought to keep his temper under control. That Luke. Sarcastic. At times mean-

spirited. Why couldn't he simply keep quiet? James looked at his feet, back at the group, then continued. "Calves are being born as we speak and in another month or two will be ready to trail west. And the grass is already rising. Since I work at the livery stable, I'm in touch with ranches

looking to sell cattle." James ignored Luke and nodded at Andy. "And maybe that new

mercantile could point to some other ranchers as well."

"How many head you think you'll buy?" Teresa jotted notes on paper. James knew her practical side would be a real asset to the group.

Trace jumped in before James could answer. "I'd say well over two thousand."

"No sense driving less than that." James nodded, glad Teresa had asked. "Have to take into account some won't survive. Or stay with the herd. For whatever reasons."

"Two thousand?" Luke shook his head. "That's a helluva lot of..." He blew out exasperation. "Sorry. That's a lot of beef to move. Don't see how it's possible."

"We can do it." James corrected himself. "*They* can do it. We'll get men. Good men."

"So, we're agreed. We're doing this." As oldest sibling, Trace took over and snatched a sandwich from the tray. He pointed it at James. "I think we should split up the responsibilities. It's too much for him to do by himself." He pointed to Andy. "You should be in charge of checking with that new store. Write down the names of ranchers."

"Think I can handle that, big brother." Andy stood, fitted his hat to his head. "I'll start first thing in the morning."

James tapped his fist against Andy's shoulder. "I'm sure you will." He turned to Luke. "Since you're freighting, could you find us a wagon? Big enough to hold food supplies and—"

"I know what you want, James." Luke scooted forward on the couch. "You want me to buy a wagon, give it to a bunch of no-good cowboys, watch 'em destroy it inside a week." He glared at James then Trace. "No. I'm not sure this's gonna work and I'll be damned spending my hard-earned money for somebody to—"

"There's enough money in the bank to buy the wagon." Teresa turned to stare at Luke,

her mouth a hard line. "You won't lose any of your precious earnings." She took a deep breath.

"Don't you see? Your family is trying to help you. Help all of us." She lowered her voice. "Sally

would want you to."

There. Out in the open. Teresa certainly spoke her mind. No wonder Trace adored her.

Luke leaned back and contemplated the ceiling.

James let a smile creep up one corner of his mouth as he looked at Trace. If Luke didn't get on board now, he never would. James looked at the women. "And if it's all right with everyone, I'd like Teresa and Morningstar to keep track of the money. That's a big job."

Teresa rubbed her hands together and glanced at Morningstar. "Love to. I like money." Her mouth rose along with a slight chuckle. She stood wrapping a shawl around her shoulders.

"Excellent." Trace and James spoke in unison, something they did often. Trace's gaze

trailed over James.

The scrutiny was familiar and he knew his brother's thoughts. They were all lucky to be here, in this house, all together, all healthy. In one piece.

Trace addressed the standing crowd now heading for the door. "We'll hire the trail boss and the drovers. Buy the supplies." He spoke mainly to Andy and Luke. "Shouldn't take all that long. Two months tops. It'll all be ready first week in April."

Pulling his watch from his vest, Andy frowned, replaced it. "All this planning is making me sleepy. It's late. Gotta get back to work." He smiled at Trace. "More whiskey to pour."

Luke lingered behind Andy, Teresa with Faith in hand and Morningstar cradling Maddie.

His gaze swept the floor then the wall behind James. "I apologize. I've done some thinking.

Guess it's an all right idea." He focused on Trace. "Can't afford to lose any money, though."

"None of us can." Trace walked him to the door. "Can't guarantee we'll make money, but

I think James is right. We'll be ace high in no time."

Wagging his head, Luke pulled the door closed and disappeared into the dark.

The house quieted. James eyed the sole straggler, Trace, their unspoken bond as

strong as ever.

"Thank you for this." Trace perched on the sofa's arm while James sank into the

rocker. Their eyes locked. Trace drew a deep breath, started to say something. He stopped, stared at his hands.

"What?" James stifled a yawn.

"I saw how Morningstar was around Maddie. Wondering how you were doing. I mean, with..." Trace's brown-eyed gaze trailed up to his brother, returned to his hands. "You seem happy. And you're sleeping, I under-stand. No more pacing the floor." His words softened. "Managed to put those Apache behind you?"

James swallowed over the lump in his throat. "As behind as they'll let me." Could he admit the rest? It was James' turn to study his hands. "Looks like Morningstar and me'll... I can't... can't seem to..."

"Still? Damn, James, it's been what... three years?" Trace lowered his voice. "Not even once?"

James wagged his head.

Trace grimaced. "Those damn Indians. They—"

"I've decided to tell Star about my dead Pima wife. She needs to know." James' trembling hand scrubbed his face. "With this cattle drive, if we go, we'll be gone a few months, and I can't leave without her knowing. It's been too long. Besides, I don't want any secrets between us. Not any more. Maybe that'll help..."

Silence stretched between the two brothers, both gazing at walls and ceiling. Trace

gripped James' shoulder and rocked it. "Think that's a good idea. Hope it helps." He let go. "Hell, I'm sure it will."

CHAPTER THREE

"Tomorrow." Whid MacGilvray spit, brown liquid dribbling from his chapped lips. One gooey tendril slid downward, burrowing into his beard. Not a traditional beard, but more like a mop of hair springing out in all directions, as if panicked to escape his pockmarked cheeks. He swiped his forearm across thin lips, spit again, this time hitting closer to the campfire. Embers hissed.

"Tomorrow." Whid dug around in his bottom lip until his finger found what was left of

the chaw. He flicked off the wad and pieces of tobacco sailed into the fire. He nodded at the flames as if they would confirm what he was thinking. "We ride to town, Pickett." He glanced at the man sitting across from him, his knife scraping bark off a mesquite stick.

Pickett didn't bother to look up, the stick appearing to hold his interest. He spoke to the wood. "Really think you can waltz into Mesilla, find this fella, kill him, and waltz back

out, pretty as you please? Think nobody'll notice?" Pickett's narrow-set eyes trailed from the stick up to Whid. "You think he's still there?"

"Uh huh."

"Really think he's worth killin'?" Pickett dug at a knot.

"Uh huh." Would Pickett, this man who Whid had picked up in Utah, stand beside him when the shooting started? Would he back his play, whatever the outcome? Or would he run away like the short tub of lard he was, and hide, afraid of being sent off to jail again? He thought he knew his partner, but that damn nagging doubt came galloping back again.

Hell, maybe he'd off him right here and now. Knife in Pickett's back like his last partner. Whid stifled a chuckle. Yeah, the look on ol' Bob's face when he stuck him, then took all the payroll money they'd just stolen, brought a full smile to his face. Between killing that ranch owner coming out of the bank, coupled with offing his partner, Whid's chest strained the buttons. He was good. Damn good. And he still had most of the money.

Pickett gripped the whittling knife in one hand. Smoke wafted over his head. A sneeze

followed by sniffles. "Look. I get what it's like havin' a gal stolen right out from under your nose, but, hell, I didn't shoot nobody over her. No angelica's worth jail." The knife waggled in the air toward Whid's face. "Fact is, I figured if she didn't want me anyhow, why in the hell'd I want her? Better off without her. I say good damn riddance."

Stars winked back while Whid studied them, ignoring Pickett's worthless ramblings. A hint of breeze cooled the anger, the frustration seething inside. Somewhere nearby, maybe behind the hill, coyotes sang. Something small skittered from one bush to another. Whid pulled his coat tighter around his body. Early April breezes still had a bite to them, and even though he was tall, there was little meat to keep his bones warm. He shivered.

"Tomorrow." Whid shoved a stick into the campfire, waited for the wood to ignite. He held up the torch. The flame danced, growing brighter, then shrinking as he waved lighted twig like a conductor's baton. "Probably won't kill him tomorrow. But soon." He blew on the flame until the fire died. "Real soon."

With Pickett yards behind, Whid rode his horse across the Rio Grande, splashing through mud and water soaking the bottom of his stirrups. He thought about ways to kill Colton. That low-down, woman-thieving, son-of-a-bitch. An out-in-the-open fight? Would he even tell him who he was and why he was fighting? Or would he ambush the rotten scoundrel alone one night and beat him to a pulp? Then kill him. Both scenarios sounded enticing. But what was the hurry? Whid's love, his girl, had been swept away by that bastard three years past, while he, Whid Amos MacGilvray, rotted in an Arizona prison. For three damn years.

Colton had put him in jail as surely as he'd opened and locked that iron door himself. And for what?

Whid gripped the horse's reins until he lost feeling in his fingers. Soon. Real soon, he'd

find James Colton, and with what he'd planned, Colton would wish he'd never laid eyes on beautiful Morningstar. A woman who, with one look, could turn a man into mush, melt him into a puddle at her feet. Nighttime stars could never shine as bright as she did.

First stop—the general mercantile. They'd have what he needed. And what he needed was information. If the mercantile didn't, he'd check with the bartenders. They knew everything and everybody. After all, it was a body he came for.

Whid and Pickett reined up in front of the Mesilla Mercantile, its door facing east into the plaza. After tying their horses, Whid sauntered into the store, his partner on his heels. A glance, then a closer look, revealed a typical mercantile, the usual goods displayed where they should be. Bolts of fabric against a far wall, boots and bonnets on an opposite wall, jars of sugar candy and licorice lining the counter.

Pickett sauntered toward a stack of ropes in the corner, while Whid made his way toward a young woman who clutched a feather duster. She worked here, it was obvious.

"Howdy, ma'am." Whid touched his hat brim and nodded.

"Afternoon, sir." She produced a smile, which lit up her clover green eyes. "Can I help you find something?"

"Matter of fact—" Whid turned at the door slamming open. A lanky man, probably six two, maybe twenty, stepped in, and ducked his head. His eyes riveted on the woman.

"Howdy, Ginny." He threaded his way over to her. "I was only passin'—" His head

snapped from the girl to Whid. "Sorry there, Mister. Didn't mean to interrupt."

For some reason, Whid knew this kid would provide the answer to the question not yet asked. There was something about him that reminded Whid of his quarry. Instead of

complaining, he stepped aside. "No problem there." He touched Ginny and the young man on the

arms, drawing them together with a gentle nudge. "You go ahead and talk, I'll look around." Whid moved a few feet away, but within hearing distance.

"Sure is nice seeing you again, Andy." Ginny's voice turned soft, velvety, that pleasant but business-like hardness saved for customers gone.

"You, too, Virginia." Andy pointed over his shoulder. "I was looking over a few last details with my brothers before the cattle drive tomorrow. James wants everything in order before we watch them head out to California."

The syrupy sweetness emanating from those two turned Whid's stomach. He knew he'd throw up if his throat hadn't squeezed tight. Could it be James Colton the kid was referring to? Could this quest really be so simple? That easy?

"Tomorrow already?" Virginia straightened Andy's vest. "Afterward, what're you...? I mean, you've been so busy getting ready and all, I've hardly seen you around. And there *is* that dance Saturday night. And since you'll be in town..."

"Shucks, Ginny, I'd take you to the dance even if my boots were on fire." Andy ducked his head. "Feel like they already are." He ran his hand down her arm.

Whid eased toward Andy and Virginia mooning over each other. What a shame to break up such a happy couple. Made him sick thinking about that gal and fella together. No telling what else they did when not in public. Were James and Morningstar like that, too? A knot clotted in his chest. Words spurted out over the lump. "Sorry, but I couldn't help overhear your conversation." Whid nodded to Andy. "Andy, is it?"

"Yes sir. Andy Colton."

The hair on the back of Whid's neck bristled. Yep. He'd guessed right. It took every

ounce of control he had not to pull his .45 and plug James' brother. Right in the heart. Deciding

against such a rash move, he lowered his voice to a neutral tone. "I heard you say something about a cattle drive." A glance at Pickett, engrossed in checking out boots. He'd back his play, but there was no need to alarm anyone. No, he'd bide his time and strike when it was right. He needed more information any way.

"Cattle drive. Yes sir," Andy said. "Me and my brothers bought a herd and they're being driven clear over to California first thing in the morning." His smile turned lopsided, but the brown eyes sparkled. "Wish it could be me with 'em, but..." His eyes trailed down to Virginia. "Well, I have a job, two jobs in fact, and a girl. Guess I don't need to be running off."

Virginia moved closer to Andy but turned her eyes on Whid. "Why're you asking? You a cattle buyer?"

"No. Not a buyer." Whid shook his head afraid he'd shown his hand way too early.

"Used to tend cattle over in Texas. There's talk of forming big drives heading up toward Kansas, but I don't think there's any money to be made driving them all that way."

"Well, Mister, my brother James seems certain the people in California are hungry for beef, and we're the ones giving it to 'em." Andy's shoulders straightened, his chest puffed out a bit. "Intend to see a profit, too." He nodded to Virginia.

"And this James understands a lot about cattle, does

he?" Whid was having fun with this boy. And why not? He was playing into his hands exactly the way he wanted. Besides, Andy would die soon enough. Might as well let him enjoy his last few days with Virginia. Such a pretty young thing. Maybe he'd take this girl, too. Morningstar and Ginny. Perhaps he'd give Ginny to Pickett. Or keep her for himself, she being so young and virtuous.

Andy fidgeted, looked at Virginia, changed his gaze to across the store. "No sir, we don't

know a lot about cattle. None of us do. But we hired us a right fine trail boss and the best crew.

They'll see our cattle get safely to Tin Town."

"Uh huh." Whid glanced right as Pickett wended his way closer. "Who'd you say your trail boss was? I might be remembering him."

"I don't think he's ever been in Texas, but his name's Zeb Perchman. He's run several herds over the years."

Whid studied the ceiling. "Perchman... Perchman... yeah, I remember him. Let's see." He met Andy's gaze. "Tall fella? Maybe six four?"

"Nah." Andy wagged his head. "He's shorter'n me."

"Beard? Dark brown?"

Andy's eyes lit up. "Yep. Big and bushy." He nodded toward Whid. "Kinda like yours."

Whid smiled. "I'll bet that's him. Haven't seen him in a coon's age. Think he'll be around town tonight? Or out there checking on the cattle?" He pointed to Pickett. "Me and my partner'd like to buy him a drink—for old times."

A shrug. "Hard to tell. He might be over at Sam Bean's, or one of the other saloons, or he

might be getting ready for tomorrow." Andy shook his head. "Sorry, Mister. I never did get your name." He stuck out a hand.

"Smith, son. Amos Smith. Pleased to meet ya."

* * *

Finding Zeb Perchman wasn't hard. In fact, none of this had been hard. Despite what Pickett had

said, he'd waltzed into Mesilla, located James' brother, learned more than he'd hoped for, and currently, sitting right over there was Zeb Perchman. The first of many disappointments for ol'

Jamey boy.

Whid leaned against the bar, beer mug in hand. He smirked at his first-rate fortune. He

and Pickett had walked in, ordered a beer, and as if he'd planned the entire affair, a fella wobbled over toward another fella with a big, bushy beard, slapped him on the back, calling him by name. Perchman shook hands with the man and gestured to an empty seat. Yep. This would be easy.

Pickett guzzled his beer, draining the glass in one long gulp.

Whid turned his back to the barkeep and leaned close to his partner. "Better watch that

drinking. Don't want you all liquored up."

"I'm thirsty. One more won't hurt." Pickett nodded to the bartender, tossed a coin on the wooden plank. He waited for the next glass, and the moment the suds arrived, he slurped the foamy liquid halfway down. His back to the barkeep, he nodded at the glass. "That was plumb fine. I was right parched."

"Now that you're watered, remember this fight needs to look like Perchman started the ruckus. And..." Whid scanned the smoky, lantern-lit room for people listening, but found none. "Break every bone in his body. We don't want him helping out poor James Colton."

Pickett fisted his empty hand. "I'm ready, but still don't see why we're hurtin' this fella."

He leaned closer to Whid. "Hell, you can take out James tomorrow at the cattle drive. The shootin' might even stampede a few. That'd be fun."

"Uh huh. But this way takes longer. We'll harass the livin' hell out of ol' Jamey boy

before we bed him down." Whid's muscles tensed. "He'll lose everything he ever loved, before

he loses his life." He turned to Pickett. "Now *that* will be fun.

CHAPTER FOUR

A hint of breeze, like cold lifeless arms, embraced James. He rubbed the back of his neck. A slight shiver sent his hands buttoning the coat and immediately diving into pockets. The warmth in those pockets relaxed his nerves, more anxious than strained. His gaze swept across the herd snorting out icy breaths in this early too-cool April morning. The sun would bring warmth later, much like early summer's. But for now, he'd have to blow on his hands or keep them in pockets.

James shifted his weight in the saddle and watched the herd, *his* herd, spread out across the pasture. The few drovers from the S Bar Cross rode on the outside of the herd, calling to the cattle, keeping them calm. From his vantage point on this low hill west of Mesilla, James surveyed the land—more than fifty square miles stretched all around. Dust raised in the south brought a smile to his face. More cattle coming in. Two small herds were already here and five more expected soon.

So much for the cattle. The ranchers were eager to

sell, with cattle at a premium price in California. He figured that by noon, the herd would be complete. Where was Zeb Perchman, the man he'd hired as trail boss? The man who'd come recommended by more than a handful of ranchers. James fought uneasiness as he gazed across the herd. Late is all. Nothing more.

To his right, James spotted Luke, sitting tall in the saddle and chatting with one of the cowhands. Looked like Luke had come through, like he said he would, finding the perfect wagon and not complaining too loudly. The company had already paid for the wagon, the supplies and a month's salary to Perchman. Not a whole lot left in the bank, but enough to see the herd through to California.

"Great, huh?"

James swiveled to his left and squinted into the rising sun. Andy, a grin as wide as the landscape, rode up next to him.

"How many you count?" Andy leaned forward in the saddle. "Looks like five thousand, maybe six. Anyway, a whole bunch, don't you think?" He pointed over his shoulder. "There's another herd coming in, too. Isn't this better than great? *'Tis gran'*, as Ma would say."

"Aye, 'tis gran'." James couldn't help but smile at the remembrance of their ma's Irish brogue. "I never imagined it'd be like this. You're right." James' grin dropped as he thought about the late crew. Where the hell were they? "Seen any sign of our wagon on your way over here?"

A wag of Andy's head and shrugged shoulders did nothing to alleviate the panic brewing in James' chest.

"Want me to see if I can find them?" Andy reined his horse around. "I bet they're simply checking and double checking their supplies. It's a long way." He gigged his horse. "Be right back."

James returned his focus to the herd. The cattle had almost doubled in the time he'd been talking to Andy. That was a lot of animals. Glad he wasn't trying to keep them in line.

A single cloud of dust approached from the south, from town. Had to be one rider, not a

herd and certainly not a loaded supply wagon. James waited until he recognized the rider. The easy way of sitting, the head lifted, the steady gait. Trace. Nobody sat a saddle like his older

brother.

Trace waved and walked his horse close to James. He reined up alongside.

James couldn't help but sit a bit taller. "Appears we're in the cattle business. Four C Square, brother. Ours, all ours."

"Glad you're sitting down." Trace's voice carried not an ounce of happiness. It was cold, official, exactly like a sheriff.

"Why?" Icy panic filled James' lungs. "What's wrong?"

"There was a fight at Sam Bean's last night."

"So?"

Trace swiped his hand across his mouth. He cleared his throat. "Arrested Zeb

Perchman. Drunk and disorderly. Broke up the bar something fierce. Took myself, my deputy, and Sam to get him to jail."

"And? What is it you're not telling me?" James leaned closer to his brother.

"Perchman broke his arm."

"He can still trail cattle with a broken arm." A cold knot clotted in his chest.

Trace looked away. "Also a bad concussion."

"So?" James wanted to grab his brother by the throat and squeeze the information out of him. Why was he taking so long? "Is that it?" He looked around. "Where is he?"

"It ain't that simple." Trace met James' gaze. "While the doc was patching him up, I spent some time searching through my wanted posters. This isn't easy to say—"

"Then don't." James slapped his open hand against his chaps. "What the hell'd you find out?"

"He's wanted in California. Seems he's done a lot of trailing cattle—like he said. But, he

didn't always share the money with the owners. He's run out on four or five. Lots of people want

his hide—or a piece of it." Trace wagged his head. "I had to charge him twice. Drunk and disorderly. Stealing. I'm sorry."

Before he could think any further, Andy rode up, the dust swirling around his abrupt stop. "Bad news, James." He looked from brother to brother. "Seems like Perchman was arrested last night, by big brother here. Rest of his crew says they're not working if he doesn't. Quite a few've already left."

Words wouldn't form expressing what James thought. What he felt. With a quick intake of someone about to plunge into icy water, he gazed from Andy, to Trace, back to Andy.

After what felt like hours, James pulled in dust-laced air. Before thoughts mixed themselves into words, Andy leaned forward and stared at James.

"What d'we do?"

CHAPTER FIVE

"What d'you mean you didn't know?" James shoved his shoulder between the cell's iron bars, his arm waving toward Perchman's face. "How the hell could you *not* know? You didn't *know* you had a warrant, my ass. You didn't *tell* me, is what you did. I swear, if I could reach you, I'd strangle you myself." Heat flushed through his body, his heart thundering in his ears.

Trace pulled at James' coat. "You'll hurt yourself. Calm down. Yelling isn't helping."

Eyes narrowed, James lowered his voice, spoke through gritted teeth. "I'm not yelling." He pushed his shoulder farther through the bars, wedging it until he couldn't move. His extended arm flapped at Perchman who stood inches away, his back against the wall. James fisted his hand. "What the hell'm I supposed to do? Huh? Tell me. Where'm I supposed to find a crew? Hell, they're all hired off. All of 'em. Some other cattle outfit came by and snatched 'em up. All of 'em. What the hell'm I supposed to do?"

Perchman cocked his head. "Ain't my fault. The fight. You heard wrong. I was—"

"I don't want excuses. I want drovers. I want wranglers. I want a trail boss, and I want a ramrod." James glared at the man who by all rights should well be on his way to Tin Town by now.

"Told you. Ain't my fault." Perchman's bushy beard did nothing to hide the bruises cascading down the right side of his face. An ugly cut puffed above his left eye.

"Dammit, Perchman. I want you to do what I paid you to do. Herd cattle. Dammit!" James clenched his jaw issuing a declaration of war. "Herd my damn cattle."

"Can't herd your damn cattle like this!" Perchman offered his wrapped arm in a sling

as proof. "Ain't my fault I'm hurt." He glared at Trace. "Hell, I shouldn't be in here. Some other

fella started it."

"Like I told you twice before, that's not what Sam and the others in the saloon said."

Trace tugged and pulled until James' shoulder popped free from the bars. James glared

from Perchman to Trace and back. He snorted anger, frustration. What could he do to make this right? James stood gripping the iron bars with Trace behind his left shoulder. Only James' steam engine huffing broke the silence.

Perchman rubbed his head with his right arm as he eased down to his cot. "Feelin' kinda dizzy. Lightheaded." His eyes trailed up to Trace. "Is that normal with a concussion, Sheriff?" The words slurred a bit.

Trace nodded.

James cringed. Apache fists knocking him to the ground. Moccasins plowing into tender ribs and thundering head. Dizzy, lightheaded, roiling stomach. Sometimes vomiting. A black eye or two. Concussions he knew.

Trace's hand on his shoulder, a slight tremble. James blinked away the past forcing his thoughts into the present. He searched the floor for answers to their current problem.

"All we can do is return the cattle. And their money." James blew out a long stream of air.

Pacing the room, Trace wagged his head. "We'll have to cancel the contract."

The office door swung open and Andy stuck his head in. "Great news." He brought the rest of him in with it. He glanced at Perchman and turned to James. Andy thumbed over his shoulder. "Luke and me found us a coozie." His chest puffed as he stood straighter.

"A what?" Trace looked around James.

"Coozie." This James knew. He explained to Trace. "A cook. *Cuisinero*. A Mexican

word." Did he dare let hope creep into his chest? "He's willing to join up?"

"Yep." Andy beamed like he'd won a trophy. "Seems he's real experienced, too. Even been to California. Three times." His three extended fingers waggled back and forth. "Looks like we have us a cattle drive."

"Who all's driving it?" Perchman continued rubbing his head.

"We are!" Andy beamed, nodding to his brothers.

"What?" Trace and James spun toward Andy who shrugged.

"Why not? Between the four of us and this coozie, we oughta be able to get those longhorns to California. How hard can it be?"

Could they? Could the four Colton brothers pack up their lives in a day to hit the trail for the next three or four months? James cocked his head and looked at Trace. Why the hell not? Because they didn't have a clue about herding cattle didn't mean they couldn't learn. The look on Trace's face said about the same. Why the hell not? Besides, what else could they do without admitting defeat?

"Convincing Luke might take some doing." James pursed his lips, scenarios running through his mind.

"About what?" Luke's voice spun all three brothers around. He stepped through the door,

eyebrows raised. "What're we talking about?"

CHAPTER SIX

James gripped the metal coffee cup, the warmth radiating up his arms. If he drank the strong brew, maybe he'd stay awake. Maybe. But he was so damn tired. The noonday sun had done nothing to help him keep his eyes open. The brown liquid lay in his cup, simply lay there as if taunting him, daring him to summon enough strength to pick up his hand and bring the cup to his mouth. Actual swallowing would be too hard.

The rock under him grew hard. It poked in two or three spots. Soon, he'd have to move his rear, get off this rock and stand, but the pain was the only thing keeping him awake. Besides, moving would take energy. Blinking didn't take much, but keeping the eyelids open used what energy was left. His eyes seemed intent on closing, like they were late for an afternoon nap. Something popped in the campfire tossing an ember onto James' boot. In his muddled mind, the only solution was to pour the coffee on the offended area. He poured brown liquid onto his boot. The ember hissed, sputtering out.

He stared at the wet boot, empty cup still in hand, a pair of legs appearing next to him. Could only be Coozie, everyone else was out with the herd.

"*Señor?*" Coozie's Spanish accent drifted over James' head, swirled, and floated into his ears. "*Señor* Colton?"

A deep sigh, then James pulled in enough air to lift his head. His gaze traveled up brown canvas pants, smears of flour and grease spread like an artist's masterpiece across one leg. What had started life as a white apron snugged around a slender body. One arm held out a coffee pot, the other a towel. Above that, a head, thin mustache penciled over curved lips, brown eyes

staring down, a furrowed young forehead under a mop of curly brown hair.

"More coffee, *Señor?*" Coozie waved the pot closer to the upturned cup. "Or maybe

already a shave and face wash?" He offered the towel. "You need rest, a *siesta*, already."

Was James' head actually bobbing? "No time. Need to keep the herd moving."

Coozie squatted, knee to knee with James. "You already fell out of the saddle already this

morning. Made the bruise on your face. Maybe ride with me in the wagon for an hour to sleep."

Dredging up strength from Lord knew where, James pushed off the rock and stood. The world wobbled like a child's spinning top. He thudded back down.

"You are not well, *Señor*. Let me call one of your brothers." Coozie gripped James' shoulder.

"No. Here." James offered the shaking cup. "Take this. I'll be all right. Everyone's as tired as me. I'll head back in a minute."

Snorting softly, Coozie plucked the cup from James' hand.

It had been what, three days since they'd left Mesilla? Since then, James had learned about a whole new world. He'd learned taking Perchman with them had been an excellent idea. The reasoning was Trace had to get Perchman, along with his arrest warrants, to California, and it seemed only logical they take him along too. His expertise was proving invaluable. The first bit of advice Perchman gave was to push the herd fast and hard for the first few days after coming together. Cattle, he'd said, preferred to stay in their own pastures with familiar surroundings. Once they were far enough away from home and comfortable being on the trail, you'd slow them down and create a leisurely stroll out of the adventure. If you traveled ten miles a day, it was too fast.

Those first few days had been hell.

The second piece of advice proved easier to figure out. Perchman had said, "Find a Judas

steer, let him lead. Those dumb critters'll follow him clear to the slaughter pens. Easy." One shoulder shrugged. "Might save him out for the next drive."

By the end of the first day, James thought he'd identified a leader and by day two, it had

become clear he was right. That longhorn steer moved to the front and never looked back.

But what he'd realized the most was that they were undermanned. At least three times as

many men were needed for a herd this size, a bit over two thousand at first count. Between walking the cattle, "driving" was a bit of an overstatement, the brothers and Perchman took turns guarding at night. The cook didn't tend cattle. He had one job and one only and that was to feed the hands and doctor them, if necessary. Everyone, including Coozie, was exhausted.

But they couldn't let the cattle bed down for a day or

two, to take a day to stay in one place and let them graze. Let the men sleep. Hell, they'd left Mesilla later than planned and July 1 wasn't all that far off. No, right now they had to push.

James allowed his eyes to close and used a hand to hold up his head. Sitting there, he

thought back to a few days before. He would laugh about it, if he had the energy. How in the world had his brothers pulled their lives away from normal and started this cattle drive? Morningstar and Teresa were angels for being so understanding and helping to pack, promising this change of plans was fine. The brothers weren't to worry. The women would manage.

Today was day number three and so far, things were proceeding right along considering they had no idea what they were getting into. And he missed Morningstar, already. The final farewell kiss lingered on his mind. The back of his neck tingled remembering her touch, the way she held him.

He jerked his head up. "Stay awake. Whole mess. My idea." Black. Swirls. Black swirls.

Leaden eyelids slammed shut.

"*Señor?*"

A nudge on his shoulder.

"*Señor*, you were snoring." Coozie leaned in, almost nose-to-nose with James. "Come. Sleep in the wagon." He tugged on James' arm pulling him to his feet.

Trace rode to the wagon, dismounted and tied his horse to the side.

"What happened?" Trace frowned at Coozie first then at James.

"Nothing. Need coffee." James shifted his weight. Standing brought energy to his sagging body. He pointed to the cup sitting on the wagon's folddown table.

Trace cocked his head. "What's that goose egg on your cheek there?" He whipped around to Coozie. "You hit him?"

Coozie, eyes wide and head shaking, released James' arm and stepped back. "No, *Señor*.

No. He fell." Both hands turned outward. "Already he simply went to sleep."

"What?" Trace moved in close and poked at the reddened knot on James' cheek. "What

happened?"

James batted the hand away. "Ow. Don't."

"You all right?" Concern edged Trace's words.

Coozie walked to the campfire and spoke over his shoulder. "Your brother, he sleeps in the saddle. Falls off the horse." He picked up the coffee pot, poured a cup, handed Trace the steaming brew.

A chortle shook Trace's shoulders. "Off your *horse*?" Louder chuckling. "I thought Pa

and me taught you how to ride better 'n that, little brother." He patted James' back harder than

necessary.

Finding nothing humorous in being made fun of, James straightened his shoulders and

stood upright. "We're all so damn tired. Need to find more drovers. With only two of us on night

guard, that means three hours less sleep." He wagged his head. "And hell, Trace, we haven't even had any trouble yet. Hell, nobody can drive all these beeves all that way, and not contact some kinda trouble."

A glance over his shoulder. The dust was more intense, more *dusty* with the herd

growing closer. He was starting to truly hate dirt.

"According to the map, the Southern Trail we're following heads on down into Mexico in a few more miles." Trace used his cup to point southwest, toward the Florida Mountains, toward the Chihuahuan desert, toward uncharted territory. "Those fellas who started that trail must've understood what they were doing. I bet there's ranches with extra hands we can hire."

"What d'you think, Coozie? You're from down around there, aren't you?" A flicker of

hope lit on his chest.

"No." Coozie shook his head. "But there are *ranchos* there already. And maybe with extra *vaqueros*."

"Ah, hell." Hope faded. James kicked at a rock. "We're still a week, maybe two

away from Mexico."

Trace snapped his fingers. "The Goodsight home station." He nodded at Coozie. "It was a

stop on the Butterfield Stage, currently the San Diego-San Antonio line's using it. And it's not too far from here. Not even a day's ride. I bet they'll have extra men. Or tell us where to find

some."

Why hadn't he thought of that? Of course. James knew right where it was. They used to

stop there twice a week, back in the day when they drove for Butterfield. And Trace was right. It was north, half a day. James let himself smile for the first time that morning.

CHAPTER SEVEN

Choosing broken pieces of mesquite to see who made the trip, James drew the short one. Bolstered by hope, he took off the next morning at daybreak, waving to Andy and Luke still riding night herd, or night guarding as Zeb Perchman called it. From the small line of horses they'd brought—a remuda—James learned, he had picked out his favorite, Pinetop, to take him to the Goodsight station. She had a smooth gait and wasn't spooked easily by rabbits or tumbleweeds.

While the ride through desert, over hills, around alligator juniper, and past a few herds

of antelope was uneventful, something nagged at James. Like someone watching. Apache? They were around. Chills rocked his body. Not again. If he was attacked and captured by Indians, he vowed he'd kill himself before being taken alive.

He'd already been a captive and often he'd wished he had died—during the captivity, and then many times later on. It was a hell he couldn't endure again, especially not without Trace. The two of them had bolstered each other for two months until released. James squeezed his eyes shut. Two months until *Trace* was released. James had stayed in camp another two weeks waiting for Trace to broker a deal with the army. It took many men dying on both sides to rescue James out of the Apache's clutches. And he sure wasn't ready to do it again.

But still, was somebody watching? He cringed at an Apache's breath on his neck. Just like before. How could his heart thunder like this when it was frozen? Afraid to glance behind him, knowing he'd see his nightmares spring to life, he straightened his tired shoulders, drew all his courage, and peeked. Nothing. A longer, slower sweep of the desert revealed no Apache, no outlaws, no body following. He shook the chills off as nerves. And fatigue. To his left, Magdalena Gap. At last. Goodsight was within a mile or two. He examined the sky. Not even noon yet. He'd made decent time. If luck held, he'd be riding back to the herd with extra hands in tow well before nightfall.

Finally there it was. As he remembered. Smoke billowed from the tin smoke pipe. He rode close. "Hello the station!" No need to be mistaken for a bandit and get shot. He reined up on a low hill several yards away.

Before he could yell again, the door opened and a man, rifle in hand, stepped out. The other hand shaded the eyes. "That who I think it is?"

James smiled and spurred Pinetop. "Sure is Tucker. It's me, James Colton." He pulled up to the hitchin' rail, tied the reins and gripped Tucker's forearm, the clasp friendly and firm.

"Can't believe it's you, Colton. Simply can't believe." Tucker pumped James' arm again and released. "Damn, it's fine seeing you. What the hell brings you out this way? You lost or something?"

James thumped Tucker on the shoulder. "How come you're still here? I figured you'd hightailed it back to that gal of yours. You hiding from her pa?" James stepped up onto the porch, the shade a welcome relief from the sun.

"There's a passel of catching up we need to do, my boy." Tucker's ample belly jiggled as he moved aside and pointed toward the door. "Sit down and take a load off." Tucker elbowed James as he stepped through the doorway. "Hell, I have a bottle of fine sippin' whiskey that needs the dust blown off. What say we have a snort?"

That Tucker. James wagged his head as his eyes adjusted to being inside. Same home

station. Three tables stood in the front room, dishes, cups and utensils set out for the next stage travelers. Off to one side sat the kitchen, the other side a bedroom.

They passed time filling each other in on their lives, while Tucker served a stew he'd

made the day before, fresh for those passengers. Two deep pulls of whiskey helped kill the taste.

At least the company, James mused, was pleasant.

Hiding a long belch under his napkin, James then turned the conversation to business. "I need some hands to help drive the cattle. We left thinking we could do it with only us brothers, a cook, and another fella. Truth be told, we had no business setting out like we did." He pursed his lips, wagged his head. "My brothers and me, all barkin' at a knot. But we can't turn around and head home. Not like a bunch of good-for-nothing loafers. I gotta see it through."

Tucker leaned back, pointed his glass at James. "That's one thing I always liked about you."

"What's that?"

"That hard-headed stubbornness you carry around. Caused you considerable amount of trouble more'n a few times, if I'm remembering right." Tucker cleaned off the table, piled the plates one on top of another, and ambled into the kitchen with them. His words boomed from there. "But you always seem to land on your feet. Kinda like a cat."

"Sometimes." James knew not to think too hard about that. He changed the subject. "So, you know anybody looking to push cattle? We're desperate."

Tucker stood in the doorway. "Let me think a minute. I need to haul more water from the well." He thumbed over his shoulder. "That whiskey's hardly been touched. Stay there and help yourself. Be right back." He disappeared. A back door squeaked open, slammed shut.

Within minutes, the aroma of boiling coffee wafted under James' nose. Banging of pans

and a tin cup hitting the floor made him turn. "Need help?" He secretly hoped the answer would

be no. Sitting in a real chair, not hard like a rock, and not swaying like in the saddle, brought a

sly smile to his face.

Without answering, Tucker walked in, a cup in each hand. He gave one to James, blew across his own cup, sipped, then nodded. "Been thinking about your predicament. There's some Mexicans around here might be needing steady work for a while." He sipped again. "Tell you what. Stage isn't due in until around ten tonight. I'll ride over to their place in a few minutes and if they're wanting to, I'll send them your way."

Even though the coffee bordered on too hot, James downed half of it and stood. "Can't thank you enough. But I do need to be heading back. Like to get there before dark." He shook hands with Tucker. "Thanks for the grub, the whiskey, and hell, for being here."

"Where else would I be?" Tucker followed him outside. "Tell your brothers howdy for me."

"Will do." James untied his horse and led her to the water trough around on the side. Within minutes, he stepped into the stirrups, waved. He put spurs to Pinetop's belly.

"*Buenas suerte*." Tucker waved. "*Adios*." He closed the door with one more wave.

The Goodsight station behind him, James set his sights on the herd. It would still be a long way back, three, maybe four hours, but then he could unwind with his brothers. What he had to tell them could be good news. A promise of more hands, although a slight chance, allowed him to relax. He eyed the expansive turquoise sky, refit his hat, leaned forward and patted Pinetop's neck.

The return trip took him the way he'd come, past the same herd of antelope, heads up, erect, ready to dart, watching him lope by. He rode down and up wide gullies, a covey of Gamble's quail scurrying out of his way.

Back a bit stiff, still not used to being in the saddle all day, he twisted to his right, placing

his hand on the horse's rump. He leaned back. Without warning, Pinetop reared. Her hooves

slashed at the air. She came down and bounced like a rabbit. Hopping sideways, she reared again

as if on fire.

James pulled back on the reins. Another buck. His knees pressed her sides. She kicked

high. Saddle horn wrenched out of his hand, he flew forward, the horn spearing him under his rib cage.

Another buck. He jerked backward, the reins ripped out of his grasp.

Tilting to the left, partway out of the saddle, he clawed at the horn, the leather skirt, the blanket. Anything to keep him off the desert. Each buck sent him farther sideways. Right leg jolted out of the stirrup, he sailed across the saddle and his foot hit dirt. He slid. His hands clawed at horse but found nothing to hold onto. Right leg plowing through sand, his left boot spur stuck in the stirrup. Face up, he sailed along the ground, kicking at air, frantic to loosen the tangle. Mesquite branches whipped his face and arms. Desert sand ran up into his shirt, down his pants.

James prayed this would end. His left leg, spur still firmly caught in the stirrup, tried to dislocate at the knee. Searing pain raced up and down his leg. A rock smashed into his shoulder. The impact rolled him over face first into the dirt.

He crashed into an alligator juniper, grabbed one branch and flipped over. He spat sand and struggled to keep one arm over his eyes. His hip popped. The entire leg caught fire.

Down an arroyo they flew, bouncing off rocks, careening through sage bushes. Up the other side, last bit of energy spent, he would die like this. With one last push, James rolled, managing to kick loose. He tumbled over and over crashing to a stop against a juniper, its branches covering him like protective arms.

He lay there, half awake, half wondering what the hell happened. A survey of his body revealed bangs and growing lumps, throbbing places, a few bleeding, a leg burning like Lucifer's fire. But despite everything, he was alive.

Minutes passed before he dared try standing. He

groaned to his knees, followed by one foot, the other. There. Upright. He grasped juniper branches to steady his shaky body, but he was up under his own power. His gaze traveled over the desert. Where in the hell was his crazy horse? What had caused her to do that? Would he have to limp all the way back to camp?

A snort from a gully on his right. Somewhere close.

One foot in front of the other, James hobbled in the snort's direction. He stopped on the

arroyo's edge and looked down. There she was, standing. Instead of yelling curses at her like he wanted to, he calmed his voice. "It's all right, girl. Relax. Won't hurt you." He picked his way down until he stood next to her. "What happened?"

The saddle hung under her belly. He checked the cinch strap. It had been loosened a notch. That would sure cause the saddle to slide and his boot to be caught. But not the bucking. James unbuckled the cinch, the saddle hit the ground, and with it, the blanket. James picked up

the blanket and frowned. A burr. A large one.

"Dammit! Somebody wanted me hurt. Or dead." James glared toward Goodsight and Tucker, currently several miles out of sight. "Why the hell would he do that?"

Leg still on fire and threatening to give out, James knew he had only moments before his muscles stiffened and cramped, making his leg buckle. He had to remount and ride. Running his hand down Pinetop's neck, his skinned palm slid over sweaty hair. "Sorry about that, girl. Let's take it nice and easy from here."

CHAPTER EIGHT

S hadows turned dark gray, while James neared camp. Coozie's crackling fire, flames glowing orange and gold against the world, and the gut-warming allure of coffee, welcomed him like a beacon of relief. Sore muscles had cramped on the ride back and his right eye, a stinging cut above the brow, had puffed to where all he could see were blurry cactus and hills. Somewhere in the desert he'd lost his hat. Sand, dirt and who knew what caked his hair. Dried blood crinkled across his forehead each time he squinted.

He reined up at the remuda line. James leaned over the saddle horn, careful not to hit his tender stomach and shifted his weight until his right foot came out of the stirrup. A voice in his ear startled him. "What's wrong there?" A hand on his shoulder. "You all right?"

In addition to dirt in his ripped pants and shredded shirt, he'd managed to swallow a fair amount of sand. James hated to admit he'd fallen off his horse *again*. But, damn, he hurt. "Horse threw me." Words gravelly, he cleared his throat. He looked over at the face close to his. Andy.

James let his youngest brother ease him to the ground. Both feet down, he stood leaning against Pinetop. "Burr under her saddle. Took off like a bolt of lightning." James handed the reins to Coozie. "Thought she'd drag me clear back to Mesilla."

He tried to smile, wanted to smile, but even his face muscles hurt. Andy's strong arm around his shoulders, a gentle nudge toward the campfire, moved him forward.

"Can't imagine what happened." Entire body on fire, James eased to the ground, leaned back against a rock. He fingered the knot above his eye and accepted Coozie's damp towel. "Would someone want me hurt? On purpose?" His gaze trailed up to Andy's narrowed brown eyes as he held the cloth against his face. "Couldn't be Tucker but couldn't be anybody else."

Andy shrugged. "So, it wasn't an accident?"

James shrugged.

Andy popped the cork of a whiskey bottle Coozie handed him. He sniffed it. "Well,

I've only met this Tucker fella a couple times, and not for very long at that. But he sure didn't strike me as the kind to... to... hell, James." Andy frowned. "Was he tryin' to kill you?"

Good question. Really ace-high question. Before he could answer, and now that he was back, James thought about Pinetop. She might've been hurt in her frantic struggle to dislodge the sticker. He hadn't even much thought about her until right this minute. Should have been taking better care of his transportation. "Coozie? Take a look at Pinetop, be sure she's all right." He nodded to the cook. "When Perchman comes in, he can take another look since he's in charge of the remuda."

Andy handed James the whiskey bottle. "Drink up. You'll be damn sore tomorrow." He produced a sideways grin. "Might as well kill some of the pain now."

James patted Andy's knee. "Be glad to. Only," he eyed the elixir, "don't say *kill* again."

CHAPTER NINE

James pulled his bandana up over his nose and lowered his head against the wind knowing the weather would only get worse. Even at this time of morning, that damn spring wind threatened to wipe out what had started as a beautiful day. The sunrise, now fading the shotgun pattern of stars, had bathed the desert in shades of gold and pink. No clouds blotted out the sun. Cattle seemed to be basking in the glory, munching on grama grass like they were at a party drinking, smoking, eating, telling tall tales.

The top of his head warmed. James chided himself for not returning the other day to pick up his hat, and the brothers certainly wouldn't hold the herd an extra day simply because of his mistake. Guess he wasn't thinking too clear then, because right now he was busy being sunburned. He'd used his neckerchief for a hat yesterday, but today's wind and dust were worse than sun. Sore places tugged with every move, but at least the cut over his eye was shrinking thanks to Coozie's cool towel and some sort of poultice he'd concocted. The world was in focus again. Even his left leg was better. He could bend the knee, although it was still swollen twice its normal size. What little time he'd spent on the ground yesterday, when not in the saddle, he'd hobbled around like an old soldier with a wooden leg. And he'd needed Luke's help to mount a horse. Today, he'd managed alone.

Thoughts returned to his visit with Tucker at Goodsight station. Two questions haunted him. Why would his friend do such a thing? He searched his memory for past injustices and found none. While they weren't close friends, still, they were friendly. The other question had been answered—looked like nobody would come help with the herd.

This morning they had already turned the cattle southwest, toward the border. According to the map, that route would provide a few watering holes as well as more grass than heading due west. Perchman had confirmed this was the best route. He claimed he'd ridden this way last year and reported plenty of water and grass but, most importantly, no Indians.

If his cattle were to arrive in California in a timely manner, they'd have to travel that way, south and west, past the Chiricahua Apache. James shivered. Maybe if they detoured south far enough, far into Mexico, maybe Cochise wouldn't find them, wouldn't bother them, wouldn't—

"Stop!" James squeezed his eyes shut and gripped the reins harder than necessary. "Stop thinking."

"Stop thinking about what, Mr. Colton?" Zeb Perchman rode close, two men riding next to him. James didn't recognize either man, Mexicans according to their deeply-tanned faces.

Not answering, James reined up and faced the three men. He pulled down his bandana and within seconds tasted sand. "Visitors?"

"Reckon not." Perchman cocked his head at the two. "Seems you invited more men to

come join this little party. They're from a ranch up around that Goodsight station you went to a

couple days back." He pointed with his left arm still in a sling. "*Señors*, this is Mr. James Colton, the man who started all this. The founder of the feast, so to speak."

A quick scan of the men revealed nothing extraordinary. Both smiled and one extended a hand as he nodded at James.

"*Señor* Tucker sent us. I am Carlos Cervantes. *Con mucho gusto, señor.*"

The grip firm, the hand revealing years of hard work, strength. Relief allowed James' shoulders to sag. Help. At last. Breath caught in his chest. Were they responsible for his event? Maybe they were in cahoots with Tucker. But to what purpose? James decided to hold off

accusations until he knew them better. At that point, maybe they'd explain.

The one closest to Perchman leaned over, stuck out his hand. James took it, the grip strong as the other. "Juan Tomás Cervantes." He cocked his sombreroed head at Carlos. "I'm his cousin. *Younger* cousin."

"Only *dos días*." Carlos produced a half smile at his relative and held up two fingers.

"*Mucho gusto, Señors.*" James' Spanish was improving. "When did Tucker talk to you?"

Maybe he'd catch them in a lie right off.

Carlos and Juan Tomás glanced at each other. Carlos shrugged. "Maybe two days. Maybe

three. He came to the *rancho*. Our boss says it's all

right we leave for a while. Most of the work, already done."

"And we are here." Juan Tomás nodded, raising one shoulder. "If you do not want us, we can return to the *rancho*."

James held up a hand. "Didn't say that. Simply curious." Maybe he had jumped at a conclusion. "Had much experience with longhorns?"

Juan Tomás and Carlos chortled and spoke in unison. "Oh *sí. Mucho.*"

"*Bueno.*" James smiled inside, relieved. A glance at the herd showed they were still in New Mexico Territory, in what locals called the bootheel. Presently heading toward Mexico, they were yet a full day from the border. The cattle seemed oblivious to the wind with their rumps turned into it. James knew the pelting rocks and sand would be almost unbearable by late afternoon, the windborne dirt blotting out the entire world. Would the cattle become restless, refusing to walk, or preferring to run? Would the horses bolt as tumbleweeds hit their legs? How much more sand would he eat before this storm was done? He hated spring.

James pointed south. "Let's catch up with Coozie, sit down at the noon meal and talk."

He tilted his head toward the end of the herd. "Perchman, tell Trace—he's riding drag—to meet me at the wagon. *Señors*, follow me." He pulled up his bandana, grateful for the small respite from the wind the piece of material gave his mouth and lips.

* * *

A tin plate of Coozie's cold stew in hand, James leaned against the end table of the supply wagon. Despite the cook's best efforts, no flames would catch in this wind. Cold food was not his favorite, but he could hear Ma saying, more than once, "Take it or leave it." He'd take it. Trace finished shoveling in his plateful and polished off the food with a tortilla, left over from this morning's meal.

James eyed the two new men, both seated on nearby rocks. They looked to be about his age, mid-twenties. Both wore the look of working hard their entire lives. Little lines fanned out from Carlos's dark eyes. Laugh lines? The man's full mustache draped over his upper lip like it had grown there since the day he was weaned. While neither man was tall, they weren't skinny. Each had muscles, or at least what James figured were muscles under their coats. Their shoulders filled out their shirts and the buttons in front strained to keep the material together. The leather vests didn't begin to meet in the middle.

Juan Tomás sipped from his cup, then pointed south, toward the herd. "*Señor* Tucker told us this is your first time with the cattle, *señor*. But looks to me like you don't need no help." His dark eyes flashed on his cousin. "But if you do, we have been only as far as Tubac."

"*No se* what is farther west." Carlos scraped the last of his stew, forked pieces of potato and beef into his mouth, and talked over it. "But we are eager to see for ourselves. This California. Maybe we see some pretty *señoritas*, no?"

Trace raised both eyebrows. "Your job is to chase cattle, not women. *¿Comprendé?*"

Grins bloomed on both faces, both sets of eyes glowing. "Oh *sí*." Carlos's shoulders shook with the chuckling. He nodded. "But there is always time for both, señor."

"First one, then the other, Carlos." Juan Tomás elbowed his cousin.

James smiled, too. "Don't get them confused." He glanced at Trace whose grin was a welcome sign. "Steers have *four* legs."

"Oh, *sí*. Juan Tomás leaned back on his rock and pointed his fork at James. "*Señor*, you'll be a good boss."

CHAPTER TEN

Where was Trace? James stood in the stirrups, squinted into the horizon, sheets of sand and tumbleweeds whipping past. Nothing but endless sand and blurry cactus, thanks to half of the desert in his eyes. An hour ago, Trace had volunteered to scout for water holes Perchman promised would be there. But he should've been back already. The cattle, spread out over half a mile, kept their pace slow but steady. Squinting harder, he could barely make out Andy riding swing up near the front, his green bandana covering his mouth and nose.

But where the hell was Trace? James twisted in his saddle until he spotted Luke back behind him, on the other side of the herd, bringing up the rear. Luke rode bent over, face down, reins held loose, letting the horse plod behind the cattle. Hat pulled low on his forehead, the figure reminded James of pictures of defeated warriors he'd seen in books. Luke hated riding drag, everybody did, but all hands took turns and today was his. James snorted. His brother would simply have to grow up and do his job. Quit complaining.

He thought about Luke and Sally, school sweethearts. She and his brother hadn't planned to marry at such a young age, barely eighteen, but before it became obvious she was with child, they had taken vows. Now even being married with two children, Luke still didn't act like a mature adult. Maybe, just maybe, after this drive was over, Luke would do whatever he could to win back Sally and bring his family to Mesilla. Or go back to Kansas and rebuild what he'd destroyed when he'd lied about riding with murdering Quantrill. Taking the side of slavers. How could he? James shook his head. Slavery was wrong. He knew the sheer terror firsthand and slavery was flat wrong.

His concern about Luke turned to Trace. Where the hell was he? Cold knots of dread

wedged their way into his chest. That same terror he'd felt when he and Trace were held captive by Cochise a couple of years ago. Back then, Trace would be sent rabbit hunting. What felt like days would pass before he and the Apache returned. The same dread clenched James' stomach now.

Swinging left, James saw Juan Tomás, or was that Carlos? Hard to tell at this distance. Juan Tomás was bigger, plus he wore a Mexican sombrero, its wide brim easy to spot. Yep, there he was. Coozie and the wagon were up ahead, which left Trace, Perchman and Carlos missing. This late in the afternoon, with the dirt and dust sailing past, distinguishing certain people proved hard. Wait. He'd forgotten he'd sent Perchman to catch up with Trace so the two of them could plot and plan tomorrow's route. Before sunset today, they'd bed the cattle about a mile farther on, and by sunrise tomorrow, this damn wind should have blown itself out.

But where was Carlos? Nagging doubts surfaced. Hairs raised on James' neck. Why was he reacting like this? Carlos hadn't done anything to deserve his doubt. Yet. Of course James had only known him two days, but Tucker had more or less vouched for them.

Tucker. James rethought. Despite his eagerness, maybe hiring these new drovers wasn't such a good idea. Maybe Tucker had sent them to finish whatever he had started. And he'd started to kill James. Or so it seemed. On the other hand, maybe the burr hadn't been intentional. Maybe the sticker had been there all along and somehow made its way under Pinetop's blanket.

Bang!

James jerked. A gunshot from over the next hill, way past the front of the herd. In this wind, maybe the sound hadn't carried the right way. Clearly, somebody was in trouble.

Signaling something. Nobody fired a weapon unless crucial—loud noises, thunder, even

tumbleweeds scared the cattle. They'd run. Nobody wanted a stampede. So, apparently, the stock

hadn't noticed.

James spurred Pinetop into a gallop riding closer to the front of the herd. Signaling Andy,

James pointed toward the noise. "Stay here. I'll go see." Andy held up a hand.

Nerves on fire, James envisioned everything wrong. No watering hole, Indians attacking, armed Mexican bandits holding Trace hostage. Trace killed. The list went on. He stretched out over his horse's neck and urged her forward.

Racing past the wagon, he waved at Coozie. The cook nodded and chucked to the team. Slow and steady.

Up a slight hill, around a couple of boulders, down an arroyo, past a stand of cholla.

He searched for tracks, traces of his brother's trail. Anything. Dust and sand blotted out any possible signs, instead creating little sand dunes piled against rocks. He pulled down his bandana and yelled into the wind. "Trace?" James yelled louder. "Trace?"

Down another arroyo, up the other side, and there, in front of him. A pond. Perchman, gun in hand, kneeling over a man lying face down on the ground. Trace.

James jerked back on the reins harder than he should have, leaped out of the saddle before Pinetop stopped. Pushing through blowing dirt and sand, James fought his way to Trace. He knelt at his brother's side, grabbed the gun from Perchman.

"You shot him?" James waved the weapon at Perchman, then gripped Trace's shoulder and tugged to roll him over. "That what you did?"

"No. Shot to warn you." Perchman's head waggled back and forth. "He's poisoned."

"Poisoned?" James pushed harder, this time his brother rolled. He looked up at Perchman, eyes wider than usual. "You poisoned my brother?"

"No. The hole. Told him not to drink." Perchman shrugged. "Don't drink, is what I said.

Look for signs around it first, I said. That's what you always do. Look. Told him."

"Liar! You're lying!" James jumped to his feet, fisted his hand and drove it straight into

Perchman's cheek. The man flew backward, his right arm flailing. He crashed next to Trace.

Was Trace dead? Hand throbbing from punching

Perchman, James used the other to pat his brother's cheeks, gently at first, then harder. "Trace? Wake up. Wake up." As much as he wanted to light into Perchman and pound him into mush, Trace needed him more than James needed to beat Perchman. There would be time for that later.

James fought to control his emotions. He pulled at his brother's shirt until James had him lying draped across his knees. "Perchman." James snarled at the former trail boss lying in the dirt, rubbing his face. "Find Coozie. Maybe he knows some medicine. Something from a *curandera* or something."

Perchman scrambled to his feet. "A *curandera*? You mean a witch doctor?"

"I swear I'll beat you senseless." James pointed northeast. "Git!"

"Wasn't me." Perchman grabbed his dirt-encrusted hat from the ground. "I didn't poison

him. Wasn't me. I didn't do it." He pulled the hat down low, mumbling as he headed for his mount. "Well, hell, if you want a medicine man, instead of a real... Don't know who'd do such a thing, but—"

"Get the hell moving. Do what I said." James fought the need to scream obscenities at the man, but instead yelled, "Git!"

Before Perchman's rear hit the saddle, Trace coughed. James propped him up farther

until he was almost upright. "You're all right. Be right as rain. Thank heaven."

James wasn't a religious man, but at times he sure felt the need to thank somebody, and

God seemed handy. Trace's eyes fluttered open. He frowned, sat up straight, leaned over and

vomited.

Spasms hit, one right after another, until he sagged back against James' chest. Trace

gripped his stomach, both hands shaking. He brought his knees up under his chin, his entire body wracked with twitching.

"Perchman's riding for help." James hoped the cook knew an antidote for whatever had tainted the water. He pulled in a deep gasp. The watering hole. The herd was heading straight for death and would be here within the hour. He had to stop them. Maybe they hadn't smelled the water yet. Somehow, these cattle had an uncanny sense of knowing where water was.

But he couldn't leave his brother. He'd rather lose two thousand steers than one brother. He untied his bandana, using the cloth to mop Trace's sweaty forehead. James surveyed the watering hole. At some distance up a small rise, lay Trace's horse, twitching in final death throes. James pulled Trace closer.

As he sat waiting, hoping, he spotted something gray sticking out from under a creosote

bush. A coyote lay on its side.

What the hell? Who would do such a thing? Before he could begin to answer the question, a whoosh of hooves galloping over sand made James look over his shoulder. Coozie, not in a wagon, but on horseback.

Coozie, canteen and small cloth bag in hand, sprinted over to James, knelt beside the two men. "*¿Como?*" His question was soft yet tinged with concern.

"Threw up everything he had." James turned to the cook, hoping he could help. "Think he'll be all right?"

Coozie peered into Trace's eyes, then felt on either side of his neck. He rocked back on

his heels and looked at James. "Could be loco weed. Could be worse." Coozie shrugged and untied the bag, gray powder floating out. "This will settle his stomach. Maybe calm him, too."

"What's this?" James peered inside. Nothing but a charcoal grayish concoction, a

powder, about flour consistency.

"Different flower seeds and leaves ground together." A half smile raised a corner of Coozie's mouth. "My *abuela* gave this to me before I left. Grandmother is *mucho*, how you say?... *full of skill* at curing people."

"What d'we do?" For the first time, James allowed hope.

"Mix some of this with canteen water I brought, he drinks it. We wait." Coozie crossed himself then nodded at Trace. "With these powders and prayers, he will be well again."

CHAPTER ELEVEN

Whid MacGilvray stretched out on the ground, propped his head up on one elbow, and tossed a small stick into the fire. Plans were proceeding fine. He glanced into the surprisingly clear night sky. The windstorm, its stinging sand and clouds of dirt, had blocked out everything including the few trees, mesquite bushes, and especially distant mesas. Everything. But tonight, the wind had blown itself into a much-needed siesta, and Whid was grateful. He hated wind almost as much as he hated James Colton. Almost.

"Think they'll spot our fire?" Pickett sat cross-legged opposite his partner, the campfire between them. His tin cup pointed west. "We're too close in my thinking. What if they wander

over this way?"

Whid used his tongue to move the chew wad over to his other cheek. "So what?" He

found mesquite beans and flicked them into the fire. "What'll they find? I'll tell you what they'll find. Two men, traveling in the same direction. So what?"

"So what if that Perchman fella recognizes us from the saloon last week? What if he tells the law?"

"What law?" Whid sat up and spat, the brown glob hitting Pickett's boot. "Hell, there ain't no law within fifty miles."

Pickett used his cup to again point toward the herd half a mile away. "That one fella is. Hell, Whid, he's the sheriff of Mesilla. And that younger pup's a deputy. Ain't much more 'law' than that."

Whid whipped off his hat and slapped it against his knee. "Arrest us for what? Huh?

What? Even if Perchman squeals, who's gonna take the word of a beat-up drunk? It's our word

against his."

"But—"

"And that sheriff's half dead, anyways." Whid stared into the star-laden sky. "Would've been full dead if that tar-sucking Perchman hadn't pushed him away from the water."

"Killed his horse, though."

Whid huffed into his mustache. "Yeah. Killed 'im good." He thumbed over his shoulder toward the tainted watering hole. "I figure those coyotes are about filled up on horse, don't ya think?"

"Deputy knows you." Pickett wiped one eye. "We saw him in town. Hell, Whid, you even talked to him up close. He'll recognize you sure as hell."

Yeah, that could be a problem. Whid shrugged. "I'll kill him if he calls me by name." He spat again. Brown liquid dribbled down his beard, a few drops splattering his trousers. He used his sleeve to swipe the spittle disappearing into the beard. Scrambling to his feet, he fit his hat

back onto his head and pointed into the dark. "I need to water a bush. When I come back, we'll

do us some more planning for poor ol' James Colton. Hell, he ain't seen trouble yet."

CHAPTER TWELVE

J ames squatted at the campfire, extended his hands, rubbed them together. Despite today's ferocious windstorm, dirt, sand and rocks pummeling his face, the night had turned chilly. The fire's heat soothed his nerves. He looked at Trace sitting on the other side of the campfire. His face had regained some normal color, and he had been able to stand by himself. Food had no appeal, but he'd taken several sips of cool water along with Coozie's special tea.

Coozie's grandmother had saved Trace's life. No denying that. James made a mental note to thank her when he had the chance. He reviewed the day. Who had poisoned the watering hole? Where had Carlos been? Was Perchman the culprit? Somebody else? But why? Two big questions—who and why. Above all else, he knew he wouldn't like the answers.

But what he did like were the people on this cattle drive. The men in the outfit were top notch. The moment Perchman left to fetch Coozie, he'd been able to turn the herd around and head them a mile away. Apparently, they'd not smelled water yet. If they had, Perchman said, there's be no stopping them.

Coozie poured more coffee into James' cup. "He's better. Your brother."

"It was close, that's for sure," James said.

"*Si.*" Coozie poured a cup for himself, sat on a rock next to Trace. "A day or two, you will be fine, *señor.*"

Trace nodded.

Near enough to the campfire to stay warm, far enough away not to roast, Carlos and Perchman lay rolled up in blankets, heads on saddles, snores wafting into the desert. They had turned in early, both now wheezing and snorting like a herd of fighting bulls. James wondered how they didn't wake each other. Andy had ambled off into the night in search of the perfect place to "help the wildflowers grow," as he'd said. James smiled.

Andy. Easy going, hardworking, straight head on his shoulders. Way too grown up for nineteen. He hadn't had any trouble taking time off from his two jobs. One was being Trace's deputy. Before leaving on this drive, Trace had appointed two men to fill in and help Sammy Estrada, Trace's other deputy, now temporary acting sheriff. And Sam Bean, Andy's boss at the saloon, had asked him to investigate the wines in California, see if they were as tasty as the wine produced in the fertile Mesilla Valley. And if Andy brought back a bottle or two, Sam said he'd appreciate it.

Two horses trotted into camp. Was it that time already? James realized the first night watch was over, and time was at hand for him and Andy to mosey around the herd, singing to the cattle, making sure they stayed bedded down until he was relieved by the third guard. But, at least with two extra hands on board, his watch was only two hours long, not three. He was sleeping more now. But not tonight. He'd agreed to take Trace's place in the fourth guard, which meant James would come back to camp in two hours, sleep two hours, and be up again well before first light.

James pushed his still-sore body off the rock and met Luke and Juan Tomás at the tie line. "Anything unusual?"

"Nope. Nothing." Luke pulled his saddle off his roan and set the leather down. "Peaceful and quiet. Like we want."

Juan Tomás, saddle in hand, glanced up. "And the stars. They shine extra hard tonight."

Luke and Juan Tomás headed toward the supply wagon. James stopped the new hand.

"Put your gear down over there. We need to talk."

James walked with him over to a mesquite bush near the fire where he set down his

saddle. Here he would lay out his bedroll and sleep tonight. Juan Tomás stretched, arching his back. "Long days in the saddle." Another stretch. "*Señor* Colton. What is the matter?"

He wasn't sure exactly how to approach Carlos's relative, so James spoke right out. "This afternoon. The watering hole. Somebody poisoned it. *Some*body. I can account for everybody but Carlos." James hated to ask. "Was it him?"

Juan Tomás ran his brown-eyed gaze up and down James, inch by inch. He shook his

head frowning. "No, *Señor*. It was not Carlos. He is my cousin. He would never do anything like that." Juan Tomás spread his arms. "He likes you and your brothers. There is no reason for him to harm anyone."

"You're sure?"

"*Si*." Juan Tomás nodded. "I know where he was, too. I hate to say this, but your cook's

stew did not agree with his stomach. Carlos was...
well, he went aways off and well...

from both ends." He hung his head. "In truth. It
upset my stomach, too."

James pulled in air. That's what Carlos had already
said. Either they were both lying or both telling the
truth. James wanted to believe that Coozie's stew had set
wrong on their stomachs. He wanted to believe. But did
he dare?

And if he did believe, who did that leave? No one. A
sudden shiver washed over James.

He patted Juan Tomás' shoulder. "Sorry you were
sick. Thanks for telling me." He pointed toward the
campfire. "Coffee or shut eye. Whichever agrees with you
more."

Juan Tomás nodded and ambled toward Trace and the
wagon. Silhouettes of the men

danced in and out of the campfire's glow. Was this the
way the entire trip would be? Afraid of

shadows on each turn in the trail? A wag of his head,
James walked toward his horse.

"Hey, James." Andy stepped into the firelight, a bit
out of breath. He pointed back over

his shoulder. "Out there."

"It's real damn dark. I know." James tightened the
cinch on his horse's saddle. "Let's go."

"No. What I mean is," Andy pointed east. "I heard a
noise out there. Over there, way past that little hill."

"What kind of noise? Coyote? Cougar?" James hoped
the cattle wouldn't be attacked

tonight. Not tonight with no moon. The world was
dark, pitch dark.

"Nope. Not animal." Andy lowered his voice and
glanced around. "Footsteps. People footsteps. I heard

stones crunching like was someone was walking on them."

"Indians? You think it was Indians?" Instinctively, James moved closer to his brother.

"Doubt it. They don't wander at night." Andy turned and peered into the darkness. "No idea who the hell it was." He spun back around. "Ghosts?"

CHAPTER THIRTEEN

"That's twice now. Twice I could've shot him." Whid aimed a finger at Pickett. "Shot him right in the heart. Point blank. *Blam!*" His hand recoiled with the imaginary blast. He unrolled his bedroll and spread the canvas blanket next to the dying campfire.

Pickett pulled his coat closer around his body and shoved his hands into the pockets.

"Hope it's worth it."

"What?" Whid frowned at his partner. That man always questioned what he was doing. And why. Couldn't he for once, keep quiet? Couldn't he come up with some ideas of his own, for a change? "What the hell you talkin' about?"

"I ain't too high on goin' back to jail. That's what I'm talkin' about," Pickett said. "Seems to me, all you wanna do is kill this James Colton, and when you do, you think that gal's gonna come prancin' back into your arms." He fed a small stick into the fire and looked over the flames.

"Well, she ain't. She never liked you anyhow. Never even gave you a second thought. That much I'm sure of."

"What d'you know?" Whid hated when Pickett started talking like this. Maybe he'd shoot his boot-lickin' partner first.

Pickett smoothed out a lump in the bedroll. "It wasn't Colton put you in jail. Give you three years. You did that all by yourself." His gaze returned to the fire. "You was always doggin' her, offerin' to help carry packages, askin' her out for supper."

"She was keen on me." Whid sneered at his partner. "Her pa wouldn't let her see me. She would've run off with me if he'd of let her."

"She wasn't going nowhere with you." Pickett sat cross-legged on the blanket. "Hell,

Whid. If you'd of left her alone, like her pa told you, more 'n once, and you hadn't torn up that saloon, nearly killing those men, you wouldn't've been stuck behind bars." He pulled in air. "Or me. It was 'cause of you I ended—"

"You deserved it." Whid snorted. "Shoulda paid the damages like I told you to."

"Wasn't worth eighteen months."

"What the hell you know about women anyways?" Whid fisted and unfisted his hands. "Her pa saying she's seeing someone else and for me to scat, stop bothering her, he says. Well, hell, that sits on a man's chest. Eats right into him. What kinda man's gonna let another man push him around like that? Huh?"

Pickett wagged his head, his shoulders sagging. "Sure didn't need to go almost killing that one fella in the bar. Didn't even know him." He picked up another stick, teased the flames. "I hear he still can't walk... or feed himself. You hit him that hard."

"So? That ain't deserving of three damn years." He snorted. "Three damn years of *my* life behind bars."

"Maybe so." Pickett lay down and pulled another blanket over his body. "All I'm sure of is I'm done with jail. Ain't never goin' back."

Whid dug around in his coat pocket and pulled out a plug of chewing tobacco. He stuffed a wad into his mouth, closed the sack of Durham, shoved the fixings back into his pocket. The acidic tobacco taste always calmed his nerves, always made him feel better. Think better.

And what he needed to think about was his next move against that stinking Colton boy. Whid squatted near the fire and pushed a small mesquite branch into the orange heat. Flames shot up, within seconds settling down into sparks of red and gold. Smoke sailed straight up. No

breeze. Not even a hint of wind.

While the stick burned, Whid thought. Originally, he'd planned to gun down James

Colton. Only him. Out in the open. In front of Morningstar and his brothers. But, Whid had been given a delicious opportunity to kill them all. The whole stinking tribe. Every last one of them. Would he pick them off one by one, like he'd been trying to? Or would he take them all down at once? Maybe when they gathered around a campfire, or a watering hole?

One thing he knew for sure. Harassing this little party was more fun than he'd imagined.

Thoughts of tormenting James Colton produced a smile so wide his cheeks hurt.

Unquestionably, the harassing needed to continue. What was one thing about James Colton that set him apart from the others? Where was he most vulnerable?

Whid turned over possibilities. His job? Nah. His brothers? A definite yes. But more than them? Morningstar. Absolutely. Hurting her or even threatening to was out of the question. He loved her too much for such extremes. But James was another matter.

Thinking back to the days he'd spent in Mesilla, he nodded. One quiet afternoon, he'd talked for hours with Sam Bean, owner and operator of the Colton family's favorite bar, the one Andy worked part time for. Sam was more than forthcoming when Whid told him their families had been neighbors in Kansas. Hell, he'd even spun some tales about him and his own brothers playing with the Colton brothers. The fact that Whid didn't know of any brother he had, didn't stop him. Playing make-believe had been fun.

Sam said he'd never seen a family of four brothers so close. Inseparable. While Whid confirmed it and bought many drinks, Old Sam had outlined, in detail, James' and Trace's lives since they arrived in Mesilla. He talked about how the two of them got captured by Cochise and how James never recovered. He described James' mental state when he got back—the whoring, drinking, fighting.

And how Trace tried to help his brother, having to clean up the destruction James had wrought on the town and himself. How James had killed the former sheriff and was ordered to join the Union Army as punishment. Sixteen-year-old brother Andy had joined the army with him. The saloon's owner made it a point to talk about the youngest Colton. What a terrific person he was, an upstanding young man. Less than a year after joining, he'd been discharged from the army due to his young age combined with a wound he'd received near Yuma.

More accolades about Andy, on and on and on until Whid knew he'd throw up. According to Sam, Andy and saints were one and the same. But, with Whid's leading questions, Sam had also mentioned how, after James had met Morningstar in Tucson, he'd become a changed man. A decent man. A good man.

Whid's stomach twisted when he considered the rest of what he'd learned. James' loyalty to Morningstar was legendary. All around Mesilla he'd heard about James' undying love for his wife. What about James being caught with another woman? Whid spat into the fire. The sizzle resonated in his head. His chest swelled. Yeah, that was the answer.

So, ol' Jamey boy's gonna fall off the wagon. And with a fallen angel in Nogales, Mexico, no less. A big, fat, ugly one... with no teeth... older than his ma.

Whid's chortle grew into a full-blown laugh, shoulders heaving with possibilities. "Got it, Pickett."

Pickett rolled over and glared at Whid. "Got what?"

"It, my friend. Got 'it'." Whid lowered his voice. "*It* involves a cantina, lots of *mescal*,

and a willing woman. All in Nogales."

CHAPTER FOURTEEN

From atop his favorite horse, James yawned. He stretched. The familiar *pop-pop-pop* of his back complaining made him stretch harder. He reached his arms overhead, out to his sides, behind him. He twisted gently, yawned again, this time longer and louder. Endless hours in the saddle. Would he ever get used to it? Spikes of sun peeked over the cactus-dotted east mesa, its warm fingers spreading like heated tendrils across the sand. James squinted. This time of early morning always made him stop and appreciate things. His family, his wife and Nature topped his list. As if right on cue, a covey of Gambel's quail scurried from under a mesquite bush. Pinetop skittered sideways. James grabbed the saddle horn. *Now* he was awake.

He turned his back to the rising sun and surveyed the herd. Spread out for a quarter mile, the white-faced cattle, long-horn as well as muley steers, sat on their bed ground, content simply to sit, chewing chunks of grama grass and whatever else they found growing within reach. So far, the cattle were peaceful with each other, even with a mixed group like this.

James rode around the tail end of the herd for the last time this morning, his two-hour watch about over. When they'd first started this adventure, James figured Perchman was crazy for suggesting the night guard sing to the herd throughout the night. The former trail boss claimed cattle were insecure and liked knowing someone was watching over them. Kind of like a "cow lullaby," he'd said. James huffed. Cowhands were crazy. They spent way too much time in the sun eating dust and bad beans. Besides, if he sang "Old Dan Tucker" once more, he knew he'd become crazy too. However, that song seemed to settle cattle faster than anything else he'd managed to croak out. Half the time, his voice sounded like a mule with a bad cold. But he sung to them anyway. "Oh! Susanna" was the herd's second favorite.

But little brother Andy had the right idea. Ginny had presented him a harmonica just before they left Mesilla. Andy had been practicing every day now, and, despite a few truly awful notes, he was getting better. In fact, the cattle seemed to prefer Andy's tunes over James' voice. He couldn't blame them there.

He patted Pinetop's neck. She was almost as worn out as he. Endless days of riding, watching over cattle, had certainly taken a toll on James' body. Not only did his back groan every time he climbed aboard or dismounted a horse, but his knees complained as well. Did cowhands who did this day in and day out also have creaky knees and bad backs? At any rate, a hot cup of coffee and a long nap were in order.

Coffee was guaranteed, but a nap would have to wait. As soon as breakfast was in his belly, it would be another long day of trailing cattle. At least the promise of money at trail's end made eating dust more palatable. Kind of like a carrot dangling over a stubborn mule. Only this time, a stack of dollars dangled over dusty trail drovers. James grinned at the image.

Quick calculations showed at this rate, eight to ten miles a day, they'd be in California in two and a half months and on up to Tin Town a few weeks after that. Perfect. Exactly what he and Trace had planned. And what Tin Town was expecting.

Carlos rode up next to James, their horses matching slow strides. "Coozie's made coffee. Better pour yourself some before Andy beats you to it!" Carlos glanced over the herd and turned to James. "Any problems?"

"Nope." James ran a hand across his face. A shave would be in order today. Or not. "No sign of Indians or cougars. Been dead quiet." For the past two weeks it had been nothing exciting. That in itself didn't feel natural. But why did he question their luck?

Flashing a smile, Carlos reined his horse toward the herd. "*Calma*," he said. "That way
we like."

"That we do," James said to Carlos's fading back. Grateful another night had passed with
no incident, he headed over to that welcomed cup of coffee. Andy, on the far side of the herd,
waved. James returned the gesture with an upheld hand. Perchman would relieve Andy any
moment.

Back at the camp and once Pinetop was fed and tied with the other horses at the remuda, James ambled over to the wagon where Coozie handed him a plate. Ham and beans, held down with a tortilla, tantalized James' stomach. Coozie was a master at breakfast, somehow making a meal out of the remnants of last night's supper without the food tasting like last night's supper. Ravenous, James leaned against the wagon and shoveled beans into his mouth. Hot coffee topped the cuisine. Coozie's secret ingredient, a special seasoning of some sort, sure perked up the flavor. Yep. Coozie was a valuable member of the team. James made a mental note to thank Andy for finding him.

Grub consumed and plate handed to Coozie, James and his coffee watched Trace rolling his canvas bedroll. James nodded, more to himself than to Trace. His brother's scrape with death back at the watering hole certainly had hung a black cloud over the group for days. James shook dark images from his mind.

But two weeks had passed since that incident. Trace was himself again. And they were making progress. Nogales—civilization—was a day or three away.

Coozie held up the enamel coffee pot. "More, Señor Colton? Time to pack things away."

"Thanks," James said as Coozie poured black brew into the outstretched tin cup. He glanced around the camp. Carlos and Perchman were already with the herd. Andy was tying his horse at the line, Coozie packing supplies. Luke and Juan Tomás were swinging up into their

saddles. Looked like everyone was ready for another day. James stood near the fire, the aroma of

burning piñon adding to the coffee's flavor.

Nagging doubt, questions wouldn't let him rest. He'd speak with Trace right away. He

waited for his brother to bring his bedroll to the supply wagon where all bedding and extras were

kept. No need to weigh down a horse.

"We need to talk," James said to Trace. He wanted this conversation to be only between them for the moment. James glanced around. Nobody except Coozie within earshot.

Trace handed the bedroll, along with his saddlebags, to the cook, turned to James. "What's wrong?" Curiosity lines raced across Trace's forehead.

Keeping his voice low, James glanced over his shoulder half expecting Andy to be standing right behind him. Instead, Andy was heading off toward another bush. James turned back to Trace. "I was thinking this morning, right before dawn, that we're in Mexico. Have been for a while. And not far from Nogales." James pointed west with his tin cup, a bit of coffee sloshing over the edge.

"Isn't that what we wanted?" Trace leaned in, his eyes fixed on James. "We're following the map, aren't we?"

"Yeah." James released his pent-up concerns, the words shooting out like bullets. "But I realized that with Perchman being arrested for keeping all those cattle buyers' money and all, what'd keep him from making a dash farther into Mexico? Hell, Trace, we've already escorted him across the border. Isn't that a head-scratching thing to do? Seems to me we brought the coyote into the chicken coop. When we ride into Nogales, how do we know he won't simply take off?"

"We don't." Trace's gaze dusted the desert floor followed by a deep sigh. "Why do you suppose he hasn't run yet? I've been thinking he might."

For this, James had an answer. "He's waiting for Nogales. It would be easier escaping from there, I'm thinking. More people to use as cover." He lifted a shoulder as Luke and Juan Tomás rode off. "One man alone in the desert is a recipe for disaster. It'd be damn hard to survive."

"That it would." Trace peered inside the tin cup, then set it empty on the wagon. "We'll have to wait and see."

"I'm not liking that idea." James glanced inside the half-empty cup he held. "What I'm truly thinking is I don't want him hurting you, or any of us, simply to run." James swallowed hard. "He might kill for his freedom."

The brothers studied each other. James knew what Trace was thinking.

A shrug from Trace. "He doesn't seem like that kind, but you never know. I'll keep a closer eye on him."

"We *all* will," James said. "I'll talk to Luke and Andy. Let's take another look at the map. If I remember right, from Nogales we head west then cut north back into Arizona Territory, follow the Santa Cruz River." He cocked his head. "Half way to Tucson we'll turn west to California."

Trace pried the mug from James' hand. He held it up. "You mind?" Before James could agree, Trace sipped. He produced raised eyebrows and a slight huff, and patted James' vest. "Let's see that map."

James fished in his vest and pulled out a cotton map. He spread the material over the wagon's table.

Mumbling, Trace ran a finger along one of the markings while Andy returned to the

wagon. Coozie handed him a plate and a saved cup of coffee.

Leaning against the wagon's side, Andy scooped beans into his mouth. "What're you looking at?" He moved in closer. "Ah, hell. Don't tell me we're already lost! Knew we should've taken a left instead of—"

"You never mind, little brother." Trace picked up Andy's cup, perched on the edge of

the table and brought the coffee to his lips.

"Mine." Andy grabbed the cup. "Find your own."

James ran his finger along the trail on the map. Barely into Mexico, their route ran west along the Mexican border, moving north into Arizona at Nogales. They'd already passed a trail, Cooke's Wagon Road, that led into Arizona, about fifty miles east. Even farther east and north lay Apache Pass in Arizona. Cochise's empire covered Apache Pass and farther south, clear down into Mexico. So far, they'd avoided those hundreds of square miles and Apache. Had dipping down into Mexico been the right idea? Another look at the map. Nogales sat at the edge of Cochise's reign of terror.

Cochise.

Apache Pass.

Memories swam before James' eyes. The map blurred. Rawhide strips sawed into his wrists, his back jammed against the prickly saguaro. Demonic horsewhip digging into flesh. A steely knife sliced across his neck. Screams. Trace's. His. Pleas for mercy. Trace's... his. Indian taunts—

A hand on his shoulder. James recoiled at Cochise's deathly grip.

"What's wrong? You're shaking."

The same hand shook him harder.

"James?"

Vowing not to give in, he wouldn't let the Apache see him weak. James straightened his shoulders. With new air came a new world. Not Cochise's world. Not his world from before. This world. The now world.

James frowned at the face attached to the hand on his shoulder. Andy.

"You all right?" Andy released James' shoulder. "Cochise again?"

Holding up a hand, James ran his trembling fingers

through his hair, then across a scar on his left cheek. He patted Andy's shoulder. "I'm all right." He looked over at Trace. "We both are."

Apache memories and images pushed firmly back into the corners of his mind, James shook his head, licking too-dry lips. He addressed both Andy and Trace. "Guess we'll merely keep on, follow the southern trail like we have been."

Trace stared into the desert, his words turning soft. "Damn Indians attack at odd times."

CHAPTER FIFTEEN

The men, antsy, as hard to hold as cattle once they smelled water, could taste Nogales. That town offered something besides endless beans, biscuits and dust. James felt the tug too. The sleepy Mexican village pulled at him, its tendrils, like soft arms, wrapped around his body, whispering possibilities. He allowed himself to be seduced. With any luck, by tomorrow at this time, he'd be there, reveling in beer and relaxation. No hard saddle. No stinging wind. No cattle rumps.

Sun straight overhead, James reined up on the left flank of the herd, stopping next to Luke, who swung one leg over the saddle horn like he'd been a cowhand all his life.

"Finally!" Luke pulled in air. "You smell it? Nogales. Just over those hills." From his vest pocket he pulled a pouch of tobacco and cigarette papers, nodded at James. "Want one?"

Back aching, James shook his head, hunched his shoulders. He twisted side to side, moving as much as sitting in the saddle allowed. His gaze rested on his brother. "Thought only dandies and doxies smoked cigarettes." Luke's glare proved James had hit a nerve. "If my reckoning's right, you aren't either one."

"I *do* prefer cigars to these. But I'm all out." Luke sprinkled tobacco over a thin sheet of paper, licked one side and rolled it. "This'll have to do 'til we hit Nogales. Plan on buyin' me a fistful of Cubans."

James couldn't resist teasing. "Why d'you think any of us are riding into town? Unless you come up with a damn fine reason, nobody goes. No need to take risks."

"What? Why the hell not?" Luke struck a match against his leather chaps. "You can't say

who leaves and who doesn't." Holding the flame to the end of the cigarette, he pulled in a lungful of smoke and immediately spewed it out. "You ain't my boss. Hell, you ain't even Pa."

"No, but we all agreed I *am* in charge." James fought a tinge of anger. Why was Luke so ornery? During the last few days he'd spent hours in sulky silence, then a moment later he'd lapse into a fit of glee. No telling which Luke would come to the table. Otherwise, he'd done his duties well, roused himself in the middle of the night to ride guard without being reminded, helped when steers strayed into the brush. So, what was wrong with this brother?

"What d'you think'll happen in town?" Luke shook out the match, pointed the burnt end at James. "Think we'll all run off, like Perchman might do? Or get drunk and thrown in jail? I hear there's nothing like spendin' time in a Mexican prison to put hair on your chest." He blew smoke toward his brother.

James fought a sneeze and dropped his voice low. "Jail? Hell, we might get killed."

Luke snorted. "Well, I'm not hankering to do either one, big brother. Merely looking for some fun. A beer. A bath. Maybe another beer."

And a woman, James thought. Another thought hit him. Had Luke been faithful to Sally

this past year in Mesilla? Did he really want to know? This brother had a reputation as a man with a quick temper and an eye for women. How much philandering had he done behind Sally's back? Hell, behind all their backs? James bristled. Last winter, while he and Trace had been up in Mogollon looking for Andy, Luke had ridden into Mesilla and tried to seduce Morningstar. Had he succeeded? Only those two knew for sure and both had denied dalliance. James wasn't sure, but he thought Morningstar had nothing to hide.

Nothing to hide. His thoughts returned to Mesilla and a few weeks before leaving on this drive. Beautiful Morningstar had sat on the sofa, James next to her, her hand in his. He stammered, "I'm sorry from the bottom of my heart, Star. I didn't have the words to tell you this sooner."

She looked at him with those bright, round eyes. Eyes that sparkled when she laughed. Star didn't say anything, but kept her gaze steady on his face.

James studied their entwined hands, his heart tap-tap-tapping, mouth desert dry. He swallowed and whispered, "I've been married before." He waited for her to cry, or scream.

Instead, she lightly squeezed his hand.

Pressure built, engulfing his chest. "When I was Cochise's captive?" He waited for her nod. "They also took a Pima girl captive." How could he look into Star's face? He couldn't. Instead, he stared at their hands. "She was maybe fourteen. It was Cochise's way of humiliating the enemy. There was no one lower than me, a White Eyes captive. So he made us marry, and then I... then... with Dark Cloud. Her name was Dark Cloud."

Morningstar placed her free hand on top of his.

James pulled in air and courage. "They took her into the desert and..." He swallowed hard. "If... if they hadn't killed her, she'd've had my child." He allowed his gaze to trail up to her eyes. "But we were married only three days. I didn't love her but needed her. By then, Trace was gone. She helped me get through..." Tears clouded his vision. No more words would come.

James flinched at a light punch to his upper arm, bringing him back to the here and now. He glared at Luke, now busy gazing out into the desert.

Luke pointed south. "Must be a mighty fine dust cloud you're staring at. Mind if I join the 'thought' wagon train, too? Feel kind of left out."

Pulled into the present, James looked away, blinked back moisture collecting in his eyes. He sniffed and shook his head. "Sorry. Just thinking."

"So, I'll ask again, since you weren't listening the first three times," Luke nudged James'

arm. "What's wrong with us riding into Nogales?"

James pushed Luke's voice aside, allowing memories to rush back in and settle on what happened later that evening. Warmth and peace wrapped arms around James, holding him, reminding him of Star's embrace. At long last he'd been able to be a man with her. Be the man he'd always wanted to be. Was Star with child now? He desperately hoped so. If anything, for her sake. For *their* sake.

And damnit! Why had he waited so long to tell her?

"Hello? James?" Luke leaned in close, snapping his fingers. "Over here. You were saying?"

James flashed the famous family grin, smacked Luke's shoulder. "Nothing's wrong. Just trying to rile you."

"Did a helluva job there, older brother." Luke rubbed out his cigarette on his chaps, flicked the butt to the sand.

"Just that, well, I have a bad feeling about Nogales, is all."

Luke swung his leg back over the saddle and slid his boot into the stirrup. "You and your feelings." He tossed a half smile at James. "I'll show you how to wrangle 'em down to size—damn fast." He gigged his horse. "Once we're sippin' that fine tequila."

CHAPTER SIXTEEN

James' jealous streak was certainly out in spades today. He fought the urge to pound his fists on the ground, hold his breath until he turned blue, and scream *it's my turn. I should be first*. After all, this entire venture was his idea. Instead of holding his breath, he let air out inch by inch. He pulled in a lungful, let that out. A third pull, his heart returned to a normal beat.

At last under control and feeling a bit silly, James surveyed the men, four holding a long mesquite stick. Trace's face beamed, as did Carlos's and Andy's. Perchman's mouth curved up at one end, lifting the mustache. They were the lucky ones. They'd ride into Nogales this afternoon, after the mid-day meal. The only consolation, if there was such, was that Luke had drawn the short one, too. Luke had to wait his turn. If he wasn't so angry, James would have laughed. So he and Luke, along with Coozie and Juan Tomás, would stay behind to watch the cattle—all night. Fair enough, tomorrow the four of them would ride into town. But still, this cattle drive was *his* idea. And he was the boss.

This morning as they pushed cattle, Andy pulled out his pocket watch, checked the sky every other minute. James considered this brother riding in front of him. The kid. Hopefully, trouble wouldn't find Andy or he find it. Big brother Trace would be sure he towed the line. Not too much drinking, probably not much gambling and more than likely no women. Of the four brothers, only Luke would be apt to take up with ladies of such persuasion. Those temptations were nothing but trouble. More than one man was killed over misplaced affections. At the very least, men wound up with serious diseases. Andy certainly didn't need that. Undoubtedly, Trace would remind Andy of his ladylove waiting back home.

Trace located a thin stream, and next to it, plenty of mesquite and low grama grass. A

perfect place to bed the cattle for a couple of days. Give them a chance to get fatter and the men to get to town.

Shortly after the noon meal, the men rode off in search of something besides cattle, waves trailing over their shoulders. James knew he wouldn't see them until tomorrow around this time. Hopefully, they'd come dragging in before then. The sooner the better. He'd leave the moment they returned.

* * *

Once the sun hit the eastern horizon, the steers blinked awake. This morning, like every morning, the saddle was hard, but the anticipation of town lifted his spirits. James shifted his weight reining Pinetop around toward the back of the herd. Although his job today was making sure they stayed in one place, being shorthanded, he'd swing back to check on the cattle. Off to his left, behind a clump of mesquite, James spotted two tails. He sighed. Why couldn't the calves stay with the others? Seemed like they were always either getting lost or ambling too far behind.

James reined his horse into the desert, flanking the calves on their right. He stopped.

Faint wood smoke floated on the air. Turning in his saddle, he lost the scent. Couldn't be from Luke's match or from Coozie—he'd packed up hours ago and rode well out in front of the herd. He wouldn't be setting up, starting a fire for another hour. James sniffed the air again. Nothing but a hint of dirt, a harbinger of another windstorm. Nothing smelling like campfire. He stood in his stirrups and sniffed.

Mesquite bushes, low hills and desert sand greeted him.

Frowning, he shrugged. "What d'you think, Pinetop? Am I crazy?" He patted the horse's neck. "Don't answer that."

CHAPTER SEVENTEEN

Where the hell were they? As far as James was concerned, by this time today, he should've been in Nogales, eating belly-satisfying grub, restaurant food, smoking the *oregano chino*, and sipping on a nice sudsy brew. He couldn't wait to enjoy the hustle and bustle a town brings. But no, so far this morning he'd had nothing but trouble. Soon, though, he'd be able to leave camp, have his

chance to tamp down his doldrums.

This morning, cantankerous steers had decided to strike out on their own, kind of like unruly school children. It had taken longer than he'd wanted to round them up, wrangling them like putting snakes into a box. And then later, a short-lived windstorm blew out the campfire. Embers popped into bushes, setting several on fire—a recipe for a stampede. After throwing saddle blankets on the mesquite, everyone had to circle the herd, singing until the cattle calmed. Worse yet, the men had to be content with cold grub.

He sat in the saddle, grumbling at the wind, the

cattle, the whole idea of trying a cattle drive, his impatience. Where the hell were they? Movement in the distance, south. Four riders plodding toward him. Finally.

James chuckled at Trace, Andy, Perchman and Carlos as they slogged back into camp, those faces glowing and yet, oh so hung over. If rumpled clothes and lingering aromas of tamales and beer were any indication, they'd taken great advantage of Nogales's hospitality. One thing was certain, though. They'd come in much quieter and slower than when riding out.

According to Trace, Perchman had been true to his word, never once straying from sight.

While they'd spent most of their time singing and hollering in Nogales's biggest cantina, *El Palacio*, they'd also found time and money to buy a bath, shave and haircut. Andy had needed a haircut more than anybody else. That boy was growing more than broad shoulders. His hair seemed to have sprung a leak when it came to adding inches. Until yesterday, it not only hung in his eyes, but well past his shoulders. Today, he was a respectable looking teenager, except for the slumped shoulders and dark circles under his eyes, which showed off a sweetheart of a hangover. And that would pass within a day or two.

Not taking any longer than necessary, James, Luke, Coozie and Juan Tomás were

mounted and whooping toward Nogales. Damn, they were late! Already siesta time, the ritual of taking a nap after dinner, the town was quiet. During siesta, everyone lay down for an hour and enjoyed a full stomach while the sun broiled overhead. People found refuge wherever they could, usually at home or in a cantina. Dogs were relegated to shade trees or under the few porches. No one paid the animals much attention, anyway, but the dogs, pigs and goats always seemed to find a spot of coolness in which to snooze. Even the chickens roaming the streets managed to stay out of the sun's way during the heat of the day.

James reined up at the edge of town and soaked in the adobe buildings, the lingering smells of various noon-day cooking whetting his appetite. Strange, he had missed being in a town. Until this moment, it had never crossed his mind. The others reined up beside him.

Luke raised his nose to the air. "Enchiladas or posole." He licked his lips. "My stomach feels like a post-hole that ain't been filled up yet. I'm finding something to eat." He flashed a wide smile at James. "Meet you at *El Palacio* later."

"I'll ride with you," Juan Tomás said to Luke and gigged his horse. "Wonder what real cooking tastes like."

Coozie stood in his stirrups. "I heard that."

"I'm sure he was funning you," James said, hoping he had muffled the snicker threatening to rise to a full-blown laugh. Never cause the cook to be angry. No telling what he'd serve.

"We need supplies," Coozie said. "Flour, sugar, but just enough to put in these saddlebags." He stuck out his hand, palm up. "I could use some *dinero*."

James dug into his vest pocket and extracted five one-dollar coins. "Use whatever's left for yourself."

"Gracias!" Coozie nodded, pocketed the money.

Picking out supplies, other than his *oregano chino*, wasn't the way he'd envisioned spending free time. James glanced up and down the street. "How long you think it'll take?"

Coozie shook his head. "Oh, *Señor* James. I can choose supplies for myself. You enjoy your time here." He cocked an eyebrow. "*Bueno suertes. Adios.* See you in camp." Coozie turned his horse toward the mercantile.

James walked his horse down the wide dirt trail that passed for a main street. Not a soul

in sight, only tumbleweeds from the damn wind. He stopped in front of the barbershop. Should he spend the remaining minutes of the town's siesta in a barber chair or a bathtub? Remembered pleasures of each couldn't help him decide.

Too bad Trace wasn't here with him. They'd have a mighty fine time taking the town by storm, like their stage-driving days with Butterfield when they stayed overnight in Tucson. Fun days.

James chose barber first. He tied his horse to the hitchin' rail down a few places from the shop, then peered in the mercantile' window. From his vantage point, he spotted calico material, bags of flour, licorice whips, guns, ammunition, boots, straw hats, sombreros like Carlos's, water buckets, shovels—the usual. If he had a chance later, he'd step in and browse, buy something pretty for Morningstar. Since Nogales was a border town, extensive trade with the *norteamericanos* led to high prices. And there was nowhere else to buy these items. Nowhere within fifty, maybe a hundred miles.

As much as he wanted a beer, James figured he'd save that for the end of the day. Besides, he didn't know how alcohol would mix with the love potion Coozie had made for him.

Standing on the boardwalk, he stretched, turned side to side, feeling the vertebrae loosening. He stretched again, wiping beads of sweat threatening to run down his temple. Ready to be clean again, he headed inside the barbershop.

The only man in the room lazed in the single chair, the barber, if looks were any indication. The apron tied around him was a dead giveaway, and he even held scissors in his sleeping hand. Whiffs of talc and shaving cream reminded James of the few times he went with

Pa into town for a "real" shave and haircut, a treat reserved for special occasions only. Usually

Ma took scissors to all the boys' hair.

James cleared his throat. No response. He opened the door again and closed it hard.

Bang! A small start, the barber opened one eye and blinked at James. *"Señor?"*

"Buenos dias." James extended his hand and was surprised when the barber grabbed, scissors still in hand. The grip was firm if not downright painful. Hand released, James fisted and unfisted the pain. "Need a haircut and shave, *por favor.*"

"Si, Verdad. Tas muy peludo." A rumble erupted from the barber's ample chest, which jiggled as he laughed. He nodded at James. *"Sientese, señor,"* and pushed his body out of the chair. "I am funning with you, *Señor.* You are not so hairy. *Sientese."*

Despite slight humiliation, James enjoyed the time spent in the chair. It was a hundred

times more comfortable than his saddle, and a thousand times more comfortable than sleeping on

the ground. He caught himself dozing more than once while the man clipped, snipped, and

scraped. James hated to see him finish, pampering come to an end. Nevertheless, he pulled in

a deep breath, stood, and gazed in the mirror. Yep.

There stood a much neater version of the man who'd walked in a half hour before. He rubbed his smooth cheeks. James left extra coins for the barber.

The bathhouse was easy enough to find. Two doors down, across the street. This time of

day, a few people were again out and about. Siesta had ended. James looked forward to catching his own siesta. Five pesos bought a tub, soap and towel.

Bath water warm, but not hot, sudsy, but not overly so, he leaned back and closed his eyes. He wished he knew who invented baths; he'd like to thank them. There was nothing better

at times like this. He let his mind wander.

What *was* better than a warm bath? That was easy. A warm woman. James thought about

Morningstar. The moment he returned, he'd take her in his arms and give her children. A yardful of children. Unless she already...

Despite the warm water, James shivered. Why had he waited so long to tell Star? Should've been before they took vows. He had to stop thinking. Why was it so damn hard to push those memories and guilty aside? His first marriage was years ago. Or was it? Sometimes the days, the months melted into each other, so much so he couldn't tell up from down.

The manager walked in, bucket in hand. "*¿Señor? More water?*"

James shook his head, trying to loosen the grisly images rather than answer the man.

"*¿Señor?*"

"No, *gracias.*" James cleared the memories. "I'm about done."

Instead of leaving, the man stood, mouth opening, then closing. He stared at James.

"Now you are clean, *Señor*, you want a woman?" He rushed his words. "I know *muchos* good

ones. Only a few *pesos*."

Yes, he did. But he desired only one special one. And she wasn't here. "No, *gracias*."

After dressing, smoothing his newly cut hair, running his hand across his soft cheeks,

James headed outside ready to meet the others. He was hoping they'd find a café or restaurant,

have a quick meal together, then head over to *El Palacio* for much needed unwinding.

James stepped down the boardwalk, careful not to trip on loose boards, and stopped at

his reflection in the mercantile's window, glowing amber and orange with the sun. He

straightened his shoulders. Peering closer, he again admired his new haircut and shave. His face,

once again smooth. And there on his left cheek—that wicked scar running almost nose to ear. Thanks to One Wing's whip. James wrestled down those memories.

Another look at his entire body revealed shoulders, broad from hard work. At six foot one, he could carry extra pounds. The canvas pants were new—he'd bought them the day before they'd left Mesilla, saving them for times like now. His brown boots were scuffed but had plenty of sole left. He ran a hand across the top of his head. A hat. He'd need a hat, something to shade his face. How many times had he kicked himself for losing his during the rampage through the mesquite with Pinetop in blind panic? He'd lost count.

"Told you he was prettier'n all of us."

Luke's voice and snicker spun James around. Even with the glass's reflections, he had been too preoccupied to notice Luke and Juan Tomás come up behind.

"*Si. Guapo, muy guapo,* this brother of yours." Juan Tomás's dark eyes sparkled.

Cheeks burning, James turned his back to his brother and stared down the street. Way

down at the end was a sign that might have said "restaurant." He wasn't sure, but squinting, he

read "...rant." Changing the subject was an excellent idea.

He spoke over his shoulder and pointed. "Looks like there's a place to eat down there.

Let's try it. And I need to buy a hat."

Luke draped an arm over James' shoulders. "Anything you say, *querida.*"

"I ain't your sweetheart!" James tried to pull away, but Luke held on.

Patting his brother's shoulder, Luke's words were soft under his cackling. "Sure you

ain't."

"I ain't!"

Luke hugged James tighter as he nudged him down the street.

CHAPTER EIGHTEEN

James patted his stomach as he stepped into Nogales's evening. *Chile rellenos* and *frijoles* had satisfied a nagging hunger for "real" food. Too bad Coozie had ridden back to camp. Maybe he could learn more about cooking from that food. Coffee afterwards had finished off the feast. If they served breakfast, he promised himself he'd be back. Despite Coozie's superior cooking, this was like nectar of the gods.

Juan Tomás and Luke waited down the block. James ambled to meet them, taking his time enjoying the sunset and supper. *Now* was beer time. The idea of a beer or two, maybe a shot of whiskey, tantalized him. The allure of a well-deserved night's sleep in a real bed pulled his gaze toward the only hotel in town. A feather mattress. Off the ground. Heaven. Would Heaven be like that? He met up with Luke and Juan Tomás.

"Juan Tomás says he has friends not far from here." Luke pointed south. "Says he'd rather spend time with them than us!"

"I'm hurt and disappointed." James hoped Juan Tomás understood the sarcasm. He
turned to Luke. "And a bit insulted."

"Me, too." Luke shrugged. "But what can we do? Appears he's a grown man. Makes up his own mind." He flashed a grin at Juan Tomás and thumped his back. "Enjoy! See you
tomorrow morning back at the herd."

"*Sí.*" The trail hand turned on his boot heel and stepped down the walk. "*Hasta mañana.*"

"Leaves more beer for us!" Luke yelled at Juan Tomás's back. A wave over his shoulder and Juan Tomás disappeared around the corner.

Sunset, orange turned pink turned purple, cast a slight coolness over Nogales. The sun slipping under the western mesa extinguished its awe-inspiring beauty. James turned attention to the cantina, his and Luke's ultimate destination.

El Palacio was no palace, not by anyone's standards. Flaking mud plaster covered the adobe walls, and overhead, lengths of canvas stretched corner to corner serving as a ceiling of sorts. The floor, packed dirt. So, not a palace, but the guitar was loud, beer and tequila flowed steadily. The patrons appeared happy to see more *gringos* step up to their bar. The bartender set out two short handmade clay glasses, poured clear *pulque* into them, nodded.

"On the *casa*," he said. His eyes riveted on Luke as the Colton brother picked up glass and downed the fire with one gulp. The bartender cheered and poured another one. This time, he held out a hand.

Luke handed him coins and smiled at James. "Your turn, brother." He cocked his head at the glass. "Only burns 'til you can breathe again." He held up the glass and clinked with James. "*Salud.*"

"*Salud,* yourself." James closed his eyes and downed the drink in one gulp. Stinging like a hundred snakebites, his breath tangled in his toes. But he wasn't about to let anybody see him cough or strangle on this cactus juice. No sir. James squared his shoulders and blinked at the bartender. "*Uno mas,*" he croaked. "*Por favor.*"

Luke slapped James' back. "Hell, brother, done like a real professional." He finished off a second drink and paid for a bottle. "Let's sit and see what comes our way." Luke aimed for a table in the middle of the room.

The table he chose sported four wooden chairs, each one more rickety than the other, but

somehow managed to hold bodies. Luke sat, facing the door. James eased down to his right and

couldn't help but smile. He hadn't realized how much he'd needed this until right now. No smelly cows, no choking dust, no endless stew. Simply music, liquor and sitting on something other than a horse.

While James topped off their glasses, Luke plucked a cigar out of his vest pocket. He slid

it back and forth under his nose, breathing in and sighing with each pass. Eyes closed, he tilted

his head enjoying the aroma. "Strong, yet gentle. Tart, yet sweet as Sally's—"

"I'll take your word for it." James sipped his *pulque,* that rot-gut cactus juice everyone drank, recognizing the fact he'd have to deal with a major hangover tomorrow if he wasn't careful tonight. But he didn't plan to be careful. He'd trust his horse to find her way back to camp. If things grew fuzzy, Pinetop could be in charge.

Luke's cigar smoke combined with his, wafted under James' nose. He fought down a sneeze. James looked up at two men, gringos he figured, standing at their table, *mescal* bottle in one hand, two *señoritas* in tow.

The taller of the men, skinny, bushy beard hiding the face, spoke. "Hey friends. Mind if me and my *compadres* sit a spell? All the other seats are taken."

While he didn't really want anybody else sitting with him and Luke, spoiling the fun,

James couldn't find a logical objection. Before he could agree though, Luke jumped up.

"I'll grab chairs from that other table." Luke pointed across the room and dashed away.

James nodded to the two empty chairs at his table. "Help yourself."

Bushy beard took the seat to the left of Luke's, across from James, while the much

shorter, but stockier man took the last seat between them. Luke slid the extra chairs across the

floor positioning them between himself and the bearded fella. He held the chairs for the women.

Once everyone was seated, the taller man extended a hand. "Amos Smith, and this here's

Serafina," he nodded to the woman on his left. "And this is..." He leaned across to the other one. "What's your name again?"

A deep sigh, but a sly grin slid across her rouged cheeks. "Rosella."

Amos pointed across the table by James. "That's right. Rosella, and my partner, Pickett

... Pickles."

"Pickett Pickles?" James glanced at Luke. What a ridiculous name. Sure sounded made

up. "How'd you come by that?" At any rate, should be an interesting story.

"Simply *Pickles*." The man nodded. "My friend here stutters sometimes."

Was that a glare Pickles tossed at Amos? James leaned forward despite an inner feeling

telling him to leave. But what had Luke said the other day about his feelings? James ignored the warning.

Pickles sipped his *mescal* and explained. "When I was a youngster, lived out on the plains. Ma would can vegetables every year. She pickled cucumbers and such." He threw back the rest of his drink and continued. "Pickles were always my favorite. I ate 'em ever chance I got." He shrugged. "Name kinda stuck."

James rolled his eyes and hid his disbelief by turning to Luke. "Hell, you've liked pickles since you were knee high to a tumbleweed. Ain't that right, Luke?"

Luke nodded and stuck out a hand. "Looks like we have something in common, Pickles.

I'm Luke Colton." He cocked his head to the right. "And this here's my older brother, James."

The men shook hands all around. Smith frowned at the brown clay glasses in front of

Luke and James. "You drinkin' *polque*? That cheap imitation liquid fire?"

James nodded.

"Hell, I have something that'll cause you to sit up and take notice, men." Smith held up a

bottle. "You ever try this new *mescal*? Imported all the way from Chihuahua City. Goes down damn smooth." He leaned across the table and filled James' glass. "Try this tongue tickler. It'll put fire in your belly."

Eyeing the amber liquid, then his brother, James reached for the glass. Should he try this? Then again, why not? Seemed like everyone else was drinking.

Smith poured some for himself and Luke. "Better'n

that watered down coyote piss you've been drinkin'." He lifted his glass. "To new friends."

Everyone hoisted glasses and drank.

"Hell! That's what I call a drink." Amos Smith smacked his lips, held up the empty glass and pointed at the bottle. "Goes down damn smooth." He used a finger to dig around in his cheek, extracting a wad of well-mashed chaw. He flicked the muck at the floor, wiping his finger on his vest.

James' stomach turned. He'd met vulgar men in his days, but this one topped them all. James chose to ignore the flicked tobacco, parts still clinging to Smith's lower lip.

Luke finished off his shot, held the glass out for a refill from Smith's bottle. After a sip,

he threw back the fire. Eyebrows shooting up, he straightened his shoulders, nodded. "Smooth." He saluted James. "Smooth as a baby's bottom, brother."

Arm wrapped around Serafina's shoulder, Smith leaned into the table like he was telling

a secret. "No, smooth as Serafina's bottom." He tossed back his shaggy head and let loose a laugh. Pickles smiled while the woman shot a seductive look at James. Her eyes softened, the corners of her mouth edged up, and the tip of her tongue ran along pouty lips.

Mouth suddenly dry, body tingling, James gripped his newly filled glass. The shot went

down like turpentine and within seconds, James grew warm. Despite the burn and, not wanting to

be outdone by little brother, he smiled and held out his glass for more.

Before a half hour had passed, the room tilted enough for James to notice. Had to be Smith's imported *mescal*. For days he'd planned to relax, to enjoy this fandango, so no harm done sitting here with these strangers. He glanced at Luke, then at Rosella next to his brother. Her arm was under the table, and, judging by the wide eyes and bits of sweat on his brother's face, that woman desired more than merely another drink.

He glanced at Serafina who raised one eyebrow, ran her tongue around the glass rim. She was ugly, fairly plain, although overweight and older than him by at least ten years. James vowed this was as far as the flirting would spread. He owed his fidelity to Morningstar.

He slammed back another drink, tugged at the throat of his shirt, the room hotter than Hades. Tables, chairs, even the walls spun. "Gotta get some air." He pushed back his chair and wobbled to his feet using the table to steady himself. He caught Luke's attention and thumbed toward the door. "Be back directly."

Knocking into chairs and one table as he went, he navigated the cantina feeling more like

marbles in a shooting gallery than a man trying to find his way outside. He pushed open the batwing doors and stepped through. Dusty Nogales air filled his lungs, bringing a bit of clarity. However, the building across the street grew and shrunk.

He leaned against a wooden post on the edge of the boardwalk, a hand slid up and down his back. Soft words fluttered in his ear.

"You are ill, *señor?*" Serafina eased around to his front and ran practiced hands over his chest. "I will help you feel better. Much better."

James pushed off her pudgy temptation. "I'm fine, ma'am." He drank in more air and

took a longer look at Serafina. Although her face softened around the edges, and her dark brown

hair cascaded over her shoulders like waves of clouds

over mountains, James had to resist her charms. But something pulled him to her. Something strong. Something feral.

He wrapped his arms around her and drew her against his body. Her smell. Lavender?

Lilac? Whatever the aroma, he was intoxicated. No matter how much he fought, her charms

pulled him in. Powerless. This feeling, this joyful sensation was magic. Comforted, he was unable to resist. And *that* was all right. But it wasn't.

Shaking his head, he pushed her away. "No. This isn't right."

Serafina melted back into his arms, her body pressing against his. "It *is* right. You feel it

too. No?"

"No." James ran his hands down her back, up to her hair. "No," he whispered. Their

lips met. He cradled the back of her head. The kiss grew warm, ravenous. Her arms around him enveloped his soul. Passion took flight.

Serafina's brown eyes met James'. She took his hand. "Come."

He shook his head, not eager for the night to end, but also something, some voice inside

warned: *don't move closer to her bed.*

"Come." Serafina pulled. "It will be *magnifico*."

Invisible fingers wrapped around his heart and urged him on. James followed her around

the corner of *El Palacio*, random bonfires lighting the way. Trusting Serafina to escort him, he glided down the alley then behind the cantina to a small adobe. Golden light poured out from the single window. She pushed open the door, coaxing him inside.

Musty adobe smells wafted around James' head,

adding to the earthy musk aroma already dancing in his brain. Like the cantina, this room sported a muslin ceiling, mud plastered walls and hard-packed dirt floor. A bed took up most of the space with just enough room to walk on

either side. Still, things were all fuzzy. Blurry. Soft around the edges.

What had he been drinking? James chided himself for not being careful. Shouldn't have drunk from both bottles. Warnings circled his head like swarming bees, but he remained powerless to control himself. Another look at the walls. They closed in while he studied the ceiling. Black streaks and dots clouded the room. It spun.

He clutched the foot of the bed as he sank to the floor. Blackness covered him.

CHAPTER NINETEEN

J ames slumped against the stable wall, shaky hands gripping his head. Here, inside, surrounded by horses, straw and manure, he fought the circling demons. His hands clenched into fists and pounded his forehead. This morning, in the light of day, he struggled to sort things out despite his throbbing, stomach-turning headache. Why had he reacted to that woman like he did?

An infinitely sorrowful spirit sat on his chest. What exactly had they done? Had he gone through with the lovemaking? Please, God, no. He squeezed his eyes shut. His heart throbbed. Thoughts scrambled back to last night. Images refused to surface. What the hell had happened? Maybe he'd passed out. Or not.

This morning, when he'd cracked open his eyes, he'd been lying on the floor, shirt pulled out of his unbuttoned trousers. But his underdrawers were on. Serafina gone.

Feelings jumbled, he slid to the ground, picked up a rock, hurled the stone across the stable. Morningstar.

Would he admit to her what had happened? Had anything actually happened? Could he tell her? He'd vowed no secrets between them. Now he could give his wife the children she'd always wanted. But holy hell! Now, he'd screwed up things. Maybe not telling Star would be best.

Would he confide in Trace? No. He'd ride back to camp like nothing had happened. No one would know. And he sure as hell wouldn't tell anyone. The more he thought, the hotter his face burned. His fault. All his fault. What had he expected? Could he hate himself any more than he did right now? He pulled at the shirt collar threatening to strangle him. He mopped his forehead.

The stable door squeaked open, and James looked up. A soft wind pushed new odors of

straw and horses under his nose. Someone stood in the doorway silhouetted by the sun. Luke.

What the hell did he want? Couldn't he leave him alone?

Luke stepped in and shut the door. The stable dimmed. He ambled toward James, his boots stirring up straw. He slid down, shoulder against shoulder with his brother, back against the wooden wall. Together, they stared into the dim stable.

Minutes passed before James could wrestle down mad to where he could speak. "You all right?" After all, they'd drunk from the same bottle. Maybe Luke had been as loopy as him.

Luke massaged his forehead. "Can you die from a headache?" He played with the hat in his hand, glanced sideways at James, then handed it to him. "Here. Left this in the cantina. What happened to you?"

"What's that supposed to mean?" James ripped the new hat out of Luke's grasp. He'd never admit where he'd really been. Besides, his whereabouts were no one's business.

"Nothing." Luke frowned and leaned away. "You went outside for some air, but didn't
come back."

"So?"

"So don't be mad. It's simply that by the time I went to find you, my world was tilting,
turning—doing a helluva barn dance." Luke rubbed the temple on his right side. "And Rosella was all over me." He raised both eyebrows. "Guess I still have the charm."

"Bully for you." James frowned at Luke and struggled to rein in his bad mood. He let silence fill the stable.

"But I didn't... with Rosella." Luke raised one shoulder. "I mean, Sally's my wife. I
love *her*, not some Mexican nymph." He glanced at James. "Been doing a mountain of thinking on this drive. Finally figured that out. Sally. I owe my fidelity to her."

Luke, the lady's man, the man with no morals, decides *now* to be faithful? And James, the man who never strayed, was now unfaithful? Or was he? Severe pounding in his ears made his hands into fists. Flashes of bright light spun around the stable. He leaped to his feet, speared a pointed finger at his brother. "Now? You choose fidelity *now*?" He ran a shaking hand across the top of his hatless head. "What the hell you been thinking?"

Luke sat, mouth opening, then closing. He rubbed his right temple.

James bit his lip, chewed on the puffy flesh, wrestling rage down to mad. No reason to take out his problems on Luke. But more than likely, James had been unfaithful to Morningstar. Unfaithful to himself. Probably. He stood forehead braced against a wooden wall, hoping, praying the stable would provide absolution. What he'd done was wrong. Undeniably wrong.

After a few starts and stops, words mumbled, Luke looked up at James. "So, what happened to you? I was worried."

"Like hell you were." James jammed his hat down tight, stormed across the stable, his pounding head still in a vise.

"I was."

Luke's words followed James as he marched to his horse's stall. He swung open the short gate and turned at the hold on his arm.

"What the hell's wrong with you?" Luke gripped harder than necessary. "I asked a polite

question, I expect a polite answer."

James fought the anger, but if he didn't leave right now, he'd punch his brother, beat him

senseless. "Nothing." He pulled out of Luke's hold. "Nothing. Happened." James faced him and growled, "Forget it."

"Fine. But are you all right?" Luke took one step back. "Where..."

More questions. Insane questions. Questions James refused to answer as he saddled Pinetop. He led her out into daylight, squinting at the brightness. Tugging his hat down farther, he swung up into the saddle and glared back at Luke, that mouth still flapping, asking dumb question after dumb question.

CHAPTER TWENTY

Whid Amos McGilvray shifted his shoulder. A lump of God-knew-what poked into his upper back, the mattress filled with cotton, straw and more than likely a million ticks and fleas. In all honesty, he didn't want to find out what was stabbing him.

Late afternoon light poured through the single window. He thought back to earlier in the day when he'd hoisted a few more beers at *El Palacio*, later connecting with Serafina to round out the day. They'd been in this bug-infested bed most of the afternoon. He itched in places he didn't realize fleas could find.

He stared up at the muslin-veiled ceiling. Yup. So far, the plan was much too easy. There'd been no challenge tormenting James Colton. He'd fallen so easily the joke wasn't even funny. Hell, tormenting Pickett took more work than Colton, that butt boil of a man. Serafina stirred, rolled over, plowing into him. Her arm slapped across his face. He shoved it off.

Whid shook her. "Wake up. You tryin' to give me a

black eye, you blubbery wretch?" He shook her again. "I ain't payin' you to sleep."

Serafina blinked, rubbed her eyes and yawned. She rolled onto her side taking the covers

with her. Whid stared at her bare back, the fat jiggling as she pulled off the stained quilt and stood.

"You done fine last night, Serafina." Whid rolled to the edge of the bed, pushed up to his

feet. Last night's *mescal* and today's beer coated his mouth. He ran his tongue around inside, passing across gaps where teeth used to stand. He spat.

He stared out the single grimy window, the setting sun's amber rose turning the adobe

next door a golden brown. "Right fine, in fact. Colton was all over you."

She laced her arms through her blouse sleeves and raised a shoulder. "That loco powder you added to the *mescal* was magic. He would do anything I asked." A smile blossomed on her face lighting up her adobe-brown eyes. "Anything."

"Excellent."

"Maybe too much." Serafina smoothed her skirt. "He passed out on the floor. Would not wake. When I left this morning, probably thinks we were lovers."

"Well, damn, Seraphina." Whid stared at her. "Didn't I pay you to make him crazy? Make him unfaithful? Pay you to—"

"He could not do... anything. Not even that." She shrugged. "He sleeps."

Muttering and without bothering to unbutton, he tugged the shirt over his head, slipped on his vest, ran his hand through his hair and beard, and cast around for his boots. After tossing aside the quilt wadded on the floor, he found them under the bed. Grunting, he tugged on both.

Serafina stood at the door, hand held out, palm up. "My *dinero, señor.*"

"Already paid you. Two days ago." Whid set his hat on his head, adjusting the fit back to

front.

"*Si,* that was for the Colton boy." Serafina planted a hand on her wide hip. "I want more for today. With you." Her fingers motioned for more as Whid pulled a dollar coin out of his vest pocket. She snatched the money from him. "*Gracias.*"

"Hell, I got change comin', ain't I?"

Serafina glared, her fingers forming a fist.

Whid leaned in close. "That's it. No more. We're even. *Comprende?*" He looked down

into her face. Despite the plumpness, she was pretty. Maybe he'd come by and visit her again some time. Maybe he'd bring Pickett. Kind of a two-for-one special.

Serafina slid the coin into a skirt pocket. "*Si.* We're even." She cocked her head toward the open door, hot wind swirling into the room. "I have to walk home to *mi esposo* and *niños.*"

Following her, he stepped into clear evening air, glad to be rid of the room's dust, which seemed to seep inside his lungs. When he hadn't been pounding Serafina, he'd been sneezing, which made for a less than satisfying romp. He nodded to her. "See ya around."

Without a word, Serafina raised one eyebrow, turned her back, chuckled, as she sashayed off.

* * *

Whid slurped his third cup of coffee, cleaned his plate of ham and pinto beans intermixed with

corn, and was starting on his second tortilla when Pickett pushed open the restaurant's door and stepped in. His tousled hair, dark circles under eyes, shirt half tucked, reminded Whid of a man who'd been to hell and back. Rosella was written all over him.

Pickett limped to Whid's table, pulled out a chair and slumped into it. He flopped his hand at the waitress across the room busy filling a customer's coffee mug. She eyed him, nodded, finished pouring and walked in his direction.

Unwilling to interrupt his supper, Whid polished off the coffee before wiping his mouth. Bits of ham, a glob of beans, and a tortilla crumb spiked in his beard like twigs and twine in a bird's nest. A glance down, he rubbed them in.

A belch. Now he was ready to talk. He leaned closer to Pickett. "Looks like you had one

helluva ride." He used the rest of his rolled-up tortilla to stab at Pickett's chest. "You managed to down some of that special juice we brewed up?"

Coffee cup supporting his lower lip, Pickett shrugged. He spoke over the half-full cup. "Must've. It'll take me a week to recover."

Head tilted way back, Whid let loose a guffaw that sent the restaurant patrons scrambling out of their seats, two bolting outside to safety. Even the cook and waitress ran in from the kitchen. He pounded the table and roared. Cup and fork clattered in rhythm with the dancing plate. Pickett dropped his forehead to the table.

A man who appeared to be the owner, if roundness of belly and stern look were any indication, hurried to Whid's table. "Something the matter, *Señor*?" The dark brown eyes fired more anger than concern. His mustache twitched.

Laughter under control, Whid shook his head. "Nah." He looked up at the man. "This fella here's damn pathetic, wouldn't you say?" He slapped Pickett's back twice.

"*Calma, calma, señor.*" The owner's gaze roamed over the patrons returning to their tables. "*Por favor.*"

"Yeah, yeah. I'm done anyhow." Whid pushed back from the table and stood. He picked ham out of his teeth while fishing coins out of his pocket. He tossed them on the table. He gripped the back of Pickett's shirt tugging until he sat upright. "*Vamos, Pickles.* There's more harassing to plan."

CHAPTER TWENTY-ONE

James cursed silently, then out loud. So loud, one steer turned to stare. "Dammit," James yelled. "Why? What the hell was I thinking?" Nagging voices in his head blamed him until he thought he'd go crazy. Maybe he already had. Maybe it was that mescal.

In the distance, clouds built, dark gray against a turquoise sky. Closer, cattle spread out in front of him, all meandering toward a dark destiny. Just like him. What the hell had happened? Just as life was looking up, now this. He bit his lower lip, narrowed his eyes, fisted one hand, and pounded the saddle horn. More cursing.

Would he tell Star about his betrayal? Absolutely not. On the other hand, he should. After all, she'd been more than understanding about Dark Cloud. And look where that had led. To Star's bed and his new-found ability to love her. They'd spent most of a day and then many more nights enjoying each other.

But this was different. Would she be as understanding? He hadn't been forced, tortured. No, he'd lain with

Seraphina of his own free will. Not exactly. Something about the mescal had made him loopy. Besides, maybe he hadn't gone through with the lovemaking after all. He'd found no evidence except for coming to on the floor, clothes more or less still on.

What if he had indeed bedded Serafina? The questions bombarded his soul. Back here with the butt end of cattle to look at all day, he had nothing to do but sit and think.

These last few days, he hadn't been easy to live with. No doubt there. No one wanted him around and he sure couldn't blame them. *Grumpy, snappish, rude, short-tempered, childish.* These and many other words had been thrown at him—right to his face. No telling what they said behind his back.

But he didn't care. This cattle drive was too much. They were already more than four

hundred miles west of Mesilla, no turning back for whatever reason. Yet Tin Town was at least eight hundred miles farther. They'd have to continue.

What the hell'd he been thinking? While he muddled about in self-doubt, James' thoughts turned to the problems they'd encountered. First, Perchman's fight—broken arm, concussion, inability to ramrod the cattle drive. Second, a burr under James' saddle, probably placed there by a so-called friend, and James ended up dragged by his horse—nearly killed. Third, Trace came damn close to dying from poisoned water. Something else? This trek into Nogales that ended so damn badly. Was Serafina part of the problem? Or was it the special *mescal*?

Mulling over the list a second time, James questioned the events. His thoughts plodded in

rhythm with his horse's steps. The cattle strolled

toward Tin Town, James rocked with them. The slow-moving rhythm usually sent James into saddled catnaps, but today he couldn't sleep. If truth be told, he hadn't slept in days.

Not since Nogales.

Caught in a time warp, he replayed that evening over and over. Something nagged at his

brain. Something big. But what? Depression clouded his thoughts. What was the use of figuring

it out? What was done was done. All his fault. He'd asked for it. So why was he so angry at himself and the world?

"James!" He turned at his name.

Trace waved from the edge of the dust as he trotted over, his horse and air the same gritty brown. "We're stopping for mid-day camp in another mile. Carlos found a meadow crammed full of grass." Trace pointed north-west. "Good place to rest, I'm thinking."

"Fine." James nodded, hoping his brother would disappear, ride off, leave him alone

again to sulk. Isn't that what Trace had accused him of this morning? Sulking? Whatever. James

turned to focus on more cattle rumps.

"We need to talk." Trace was still there.

James glanced at his brother whose narrowed eyes revealed worry. Worry James had caused way too many times. He didn't want to talk to Trace. Or anybody else. But this brother always knew the right things to say for James to spill his guts. And Trace was relentless. Eventually, James would have to tell. But not right yet. "Later." He tugged down on the reins to head left, softly gigged his mount.

"No. Now." Trace gripped James' reins. Both horses

stopped and within seconds munched on stirrup-high grass.

Maybe he should hear his brother out, and then continue sulking. Or contemplating. Or whatever the hell he'd been doing. James reined his mount around to where he and his brother sat shoulder to shoulder, both facing away from the herd. With his back to the dust, James pulled down his bandana, chewed on dirt, spat. He held Trace's gaze. "What?"

"Good question." Trace fished sand out of one eye. "What's with you? Ever since you

got back from Nogales, you've been—"

"Rude. I know." James shrugged. He didn't care. Maybe later he would, but right now they could all rot in hell. "So?"

"So?" Trace sat up straighter. "So, what happened to the James Colton I know?" He lowered his voice. "What happened back there?"

"Nothing. Leave me alone." James gripped his reins ready to head back to the herd. Why couldn't Trace do what he asked? Let him finish this damn life once and for all. A hand on his forearm stopped him.

"Look," Trace said. "I know you better'n anybody. Even better'n you know you."

He was right. James hung his head. A piece of the hurt heart chipped off. Corners of his resolve crumbled. He fought to keep distance between himself and the world.

Trace's hand moved up to his shoulder. "I know something happened the other night.

Maybe something you don't understand. And I know you don't want to talk about." He paused,

pulled in a deep breath. "But with all you and me've been through together, there's no secrets.

You can tell me anything." He leaned closer. "Trust me."

Pressure pushed against the back of James' eyes. More crumbling.

Silence.

Trace rocked James' shoulder, the grip brotherly but firm. "Let me help."

Maybe if James changed the subject, Trace would quit the questions. Let him figure this out all on his own. "What'd Luke say?" His voice quivered, sounding more like sobs than words. A tear threatened to run down his cheek.

Shoulders slumping, Trace wagged his head. "Only that you two had ended up with damn

powerful *mescal*." He raised one eyebrow. "Think he's about over it. Threw up for a whole day."

James nodded. Yeah, he had, too—in between gripping his head, which he knew would

explode. "Anything else?"

"About women?" Trace raised both eyebrows. "Yeah. Said there were two. And I'm

guessing he bedded one of them." He shook his head. "Hell, maybe both, knowing Luke."

Despite the voice telling James to shut the hell up, confessions poured out. "No. Not both. None." He stared down at his trembling hand. "Me. I had one." He mumbled. "Probably."

There. It was said. Out in the open. Would Trace ever forgive him? How about

Morningstar? Hell, how about himself? Maybe he *should* whip out his gun this minute and be

done. Why draw out the agony?

Cattle bellowing. His heart pounding. The horse shifting its weight under him. The saddle creaking.

He lifted his head, meeting his brother's gaze. Instead of anger and loathing, he saw...

compassion. Was there a hint of shock, too? Or amusement? Hard to tell.

"I'm not proud of it." James cleared his throat and realized his cheeks were wet. He

couldn't stop the tears. "I think it was the *mescal*."

Trace rubbed his face, massaging his chin. His eyes trailed along the horizon, his gaze toward Mexico. "'Probably'? You're not sure?"

Pushing down rising bile, he wagged his head, one shoulder rose. "I blacked out. Woke up on the floor. Still dressed but unbuttoned." Maybe James couldn't figure it out by himself after all. He had to explain. "I didn't mean for that to happen. Hell, Trace. Just when I could love Star properly—"

"You're cured?" Trace leaned back.

Hadn't he been listening? James nodded. "Told her about Dark Cloud. Looks like keeping that secret was the problem. But now... I mean now... how do I...?"

Anger built, but that didn't keep tears from flowing. Desperate, he could not reel in the passion burning in his chest, rising to the surface. Trace's hand on his shoulder, the understanding grip stirred the angst. James glared at blurry distant mesas, cactus, rocks.

Pulling out of the brotherly hold, James clenched his fist and pounded the saddle horn. "I've ruined everything. Everything." He swiped at a tear. "I promised her no more secrets." He mumbled into his chest. "How do I tell Star about this?"

CHAPTER TWENTY-TWO

"I dunno, Whid. Sure wish you hadn't killed him." Pickett gazed down at the Indian sprawled on the ground. Blood soaked the buckskin shirt around the bullet hole in his chest.

"Hell, if I hadn't shot him, you wouldn't have any hair to decorate your scalp with." Whid kneeled next to the Apache and poked him. "You. Hey you. You dead?"

Pickett turned his back on his partner. "Hell yeah, he's dead. What d'you expect? You

used that buffalo rifle on him, didn't you?" At times he hated Whid MacGalvray. Like now. Times when his partner didn't think things through, didn't think about consequences. Sure, there was the chance the Indian would've killed them, but it looked to Pickett like he was too busy aiming at a herd of antelope to spot two White Eyes riding several yards away. Besides, the sun

was in his eyes. Who could shoot well with sun in their eyes?

"Look what I found." Whid held up a bow and two arrows, the rest crushed under the dead man's weight.

"He ain't using these anymore and I always wanted to learn me how to shoot one of these things." He held them high, like gripping a trophy.

"They'll bring us bad luck." Pickett headed for his horse tied to a mesquite. What the hell was wrong with Whid? For sure, he'd get them both killed. He swung into the saddle. "I say let's ride the hell outta here before his friends come looking for him." He surveyed the flat desert, grama grass stirrup high. Were more Indians hiding, waiting for the chance to attack? Or was this brave out alone? A closer look from atop his horse down to the dead man revealed an Apache boy, on the cusp of manhood.

Pickett untied the reins of the other horse, offering them to Whid. "Mount up and let's

ride. He's only a kid. I don't want no part of killing kids. *Really* bad luck."

A glare and frown from Whid as he looked up into Pickett's face. A final glance at the

Apache, Whid stood, clutching the bow and arrows. He swung up into the saddle settling his weight and turned to Pickett. "Let's go have some fun."

CHAPTER TWENTY-THREE

Running Wolf darted between mesquite bushes, around alligator juniper, loped past granite boulders jumbled together reaching high, blocking out the sun. Blue-tailed lizards and a covey of quail scattered as he raced by. He'd run his entire life, and these miles were easy. Apache didn't often use horses for riding, only when raiding far away, far over hills and valleys. No, his tribe

used horses for food, not as transportation like the White Eyes.

Light shimmered across the desert sand, reflecting the golden glow of the sun setting on

his back. Ahead, he spotted a dark spot up against the mountains. His camp. Cochise's camp. His leader knew how to choose campsites no prying White Eyes or Mexicans could find. The Chiricahua Apache raided at will, always disappearing into the desert or mountains, never to be seen except when they, the Apache, chose.

As he ran, he thought of the news he would bring Cochise. And it was he, Running Wolf, who'd discovered

Gray Fox's body, the cattle and the men. And again it was he, Running Wolf, who'd crouched low as the men rode past. Men he recognized. Men One Wing had tortured sun after sun until they both begged to die. Men he himself had helped torture. Had they been the ones to kill the son of One Wing?

A sneer crawled up one side of his face. He thought back to this morning when he crouched in high grass as James Colton passed near. So near in fact, sweaty odors from the horse

wavered under his nose. The tail flicked in his face, brushing his cheek. And with Colton's head down, eyes not watching the cattle or the land, but intent on something far away, it was easy to avoid being seen. Running Wolf knew if he'd wanted, he could have stood and counted coup on Colton. But he didn't want to simply touch him. Not at that moment. He hadn't known about

Gray Fox.

Anger and outrage grew. How dare they return. Return to kill. His chest thrust out as his

shoulders pulled back. This would be the last time James and Trace Colton passed across Apache territory. That was a promise he vowed to keep.

Camp materialized as the sun dipped below the hills, wickiups blending into the bushes. He rushed past women who stopped to stare. Past men who nodded a greeting. Running Wolf threaded his way through the encampment and stopped in front of the revered Apache leader, stew bowl in hand, sitting near a fire. The warrior sucked in air and calmed his breathing. "Cochise? I have news." A glance over his shoulder. "You will find this hard to believe."

Campfire smoke blew across Running Wolf's face. He squinted to keep his eyes from burning and waited for

Cochise to speak. Custom dictated standing quietly as long as necessary. How long would this leader take? People stopped to watch. He took several deep breaths to stay calm.

His gaze stretched across the wickiups, each laced with branches and leaves from the pines and cotton-woods in this canyon. Evenings were always busy and today was no different. Children toted water in earthen pots or carried sticks to poke into nearby campfires. Women stirred aromatic stews while warriors sharpened their lances. Two men ran cloths up and down rifle barrels.

Like a mountain lion awakening from a nap, Cochise rose from his blanket, stood and nodded at him. "What news is so important that my meal must wait?" His black eyes bore into Running Wolf's heart.

"Gray Fox, Cochise."

"What about him?" Cochise frowned.

"He is dead." Running Wolf felt the camp freeze.

"Dead? How?"

He hesitated. What he was about to say next was so unbelievable he was afraid Cochise

would kill him, thinking he was lying. The scowl was not a welcome sign, but he was obliged to tell. "Those two White Eyes you held captive three winters ago?"

Cochise nodded.

"It was one of them, Cochise." His eyes stayed riveted on the leader. "They have returned and are driving cattle. They are close by."

The leader's eyes opened wide, and his shoulders snapped back straighter than usual. A

frown knitted his eyebrows. His body—like a bear on its hind legs—stood tall, imposing.

Running Wolf kept his voice low hoping to inspire

Cochise to respond. "There are cattle, enough to cover many hills. Eight men ride with the cattle. Two I recognize as the Coltons, and two others look like them. Cochise, they carry guns." He looked at the crowd forming. "One of them killed Gray Fox. I am certain."

Cochise gazed into the desert. "Where are they?"

"A day from Tubac. I could not bring Gray Fox back with me. His weight would slow me down. But in first light, we can declare war on them and return to camp before dark." His words were true and not merely wishful boasting. Before, he'd run farther, killed soldiers, and returned to camp when the sun was still shining. This would be easy. Maybe too easy. Where was the challenge? Tomorrow, they would sing around the campfire. Sing about his bravery, his treachery, his killing the white man.

Cochise turned his gaze on Running Wolf, then at the warriors and women who had gathered around. "Where is Naichez?"

"Here." A voice rose above the murmurs. Naichez, Cochise's war leader, pushed his way through and stood in front of Cochise. "What? Have the soldiers returned?"

Giving a low grunt, Cochise explained. "Our White Eyes prisoners, who brought
    the army to us. *They* have returned." His eyes flitted to Running Wolf and back. "They killed
    Gray Fox."

Naichez's eyes narrowed, firing hate. He spit. "Trace Colton." He ran a hand across his
    scarred chest, over his left arm.

Running Wolf wasn't sure whether to explain any further or let Cochise do it. After all, it
    was *his* news, but Cochise was in charge. He decided to stay silent and watch the two Apache

leaders make plans.

Murmurs from the crowd, one woman's voice rising above the noise. "My Gray Fox? My son is murdered?"

Running Wolf turned at the voice. At the edge of the gathered tribe, stood Danché, Gray Fox's mother and One Wing's widow. She gripped a knife in one hand, a bowl in the other. Of all the women in camp, she would be the one, if Cochise agreed, to kill Trace Colton. One Wing had been the war leader responsible for tormenting and torturing both Coltons. Running Wolf remembered the day James stabbed and killed her husband. And now her son. James would pay with his brother's life.

"I kill him, Cochise." She dropped the bowl and held the knife like a sword. The other hand clutched her heart. "My son, my son!" Another woman slid an arm around the sobbing

woman's shoulder.

Before Running Wolf could expound on his adventure, the tribe burst into threats. "Death to White Eyes! Kill! Kill!"

Cochise, still standing next to Running Wolf, nodded to Naichez. "Tomorrow," his words were measured, decisive. "Bring me Trace Colton. Alive." He turned to Running Wolf. "You go too."

"And the other White Eyes?" Naichez's face beamed with the challenge.

Good question. Running Wolf wondered as well. Why Trace and not James? Why not both? Hadn't James been the one to kill One Wing? To stay in camp weeks longer than Trace? The one that would have died within a sun before the army came and released him? But Running

Wolf would not ask Cochise. One time many seasons ago he'd learned a lesson. Never ask.

A long silence fell over the crowd as night darkened the camp. Cochise drew in a breath,

nodded. "A few cows would taste good over our fires." Another pause, he added, "If the other men fight, kill them."

CHAPTER TWENTY-FOUR

"Hell's bells, Pickett," Whid tongued his chaw over to his left cheek. "Have me a bucket full of fine ideas." He spat a stream of lumpy brown into the desert sand and swiped a sleeve across his mouth. The plate in his hand tilted as he gestured. "Have me a damn fine, excellent one this time." He spit again. "*Damn* fine."

Pickett looked up over his plate, fork held halfway to his mouth. "Hope it don't involve more women." Beans and bacon dripped from his fork before he wedged it into his mouth. "I ain't quite recovered from the last one."

A snort. Whid's brown eyes narrowed in on his partner. "Nope. No women." He lowered his voice, the campfire's smoke billowing around his head. "Had me an inspiration from this morning." He rubbed one smoke-filled eye. "We'll be Injuns."

"What?" Pickett's open mouth spit out beans. "We'll what?"

Whid nodded. A mop of hair, sticking out from under his hat, waved in the breeze. "Yep. Injuns. And not just any Injun. We'll be Cochise." He jabbed his chest with his fork. "Yep. Fiercest Injun around. Wanna do it up right. We'll harass and whoop and holler and take on."

"What?"

"Might even send an arrow or two into one of 'em."

"What?" Pickett leaned closer.

Whid held up his fork. "I'll be Cochise and you can be... well, I dunno. Oh, hell, who d'you wanna be?" He set his plate on the ground, the excitement of the impending masquerade replacing hunger. "How about Limping Horse? Or... or Standing Dog?"

"Or how about none?" Pickett shoveled in the last forkful of supper, tossed his plate near Whid's. "What the hell we wanna play Injuns for? We've been damn lucky the real ones haven't lifted our scalps yet." His voice rose. "And you wanna *be* one? You're asking for trouble."

"It'll be great. Trust me."

"Don't wanna play this time." Pickett frowned into the evening desert as if Cochise and his entire tribe stood five feet away. "Gives me shivers thinking on it."

Whid ripped off his hat and slapped it against his knee. He scrambled to his feet and tugged the hat back on. "Don't you see how perfect this is? What the hell's wrong with you?" He turned his back on his partner and stared into the graying Sonoran Desert. Saguaro cactus stood proud in the cooling air. Something small darted into sagebrush.

"Nothin's wrong with me. But perfect or no," Pickett pushed up to his feet, "I ain't in favor of playing Injun. It'll only bring us bad luck."

Whid spun back around, anger surfacing. "Bad luck? Bad luck?" He moved in closer to Pickett. "What d'you think James Colton's done to *me?"* Pieces of leftover supper shot out as he yelled. "Can't get more 'bad luck' than sitting in prison for three years when I didn't deserve to. 'Bad luck' for losing the only gal who ever loved me. 'Bad luck' for having to walk behind Colton, instead of in front where I should be."

"I ain't willing—"

"From what I hear, the thing he's most afraid of is ol' Cochise." Whid snorted and lowered his voice. "I'll make sure he's more afraid of me."

CHAPTER TWENTY-FIVE

Running Wolf, Naichez and another warrior ran, their breathing like the camp drumbeats. Drums marking rhythm to men's dancing feet. spurring warriors into battle, telling of victory—victory against anyone who was not Apache.

Sun warming his back, Running Wolf trotted next to Naichez and another warrior a few steps behind. Running Wolf had spotted the dust cloud earlier, but they'd be able to reach the cattle and his target in no time. Why was this so easy? Surely Trace Colton knew Cochise still hated him and all White Eyes. Didn't he have enough sense to stay away while skin remained on his body? And why had he killed Gray Fox?

Naichez slowed, stopped at a spring. Tall grass cloaked its presence—no one would suspect water bubbled here—right in the middle of a narrow valley. Running Wolf wasn't thirsty, but here in the desert no one ever passed up the chance to drink. He and the other two cupped their hands, drank, reveling in the cool moisture.

Sated, Running Wolf stood and surveyed the surroundings. Mountains the White Eyes called Santa Rita, rose behind him. At their foot, sat Cochise's camp waiting for his return. The hidden hills and valleys in those mountains, full of tall trees, sweet water, and white-tailed deer, stretched as far as he could see. The sun, now overhead, played on the jojoba and mesquite bushes turning their thin green leaves into shimmering emerald.

Naichez stood, water drops glistening on his chin, grama grass high as his waist. "Running Wolf. You were the one to find Gray Fox's body and you were the one to tell Cochise." He lowered his voice. "Then you are the one to capture Trace Colton."

Running Wolf nodded. This was an honor. An expected honor, but still, an honor. He

would not let his tribe down.

"I will take Trace Colton." Running Wolf's chest expanded, straining the stitches in his leather vest. "I pull him out of the saddle so quietly no one will miss him until the sun sets."

Without another word or direction, he sprinted away, toward the dust cloud.

Running Wolf trotted, thinking how he would capture this prey and the many ways he could torture him again. One Wing had been adept at torturing, but only after tens of days had he been able to break the captive's will. Running Wolf would be better, faster than his dead warrior friend. Yes, he would break Colton in a day. And the pitiful White Eyes would pay for Trace killing Gray Fox.

CHAPTER TWENTY-SIX

"Something's not right." Juan Tomás gripped the spoon over his plate of stew. He wheeled around on the rock under him and peered over his shoulder. "Can't explain. Have a feeling."

Carlos spoke over a mouthful of potatoes and corn. "Like the time you thought Maria—"

"Not like that!" Juan Tomás picked a bean out of his stew and tossed it at his cousin. "I'm serious. Like we're being... *no se*... like... like being watched or something."

"Like a bad feeling? *¿Muy malo?*" Carlos regarded his cousin.

Juan Tomás nodded.

James studied the tiny noon-day campfire sparking and crackling with life. Interesting that Juan Tomás felt uneasy. He did, too. He didn't have the nerve to tell anybody, especially

after he'd been so sullen the last few days. Nobody really wanted to talk to him, much less

discuss feelings. The rock under his rear grew hard. He pushed to his feet and held out his cup when Coozie offered coffee.

"Coozie, how are you feeling?" James glanced at the cousins, their eyes on the camp cook.

"*Bueno, Señor*. Why do you ask?" Coozie held the pot shoulder high, his black eyebrows raised within inches of his hair.

With Trace, Perchman and his other brothers still out with the cattle, James hoped these men would speak more freely about superstitions and gut feelings. He'd watched them clam up around Perchman and Luke, especially. Those two tended to ridicule anyone who had any feelings about anything.

James cocked his head. "I mean... do you feel like something's about to happen? Like Juan Tomás here?" He pointed his filled cup at the cowhand. "Something strange or maybe even bad?"

Coozie licked his lips, lowered his eyes, nodded. "*Sí*. Since yesterday, or maybe the day before. Not an enjoyable feeling. *Muy malo*."

"Carlos?" James faced him, hoping he'd shrug it off. "What do you think?"

Carlos stood, gripping his plate. His eyes trailed along the ground, up to Juan Tomás, and over to James. "My cousin is rarely wrong." He shrugged. "I trust how he feels."

Something hard hit James in the pit of his stomach. Was it Coozie's stew? A repeat performance of the *mescal*? Or the fear of impending... Storm? Attack? Death?

Eying the sky, bright blue with wispy clouds lingering on a gentle breeze, James found imagining a storm difficult. But what of an Apache attack? Their territory ended not far from here. Maybe another twenty, thirty miles to Tucson and that was the edge of Cochise's reign.

Would they strike soon?

Juan Tomás was on his feet, the four men standing around the campfire, smoke spiraling

upward, each lost in what ifs. James shook his head. He was still in charge, but while he and Trace made joint decisions, his brother wasn't always open to taking action against unseen threats.

"Any idea what we're up against, men?" James hoped they'd agree on the threat, real or otherwise.

Juan Tomás shrugged in between a headshake. "*No se*. But the feeling won't leave. No matter how much I try."

James turned as Perchman and Andy rode in. No need sharing the conversation with

these two. Perchman wouldn't believe him, and Andy would become overly protective. Before

the two dismounted and tied their horses, James lowered his voice. "How about we all keep our eyes wide open?"

CHAPTER TWENTY-SEVEN

Running Wolf knelt in tall grass and quieted his breathing. A stand of mesquite bushes in front helped cloak his tensed body, but he knew even without the mesquite, Trace Colton would not spot him. Not in time, anyway. Not in time for him to yell out, call to his brothers, save himself. No, nothing would save this White Eyes.

At sunrise, he'd watched Colton talk to the men around the campfire the way a man in charge does. Like Cochise. Running Wolf envisioned Colton begging for his life instead of giving orders.

Moments ago, he'd also watched Trace Colton climb into the saddle and meet up with brother James. They'd spoken a short time before James headed into camp with a slight wave over his shoulder. Trace was now alone at the end of the cattle herd, eating their dust. That was not all he would eat before he died. Not all.

Moving from behind the mesquite bushes, Running Wolf knew Naichez and the others were nearby. They wouldn't give away their location any more than he would. No, each Apache knew what to do. And they would do their jobs well.

With stealth learned as a child, Running Wolf crouched low. Colton would pass close. Still in grass high enough to brush under horses' bellies, now crushed under his moccasins, he waited, watching his prey. Before long, the horse's plodding steps grew louder.

There. Almost close enough to touch. Running Wolf still waited. He parted the grass brushing his face, tickling his cheek. Trace Colton passed within arm's reach.

Now.

Running Wolf stood, jerked Colton from the saddle, clamped one hand over his mouth.

Colton hit the ground. Running Wolf slipped a knife out of his leggings, held it tight against Colton's throat. He laughed at the wide eyes, the terror. The body trembled, not trying to escape. Colton was smart. If he'd tried anything, Running Wolf would have used his knife, despite Cochise's orders. After all, there were other Colton brothers. Easily, he could capture another.

* * *

Before Trace could call out or catch his breath, a knife at his throat kept him frozen. He peered

up into the dark eyes of an Apache, a sneering scowl narrowing those eyes.

The Indian's knee in his chest kept Trace's breathing short. The blade stung his skin

exactly as he'd remembered—and tried to forget. Was he dreaming? No. The sun in his eyes and the acidic taste of fear in his mouth kept him in the present.

The Apache leaned forward, his entire weight on Trace's chest. "Move. I peel your skin from your body."

Trace nodded, swallowing impossible.

The knife's pressure lessened. "Sit." He pulled Trace's shirtfront until he sat upright. The Apache grabbed a length of rawhide from his legging and tied Trace's wrists behind him. Tight. Rawhide cut into the scarred flesh. He jerked.

Memories and terror collided. Trace fought panic, his wrists throbbed, burning like they'd done hundreds of times before. Would he be killed this time or did the Apache want something more? Maybe ten or twenty steers could be traded for his release. Maybe that's all they wanted—food. Something besides deer meat. Besides horse meat. Something—

James. What about his brother? Was James captured, too? Trace ran through several

dozen reasons why James would be captured, but failed to come up with even one as to why he

would *not*. More than likely he and his brother were captives again. But what about the others?

Caught or simply outright killed? He couldn't see anything sitting here in the tall grass with this Indian kneeling next to him. Chances were everyone else was captured, too. But he hadn't heard shrieks or gunshots. Maybe the trail hands and brothers were still alive.

A mighty grip on his arm, a tug. "Up." Trace was on his feet.

The Indian unbuckled the rig around Trace's waist, pulled the gun out of the holster and

held it up, examining the firearm. "Makes you weak. Not strong like Apache." He tossed the gun

and leather rig onto the sand. "No honor in bullets."

"You speak Engl—"

A backhand to his face stung like a million fires. Tears clouded Trace's vision.

"Do not speak to me, Trace Colton." Running Wolf pushed a knife into Trace's ribs, past the vest and shirt.

Trace winced and jerked, the blade's tip piercing his skin.

"Come." The warrior pushed harder. "Or die." His hot breath blew on Trace's neck. Running Wolf shoved him away from the herd.

They jogged their way through tall grass, around mesquite bushes and piñon trees, past

boulders and down into a wide gully. From there, they ran full out. How far would they run and what would happen when they reached wherever they were headed? Thoughts and images raced across his brain, but most of his concentration centered on staying on his feet and running as fast as his captor. Escape wasn't part of the plan. Yet. He'd have to wait.

* * *

Sun at his back threw shadows over Trace while they'd run for what felt like hours. How much farther? Would they soon stop? A ways back he'd lost all energy. How he'd made it this far he didn't understand. In fact, he'd already fallen once, collapsing onto the hard desert, only to have Running Wolf tug him to his feet and prod him. So, he ran. One foot in front of the other. Over and over. Again and again.

As he ran, he'd recognized Running Wolf and put a name to his face. A name and face

he'd spent years trying to forget, an Apache who'd been as brutal as One Wing. The devil of his nightmares. A man he wished he'd never see again. How could he forget someone as sadistic as Running Wolf? This Indian had put many scars and swollen eyes on Trace. Even more on James.

When he knew he couldn't take another step or pull in another gasp of air, Trace spotted

campfire smoke. Once he concentrated, the smell of mesquite and stew was undeniable. They were close. In an odd way, the smell was welcome. With the camp nearby, he'd quit running for the day and could rest, slow his pounding heart and let his feet cool. He'd prayed hundreds of times today James and the others were still with the cattle, no one else captured. Maybe he'd find out soon.

And suddenly, like a mirage, a camp appeared in the distance, a mere hundred or so yards

away. Children laughed. Women called. Distinctive thrums of drumbeats cut through his soul.

Cut clean through. He was back. Back in Apache clutches. Cochise's clutches.

Talon-like fingers dug into his upper arm, slowing him to a walk. He pulled his shoulders back allowing room in his lungs for extra air and, admittedly, all the bravado he could muster. Smoke seared his throat and he coughed. Heart thundering, nerves on fire, sweat pouring into his eyes, Trace held his head high and marched into Cochise's camp. He hoped his legs would keep him upright.

Memories, images, nightmares flooded his body. He shook so hard the entire world shuddered. Men, women and wickiups pounded in time to his heart. Images grayed and then, one by one, melted into colors, desert colors. Warriors glared, their eyes drilling holes into his heart.

Could he simply curl up and die, or did he have to wait? Wait until he'd been humiliated and

tortured again? Wait until he was broken, worn down so hard he couldn't tell up from down, right from left? Until Cochise had used him before throwing him to the coyotes?

Trace and Running Wolf stopped near the center of camp. Men muttered, their language, once part of his three years ago as a captive, was now unrecognizable. Probably just as well. He didn't really want to understand what they were saying.

Able to breathe again, Trace dared scan the camp for a glimpse of James. Or any of the other men. No one. At least not nearby. As much as he was relieved, somehow it didn't feel

right.

"Trace Colton." The voice over his head spun him around.

He gazed up into Cochise's face. Was that a hint of a smile on his lips, a welcome glint in

his eyes? Trace couldn't tell and didn't dare hope. "Cochise." Did the word come out or stick in

his throat?

Cochise's eyes swept over the growing crowd until they rested on Running Wolf. "The

others?"

"Soon, Cochise. They will be here before the sun sets." Running Wolf tilted up his head.

Trace couldn't breathe. Could the 'others' be the rest of his crew? His brothers?

Cochise dismissed the gathering with a nod. The revered Apache leader turned, marched away, disappearing into a wickiup.

CHAPTER TWENTY-EIGHT

Whid crouched behind a mesquite bush, parting the spindly branches for a better look. Luke napped in the saddle. Those steers moved at such a slow pace, the plodding would put anyone to sleep. Hell, if Whid'd been in charge, he'd run those four-legged devils diagonally through this furnace of a desert. Have them cross before the weather turned hell-raising hot.

Luke's head rested on his chest, the reins hanging limp in one hand, the other arm down by his side. Whid snorted. Same posture he'd seen in Nogales at *El Palacio*. No wonder he hadn't bedded Rosella. Probably couldn't perform like a man. And hell, he certainly couldn't hold his liquor.

No, Whid could waltz right up, pull that sleeping varmint out of the saddle. He'd put his hand over his mouth and threaten him. That would be fun. But he wasn't here to cause a little trouble. No, he wanted bigger. Harass and terrify a Colton.

Several yards to Whid's left, Pickett crouched. Black

streaks across his face made Pickett look more like a coal miner than an Injun. But they had to use what they'd found—a burned stick from Colton's morning campfire. At least the ash was black. Red or any other color proved impossible to find. But maybe the arrows and bow taken from that dead Apache would do the trick. Convince the Coltons Injuns were about. Injuns who weren't hunting only antelope.

He'd send an arrow or two their way, have the pleasure of panicking Colton and his men. Watching them pull out the arrow from whoever was lucky enough to be the recipient would be downright joyous. The black lines he'd drawn across his cheeks above his beard itched. Whid wiggled his nose and snorted.

He stood. Bow held shoulder high, he took his time placing the arrow into the string.

He'd already tested shooting twice today and did well at close range. Fortunately, Luke was close enough to shoot and yet far enough away from the others they more 'n likely wouldn't hear him yell. Whid looked left, right. Was that a riderless horse far off to his right? He squinted. Yep. Probably James' horse, loose while that woman stealer pissed all over the cactus. This was a perfect time to attack.

He pulled back on the string, took aim, and let the arrow fly. It sailed a few feet plunging into Luke's upper arm.

"Owww! Dammit!" Luke jerked upright clutching his arm. Surprised at the sudden movement and holler, his horse reared, throwing Luke over backward. Nearby cattle bolted, spooked by the noise and startled horse. More cattle joined the run and within seconds, the

entire herd thundered off, heading every which way, trampling grass and bushes in their path.

Pickett, eyes trained on Whid, stood, arms out, palms up. Pickett gave a mighty shrug.

Ignoring his friend, and, for extra measure, Whid aimed his second arrow at an alarmed steer, and released the tension. The arrow found its mark. The steer bellowed and galloped into undergrowth. Whid smiled waiting for Pickett to wend his way over. Together they'd have a hearty laugh while standing over Luke. They'd pretend to scalp him. Or maybe they really would. The best part would be the terrified look on his face.

Scalping Luke *and* a stampede. So much better than he'd ever imagined.

CHAPTER TWENTY-NINE

Andy reined his lathered horse to a stop and gazed across the backs of the herd. Most were now standing around, grazing idly as if nothing had happened, as if they hadn't run in a blind panic five miles in every direction. He shook his head and popped the cork on his canteen. Water sliding down his throat soothed his whole body. He'd eaten and breathed in nothing but dirt and dust for hours. In fact, he hadn't eaten anything except this morning's predictable stew and biscuits, and soon dark was coming.

For hours Andy and the crew had ridden alongside the running cattle, turning them back to where they circled in on themselves. Some had bolted for freedom, but the hands whooped and hollered, coaxing the doggies to cooperate, to join their friends. After what felt like days and then, as if responding to a silent signal, the cattle stopped, took to grazing like nothing had happened.

Without a chance to do much thinking, Andy had

simply reacted to the stampede, but at this time, he could ponder. He stood in his stirrups. Where was Trace? James? Luke? Far ahead, he spotted the chuck wagon's white canvas top. Always a welcomed sight. He frowned. He hadn't seen his family since early this morning at breakfast. While he found that a bit odd, he knew the cattle had covered a lot of territory. Separated by as much as ten miles was normal. Relaxing back into his saddle, he'd catch up with them later.

After a second long drink, he corked the canteen and hung the strap around the saddle horn. On his right, up ahead several hundred feet, Luke, bent over as if studying grass, rode toward him. Andy gigged his horse.

Luke held his arm, clutching the appendage like it would fall off. Andy rode closer.

Maybe he'd been thrown during the stampede. Run into a cactus. Fallen down a ravine. Now within shouting distance, he held his breath. Blood coated Luke's shirt, his sleeve dark red instead of the blue he liked to wear. Andy set spurs to the horse's side.

"What happened?" Andy reined up next to his brother whose ashen face glowed in the

setting sun.

Luke squeezed his eyes shut and swayed in the saddle. "Indians."

"What? Jesus!" Andy swiveled in the saddle, his gaze sweeping the valley on the right,

the hills behind, the stand of piñons to his left. Nothing out of the ordinary. "You sure?"

"Dammit, Andy! I didn't shoot myself!"

Of course he was right. Stupid thing to say. Andy rode to the other side of his brother. He inspected the right arm, shirt sleeve torn, dried blood stiffening the material all the way down to the cuff. Gently gripping

Luke's arm, he ripped away more of the material revealing swollen flesh, ugly red and blood still oozing. Andy's stomach clenched. He wasn't squeamish, but this was worse than he'd imagined. He turned the arm while Luke sucked in air. There, jutting out of the skin, the arrowhead, its black flint tipped sideways.

Luke grimaced. "Shaft broke off when the horse threw me. Tried to pull it out." He gritted his teeth. "Hurts like hell."

"I bet." Andy leaned in closer and squinted. Jammed in tight. Digging it out would hurt like a son of a bitch. "Let's get you to the wagon."

Full dark would be on them soon and operating on his brother would be hard, even in full daylight. He reined his horse toward the wagon. Another quick scan of the desert. No sign of Indians, Apache or otherwise. "You seen Trace? James?"

Luke used his other arm to point toward the far side of the herd. Relaxed, Andy gripped

Luke's arm, keeping him upright in the saddle. He spurred his horse's flanks. "Let's ride."

It wasn't far to the chuck wagon, but Andy kept the pace slow. As they rode, he searched for his brothers, but spotted only Carlos with the herd and waved him over.

"Need some help." Andy thumbed at his brother. "Luke took an arrow."

Carlos wagged his head. "Aye." He furrowed his forehead. "*!Qué lástima!*"

"Whatever you said, it hurts!" Luke frowned at Carlos, who countered with a nod.

Reaching camp, Andy helped Luke off his horse, guiding him to the wagon. He slumped to the ground, back against a wheel. Carlos and Coozie spoke quickly, quietly in Spanish.

Coozie headed for the back of the wagon while Carlos knelt, ripping the rest of Luke's sleeve. He glanced at Andy, kneeling on Luke's other side. "Done this a few times before, amigo. Back at the ranchero. The arrows, they come out like this." Carlos snapped his fingers flashing a quick smile at Luke. He nodded at Coozie who was searching in the wagon bed, and turned to Andy. "No worry. He will be fine."

Luke gripped his arm. Beads of sweat ran down his face, some pooling in his mustache. A soft groan. "Need water. And a smoke."

"You can have water, but smoking will be later," Carlos said. Andy passed Luke a canteen Coozie gave him.

While his brother drank, Andy fought rising panic. He'd have to find his other brothers. Things would be all right if at least one was here. Luke wasn't dead, not even close, but James and Trace would be confident in his recovery. Andy needed them to be here, to help him grasp the certainty Luke would survive. But they weren't here. He'd have to take a deep breath and do what was necessary. He pulled Luke's shoulder. "Lean up so I can get that vest and rest of your

shirt off. Might hurt a bit."

Luke's breaths spurted out short. "Already does."

"Here." Coozie handed Luke an amber-filled bottle. "Drink as much as you can. Carlos

will use the rest on your arm."

Patting his brother's shoulder, Andy raised both eyebrows. "Enough of that and you

won't hurt... 'til the hangover."

"Not funny. Remember Nogales." Luke glared at Andy. After gulping over half the bottle, Luke licked his lips, handing what was left back to Carlos. "Pull it outta there. Arm's on fire."

"*Sí*," Carlos said. "Relax. It's not deep."

"The horse tail hair is soft now." Coozie pointed to a pot hanging over the campfire. He shrugged at Andy. "The hair is strong enough to close wounds. Boiled, it softens, and infection does not set in. And the horse... he does not mind." He smiled. "Trust me."

Did he have a choice? Andy placed much stock into what Coozie had done so far. Hell, he'd saved Trace from dying from that water poisoning. That in itself was praiseworthy. Andy nodded. "Never seen it done. But go ahead."

Glad to turn over surgical duties, Andy held the lantern high. It shook.

Coozie poked a knife into the fire, turning it back and forth a long minute. Satisfied, he handed the blade to Carlos.

If this hadn't been so serious, Andy would have laughed at Luke's glassy eyes, the same

faraway stare he'd get after hoisting a few too many in Mesilla. The man was drunk. So drunk he'd start seeing things that weren't there. Andy hoped he'd pass out before Carlos started to dig.

But he didn't. Andy set the lantern on the ground and held his brother as still as possible.

Luke flinched each time the knife blade hit skin.

"Hold still, Luke. Hold still." Andy pushed his brother's shoulders against the wooden wheel as hard as he could. Luke was stronger than he looked.

Carlos gritted his teeth, narrowed his eyes and dug.

"Gawddammit!" Luke closed his eyes and relaxed, leaning into Andy. Passed out. Andy sent a silent thanks upward.

At length, the arrow came loose, the stitches were in, and Luke's arm wrapped in white
gauze.

Done, the three men carted Luke to a canvas bedroll Coozie had already spread out.

Andy covered him with a blanket, and with a final pat, left Luke sleeping.

He joined Carlos and Coozie at the fire. "Can't thank you enough, men."

"*De nada*." Carlos nodded. "Glad to help."

While a strong cup of coffee would taste like Heaven's nectar, Coozie hadn't had time to put any on to boil. Andy's gaze trailed over the cattle bedding down. Where were his brothers? He turned to the men. "I spotted Juan Tomás and James out with the herd, but where's Trace? And Perchman? You seen them?"

Vacant stares. Shrugs. The answer not what he wanted. He surveyed the graying desert once more. Where the hell was everybody?

Before he could worry any more, he spun at a horse plodding into camp. Despite the dark, he made out James. Finally.

Andy trotted over, relief relaxing his stomach.

James tied the reins, pulled off the saddle and blanket. "Damn cattle 'bout ran clear up to
Canada. Thought I'd never find them all." He pointed his chin toward the campfire. "What's
going on?"

"Luke." Andy took the saddle from James and set it on the ground. "Come. He's been shot."

"Shot?" James' voice echoed across the campsite.

"Took an arrow."

James froze. "Arrow?" He turned to Andy. "Indians?"

CHAPTER THIRTY

Trace hung between two evergreen oaks like a shirt on Ma's clothesline. The rawhide rope around each wrist burned like the red-hot end of a branding iron. His legs had given out sometime in the middle of the night. Despite his shoulders taking the brunt of his weight, the joints popping, he couldn't stay on his feet. Entire body shaking, he knew he showed weakness. Somehow, he'd dredge up enough strength to prove he was still strong.

So far, early this morning, women had scowled at him, spitting, one glob hitting his face. Three men had kicked him, one bringing pain to his numb leg. Two of the camp dogs had wandered past, sniffing.

Pine smoke wafted across his face, stinging his eyes, making him cough. He blinked into the rose and gold world and turned his head trying to find his bearings. All he knew for sure was several wickiups formed a big camp, bigger than the one he'd last been in. And, Running Wolf had tied him here shortly after sunset last night, leaving him with only one bodyguard.

If his chest and face weren't throbbing, he would've grinned. *One* bodyguard. As tired as he was, he didn't need *any* bodyguard. He wasn't escaping. Hell, he probably couldn't even crawl away if they'd cut him down and point the way out. No, he was here until he regained feeling and strength in his body.

But, he wouldn't let them see him weak. No, he would hold his head up and speak with

the bravery and fortitude he'd conjured up earlier, during his last captivity. He would be strong.

His thoughts turned to James. Had he been captured, too? Trace remembered, sometime

after full dark, shouting and drumbeats filling the camp. The drumming continued for several hours—exactly like he remembered. But either Trace had slept or passed out at some point. He

couldn't be sure when the noise had stopped.

Pulling in a lungful of air, he tried the legs again. How could something so weak, so

wobbly, support him? He dragged his feet under his body and pushed up, locking his knees.

Maybe that would work for a few hours. Give his shoulders a break. Maybe he'd even get fed. His stomach rumbled but he fought down the craving, turning his attention and thoughts elsewhere.

Were those cattle he heard bellowing last night? He could've sworn he was back in his

own camp listening to Carlos or Zeb Perchman singing to the herd, listening to a calf calling its ma. Images of being prodded across the desert, Running Wolf's knife in his back, elbowed into his thoughts. Must've imagined the cattle because he sure as hell was in Cochise's camp. Cold shivers ran down his spine; heartbeats thrashed in his ears. The world spun, alternating with shades of graying black and lightning white. Sweat dripped into his eyes. He strained against the ropes, trying to spin around, to escape.

Wails and shrieking jerked up his head. Rocked back into the present, it had come from

the far side of camp and the voices were female. Memories hit. Women who'd lost someone in battle or from an accident carried on this way. It was their way of mourning. *Someone died.*

The drums started. Trace strained to see around a mesquite bush but caught only glimpses of people moving. He turned to his guard, figuring he knew no English but decided to try anyway. "Who—?"

The Apache leaped to his feet and gripped Trace around his throat, cutting off any air.

He squeezed harder.

Floundering in the grasp, the world grew gray with sparks of bright flashing white. He twisted but the hold was Herculean. Nobody could be that strong. Trace's body went limp, his knees plowing into desert sand, his shoulders popping. Burning numbness cascaded down his head, past his chest and into his legs. How soon would his life be over?

Something jabbed Trace's chest. A stick or club maybe. Something hard. Lifting his head, he opened one eye. A broad chest, a beaded buckskin shirt fitting taut over muscles, filled his view. Both eyes now grudgingly open, his gaze trailed up to Cochise's face, a face Trace had worked to forget but knew he never could.

Leaning down, Cochise used his long finger to poke again. Hard dark eyes drilled into Trace's soul. He lifted his chin, vowing to stay calm and hoping to show this Apache leader he was not afraid. Cochise gripped Trace's jaw in his powerful grasp, turning his head side to side. "You are strong, Trace Colton. But I see marks my warriors left on you." A snort and he released him.

Realizing Cochise hadn't really crushed his jaw, it simply felt that way, Trace pulled his shoulders back, as far back as possible and stood taller. "Yes, your men gave me scars, but they also gave me strength. Strength to keep on." Another look and the Apache leader's face had softened. Trace knew to speak from his heart. "I am glad to see you are strong, also."

Cochise's relaxed features turned to iron. "Why did you kill Gray Fox?"

"What?" Had he heard right? Accused of killing an Indian? He shook his head. "I didn't kill anyone. Who's Gray Fox?"

"One Wing's only son." Cochise's finger drilled into Trace's chest. "Why?"

"What?" Trace licked his split lips, but there was no moisture, his tongue thick. The scowl on Cochise's face brought Trace to full attention.

Cochise glared. "Why do you come back? Why do you kill Gray Fox?"

Words made no sense. He squinted at Cochise. Maybe that would start firing up the brain

again. "I didn't kill anyone." Did those words come out like he thought they did? "Water. Need

water."

The lone bodyguard held a gourd dipper full of sweet water. Trace swallowed until the

cup emptied. Even drops running down his chin were welcome.

Drums beat while he fought to bring sense to his

world. Or was that his pounding heart? No, drums. And this wasn't a dream, a nightmare. This was real. He thrust out his chest straining the buttons on his torn shirt. "Cochise, let me explain." More water would help, but he knew he'd be lucky if he ever got more. He'd have to survive with what he had. "My brothers and me are driving cattle to California."

"Many cattle." Cochise locked his gaze on Trace.

He nodded. "Yes, many. Hundreds." Fear of past abuse knotted and writhed in his stomach. "We mean you and your tribe no harm."

The Apache leader snorted. "You killed Gray Fox." His finger poked Trace's chest

again. "You die for that."

Paralyzing heat flushed through his body. His heart thudded. Trace hung his head. Somebody would pay for this. Pay with his life. And, more than likely, it would be *his* life. "I didn't kill anyone. No idea who did. I'm... I'm... sorry, Cochise."

"You lie." Cochise clutched the front of Trace's shirt and vest, bunching it, twisting until seams ripped. "Then who?" He pulled Trace close. "You and your brother had reason to kill Gray Fox. Only you." He squeezed tighter, his knuckles turning white.

Trace stood as tall as pain allowed and looked up into Cochise's sober face. "Thank you for trusting me, Cochise. I tell the truth. I don't lie. You know me. I do *not* lie."

Searching Trace's face, Cochise nodded, releasing the shirt.

Trace mustered more courage. "Believe me when I say I did not kill Gray Fox." He licked his too-dry lips. "I did not know he was near. I did not want him dead."

Half a minute dragged by. Cochise folded his arms across his chest. "Your brother?"

"No. Never." Chills engulfed him. Trace shook his head and raised one shoulder. "I promise to find out. Release me and I'll find the man who did."

"Bring him to me." Cochise narrowed his eyes, something Trace had seen him do before, but only on rare occasion.

Could he turn over one of his men to Cochise? Trace knew what the Apache would do before killing him. He wouldn't allow that to happen to anyone, especially one of his own trail hands. But, if he didn't find the killer, Cochise would slaughter everyone in his way. Many

people were apt to die in the next few days.

"I won't bring him here, but I promise to take him to the lawmen in Tubac or Tucson. They will put him behind bars, and he will pay for killing Gray Fox." Trace hoped this would work. Otherwise, it was no deal. He couldn't bring himself to turn over anyone to the Apache for torture and death. He couldn't.

"No," Cochise said. "He is brought to me. Only me."

"We have no deal." Trace's heart thundered. His fate was sealed. He'd die at the hands of the Apache after all. He'd never be able to go home and see Teresa and his two beautiful daughters again. "I'm sorry."

"So am I, Trace Colton."

CHAPTER THIRTY-ONE

ndy fought to push down panic. Trace, and especially Pa, would expect him to pull back his shoulders, take a deep breath and continue on with whatever needed doing. No wallowing in self-pity, self-doubt or whatever it was called. Dammit, he was a grown man and needed to think—to act—like one. From now on, no matter what he had to do, whether grueling, disgusting or in between, his family would be proud of him.

He thought back to dawn this morning and the conversation he'd had with James.

"That's crazy!" Andy gripped his brother's shirt-sleeve. "What makes you think riding into Cochise's camp, if you can even find it, will help find Trace?"

James, reins in hand, swung up onto Pinetop's back, the saddle creaking. "If he *is* with Cochise, that Apache leader will talk to me. Only me. Not you. Not Luke. Not—"

"Understand. But... what if he won't let you go? Then what?"

James leaned over and patted Andy's shoulder. "Then you get these cattle to market, divide the money, and go have a great life." James flashed a grin. "Tell Star I love her." And with that, James gigged his mount east, toward the mountains. Toward uncertainty.

Andy shook the memory loose. He'd watched James ride into the sunrise and didn't do a damn thing to stop him. But, even if he'd ridden after his hard-headed brother, James wouldn't have changed his mine. No, there was nothing Andy could have done then.

But right now, he could be the best brother possible. Do what they would want. Despite his new vow to stay strong, Andy's shoulders slumped, his posture more like an old man rather than someone with nineteen years on his frame. The fact he hadn't slept at all the night before, added to the pose. Last night, with only Juan Tomás, Carlos, James and him to night guard the cattle, he'd been out most of the night. Fortunately, the cattle were too worn out from stampeding to do much more than sleep.

Where the hell was Trace? Was he really captured again? How about Perchman? Despite what James said, as soon as he could, he'd ride out to find them, go looking under rocks and mesquite bushes if necessary.

But Andy knew to keep calm around the cattle. They didn't need to go running all over

Creation again. So, he had watched the cattle all night, playing his harmonica, trying to remember the quiet, sad tunes. He'd found himself asleep in the saddle a time or two. At present, the rising sun bathed the desert in gold and crimson hues. Like a sweet Siren's voice beckoning, sleep serenaded him. He craved lying down, head on his saddle, light blanket over his shoulders, stars overhead, Coozie's campfire smoke drifting under his nose... Trace snoring...

Andy jerked up his head and gazed across the backs of the herd. Most still sat, their legs

folded under their bodies, munching on grass or whatever they'd found within reach. They were

too lazy to stand and wander away in search of better grass. At this point, he was tired enough to

understand. That's what he'd do, too, if he could. His horse shifted her weight under him, jarring

Andy truly awake.

A gentle nudge with his spurred boot heel and Andy's horse moseyed off toward Carlos, who now sat watching the herd. Andy remembered sending Juan Tomás back to camp for sleep right before dawn this morning. Somebody besides Luke needed to be rested. Coozie had spent some time in the saddle also, singing to the cattle and keeping them bedded down. Nobody wanted a repeat stampede.

Andy reined up next to Carlos. "Any sign of Trace? How about Perchman?"

Carlos's shoulders rose. "I think... Perchman vanished. Took off." He pointed south.

"Mexico."

"Mexico?" Andy followed the pointed finger.

"*Sí.* That's what I would do. Why go to prison when I could visit *señoritas* and drink

mescal?" Carlos chortled, wiped his mouth. "For me, sounds *muy bueno.*"

"Why didn't he take off when we were in Mexico? When he had the chance?"

A grin lifted one end of Carlos' mustache. "Don't you remember? Your brother, Trace. He kept one hand on that man at all times. Said it was either his hand or handcuffs."

"Handcuffs probably wouldn't have pinched as much." Andy produced a half grin, too. He peered across the awakening desert. A knot balled in his stomach. "I'm thinking Trace was captured. Again." He tried to swallow, but his throat closed. "Since I hadn't seen any Indian sign, figured we were well past Cochise and his tribe. But with Luke being shot and all, guess I figured wrong."

"So, your *loco* brother went *looking* for Apache?" Carlos swiped a hand across his fough chin. His gaze soared upward as he made a sign of the cross. "Aye, *muy loco!*" Carlos' eyes grew serious, his mouth a tight line. "What do you want to do?"

"Like I said last night, we won't leave my brothers behind. Gotta find them before moving on. Tin Town be damned. Besides, the herd could use a rest. I'm gonna find them."

Carlos nodded. "Maybe one of us travels to Tubac, find some help. Maybe some *soldados* at the presidio." He pointed north. "Perhaps Tucson where James' father-in-law is a doctor."

Andy took his time thinking about riding off for a few days, hoping Doc Martelli was available, or searching for soldiers and lawmen to help rescue his brother. Nagging feelings told him to sit tight and wait. He wagged his head and watched a hawk circle something about to

become breakfast.

Carlos followed his gaze. "Juan Tomás, Coozie and me can watch. If you leave, we'll manage. Luke is in *excelente* hands."

"Thanks, appreciate it." Pa's words— *'dig your boot heels in and bear down like you're roping a bronc'*—pushed into

Andy's head. Could he find help for his brothers? And if he didn't, could he go alone in search of Apache? Alone. No need anyone else being captured. He'd kill himself before letting that happen. Andy had overheard James making that exact declaration to Trace. And even if James lived, the past three years he'd spent recovering would collapse in on him. Spin him into another drunken depression. But what would James discover in the Indian camp?

Andy shook his head desperate to dislodge gruesome images. Yep, Pa would be proud. Andy met Carlos' stare. "Let's give it a while longer."

CHAPTER THIRTY-TWO

Trace fought last night's stew rising in his throat, threatening to erupt and spill down his bare chest. Earlier this morning, Running Wolf had sliced his vest and shirt, tossing the remnants aside to show off the scars he and One Wing had put on Trace's body a few years before. Running Wolf had presented Trace's scarred chest and arms with glowing pride, the gleam in his eyes like a hot poker. Apache boys, those close to manhood, and those still a few summers away, had touched, poked, prodded, run their hands around his chest and back. All stood and pointed, laughed, and chattered about Trace. A few spat on him.

Humiliated again. Trace pushed away his previous captivity. That was bad enough. But the mortification afterwards, being shunned by the men and women of Mesilla who at first thought James and he were crazed white men turned Indian, brought anger to his fists. He balled them tighter and met the eyes of Running Wolf. Those black daggers drilled into him, finding raw spots that had never healed. They dug around until tears pressed against Trace's eyes.

He blinked back the moisture. He wouldn't let them see him hurt. Afraid. Degraded. No, he vowed they'd see him strong, brave, proud. He wasn't the same Trace Colton who'd been taken prisoner three years ago. This Trace Colton was a different man. Damaged, but different. Better.

And now, yet another group of boys stood in front, one pointing at the largest pink line radiating from Trace's lip, when whooping and hollering broke the camp quiet. The boys backed away and turned their attention to the activity. They scampered off with Running Wolf on their heels. Trace strained to see around the wickiups, undergrowth and cottonwoods in this canyon, but he still couldn't see what was happening. Prayers that the activity wasn't about James,

sprung to his lips.

Trace's guard tugged on the knotted ropes. Firm. Before he could ask, the man trotted off leaving him alone. He'd simply have to stand or hang here and wait, until he was fed, released or killed. Right now, he'd choose food. So far, he'd had one meal, tasty rabbit stew and a bite of bread. His stomach rumbled at the thought. For the moment, there was nothing to do.

He didn't wait long. Running Wolf marched into view, a man in his grip walking alongside. James! Trace smiled, panic and dread fading. His brother was still alive and looked to be in good shape. But what would being again do to him? Would he survive? Mentally?

Trace and James locked eyes. They nodded. One side of James' mouth climbed toward his cheek. They would be all right, Trace knew, or they would die together.

Running Wolf steered his latest captive to where

James stood facing Trace. "Now," the Apache sneered, "we will find out which of you killed Gray Fox."

"Gray Fox?" James straightened his shoulders, stood tall. He screwed up his face. "One Wing's son?" He looked at Trace for confirmation. "Neither of us killed him. We have no reason to."

A long shadow crossed Trace's face. He looked up to see Cochise, standing, arms folded, glaring at him and his brother. Running Wolf eased back, releasing his grip on James.

Cochise frowned a deep, brows-furrowed, anger-like-thunder frown.

Silence stretched into years. Trace squinted up at Cochise, over to James, then to Running Wolf. He didn't care even flinch. No telling what the Apache would do.

His long, muscular arms unfolding, Cochise moved with the grace of a bobcat. Slow, steady, deliberate. He looked at Trace, then stared at James. "You have much nerve to intrude in my camp, James Colton. Harass my women and children."

James noticeably swallowed, pushed his shoulders back. "I was searching for my brother, thought he might be here. As you know, I brought cattle. Enough to feed your tribe for many suns."

"You trade cattle for your brother?" Cochise pointed toward Trace. "What if we eat them and kill you both?"

"You won't do that, Cochise." James eased a step closer.

"Why not?" Cochise's baritone words sailed across camp.

Half a smile raised James' scarred lips. "Because you are Cochise. A fine leader. An honorable man. A man I know." James held out a hand, ready to shake with the most feared Apache in the territory. "And I will trade for my brother."

Cochise glared at the outstretched hand. "No. He killed Gray Fox. He must pay with his life."

"No." Moving even closer to Cochise, James lowered his hand. "Let me take my brother back to camp. You know he did not kill your warrior."

"Then you, James Colton, you killed him."

Instantly, Running Wolf gripped James' arms, pinning them behind him.

"Neither of us!" Trace's words spouted over a dry mouth. "We didn't wish him dead. I already told you."

James struggled against the hold. "We will find who did, Cochise."

A warrior trace didn't recognize trotted up to the Apache leader. "Cochise. There is news." He pointed north. "Come."

Without a word, Cochise spun, trotted off, the other Apache beside him.

Now all he could was wait. He and James. Would Running Wolf torture his brother

again? Would either of them get home? Would James be able to push this capture aside, or at least to the far corners of his mind, and live his life well? Trace had no answers.

The brothers looked at each other, James saying so much with his eyes. Was it fear? Of course. But Trace saw something new there. A strength of character, determination, a man who knew where he belonged. A different man emerging.

More squirming, fighting the ropes that kept him hanging, helped pass the time. How could Running Wolf stay so still? He and James hadn't moved except for the rise and fall of his brother's chest.

Sun now well overhead, Cochise strode into view. Trace pulled in air, bits of campfire smoke swirling under his nose. Hints of pine sweetened the aroma. Within seconds, Cochise's long legs brought him to where the brothers waited.

Cochise pivoted, stepped in close to James, and pointed at his chest. "You, James Colton. You are well?"

Head bobbing, James stood straighter. "I hope to be a father soon. I wish to be as good a father like you. A good man. A respected man."

Cochise blew out air. Silence. In camp, children laughed, chasing the camp dogs. Women called to them, scolding when necessary. Trace singled out each sound, one or two Apache words now remembered, and yet Cochise remained silent.

When Trace thought he couldn't wait any longer, Cochise stepped back. "White Eyes who killed Gray Fox confessed as he died." He sneered, looked away, regarded Trace again. "Since you did not kill Gray Fox, you are free."

Trace swallowed. "My brother?"

Cochise nodded. Running Wolf released James' arms.

Despite knowing to keep quiet and appreciate the freedom, Trace had to know. "Who confessed?"

The leader's gaze traveled up and down Trace's body. Cochise measured his words. "The man stood over Gray Fox's body when Naichez captured him." He snorted. "Too easy. The man did not give a good fight. Naichez received little honor."

Giving one last glance at Trace and James, Cochise said, "We keep cattle." He stalked away, disappearing into camp.

Running Wolf pulled a wide knife from his waistband. Trace turned his head, knowing he couldn't watch this warrior slice him. Instead, he slashed the rope. Trace's numb left arm swung down and hung at his side, allowing him to sag to his knees. The one tied wrist kept his entire body from hitting the dirt.

James rushed to help. Running Wolf shoved him back hard, James thudding to the ground. Running Wolf speared a pointed finger at his face. "*I* release him. Only me."

While Trace hung, knees on the ground, he tried flexing his free arm, but managed only slight movement. The numb limb dragged on the ground like the rest of his body. A woman's voice made him turn. Danché, One Wing's wife. Clutching a well-honed skinning knife, the widow stood next to Running Wolf.

She snaked in close, lips curling into a snarl. "You, your brother kill my son, my husband." She spit at Trace. A wad of goop slid down his face. "It is my right to kill *you*."

Running Wolf turned to the woman. "Cochise has allowed this one freedom." He tilted his head and lifted one shoulder. "They did not kill your son. Only your husband."

She moved in close and plowed her moccasined foot into Trace's stomach, choking off

air. Before he could move, the same foot slammed under his chin. His teeth clacked.

He spun on the ground, one tied arm dangling him like a trout on a line. Trace knew he'd lose breakfast if he'd had any. He focused on her fiery eyes, the white knuckles clutching the knife, her body bent, ready to lunge.

She growled like the camp dogs. "He must die."

James scrambled to his feet, rushing the woman. Knife in hand, she turned and slashed at him. The edge of the knife ripped through his vest, into his shirt. Blood spread across his chest. He gripped the wound and swayed.

Frantic, Trace fought to regain feeling in his body. If she moved a foot or two closer, he could take her down at the knees. Knock some sense into her. Cochise had freed him. Would she dare go against his wishes? Yet, what would the Apache leader care if Trace died?

Running Wolf snarled. "We should let the wolves tear him apart." He nodded to One Wing's widow. "But these two die soon enough."

"No. Now." The woman narrowed her eyes, then sprung, lashing out, slashing in rage. Crazy, full-throated shrieking.

Searing fire raced across Trace's chest. He sucked in air and strained to put his feet under him, to run. Numb legs refused to help.

She moved in closer, so close Trace smelled stew. Gripping the wrist still tied, she started at the elbow, running the knife down his upper arm, ending in his armpit. Trace screamed.

Hanging by his one burning arm, Trace twisted and turned, kicking out. Using his useless arm as a bat, he swung at Danché, knocking her back. She stumbled, moving close to James, landing in the dirt.

Running Wolf's open hand whipped across Trace's face. Fire. And more fire—again to

his cheek. Trace squeezed his eyes. Heart thumping against his rib cage, he struggled to keep

from passing out, to keep his world from turning gray and black. Afraid to look at his sliced chest and arm, but realizing he must, Trace made his world focus.

Arm raging pain, Trace looked at the cut. More than a

cut, more than a slash, it was bad. He bunched his fingers. They still moved but burned like Lucifer's fire.

Blood ran from his throbbing elbow to his chest, a line of red dripping onto the sand.

He forced his focus to return to his brother. Still clutching his stomach, James head-butted Danché from the rear, both sprawling into the dirt. Sitting atop her back, he held her arm above her shoulder, grasping the hand with the blade. Again and again he banged both hand and knife against the ground. Finally, she let go, her iron grip weakened. Apache curses, snarls, warnings, more curses flew into the air. Like a bucking bronc, she reared, rolled over, throwing James off.

James scrambled to his knees. Before she got to her feet, he pulled her down, straddled her, pinning both arms to the ground. He growled, "Cochise says we're free. We didn't kill your son. Leave us alone. We didn't do it!"

She wiggled and bucked, but James wouldn't let go.

Sharp words to Trace's right. He sucked in air. There Cochise stood, hand up, eyes fixed on One Wing's widow. More angry words. Cochise. Danché. Cochise. He pointed at James. Without words, James rolled off. She clambered to her feet, marched to Trace and once more spat on him. Grumbling, she turned and stalked off.

Before Trace could thank or even talk to Cochise, the Apache leader walked away.

Running Wolf took his time slicing through the other rope. With the last little strand cut,

Trace crumpled to the ground, his arms, hands, feet, legs useless. Like a rag doll, he lay there,

curled in the dirt. James knelt beside him, closed his eyes, and mumbled a quick prayer.

CHAPTER THIRTY-THREE

Andy paced supply wagon to horse, to campfire and back. With each turn, the cold coffee in his cup sloshed over the rim, spilling onto his hand and boots. Sun would set in a few hours and still no sign, no word on his brothers. Zeb Perchman was another concern, but not like Trace or James. Where were they? Were they still alive? They'd cheated death before, more than twice, and they were strong. If there were any chance of survival, he'd bet on his oldest brothers.

He thought back to earlier today when he'd found Trace's gunbelt in between mesquite bushes. The gun, cartridges still in the cylinder, lay a couple yards away. Had he thrown the gun? Why had he left the rig behind? Andy knew the answers. And hated them. He paced.

With Carlos, Juan Tomás, and Coozie out with the herd, only he and Luke remained at camp. And Luke wasn't talking. He'd been unconscious since Carlos had taken out the arrow last night and needed to heal. His arm didn't show any signs of infection yet, thanks to Carlos's whiskey and expertise.

Too much coffee. Andy glanced at his brother and knew he'd have to step away from

camp and water more sagebrush. He set his cup on the wagon's makeshift table, wandered several yards through the grass, stopping at the edge of an arroyo. Finished, he turned and sniffed the air. Smoke. His campfire? No, he was upwind. Had to be someone else's. Another sniff and nothing.

His hand automatically brushed the butt of his Colt. Whoever was out there wasn't showing themselves. Or were they? As much as he wanted to search for the fire, he wasn't about to wander too far from Luke. A thought, dark and scary, brushed across his mind and stuck. Maybe whoever shot his brother was coming back to finish the job. Andy shivered, turned and

trotted back to camp.

Luke lay near the fire, blanket pulled up under his chin, head on his saddle. No new

arrows stuck in him. Andy knelt and shook his shoulder. "Luke? Luke? You hear me?"

Mumbling and unintelligible noises fell from Luke's lips. Andy grinned and sent a thanks

upward.

CHAPTER THIRTY-FOUR

S quatting by the campfire, Andy ignored the wispy reds and oranges of this morning's sunrise, focusing instead on pouring coffee and fighting depression. Gray tendrils of smoke snaked skyward taking with it shreds of bark and grass twisting and turning, reminding him of life's end. Was that all there is? Nothing but gray smoke and ash? Every passing minute was one more without Trace and James. Were they suffering now or was the torture all over? He prayed the ending was quick, painless. Breezes pushed smoke into his eyes. Another day lay ahead with nothing but dirt and sand in his face. He hadn't told Luke about Trace and James. Nobody had. Then again, Luke hadn't been awake enough to understand.

Propped against a rock near the fire, Luke squinted into the rising sun. Andy, two tin cups in hand, knelt, offered one to his brother.

"Thought you might need some warming up there." Andy hoped his words were not as somber as they sounded to him. The news he had to share with Luke was grim, and the words would not be gentle.

"Thanks." Luke adjusted his arm in the neckerchief sling, grimaced, sipped the steaming

liquid. He glanced around camp. "You really think those Indians went home?" Knitted eyebrows high-lighted the worry in his eyes.

A shrug. Andy gazed into his cup. Maybe an answer floated in there. Nope. Nothing but dark-brown liquid. "Like I said, I'm thinking they would've attacked again. Probably killed everybody. So, I think we're all right."

Luke fidgeted with the blanket around his shoulders, pulling it tighter. He brought his cup to his lips. "Since we're not dead, where the hell *is* everybody?" After a sip, he set the cup on the

ground.

"Out with the herd." Andy sat on a rock across from Luke. "We need to talk."

"Uh oh. *That* look," Luke said. "It'll be bad." He glanced around again. "Where's Trace? James? Both out?"

Andy pulled in air, slurped two gulps of coffee, turned to Luke. "They're not here."

"What d'you mean, 'not here'?"

That persistent knot grew in Andy's chest. "I think Trace was taken by Apache again. Haven't seen or heard from him since the stampede. Found his gunbelt and gun under mesquite. His horse came back to camp, but he didn't. We're bedding the herd here 'til we figure out what to do."

"And James? He got taken, too?" Luke blew a stream of air and gripped his bandaged arm. "Dammit!"

Andy pursed his lips, desperate to reel in anger and

frustration. "Only Trace. James went to find him. Rode out yesterday morning."

Luke glared at the desert, back at Andy. "You at *least* go look for them?"

Sarcasm. Andy hated that about Luke. He pushed down irritation at the tone. "And yeah, went looking. Made a wide circle around the herd." He shrugged. "Nothing. Just James' tracks heading east. Toward the Chiricahua Mountains. Found nothing else except Trace's gunbelt."

Luke bit his lower lip. "Ho-ly hell!"

"Perchman's not here, either."

"Perchman?" Luke scrubbed his face. "Gawd almighty!" He glared. "You have any *more* outstanding news?"

As much as Andy wanted to stalk off, leave Luke to grumble, he wouldn't. Andy chewed

his words carefully. "Carlos thinks he's run off to Mexico, what with Trace absent and all. Thinks that's the last we've seen of him."

"Well, hell! That leaves us even more short-handed." Luke rubbed the back of his neck and turned angry eyes on Andy. "What're you planning to do?"

"You see the Indians who shot you? How many were there?" Andy realized he'd come

close to shouting, lowered his voice. "How come nobody else got shot?"

"I don't know, and I don't know," Luke shouted. "Any other stupid questions?"

Heat flushed over Andy. His cheeks burned. Balling his fists, he poked his tongue into his cheek. Luke was in pain. Scared. But sure as hell didn't need to take it out on him.

Unclenching his fists, Andy ripped his hat off his

head and ran a hand through his hair. "We can sit here and fight, or we can figure this out together."

Birds flitted bush to bush, cattle called to each other, the sun warmed Andy's hands. He reset his hat, contemplating the next move while Luke rubbed his arm.

After a long, deep breath and sip of coffee, Luke furrowed his forehead. "How far's Tubac? Don't they have soldiers or the law there? Maybe they'd come help us find Trace and James. What d'you think?"

A dash of relief swept over Andy. At least his brother was rational again. Maybe he

couldn't sit a saddle quite yet, but he was up and talking. For that, Andy was grateful. He sipped more coffee. "Considered it. Didn't want to leave until we knew you'd be all right. It's a day's ride from here and we're not sure about law or soldiers. If they even have any."

Light wind kicked dust around Luke. He pulled the blanket closer. Andy let his gaze trail to the campfire, now sputtering in the breeze. What would Pa expect him to do? He already knew. *Find your brothers by any means necessary.* Andy nodded at the voice in his head, turned

his eyes on Luke. "You think they're still alive?"

It was Luke's turn to gaze into the fire. A shrug. "I'm hoping so."

"Me, too." Andy sat up straight, pushed to his feet. "I'll bring you some food, put a

gun in your hand, and talk to the men." He pointed toward the Santa Rita Mountains. "Afterwards, I'll ride east. See what I find."

"Indians is what you'll find." Luke squinted up at Andy. "You don't need to get all shot up, too. You don't wanna find help?"

"No. Take too long. Hell, it's already been close to

two full days. If Trace isn't dead yet, will be soon enough." Andy pulled a shotgun out of the supply wagon. "This thing's loaded, ready to go." He handed the weapon to Luke. "You can shoot with one arm, if you have to."

Andy swung up into his saddle, picked up the reins and nodded to his brother.

Before Andy gigged the horse, Luke called out, "Watch yourself."

CHAPTER THIRTY-FIVE

ndy thought as he rode. His brothers could be anywhere. Boulders, washes, stands of piñons, mesquite bushes, waving grama grass, all of it enough to hide men. Even if they were on their feet. He shuddered. What if they weren't?

And what about Indians? No doubt they were hiding behind the mesquite, in the tall grass, over the rise. His heart pounded at memories of his brief encounter with Cochise two years ago, coupled with his few days being captured last fall. Snarling faces spitting at him, angry hands punching, moccasined feet plowing into his stomach—the images sat in his chest, gnarled into one giant ball.

Mouth dry, he wished he'd brought two canteens. Andy unwrapped the single canteen from the saddle horn, gulped cool water and rode.

Taking extra time, he inspected every bent branch, each marking in the dirt. He didn't call out, afraid Apache would find him that much more easily. And what would he do if they never found his brothers? After all,

Trace and James had spent over two months as captives, and nobody'd found them. Andy vowed this outcome would be different.

A breeze kicked up. Far off to his right, a dust devil, a mini tornado, stirred the desert

dirt, swirling tumbleweeds high into the air. Andy remembered real tornados from his days back

home in Kansas. Several scary times Ma and Pa had herded all four boys into the cellar when the sky turned greenish black, thunder rumbled, and hail beat the crops. Thankfully, each time their farm survived.

Andy pulled in another lungful of desert air and said yet another prayer. While he wasn't

religious, still he needed all the help available. This was a big desert and his brothers small in

comparison. Were they together? Had James found Trace? They had to be here somewhere. But where?

He'd ridden close to due east all morning and half the afternoon. If he kept going, he'd likely be in Apache hands any moment. His horse needed a rest and Andy's rear end demanded one as well. He reined up next to a large mesquite bush, eased out of the saddle, wrapped the reins around a branch, and uncorked his canteen.

Andy held the canteen rim to his lips. Movement in the distance caught his attention. Close to half a mile off, far to his right, something moved. Indians? Maybe, but not animal; it was too tall. Andy squinted. A person.

He blinked, sweat running into his eyes. Image gone. He squinted harder. There. A mesquite bush moved. Did he dare hope? Could it be? A sip, he corked the canteen, wrapped the strap around the saddle horn, and swung up. "Come on, Brownie. Let's go see what I'm not seeing." He set spurs into the sides, harder than necessary.

Andy lost sight twice before he was close enough. Thoughts jumbled, he took a second long look at his brothers, hoping they weren't simply an illusion. He glanced skyward as he gigged his horse into a gallop. Would Trace and James really be there when he reached him?

They were.

Andy flew out of the saddle before the horse stopped. "Trace!" He lunged in for a bear hug, then froze. "You're hurt." He turned to James. "You are, too."

Trace sagged to his knees. James gripped one of his arms, Andy the other. Trace sank to the ground. James sat next to Trace.

Andy's gaze swiveled from brother to brother, to the horizon and back while he retrieved his canteen. He frowned at Trace's arm and chest, strips of a shirt wrapped haphazardly around

both. "What happened?"

Trace gripped Andy's shoulder. "Met Cochise again." He uncorked Andy's offered canteen, drank as if he'd never tasted water. Trace nodded at the fabric strips. "One Wing's widow. Sliced the arm."

"Damn." Andy cringed and looked closer at the bandages, dark red soaked into the material. He turned his attention to James. "You're hurt, too. What—"

"Same thing. That woman turned into a she-devil with a knife. Slashed me, then him. Thank goodness most of the blade sliced my vest, not too deep into skin. That hurts bad enough."

"I bet." Despite the news, damn, it was good to see them. Andy shot a smile and a thanks skyward.

Trace passed the canteen to James, who took one large swallow, then returned the empty container. James glanced behind him at the mountains, then raised his eyes to Andy. The stoic look on his brother's face, the one he'd seen too many times, tightened Andy's stomach. James distancing himself from humiliation and pain. What would this do to him? To Trace?

Trace patted Andy's leg, the part he could reach. "Glad to see you're in one piece. Kinda afraid of what I'd find. He corked the canteen. "Everyone safe?"

"Fine. Better shape than you. James probably already told you, but Luke's been shot—with an arrow. He'll be fine." Andy hesitated with more news. "Don't know if he told you, too, but Perchman's gone." He lifted Trace under both arms while James pushed up to his feet. Trace winced, sagged in the hold, but managed to stand. "Not gone. Dead."

Hand on Trace's arm, Andy froze. "Dead? Perchman's dead?"

Nodding, James wobbled to his feet, while Andy helped Trace stand. "Looks like we got a bunch of catching up to do."

CHAPTER THIRTY-SIX

Pickett thumbed over his shoulder. "My vote's riding into Tubac, Whid. Get us a room. A real bed. Real meal. Hell, maybe even a real bath." He pulled at the skewered rabbit, stuffed a piece of seared meat into his mouth and spoke over it. "Hell, them Injuns spurred me to plumb rethinking. I don't like seein' them out here. It sets uneasy on me. And I sure as hell don't like remembering what happened to that Perchman fella."

The setting sun bathed Pickett and Whid in shades of purple and rose. Despite the warmth radiating from the sand, combined with the small campfire, Pickett shivered. Clouds to the west turned dark gray. Rain, maybe. He pushed aside images of Perchman.

"For once, you're right." Meat held between Whid's fingers remained mid-air. "That wasn't *nothing* I ever want to see again."

"And it was too damn close, if you ask me." Pickett swallowed, followed with coffee. "I mean, there we were, standing over that Luke Colton, pretending to scalp him, when them real Injuns grabbed Perchman just standin' way over there, lookin' at that dead Injun."

"Yeah, he screamed damn fine." Whid shook his head. "I almost couldn't sleep the last two nights thinking on it."

Pickett glared at his partner. "Sure couldn't tell by your snorin'." He pointed his cup west. "I say, let's get the hell outta here while we still can. We'll catch up with those Colton boys later."

Whid spit out a piece of bone, swiped his hand across his mouth. "All right. But not Tubac. Tucson. See my ol' amigo, Doc Martelli."

"Hell, you ain't sick. What you wanna..." Pickett plunked his cup onto the dirt. "Hell,

Whid. Ain't that Morningstar's daddy? The one who—"

"One and the same. I'm figurin' after doing some persuading, talking to that old man, he'll about beg his daughter to dump Colton and marry me. Convince her she made a terrible mistake."

"How you gonna do that?" Pickett leaned away from his partner. "You ain't planning to kill him, now are you?"

A long silence cut by Whid's slurping coffee. "Kill him? Probably not right at first. But you never can tell." He pointed one greasy finger at Pickett. "Told you I have damn fine plans."

CHAPTER THIRTY-SEVEN

Andy walked, reins in one hand, the other propping Trace, who hung onto the saddle horn. He swayed like a ship in rough water. Andy led them around grass clumps, juniper and jojoba bushes. Conversation was short, Andy struggling not to ask a million and one questions. The stoic glaze over Trace's eyes, the way he glanced behind him every two minutes, told Andy everything. Details could wait.

Long gray shadows threw eerie patterns on the men by the time Andy caught the low *mmmaaaw* of contented cattle before spotting a few. "Not far now." Andy hoped his encouraging words hid the apprehension crowding his chest.

When Juan Tomás waved, riding to meet them, Andy sagged against the horse and waved back. More help. Exactly what they needed.

"*¡Hola!*" Juan Tomás' smile lit his entire face, a mustache accentuating the curved mouth. "Glad you are back!"

"Took a while convincing the Apache to let us go." Trace's voice, gravely.

"Apache." Juan Tomás crossed himself, raised his eyes heavenward. He frowned at Trace, then James. "You're both hurt. Knife?"

Trace gave a quick nod, bit his lower lip.

Andy pointed toward the wagon, the white canvas stretched over the top, visible hundreds of yards away. "Need to get to camp. Get them patched up." Andy hoped this would be the last time Carlos' surgical skills would be needed.

"I'll get Carlos." Juan Tomás reined around and headed into the herd.

By the time the brothers made it into camp, the sun had dipped below the horizon. The campfire's glow radiated hope and strength, a welcoming beacon. Andy and James eased Trace from the saddle while Luke scrambled to his feet, patted Trace's shoulder.

Luke's eyes locked on Trace's. "Hell and damnation, big brother! You came back! Thought you'd left for Mexico. What? Not enough tequila and señoritas?"

"No such luck, *little* brother." Trace leaned against the wagon bed. "How's your arm? Heard you were shot."

Luke's grin plummeted. "Arrowhead decided to plant itself in there." He glanced at his right arm resting in a red bandana sling. "Hurts damn fine."

Trace winced, nodded

Trace limped to a blanket spread near the campfire. Andy's gaze ran across his brothers. Relief, pride, love... all those feelings paraded across his chest and rested in his heart. He loved his family, and at times like this, emotions surfaced. Tears pressed against his eyes. He blinked. *Men don't cry at times like this. They shake hands and mumble gruff things to each other.*

With Andy's and James' strong arms steadying him, Trace sank to the ground and

leaned back against a small boulder. His eyes closed followed by a sigh and grimace.

"Let me look at those cuts," Andy and James said in unison as they knelt on either side of Trace.

Andy glanced at James, whose eyes squinted with worry, then touched Trace's good arm. "I'll bet Carlos can sew you up. Arm and chest. Be right as rain soon." He fumbled with the material, pulling an end of the knot under his arm. Dried blood coating the cotton fabric made it stiff, difficult to undo. Trace shook. Andy tugged at the material. "Hold still now. Can't get hold of the bandage."

"Let me." James brushed Andy's hands away, ripped the material, bringing soft moans

from Trace.

Half of Andy was glad to have James in charge again, the other half resented how he'd been pushed aside. Then again, Trace was safe. James was safe. That was most important. Andy swallowed frustration.

Every time James or Andy touched Trace, he groaned, but there was no other way. He would simply have to bear the pain. Dark-blue bruises marred Trace's gray face. An especially large one outlined a fist. Trace's eyes, normally light brown, were now red, except for the dark rings forming under both. Beads of sweat covered his face.

Luke moved over to sit near Trace when Carlos rode into camp.

Carlos squatted by Trace. "¡*Dios!* You're alive." He

crossed himself. "My cousin tells me you are cut." He studied James. "Both of you."

"Don't worry about me." James nodded toward Trace. "I'll be all right. He got sliced damn bad."

Trace stretched out his unwrapped arm, grimacing at the movement. "One Wing's widow sliced me... chest and arm."

With the brothers watching, Carlos unraveled the rest of the material. The slash across the

chest was long, ten inches, Andy guessed. He winced at the swollen skin, angry redness radiating in every direction. But when Andy looked at his brother's arm, slashed deep, elbow to arm pit, he thought he'd throw up. He chided himself for looking away. Too bad they'd used all the whiskey on Luke. Trace could use a whole bottle, but even if they had one, Trace probably wouldn't drink it all. He'd save some for the others. As it was now, he would have to endure this round of stitches stone-cold sober.

"*Aye.*" Carlos whistled through his teeth. "She was *loco*. That *bruja* who did this."

"That's for sure." Coozie knelt next to Andy. His eyes narrowed and lips pursed as he studied the wounds. He glanced at Carlos. "You want me to get more horse hair?"

A nod.

"Maybe four?"

"A *big* handful."

CHAPTER THIRTY-EIGHT

Wind kicked up dust as sun blazed straight overhead. Andy rode into camp, James a horse length ahead. Both tied their mounts to the rope line, Andy's stomach rumbling, complaining. Breakfast had been a scoop of last night's stew, a quick slurp of coffee and nothing else. Beans, biscuits, a steak, and a big slice of apple pie would slide down the throat without a fuss right about now. But, with a louder grumble from his stomach, he'd settle for about anything that wasn't moving.

With Carlos and Juan Tomás out with the herd, Andy knew he'd have half an hour to fill his belly, and return. But he also knew today was the end of "sitting around," doing "nothing." They had a herd to get to Tin Town by July first and they'd already lost precious days. If they pushed, and pushed hard, they'd be there on time.

They'd decided this morning that everyone was well enough to get the cattle moving by first light tomorrow. Trace's bruises had turned dark blue and purple, and he had moaned off and on throughout the night, fever still high. Luke's arm was healing well, and he could ride. They couldn't waste any more time. Tomorrow, Trace would ride in the wagon with Coozie and if he worsened, someone, maybe Coozie or Juan Tomás, would take him north into Tucson, to James' father-in-law, the only doctor within hundreds of miles. They were two, possibly three days's ride from there, and it was out of their way, but if Trace got worse, they would.

Coozie handed Andy a steaming bowl of stew. Aromas of beef with vegetables and whatever seasoning he put in there, made Andy's mouth water. Tortillas on top of his stew,

coffee cup in hand, he sauntered to the far side of the campfire and perched on a rock.

Luke, then James, did the same. The four brothers sat in a circle, eating, talking. Trace sat, an untouched bowl at his side. The cup in his hand shook, but his eyes were clear.

"Miss you out there." Andy cocked his head toward the herd. He shoveled stew into his mouth and tore off part of a tortilla. "How you feeling?"

"Ace high."

Fortitude emanated from those eyes despite the wince Trace gave when he moved. But, Andy thought, sheer determination covered his brother's face. If nothing became infected, he would survive, yet again, another capture by Cochise. Andy decided his brothers were either incredibly lucky or blessed all three times they were in Cochise's grasp. They'd come away with scars, but at least they were on their own two feet. That sure couldn't be said about most men

who met up with Apache.

Luke held his spoon mid-air and waved it at his brothers. "Meant to tell you. I had a

weird dream. I mean *weird*. After I was shot, lyin'
there, or maybe it was later, I dunno, I had

this crazy weird dream."

"Yeah?" James raised his eyebrows. "Sheep or
cattle?"

A glare from Luke. "I'm serious. Listen. This was
weird." He spooned more stew into his mouth, spoke
over it. "When I got shot, hit my head on the ground,
must've passed out, 'cause I swear there was two Indians
standing over me, like angels come to call. But these
angels were ready to scalp me."

"This your dream?" Andy lowered his cup as Luke's
eyes dug into the past.

"Guess so." Luke shrugged. "Anyway, there they
stood, but they didn't really look like

Indians. One had a beard. Full beard. The other kinda
rounded." He ran a hand across his face.

"War paint smeared across their cheeks. Not sure if
they had knives or not."

"They try to scalp you? Like grab you or something?"
Trace frowned at his brother.

Luke shook his head. "No. But sure feels more like...
it's real... than a dream.

Couldn't be real, could it?"

"They say anything?" James asked.

"Don't think so." Luke closed his eyes as if replaying
the event. "No."

The brothers exchanged glances. Trace shrugged at
James and then at Luke. "Never seen any Indians with
beards. Not that I saw in Cochise's camp, anyway."

"Keep thinking I've seen them before." Luke gazed
into his bowl, changed direction, looked up at Trace.
"Couldn't be, though."

"So, must've been a dream," James said.

"Good thing you weren't scalped." Andy scraped the bottom of his bowl. "But I'm

wondering why not." He glanced at his brothers who'd stopped to stare at him. He met their hard

eyes. "I mean, them being real Indians and all."

They sat in silence.

Half a minute ticked by before Andy sat up straight. "I almost forgot." He pointed his

empty cup over his shoulder. "The other night, before Trace got back... well, I smelled campfire smoke again. Not ours. Somebody else's."

James looked up, frowning. "Where? Close by?"

Andy nodded. "Small fire. I'm guessing not Apache."

All four men turned, following where Andy pointed.

Luke lowered his voice. "If it ain't Apache, who?"

CHAPTER THIRTY-NINE

Trace rocked on the hard wagon seat, the wood creaking while Coozie navigated around holes, dips and swells in a trail made by Spaniards coming up from Mexico two centuries before. Trace thought about the explorers' travels. They'd discovered watering holes and an easier path than straight over mountains. The sketches, maps and diaries the parties left behind certainly had helped the next generations of travelers. The trail they'd forged led to Tubac, and on up to Tucson.

Trace and his brothers had talked at length last night about which trail to take. July first was fast approaching and they weren't anywhere close to Tin Town, California. They decided to bypass Tucson altogether, opting to swing west a bit south of Tubac. Despite what they'd thought earlier, they'd send Trace and Coozie into Tucson to get supplies for Coozie and a doctor for Trace's wounds. A quick visit with his James' father-in-law would be welcome.

They agreed to head out at sunrise tomorrow morning.

Figuring Tucson had some sort of mail service, each man had written a letter home. Trace glanced at the stack of envelopes at his feet. He glanced over his shoulder at the cattle. Would his letter smell like beeves? Probably. The smell permeated his clothes, his hair, even the stew. And maybe Teresa would get his letter before he returned from Tin Town. Sometimes, letters took a month simply to travel a few hundred miles. But still, he had faith.

With the sun directly overhead, its heat shimmering across the desert, Coozie wiped his forehead and pulled back on the reins. "This place'll make do to set up mid-day camp." He pointed at a row of bushes zigzagging across the desert. "A stream with sweet water."

Wanting to help, but still weak, Trace fought to stay upright on the wagon bench until

Coozie helped him down. His pride had taken another beating, but he knew at times like this,

he had to be grateful for the help. Arm throbbing, he flexed his hand, but it refused to form a fist. Four attempts later, he closed it almost completely. Arm on fire, Trace leaned against the wagon, pulled in gulps of air until the pain lessened. He tugged off the hat Carlos had loaned him, his own being lost somewhere between here and the Apache camp. The wide brim afforded protection from sun, and Trace again mentally thanked the invaluable trailhand for remembering he needed a hat, because he had certainly forgotten.

A cool hand on his forehead brought his attention to the present.

"Fever." Coozie wagged his head. "You need water

and rest." He pointed over his shoulder. "You sit, I'll get water."

"No, I'm fine." Did Trace really believe his words, because Coozie certainly didn't. The pursed lips, the shaking of the head, the raised eyebrows served to reinforce that Coozie saw right through the bravado. A bravado Trace thought he'd perfected.

A grip on his arm, a nudge and Trace found himself shuffling toward a blanket Coozie had spread out. He frowned wondering when Coozie had done that. Hadn't they stopped a moment ago? He eased to the ground, Coozie at his side, canteen in hand.

While Coozie whipped up the noonday meal, Trace peered at a map. They were still hundreds of miles from Tin Town, but it looked like they were on the fringes of Cochise's territory. Visions of Perchman's tortured body still disturbed Trace's dreams, haunting his awake thoughts as well. While in camp, the Apache had indeed made Trace watch the women mutilate Perchman's body. He knew he'd never push those images out of his head. Had Perchman really killed One Wing's son? No one could be certain, but his death was the only reason Trace was alive today. For being alive he was grateful, but still, he agonized over how he'd gained his

freedom.

Juan Tomás and Andy rode into camp, tying their horse's reins to the tie line, then headed

toward the stew. Andy sniffed at the pot before turning his wide grin on the cook.

"Ah... nectar of the gods, Coozie." Andy patted his stomach. "Been tasting your cooking all morning."

Juan Tomás thumped Andy's shoulder. "Been comin' back on me, too." He turned to Coozie. "What d'you put in there, amigo? I taste it for days."

Spoon held halfway to his mouth, Andy balanced his bowl in one hand. "Makes it extra

tasty, don't it?"

Both men dug into their stew bowls, Andy shoveling faster than Juan Tomás. With most of the meat and beans consumed, Andy took a breath, his gaze traveling to Trace. He nodded as he sat by him. "You're looking better." His spoon waggled near Trace's cheek. "I see regular color under those bruises."

"Never been better." Was Trace lying to himself as well? Each movement produced fire, raging hot pokers in his arm, across his chest. He swallowed hard.

"Like hell." Andy scraped the bottom of his stew bowl. "If you're fine... I'm the Queen of England."

Before Trace could rebut, James rode into camp, faster than he should, his mount snorting and puffing. As soon as his boots touched ground, he marched over to Trace and Andy, knelt facing them.

"Talked to a caravan behind us." James pointed over his shoulder toward the southeast. He dropped his voice. "'Bout half of them were killed by Apache. The other half ran for it."

"Damn, we were lucky." Andy sighed.

"There's more." James' words turned hard. Iron hard. "They also say there's a renegade

band of cutthroat bandits heading up from Mexico. Their leader's some army commander turned

bad. Apparently, he stops at nothing to get what he wants."

Juan Tomás held his bowl mid-air. "What is it he wants?"

James looked behind him. "Everything."

CHAPTER FORTY

"Check your ammunition, men. Put extra cartridges in your pockets." James' gaze trailed over his crew. Juan Tomás, Carlos, Coozie, Luke, Trace, Andy. Everyone stood by the chuck wagon, the herd left alone for the moment. James pulled in a deep breath. "If you see anything, anything at all, holler out. You don't wanna spook the herd, but if there's any shooting... well, you know what'll happen."

Luke gripped his arm still supported by the sling. "You think maybe they'll simply take some cattle and leave? I mean... we don't have any money to give them. At least *I* don't." He shrugged. "They'll probably slice us up like what the Apache did to Perchman. Kill us all for fun."

"Maybe they'll leave us alone. Not come this far." Juan Tomás raised his eyebrows along with one shoulder.

Carlos shook his head. "They'll come."

A long look to the south, Andy turned back to the group. "Sure as hell can't outrun them. Probably can't outshoot them."

Trace pointed at Andy. "We'll have to outsmart them." Beads of sweat glistened his face, one rolling down his right temple. He swiped at it. "Maybe we can tell them we're all sick.

Diphtheria, measles or such?"

Coozie snapped his fingers. "Anthrax."

At last, a bit of hope wedged into James' chest. Maybe Trace and Coozie were on to

something. Maybe they'd get out of this alive, after all. James nodded and considered. "Anthrax

would scare off most people."

"Long as it doesn't rain." Carlos glanced into the cloudless sky. "Rain clears off the

infected dust and soaks back into the earth."

Luke snorted. "You really think those bandits'll fall for some dumb excuse why they shouldn't rob us? I mean... you think they have nothing under their hats but hair?"

Andy's long legs brought him right up nose to nose with Luke. He poked his brother's chest with his finger. "You come up with a better idea? A plan to keep us alive? Something to keep us breathing and our cattle moving? Do you? I'd like to hear it." Both arms flew out to his side. "Go ahead. Tell us, mister bad attitude."

"Andy, back off." James wedged between them. What had set him off? Usually the youngest of the Colton clan was laid back, slow to rile. This wasn't like him, but Luke's poor attitude deserved scrutiny.

James turned his thoughts to the idea of anthrax. That was an excellent one. As far as he could tell, this plan was the only idea that didn't involve a lot of shooting and probably death. If they played it right, those bandits would steer clear when they found out deadly bacteria was infecting the herd. Nobody in their right mind wanted to be anywhere close to anthrax.

"All right." James cocked his head and looked at everyone again, focusing on Andy who had backed away. "What do we know about anthrax? We need to have our stories straight."

"It's deadly to cattle and spreads quickly," Carlos said.

"Symptoms?" Trace leaned back against the supply wagon.

James gripped Trace's arm to steady him. "I've heard they call it 'getting the staggers.' That's because the animals are wobbly, before they die. And they die quickly." He regarded his brother. "I think we might pull this off."

Carlos nodded. "Also, there could be sores on the body. *Vacas* or men. With Luke and

Trace bandaged like they are, maybe the *bandidos* will believe us."

"But it doesn't spread from man to man too fast." Coozie's shoulders rose and fell. "Maybe they won't know that."

"Let's hope so." James ran a hand over his unshaven face. "All right, men." He took a deep breath. "Looks like we're in for some play-acting. Think you can do it?"

"Keep your eyes peeled, your guns loaded, and start feeling sick." James brought his shoulders back. "Questions?"

Quiet "no's" rumbled around the group.

"Let's get back to the herd." James turned to Andy. "Need to talk to you." Their eyes met. "Alone."

Juan Tomás, Carlos and Luke swung up into saddles and headed back to the herd, while Coozie broke down the mid-day camp. Trace helped by putting away what he could. James and Andy walked off, stopping near a stand of scrubby piñon trees.

James knew to phrase his question exactly right. Something was obviously eating at Andy. Maybe he would say and maybe he wouldn't. However, with Andy, you could usually

come right out and say what was on your mind. James chose the direct route. "What's the problem? What's wrong?" He frowned into his teenage brother's face. "This isn't like you."

Andy's hands fisted, relaxed. Fisted, relaxed. He glared into the desert and sighed. "I'm

so damn tired of him finding fault with everything. Nothing we do is right or good enough. I'm sick of his attitude. Sick of it."

"I see—"

"And he may get us all killed if he don't play along with this little act we're putting on."

Andy gritted his teeth. "Killed dead." He turned his eyes on James. "Hell, I don't wanna die."

James held Andy's shoulder and squeezed. "None of us do." He rocked the shoulder. "I'll do everything I can to be sure we don't. All right?"

Andy looked at the ground, nodded.

"Fine." James released his grip. "I need you to ignore Luke. No excuse, but he's still in pain from that arm, and since we're out of whiskey—"

"But you don't hear Trace complaining or whining." Andy shrugged. "Hell, it was even his idea to be sick. And he's hurt worse, a lot worse than Luke."

As he spoke, James realized exactly what he was saying. The gravity of the situation. "Your two brothers will likely be the key to keep us all breathing. If those outlaws want proof we're all sick, it's up to them, with their bandages and all. Those bruises on Trace's face and neck look nasty."

"Sure do." Andy winced. "Face is all swoll up. Bruises on his cheeks're black as the bottom of Coozie's skillet."

"Those bandits won't know Apache put them there." James pushed down panic for the moment. "Your brothers are well aware this whole thing is up to them." He shook his head. "That's a lot for anybody to take on."

Andy toed the dirt. He turned to James. "You really think they can? Think it'll work?"

He didn't have to think. James knew. "Yes." He slid an arm around Andy's shoulders, nudging him back toward camp. "It has to work. It's the only plan we have."

CHAPTER FORTY-ONE

The afternoon dragged, one long minute following another. As they rode, each little dust cloud brought a knot to Trace's stomach. Frequently, he turned on the wagon seat staring back to the south, back toward the bandits' path. Plans to ride into Tucson were set aside. If these Mexican outlaws attacked, he and his brothers would need every gun available. There would be time to get to town afterward. If there *was* an afterward.

Rubbing the back of his neck, he jumped every time a lizard darted under a bush. A startled covey of quail pushed him to the edge of the wagon bench. Every branch snapping, sagebrush rustling, even hawks flying overhead set him on edge. Wish they'd come on. Wait. What was he thinking?

Coozie turned his eyes on Trace. "Don't worry. We're ready."

The wagon lurched and bounced. Trace sucked in air, desperate to fight the agony each movement brought. He gripped the wooden seat managing to keep his balance. Turning right, he examined the horizon behind him.

Like a nightmare, in the distance, unmistakable clouds of dust—a line of riders. Coming fast. Most of the herd scattered, a few darting ahead of the wagon. Trace swiveled back around. "Company's here. Hope this works."

Coozie tightened his grip on the reins, the other hand crossing himself.

Before the chuck wagon had covered a quarter mile, three riders galloped up. Trace stared into their scowling faces and down to guns pointed at his chest. Coozie brought the team to a quick stop while he and Trace raised hands.

"*¡Abajo!*" A bandit waved his gun from the men to the ground. "*Los dos.*" A thick black

mustache drooped over his lip, a wide-brimmed hat shading the face.

He knew it was time to be sick. Fortunately, that wasn't hard. Trace's stomach roiled, mouth dry. Instead of complying, he tried explaining. "Anthrax. We're sick. Contagious. Stay away."

A second Mexican spurred his horse to the side of the wagon. "Shut up, *gringo.*" He grabbed Trace's bandaged arm and pulled. He flew off the seat, slid down along the side of the wagon, plowing onto the ground. Wedged between the bandit's horse and the wagon wheel, Trace fought to stay conscious.

Stars spun. Icy hot white stars. Agony roared up and down Trace's arm, across his chest. Dinner surfaced. Shaking, he vomited until nothing came up. He lay on the ground panting, curled up against the wagon wheel. Little by little his world quit spinning. Stars faded.

Coozie scooted across the bench and jumped to the ground. "Anthrax. Full out anthrax." He pointed to Trace. "*Mira*."

Groans rattled Trace's chest. He tried to stand by pushing up against the wheel, but his legs turned to rubber. Still on the ground, he reached up to Coozie whose strong arms would get him on his feet. So far, he realized, none of this was acting. He really was sick.

With Coozie's pull, he stood.

The mustache-draped Mexican made a show of cocking his pistol and leaned in close. "Lying *perros*. You say anything to keep from dying." He snickered and turned to his companions. "What say we shoot them now and be done?"

Launching off his horse, a third bandit threw back the canvas covering the back of the chuck wagon. "*Aye, compadres*." He extracted a canvas sack of tortillas. "*¡Comida!* He cooks us food now."

"*Sí*. I could eat." Still astride his horse, the second bandit, his cartridge-filled bandolier stretching across his expansive stomach, nodded and waved a pistol at Coozie. "After, we take all their monies." A grin crinkled his dark brown face. "And their whiskey!"

"You." Tall and toughened like a dry hide, the third bandit stood next to Coozie. He shoved his revolver into the cook's chest. "Cook us foods. *Andele*."

Coozie stepped back from the bandit and held his arms out at his sides. "All our food has anthrax. You eat, you die."

"You lie." The Mexican shoved Coozie toward the end of the wagon. "If you can't fix food, what do you eat?"

"Nothing." Trace glanced at Coozie. "We're headed for Tucson. The cook and me. For more food and a doctor."

"You lie." The same bandit stepped in closer to Coozie who moved back.

"No. Anthrax. *Muy malo*. It kills." Coozie waved his arm toward Trace. "He is dying. Look at him. Sores, coughing. He lives maybe a day longer."

Trace stared into the bandit's black eyes. They narrowed, but the cruel mouth formed words. "Why wait? I kill you now."

Somewhere a gun cocked. Trace realized he'd have to sell his illness. *Now* and with

everything he had. Would they call his bluff? He leaned against the wagon wheel where a cough

spasmed his chest. He held out his bandaged arm. "Go ahead. Don't have long to live anyway." He set his gaze on the closest Mexican. "But, now neither do you."

Guffaws shook the man's chest while he wagged his head. Bushy eyebrows rose over cold, black eyes.

Nose to nose with the bandit now, Trace coughed. Loud and long. He trembled.

The Mexican shoved Trace back so hard he hit the dirt. He lay still hoping he'd been

convincing.

A sneer raised the outlaw's lips. "I think you still are lying, *gringo*. Now we take your monies, food and whiskey." The Mexican cocked his head to the man remaining on his horse. "Guillermo, come." He waved to the other. "Miguel, we fiesta!"

"*Aye, aye, aye*. Fiesta!" Guillermo launched himself off his horse and strutted past Coozie at the open chuck wagon. "Whiskey." He rummaged through the containers, tins and utensils. "Where's the whiskey, *gringo*?"

Guillermo, a jagged scar running across his cheek, grabbed Trace and hoisted him to his feet.

"No whiskey," Trace said. Guillermo tightened the

hold until Trace knew he'd pass out. "Used it all to clean out the anthrax." His words spurted over his moans.

Coozie held his arms out at his sides, palms up. "All of it. That's why we were riding to Tucson."

Before Coozie could explain further, the other bandit backhanded the cook, who tumbled to the ground and rolled. Coozie jumped to his feet holding his reddened face.

Guillermo, with Trace still in his clutches, pointed to Coozie. "Food. Now!" He turned to the other Mexican who sported a whisk-broom beard. "Miguel, watch this one." He shoved Trace.

Spinning, Trace sailed several feet into Miguel's arms. Whiffs of old outhouse and dusty sweat penetrated Trace's nose. His eyes watered.

While Coozie set about building a fire and putting together stew and tortillas, Trace

formulated more plans, rejecting them all. He thought and thought, but nothing else came to

mind. Maybe he could keep up this charade. Maybe he'd given up too soon. Peeks into the

desert, toward the herd, revealed nothing but more cattle. No brothers or drovers coming to the rescue.

Unable to stand any longer, Trace slid out of Miguel's grip, hit the ground, and leaned back into a mesquite bush, spindly branches holding him upright. He looked up into the Mexican's pockmarked face. "Doesn't matter how much you eat," Trace said. "Or how much whiskey you drink. You're still dying. By tonight, you'll be coughing, itching. The sores.

Anthrax. Real contagious."

Trace saw the boot too late. It sent him careening across the ground, his face plowing into desert. He lay still, hoping this would end soon. Big blinks, he pushed himself up, and sat, thinking about other ways to get rid of these renegade outlaws.

CHAPTER FORTY-TWO

Luke shook until he thought he'd fall apart. The Mexican holding a gun to Luke's head had an arm around his chest. Back jammed tight against the bandit's torso, Luke felt the man's heart beat. And with the .45's barrel pushed hard against his temple, all Luke heard was blood whooshing in his ear. Try as he might, there was no way he could breathe wrapped up like that. Caught in the arms of a nightmare.

A long look at James. His arms reached skyward as he faced another bandit. Luke spotted Juan Tomás and Carlos, their hands up, peering down a gun barrel as they stood on his far right. The only one missing was Andy. Maybe he'd escaped. These outlaws had netted everyone riding drag and swing on the herd, except him. Luke prayed Andy had gotten away or at least was safe. All he could hope for right now was Andy's safety.

It was up to him to keep everyone here alive. Luke counted four bandits. They'd come up fast, before James had had time to ride to the chuck wagon and warn Trace. Were his brother and Coozie still in one piece?

With the ferocious grip and the way this Mexican held him, all feeling drained from his arms. His shoulder throbbed. He squirmed, but nothing moved except his head.

James nodded toward Luke. "He's sick. We're all sick. Anthrax." He trained his gaze on the bandit directly in front of him. "Now you have it, too."

"Liar. *Caca de pero* liar." The Mexican cocked his pistol.

"Anthrax?" The bandit holding the gun on Juan Tomás frowned and turned his attention to Luke. "You have anthrax?"

Luke swallowed best he could and nodded, mumbling something that sounded like a

strangled *yes*. He shook harder. None of that was acting. He couldn't remember the last time

he'd been this afraid. Sick. He was sick—and afraid.

James shifted his weight. "That's right. Cattle came down first. We're hoping there's a doctor in Tucson to treat us all, but it spreads so fast—"

"Anthrax!" The man stepped back, pulled his neckerchief over his nose, looked at the bandit holding Luke. "Diego, they are sick. I don't want to die like them."

"They're not sick, *stupido*!" Diego jutted out his chin. "They lie to save their skins."

Realizing it was now or never, Luke groaned, growing limp in the man's arms. He collapsed back into the Mexican as he slid to the ground. Coughs and groans rattled his chest. His body twitched.

"Cattle die quickly, but people..." James leaned toward the man still holding the gun. "First sign is bruises. I have many on my legs. Second, open sores." He pointed to Luke. "See the blood oozing on his shirt?" He pointed to Luke's arm, dried blood coating the sleeve. The sores bleed."

The Mexican standing above Luke kicked his arm, snickered. "*Mentirosos*. Liar."

James tried harder. "Stay any longer, you'll end up like us."

"I'm dying!" Luke held his stomach, writhing as in final death throes. "Please shoot me now! It hurts! It hurts!"

Before Luke could moan louder, two horses galloped into the circle. Andy on one, another Mexican, this one skinny and sickly looking himself, on the other. Without a word, he launched himself out of the saddle and jerked Andy down out of his. He pushed him toward Diego.

"Found him trying to escape."

Andy crumpled to the ground, a red welt glowing on the side of his face. Pistol whipped.

No hand would leave a mark like that.

Diego marched over to Andy and knelt, turning his face back and forth. "No bruises.

No sores. No nothing." He stood pointing his gun at Andy. "We shoot you first."

Right on cue, Andy doubled over and vomited. He coughed up dust and dinner.

The skinny bandit pointed over his shoulder. "Diego, I tell you. I found *vacas*. Dead ones."

A frown. Diego followed the hand. "*Vacas* die, Gonzales. That is not unusual."

"These still twitched." Gonzales's stick-like arms moved up and down like marionettes. "Like this."

Sniggers rumbled around the men.

"Anthrax, Diego. I *tol'* you." The bandit holding the gun on Juan Tomás shoved his weapon into the holster. He bolted for his horse as he crossed himself. "*Vamanos*."

Diego grabbed his partner's shirtsleeve. "They are

lying, Roberto. You *will* stay here or," he lowered his voice, "I shoot you myself."

"A chuck wagon's not far from here, Diego" Gonzales said. "We get some whiskey. And food."

Diego's coffee-colored eyes lit up with his nod. He turned to James. "Your cook fix us food. We drink *all* your whiskies, take *all* your monies." He leaned in close, spitting as he talked. "We kill *all* you men."

His arm shot toward the chuck wagon. "*Vamanos.*" He swung up on his horse, wagged his gun at James. "You. In front. Walk." He reined his horse up against James and addressed the group. "One wrong step, I shoot him dead. *¿Comprende?*"

Forming mental escape plans, and discarding them one by one, Luke kept one eye on the leader and another on James as they trudged across the desert. If his brother made a play, Luke had to be ready to back him. As they walked, leading their horses, he hoped they could convince these Mexicans to leave. So far, he doubted their play-acting had worked. Nobody but one, possibly two, seemed bothered.

Smells of Coozie's stew invaded Luke's nose. Could it be? He was cooking? Of course. But what about whiskey? There was none and that fact alone was enough to get everyone shot. He hoped somehow Trace and he could convince the bandits they were in real danger.

Now close to camp, Luke spotted the cook ladling out a plateful of stew to a big Mexican, his gun belts forming an *X* on his chest.

Glad to see his brother and Coozie, neither one sporting extra holes, Luke then spotted the other outlaws. His stomach clenched.

"Diego, *mi compadre*, you come to join us for *comida*?"

The Mexican, arms waving, motioned toward the stew. "No whiskey, but the food is *bueno.*" He patted his stomach.

Wracked coughing turned Luke's attention to one of the bandits. The stew plate clattered

to the ground. Clutching his throat, Guillermo choked, coughed and jumped to his feet.

Staggering toward his horse, he fell to his knees.

"¿Guillermo, *está bien?*" Diego pounded his friend's back.

"Anthrax! *¡Madre de Dios!* Anthrax!" Gonzales swiveled his head from man to man.

Miguel jumped to his feet, scratching at his arms, his legs, his face. "Get them off. Get the ants off!"

More uncontrollable coughing, fits of scratching sent Guillermo into the desert. He staggered into a mesquite bush.

"*¡Vamanos, hombres!*" Two of the Mexicans bolted for their horses, leaping into the

saddles and kicking their sides before the other men could find their feet.

Within moments, the bandits, including the coughing and itching men, galloped away, all

disappearing into a cloud of dust.

Luke frowned at each brother, the others, his gaze resting on Coozie, wooden spoon still in hand. Luke stared at the bandits' tail end. "What happened?"

A smile blossomed on Coozie's face. He held up a spoon and shrugged. "*No se.* Maybe I put in the wrong spices?"

CHAPTER FORTY-THREE

Memories of the bandits pushed to the back of his mind, and with their Tucson visit behind them, Trace swayed and bounced. Swayed. Bounced. A rhythmic clop clop clop of the mules' gait pulling the supply wagon jarred his entire body. The jolting slumped his shoulders, his back. Trace slid right to the seat's edge and watched the ground flashing past the wheels, swirling sand running under the wagon making him dizzy. He straightened and scooted to his left, his shoulder now planted against Coozie. Rear end almost numb, he regarded the wagon bench. Hard. Too hard. The past two days of riding on this board had flattened his backside, certainly straining his back. Time for a stretch. He rose to his feet, but Coozie grabbed his arm, easing him down until his rear end hit the seat.

"If you want to get down, let me stop first." Coozie released Trace's arm. "Don't add a broken leg to your troubles."

Warmth flushed over Trace. He reached out and gripped Coozie's shoulder. That cook had saved his life again. Times like this made a fella glad to have friends. "You're a ace-high man, yeah you are." He produced a half smile. "Always watchin' out for me. You're swell."

One of Coozie's eyebrows arched as he returned the smile. "*Gracias*. And I think the medicine is working." Reins in hand, he flicked them, urging the mules to pick up the pace.

"No, I mean it." Trace nodded and patted Coozie's shoulder. "What would've I done without you?" He used his unbandaged arm to wave at the desert, its cactus and rocks glowing with June sun. "Look at all this. Thanks to you... it's still here."

Coozie cut his eyes sideways. "*¿Como?*"

"Simple." Trace held out his bandaged arm and studied the gauze. With the other hand,

he gripped a whiskey bottle and drank. Warmth flooded his stomach, tingled his toes. He corked the bottle, held it up toasting the hills, the mesquite, the sky. "No. *I'm* still here to see this, my friend. *Mi compa... ñero.* And James' still here. *Mi her... man... o.* And Luke... and Andy... and Juan—"

"*Sí.* We're all still here."

"Yessiree," Trace grinned. "Simple." A hiccup. "Without you, I'd be dead. Or *worse.*"

"You should thank my *abuela*. Grandmother knows all the herbs and spices to heal anybody." Coozie's tanned face softened. "She is the life saver, not me."

"Exactly like that... that *curing deer* back in Tucson." Trace looked over his shoulder at the town, now only a memory. Coozie's tight hold on his shirtsleeve kept him upright. Trace gripped the seat railing and glanced down at his freshly bandaged right arm still resting in a sling.

Coozie's shoulders bounced with a snicker. "You mean the *curandera* there in Tucson?"

"Yep. Ol' what's her name. The one you found 'cause regular doc wasn't home."

"He was due back this evening." Coozie glanced at Trace. "Babies come when they feel like it, not when the doctor has time."

"And that new lin-ment tastes first-rate." Trace leaned closer to Coozie. "Wanna smell?" He offered his bandaged right arm.

"No, *gracias*. I helped her put it on." Coozie leaned away. "Better go easy on that bottle. We only bought five and you've about drained one. Your brothers'll be *muy descontento*... angry, if you drink all the whiskey before we get back."

"Oh, p-shaww." Trace flapped his hand, watched fingers flutter in front of his face. "How much more miles you think?"

"One or two hours. They're not far ahead of us now. We've only been away *dos dias*."

Trace offered the bottle to Coozie who shook his head. He sniffed it, then a long satisfying pull drained the bottle. Trace held up the amber painkiller, like presenting a trophy. "Here's to you, Coozie. And Grandma." A grin stretched his cheeks.

CHAPTER FORTY-FOUR

Whid brought the shot glass to his mouth, whiskey lapping against his lower lip. He threw back the satisfying tonsil varnish, swallowed, and smacked lips hidden under the mop of mustache. Glass held up, he spoke to it. "Only thing better than a shot of high-quality whiskey is a high-quality woman." His eyes cut sideways to Pickett, sitting to his right. "But not *any* woman."

From Pickett, he shifted his gaze to the grayed air of *El Diablo,* the largest saloon in Tucson. Smoke hung from the ceiling like gray icicles. The only light source, two kerosene lanterns placed at either end of the bar, splattered odd patterns of illumination. The bare walls of the adobe room soaked in the meager glow. Patrons groped their way around the saloon, knocking into chairs, tables, and other patrons along the way. Curses rolled as thick as the smoke.

A half-empty whiskey bottle sat on the table, as irresistible to Whid as a flapping cape to an enraged bull. Whid poured himself another glass and held it up. The kerosene flames turned the amber liquid golden. He turned to Pickett. "Nope. I lied. The only thing better than this whiskey is killing James Colton." He gulped the liquor in one swallow. "Soon."

Whid's cigar added to the air's stagnation. When the shot glass wasn't perched on his lips, the cigar took its place. He puffed like a blowfish enjoying the thick smoky rolls circulating around his head. Pickett coughed and rubbed his eyes each time Whid turned into a smokestack.

Pickett played with his half-full beer glass. He spun it, sloshing the contents onto the table. "Glad that Colton fella didn't spot us in here yesterday. He'd of probably figured out you were the same fella from Nogales what set his brother up with that whore." Pickett wagged his head. "Bet he's still mighty upset. James bedded by that woman and all. Probably wanna fight

you right here. Call you out to a duel."

"A duel?" Whid puffed, producing smoky o's. "You been readin' those history books again?"

"At the very least, he would've called you out to the street." Pickett lowered his voice. "I hear he's fast. Real fast." He pointed his finger at a light and fired. "They all are."

"He ain't usin' but one arm." Whid's loud words turned a few heads. "And it's his shootin' arm that's all cut up. Hell, he's as harmless as a one-eyed kitten."

"Still." Pickett slouched back into his wooden chair. He picked up the beer glass. "Watch yourself. If it ain't him, it's one of the brothers."

Whid snorted into his newly filled shot glass, leaned back against the chair and thought.

A drink, a few more puffs, he nodded. "His brothers. You're right, Pickett."

"I am?"

"Yep." Whid rubbed dribbled whiskey into his beard. "Ain't nearly killed but three of 'em so far. There's still the youngster to take care of." He turned his full attention on his partner. "Hell, I'm tired of sittin' around, waitin' on Doc to come back. Have me a hankerin' now to kill Andy."

Pickett leaned in close, his eyes darting right and left. "Thought you was killin' only James." He glanced toward the door. "And if you do kill either one—any of 'em—you'll have the rest of the whole damn family and those cow hands down on you. Hell, on *us*."

"So? We kill 'em all."

"I don't want no part of killing. Told you before. What's the point? You ain't never gonna get Morningstar. Even with James dead, she ain't loving you. Give up."

"Give up?" Whid jumped to his feet, launched his empty glass across the room, shattering

against a wall inches above a cowboy's head. "Give up? What the hell you talkin' about?" He grabbed Pickett's vest and tugged. They stood nose to nose. "Whid Amos MacGilvray don't *never* give up. *Never ever.* Understand? *¿Comprende?*"

Pickett nodded.

"Got it?" Whid shook his partner.

Pickett nodded harder.

"'Bout time."

Before Whid released the vest, the barkeep, backed by the glass-christened cowboy, moved in close.

"Best be getting on somewheres else, fellas," the bartender said. "Don't need no trouble

in here." He pointed toward the door.

The cowboy brushed glass off his shoulder. "He found trouble with me." He stepped nose to nose with Whid.

Whid blew out whiskey-laden smoke. "I'll see your trouble and call you."

"Hold it, boys." The barkeep shoved his way between the two men. "We all wanna live to see another day. Right?" He waited for heads to bob. "How about the next round's on me and we tell some jokes 'stead of plantin' each other in Boot Hill. All right?"

Pickett nodded faster than the other men. "Sounds fine. Thanks."

Silence filled the room.

A snort. A quiet curse.

The cowboy stuck out his hand. "No hard feelings. Guess it was an accident."

Whid accepted the hand and squeezed harder than he should. "Yeah."

"Fine." The bartender turned to Whid and Pickett. "Soon's you drink up, I suggest you go

on about your business."

"Fine." Pickett headed toward the bar.

"Fine." Whid wiped his hand on his pants and followed him.

CHAPTER FORTY-FIVE

Andy lay his head on the saddle and pulled a wool blanket up around his shoulders. Even though the stars were out in full intensity tonight and Trace and Coozie were back from their adventure in Tucson, nagging dread and doubt kept him awake. Something wasn't right.

He turned onto his side and envied Juan Tomás sleeping a few yards away. His soft snores sailed across the quiet desert but failed to soothe Andy's raw nerves. No matter what he did, he couldn't ignore the feeling or get to sleep. Eating? Nothing appealed. Trace had mentioned only this morning that, despite the Arizona sun, Andy was pale. He remembered Trace's scrunched eyebrows, frown, warm hand pressed against his forehead. Exactly like Ma when he was sick.

But was he sick? No fever. No aches and pains. No broken bones or deep bruises. Where he'd been pistol whipped was still tender, but a long look into the shaving mirror this morning revealed a fading mark.

Andy rolled onto his other side and thought about

Ginny. Ginny far away, far back in Mesilla. Ginny with that honey-brown hair, those mesmerizing green eyes set off by sweeping eyelashes. Her captivating fragrance— like lilac soap. Besides all that, he loved the way she laughed, crossed somehow between a giggle and a full-blown guffaw. Every time something struck her funny, which was often, her eyes lit up and danced. Pulling in remembered smells and images, his chest tightened.

I miss her.

Maybe that was the problem. Maybe it was a case of wanting to hold the girl of his

dreams again. Wrap his arms around her and feel her soft curvy body melt into his. His brothers

hadn't said much about their women, but he guessed they missed them, too. Of course, Trace and James and Luke didn't have to worry about their women finding another man. They were already married. Andy hadn't put a ring on Ginny's finger yet. There was always the danger someone else would.

Thoughts turned lustful. He could share her bed any time he wanted if they were married. *Any time.* He hadn't suggested the idea of bedding to Ginny yet and certainly wouldn't until after they were officially married. Pa taught all his boys about restraint. And as far as Andy knew, they'd done what Pa said. Except Luke. He'd always been the family renegade.

Maybe James could share some insight. Andy knew his brother had had bedroom

problems, but by now they were sure to be fixed. It'd been so long now. Yeah, James would be

the brother to confide in.

Andy turned again on the hard sand, the saddle blanket under him. Visions of Ginny teased his senses, sent heat surging through his body.

* * *

Sitting at the campfire next morning, breakfast plate in hand, Andy waved his spoon at James, who was making his way over. "Plenty of room. Let me pull up a rock for you."

He pointed to a flat rock Carlos had situated near the fire the night before. Andy surveyed the campsite. Coozie, way over by the string of horses, stood talking to Juan Tomás. Luke and Trace were already with the herd. Carlos had wandered off in search of the perfect bush to water. That left Andy and James.

James eased down to the rock. "Fire's warming my outsides this morning and I'm glad for it, even though it'll be stinking hot by noon."

Andy used the spoon to chase beans around in the bowl until he tired of the pursuit. He

still wasn't hungry and sleep had evaded him most of the night. He dropped the utensil into the

bowl and sighed.

James dug into his stew. "Trace tells me you haven't been yourself." He glanced up. "I noticed it too, didn't say anything." He waited. "So... what's the problem?"

How could he unscramble his thoughts? Andy looked down at his hands.

James pointed his spoon at the herd. "I sympathize with how you feel... killing the cattle and all. Had to be done. Mighty convincing they had anthrax. How'd you do it without those Mexicans finding out?"

"Cut some leg tendons, necks. Needed lots of blood." Andy sighed. "Sure hated to."

"I agree." James nodded. "But the padres at the mission in Tubac truly appreciated the meat. It won't be wasted."

A longer sigh from Andy. His shoulders rose and fell. He glanced toward his brother. "I miss her."

"Virginia?"

Andy nodded. "Think about her all the time. My heart hurts." The campfire's flames sputtered, one twig igniting into a flume of red, then as dramatically dying.

"You in love?" James' words were soft.

A shrug, a smile. "Think so." Andy set his untouched bowl on the ground and gave his

brother full attention. "How do you know when it's right? When she's the one? How do you... how do you... *love* someone?"

James cocked his head.

"I mean..." Andy swallowed hard. "And how do you *bed* a girl?" His cheeks warmed.

"I mean I know how... to..." He simply couldn't keep eye contact with James any longer.

Instead, he stared into the fire. "Did you... you... with Morningstar before you married?"

"No." James stared into the fire, too. "Damn no."

Andy's words quietly tumbled out. "I knew you had troubles a few years back after being held by those Indians, but I figured you were all right by the time you married. I mean, I remember you and me talking when we were in the army together over in Arizona City. And you said—"

"Nothing changed until a month or so before leaving Mesilla." James picked up a rock and threw it across camp.

"You mean..." His words faded into the desert. Surely his brother was joking. He studied James. Tight lips, clenched hand... Damn. He was serious.

James chucked a larger rock at a piñon tree. "I finally told Star about my Pima wife when I was a captive.

Guess that made a big difference." He tossed raised eyebrows at Andy. "Sure changed things."

Now that was something he'd never expected. How frustrating and maddening for his brother. No wonder he turned moody sometimes.

James pushed himself off the rock, stood staring down at Andy. "And no, I wouldn't have bedded Morningstar before marriage. I sure thought about it. A lot. But it's not right."

Andy closed his opened mouth.

"And you *know* when she's the right one." James walked away, turned back. "You simply know."

CHAPTER FORTY-SIX

Whid clutched a tin coffee cup in one hand, used the other to push himself up off his rock seat. On his feet now, he twisted his back creating pops and pings so loud Pickett looked up from his own cup. Whid rubbed his lower back while slurping the remaining coffee. "Damn, I hate sleepin' on the ground." He rubbed harder and pointed the cup at his partner. "Andy Colton."

Pickett cocked his head. "Huh?"

"Figured it out."

"Figured what out?"

"How I'm gettin' rid of Andrew Jackson Colton."

"How?" Pickett frowned into his cup.

Whid wandered away from the fire. "We're what, a hundred, two hundred miles east of Fort Yuma?"

"About."

"Perfect."

Pickett stood, cup still in hand. "What's perfect?"

"Gives us enough time. See, poor little brother Andy? Why, Fort Yuma'll find out he's a deserter." Whid turned his focus on Pickett whose eyes had narrowed. "Those soldier boys will get to arrest and hang such a low-down criminal." His chortle grew into a full-blown laugh. "Damn deserters ought to be shot *then* hanged."

"But—"

"Yeah, a pure damn shame, it is. I mean those Colton brothers will have to choose between trying to save little brother's life and saving their herd." Whid laughed again. "Damn

shame. Hard choice, I'd say."

CHAPTER FORTY-SEVEN

They had pushed cattle for what felt like years. James, relieved nothing else had happened over the past three weeks, realized the drive had sunk into routine. Life was predictable. Up before sunrise, hot sun, dusty wind, rousting renegade steers from mesquite undergrowth, long hours. But from here in the saddle, despite the rain, he sure as hell couldn't and wouldn't complain. A whole lot of "nothing exciting" was welcome. Maybe their run of bad luck was over. Maybe it would be smooth sailing to Tin Town.

James re-wrapped the black gum blanket around his shoulders, tugged his hat down lower. The incessant rain, starting before dawn this morning, cooled the after-noon air. For that, he was grateful. The last few weeks had become scorchers, close to unbearable. He knew firsthand now what the preacher meant when he talked about hellfire. Damnation and hellfire—that was summer in southern Arizona rolled into one. And they'd been right in the middle of hellfire for days as they plodded west across the Sonoran Desert. Hellfire followed his crew, his brothers, and close to three thousand head of beef.

Three thousand. That in itself was a head-scratcher. When they'd started off from Mesilla in April, they'd counted two thousand, five hundred and twenty-six. Along the way, some had calved, and some were Mexican cattle wandering into the herd and staying. The rest... he had no clue, but even the new ones, all three thousand, now wore his road brand. The 4C Square. James threw his shoulders back as he remembered when his brothers all agreed on this venture. Yep. It was certainly turning out to be an adventure of a lifetime.

Despite his wide-brimmed hat, thick raindrops splattered in his eyes. He reined up and wiped the water off his face. Vision now clear, his gaze trailed across the herd until he spotted Trace, way off on the other side, opposite him. Today, he and Trace rode swing, either side of the herd. Up ahead rode Juan Tomás. His position as lead worked well. He kept his eyes open and guided the beeves across the terrain. Andy rode opposite him.

Way up ahead, out of sight was Coozie, looking for a place to stop and set up camp for the night. With the rain making things wet and muddy, when they'd stopped at noon, he hadn't bothered to light a fire. The drovers settled for a fistful of beef jerky and cold tortillas left over from yesterday's supper. James hoped the rain would let up enough this afternoon for Coozie to light a fire and toss more beans into his famous stew. James' stomach rumbled at the thought.

Today, Carlos rode point and scout—way out in front, checking for better passages,

better feed, fewer Indians, hopefully water. That left Luke. One side of James' mouth drew up. Now with his arm healed, Luke was expected to do his full share. This morning he drew the short straw and had to ride drag. Bringing up the tail end. Eating everyone's dust. Luke hated riding drag. Absolutely *hated* it and told everyone every chance he got.

James shook his head, turning halfway around in his saddle. Yep. There was younger brother Luke, hat down around his ears, slicker pulled up to his neck, bandana covering his face—like those bank robbers he'd seen pictures of in newspapers. Instead of dust today, he'd been fighting mud. James swung back around and nudged Sophie.

Another mile, Trace called for a stop. Today's gray skies turned darker. Sunset wasn't too far off. By James' reckoning, they'd covered eight full miles today. With a few more under their belt, they'd be across the desert. His shoulders slumped. Even so, no way in hell they'd get to Fort Yuma, and north to Tin Town by July first. No way. Not at this pace.

Coozie's camp consisted of a canvas tarp strung from the top of the wagon to two poles stuck in the ground. James ducked to get under. Always the miracle worker, somehow Coozie had managed to find dry wood and build a fire. Not big enough to set flames to the canvas, but enough to heat up the stew. The aroma of boiling coffee brought a sigh and smile to James.

James, Andy—appetite again hearty—and Juan Tomás hunkered down shoulder to shoulder around the fire. Stew bowls in hand, they shoveled in spoonfuls of warm beef. James spoke over his full mouth.

"Best stew for a hundred miles." The spoon in James' hand slid out of his grip. Bits of gravy sloshed onto his slicker. "Damn. How slick can a spoon get?"

"Mixes in perfect with the mud," Juan Tomás used his

spoon to point at his own mud-splattered slicker. "Who can tell?"

James would never tell this crew, especially his brothers, how tired or how convinced he was this cattle drive was a huge mistake. They'd never get there on time and they'd end up selling the cattle at a loss. Bad decision to even start out. What had he been thinking?

Any extra space in his brain was now crammed with Andy's recent questions about marriage and bedding. Old hurts and misgivings had been thrust to the forefront, making him think about things he'd tried hard to push to the back—to eliminate, erase from his life.

On the other hand, he'd at long last been the lover he'd always dreamed of being and with a woman he cherished beyond his own life. He'd do anything for her. Except tell her about Nogales. Probably. Maybe. He'd spent hours questioning what had transpired after drinking the mescal. Probably nothing. No, in fact, he was sure it was nothing. Unless...

"You all right?"

Andy's voice and shoulder bump jarred James. He dropped the spoon again. "What?"

"You all right?" Andy cocked his head and dipped his eyebrows. "You're sitting there like you'd seen a ghost." He moved in close.

His brothers knew about his recurring nightmares, which also appeared in bright daylight, many coming hard and fast with Trace's recent capture. Most times those demons hid out of reach. But they came swooping in at odd moments, especially when James least expected, and he'd end up shaking or yelling out in his sleep. Or simply crying. Or fighting. Andy had experienced the receiving end of those nightmares a time or two. Thankfully, the bruises were long healed.

"Thinking, Andy. Only thinking." James picked up the spoon, wiped it on his slicker and stuck the spoon into the stew.

"*Señor* James?" Juan Tomás handed Coozie an empty bowl and turned to James. "We are not far from Arizona City." He paused, shot a look at Andy. "Will we ride into town? It's been over a month since Nogales."

"I could get more supplies," Coozie said.

"And I haven't been there in ages," Andy said. "What'd you say, James? Are we?"

Bad thoughts of Nogales—not only the woman, but the whiskey—tightened James' chest. "Let's talk it over with Trace. Can't afford to lose any more time, though."

"We'll be quick. Don't worry." Andy stretched out his bowl for a refill while Coozie ladled another steaming mound into the dish. Andy licked his lips.

Waving his spoon over his shoulder, Juan Tomás tried to hide a burp. "Carlos says Siphon Spring is less than a day away. Should be plenty fresh water there."

"Great!" James allowed a smile, even though with all the rain, the idea of water wasn't too appealing right now. "How big's the spring? Did he say?"

"Enough to water maybe a hundred at a time." Juan Tomás nodded. "Big enough."

James handed his bowl to Coozie. "We can refill the water barrels and wash dishes and

clothes."

"Refill the barrels, *verdad*," Coozie said. "But *you* can wash dishes and clothes, *mi*

amigo." A solid pat on the back sent James forward. Coozie pointed his spoon at his own chest.

"*I* will sit and watch how you do it."

CHAPTER FORTY-EIGHT

Whid tucked the new blue shirt into his new twill trousers. He spread his arms out wide and presented himself in front of his partner. "How do I look?"

Pickett stumbled backward out of the mercantile's door. "That you, Whid?" He frowned.

"Ain't never seen you all duded up before."

Whid stepped into daylight and gave the street a long look to his left, a quick glance right. Would anybody recognize him? Probably not. More than several years had passed since he'd been here in Arizona City. Plus, few people chose to be outside during the heat of the day. And today was the hottest yet. Whid let the heat fall off him. A second long look. One man stepped across the street disappearing into the saloon. Otherwise, town was deserted.

Whid smoothed his beard. "Yep. Even the barber tamed this a bit." He pulled off his hat, revealing cut and oiled hair. He stuck out one leg. "New boots even."

"Hell, Whid. You don't look like yourself at all. Don't

even smell right. I'd never recognize you." Pickett whistled as Whid held up his other boot. He followed Whid down the dirt street. "Tell me again. Why're you troubling yourself? Aren't you planning on only talking

to the Army?"

Whid let out a long stream of air and a solid curse word. Pickett was so dumb he couldn't teach a hen to cluck. He turned to his partner. "Only tell you this one more time." He lowered his voice. "Need to convince the Army I'm a lawman. So they'll believe me. You seen any lawmen with unkempt beards and dirty clothes?"

Pickett shook his head.

"Me neither. If I'm to be the law, I need to look like the law—as much as it gives me the

shudders thinkin' on it." Whid marched down the street, Pickett on his heels, until he reached the livery stable. He stopped. "What'd you find out about the commanding officer?"

Standing, one hand on hip, Pickett sighed. "How come you get all duded up, new clothes and such, and I don't get nothing? Not even a bath?"

Muscles constricted across Whid's shoulders. A deep breath in, a long one out. His words were loud, measured. "'Cause you don't need to." He leaned in close. "Get it?"

"Yeah." Pickett backed away. "Could use a bath, though. Been scratching somethin' fierce." His eyes lit up. "Maybe after we talk to the army, we can come back and I'll take me a long, soapy one. All right?"

"Fine." Whid shoved down his anger. "Now, about the officer?"

"Fella named Rickman. Lieutenant Rickman." Pickett followed Whid into the stable. "Apparently been in the army for years, but this's his first command. Word is he's a fella that lives by the book."

"Perfect." Whid saddled his horse, led her out into the sunlight. Reins in one hand, he used the other to scratch his chest. Even from this area of town on a slight hill, he could spot the Colorado River, its blue ribbon snaking past. If he listened hard, he could hear its roar.

Pickett led his horse into the sunshine also. He cocked his head. "You really think your

plan'll work? I mean, Fort Yuma's regular army. What if they don't care about Andy? Or they learn he didn't really desert? What then?" Pickett's Adam's apple bobbed up and down. "I still don't think it's one of your better ideas. Purely ain't happy about comin' along."

"You worry too much." Whid swung into the saddle, smiling at the creaking leather. He dug around in his vest pocket and extracted a tin star. It looked real enough, even this close. His days rotting in jail had paid off finally. How many hours had he and his cellmates, when he wasn't in solitary, spent bending cans, scratching on them? Who said jail was a waste of time? He examined it closer. No one would ever suspect it started life as the lid of a green beans can. He pinned it on and nodded. "I'm official now."

Laying on the banks of the raging Colorado River, Fort Yuma sat directly south and a bit west of Arizona City. The fort defended southern California and Arizona Territory from marauding Indians, hostile Mexicans, rampaging prospectors, and other people looking to get rich without the sanctity of law on their side.

Whid reined up a quarter mile from the gate. He turned to Pickett. "Got your story straight?"

A nod.

"You remember everything I told you?"

Another nod.

"You sure?"

A third nod.

"All right. Let's get to 'er. I'm looking forward to watching Andrew Colton swing. Or face a firing squad." Whid pushed his shoulders back, leaned over and spit. Brown tendrils hung from his beard before he scraped them off. He wiped his hand on his new pants. Pushing his chaw to his other cheek, he spoke over the wad. "Yep. Looking forward."

* * *

Whid and Pickett followed a sergeant into an office reeking of military. Diplomas, pictures of recently-slain President Lincoln, and several rifles stacked in the corner reminded Whid why he hadn't joined. He hated anything that organized, that regimented. No, he was his own man, and, by God, he'd stay that way.

He stopped in front of a paper-laden desk. A man in a blue uniform, one silver bar on each shoulder strap, lifted his head and locked eyes on Whid. For a split second, Whid questioned his choice of harassment. Could Pickett possibly be right? Maybe this plan would backfire. He rethought. No. This was too worthwhile to pass up.

Whid extended his hand as the lieutenant stood. "Amos Smith, sir. Sheriff, Utah Territory." He nodded toward his tin badge, tilted his head at Pickett. "And this here is a fella I brought with me to back up what I'm about to tell you. His name's Pi… Pickles."

"Odd name."

"Kinda nickname, sir." Pickett threw back his shoulders, drew in a long breath. "See when I was a kid—"

"Pleased to meet you. I'm Lieutenant Josiah Rickman." He pointed to two wooden chairs in front of the desk as he retook his seat. His hooded gray eyes trained on Whid. "What can I do for you, gentlemen?"

Whid chose the chair on Pickett's right, sat, and leaned back against the creaky wooden slats. "Was on the way down from Utah to pick up a prisoner over in another county, when I was passing time with him." He pointed to Pickett.

The commander frowned. "Excuse me. You're from where?"

Whid felt himself slouch. Wouldn't do for such an important man. He pulled in air, sat up

straight, and jerked his thumb north. "Utah Territory. I'm a marshal up there."

"Thought you said you were a sheriff." Rickman's eyes traveled to Whid's badge.

"I am." Whid almost stuttered and hated himself for it. "Fact is, I'm both. We call ourselves marshal-sheriffs up there."

"Hmmm. Never heard of it." Rickman nodded. "And?"

Whid turned to Pickett. "This man right here was sitting at a bar down in Nogal—"

"Excuse me, Marshal Sheriff." Rickman picked up a pencil, smoothed out a piece of

paper, exhaled. "I'd rather have him tell it." He glanced at Pickett. "Please tell me what happened... Mister... Pickles."

A start and stop. A stare at Whid.

Not wanting to lose this chance at doing in Andy Colton, Whid nodded. "It's all right, Pickles. Tell him what you told me. You won't get into trouble. It's that deserter, Andrew Colton, that'll be in trouble."

Pickett slid slightly forward in his chair. "I was down in Nogales few weeks back. Started talkin' with a fella braggin' about desertin' from the Army."

Rickman scribbled, dotted a few i's, looked up. "Go on."

Why give Pickett all the fun and glory? Whid jumped in and spoke over his partner's words. "Fact was, this fella says he spent some time right here in Arizona City. Before the Battle of Picacho Pass. Claims he was shot not too far from here. Some Rebs ambushed him and some others."

More writing. "Uh huh." Rickman re-read his notes. "What's this man's name again?"

Whid knew he had him. At least his curiosity was piqued. "Says it was..." He searched the ceiling as if it held the name. "Colton. Andrew Colton."

"Andrew *Jackson* Colton." Pickett glared at Whid.

"What exactly did he tell you, sir?" Rickman trained his eyes and pencil on Pickett. "Please try to remember details."

After a glance at Whid, Pickett began. "I was sittin' in a saloon, down in Nogales,

talkin' to this fella when all of a sudden like he started braggin' about bein' in the Army a year or

so back but didn't like it. So once he made it to Mesilla, he left. High tailed it to Mexico." Pickett nodded. "That's where I run into 'im. Mexico."

"I hate deserters. Scum of the earth." Rickman's lips curled into a thin sneer. "Nothing

lower than—" He snapped back to the present. "What I mean is, the Army has no tolerance for deserters. Where would the Army be if people merely came and went at their pleasure?"

"My feelings exactly, Lieutenant." Whid's shirt strained across his chest. "Knew you'd want to find out soon as possible."

"Absolutely. We could use more respectable citizens like you." Rickman scribbled a few more words, looked from Whid to Pickett. "Anything else?"

Before Pickett could start, Whid jumped in. "Besides his bein' at the battle of Picacho Pass, said he was down with the Apache back in '62. Killed a handful of Rebs, a few Indians—"

"He ain't a hero, though." Pickett leaned closer to the commander. "Said he grew tired of being ordered to march here, march there, march back and forth, so he simply marched himself down to Mexico." Pickett leaned back. "That's where I met him."

"And he was never officially discharged, sir?" Rickman scribbled on a second piece of paper, his eyes scanning the new lines of writing.

"Nope." Pickett brought himself fully upright. "Said he didn't."

"Made it real clear he hadn't," Whid said. He'd be damned if he'd let Pickett steal his

thunder. "Seemed to take pride on it." He gave his partner a quick smirk.

Rickman dotted the last sentence, looked up. His eyes danced with excitement, his mouth curving up at one end. Even his brown hair seemed to glow with anticipation. He was young, Whid realized. Maybe not real young, closer to the long side of thirty.

Pencil tapping brought Whid's thoughts back to the matter at hand. Did this soldier

believe the story? Parts were true. Whid congratulated himself again for paying attention when asking around Mesilla about Andy. Pretty little Virginia had been more than forthcoming with her knowledge about him. Her beau. She'd sung his praises and couldn't stop talking about how wonderful he was. Well, Miss Ginny, thanks to you, your precious beau's about to die.

"Anything else you can remember? Either of you?" Rickman's gaze trailed from Pickett to Whid and out the small window. He turned back. "Guess I should ask you what he looks like."

"About six one, six two, maybe." Whid held his hand up over his head, pointed to his own eyes. "Brown."

"Brown hair, hits his shoulders," said Pickett. "Young. I believe he said he's nineteen."

Rickman jerked back at that. "Nineteen? He was in the Army in '62?" A few blinks, a frown, he continued. "That'd make him sixteen when he joined."

"Does it?" Whid glared at Pickett. "Maybe you didn't hear right, Pickles. He might've said he was nineteen when he *joined* the Army." He leaned forward and with that movement kicked Pickett's foot.

Pickett slid both legs to his left. "That might've been what he said." He lowered his

voice. "We'd had a few beers."

"Uh huh." Rickman stood. "You have any idea where he may be right now? I'd like to find him soon as possible."

A strange, hot excitement tingled Whid, filling his whole being. This was it. James Colton would pay. And pay dearly. He didn't try to hide the smile crawling up his face. "I hear he's taken up with a cattle outfit down about Siphon Springs. They were headed that way when I passed them. Fact is, should be coming by here in a week or two. Said they're on their way to California."

Lieutenant Rickman pursed his lips and stared out the open door. "Hate deserters. Hate 'em."

"Don't like 'em much myself either," Whid said.

"Seemed like a nice enough fella, though." Pickett eased to his feet.

"Nice doesn't cut it in the army, sir." Rickman walked Whid and Pickett to the door. "Can't tell you how much I appreciate you coming in to tell me. Deserters. Nothing but scum." He stood at the door. "I'll see to it he hangs."

"Firing squad's not a bad option, either," Whid offered.

Rickman extended a hand to Whid. "I like you. We think alike." He shook with Pickett.

"Take care."

Once Whid and Pickett were safely on their horses and outside the fort's gate, the men's shoulders slumped. Whid led them into town, to the livery stable. Neither spoke during the return ride.

Whid tossed a coin at the stable boy and turned to Pickett. "What was that? *Seems like a nice fella?* What the hell you thinking? You turning soft on me?"

"He *was* a nice fella. Don't see why he'll hang, though."

Daylight blinded Whid. He squinted at his partner. "'Cause he's a Colton, that's why." He unpinned his badge and shoved it into his vest pocket. "Come buy me a beer. Looks like I done my most virtuous deed for the day."

CHAPTER FORTY-NINE

Andy sat under a cottonwood and watched the cattle drink. Normally, he'd be smiling at the cows pushing their way into the water, their bellies skimming the pond's surface, slurping water as it dripped off their noses. But despite the blue skies, warm weather, and all the clear water anyone could drink, Andy's shoulders sagged. Images of Perchman haunted his dreams. More than once these last few nights he'd been roused out of fitful sleep by someone shaking him, admonishing him for yelling, waking everyone.

More and more often Perchman's face appeared in the clouds, in the swirling sand, hell, even in his stew. Only this morning he was visualizing Ginny's pretty face, when Perchman's took her place. Andy remembered scrambling back from the fire, coffee cup in hand. In fact, the burn on two of his fingers from the sloshed coffee still hurt, still red. He picked up a stick and drew circles in the dirt. Lines and figures. More circles. Unsatisfied, he tossed the stick away. Andy chose a rock and examined it. An ordinary rock. Nothing special about it. Gray with tiny flecks of black. Not even a river rock, smooth, round. Simply a damn boring rock. Like him.

He sighed. Loud. His fingers folded around the rock. He rested his forehead on that hand, closed his eyes. Cows slurped, crows cawed, and boots scuffled through the sand his way.

Andy didn't bother looking up, didn't want to look at whoever was heading toward him. He wanted to be left alone with his thoughts. Dark thoughts. He couldn't be suitable company. Maybe if he ignored whoever it was, he'd leave. The boots stopped less than a foot in front of him.

Silence. Breathing. Andy squeezed his eyes tighter. Perhaps as long as a minute passed

before that same someone slid his body down against the trunk of the cottonwood. Warmth

radiated from the shoulder touching his.

Words. Quiet words filled Andy's ears. "What's wrong?"

Trace. He recognized his oldest brother's strong voice, that baritone, so much like Pa's.

Could he tell Trace he was so damned depressed he had to keep from lying down and crying? That he had no idea why he was feeling this way? And he saw Perchman everywhere?

A hand on his leg. A gentle shake. A nudge. "You sick?"

Andy's head wagged and shoulders rose up and down before he could think of the right

answer. Knowing Trace wouldn't go away, he gave in. He opened his eyes and looked at his brother. Brown eyes searched his face.

Something about Trace always made him tell the truth. Bare his soul, so to speak. And this time was no exception. One look at that face, those concerned eyes, Andy poured out his heart. "Perchman. Why'd he have to die? What gives anyone the right to take another man's life? And what do we really know about Perchman? Didn't he deserve at least a little respect?"

"Why're you—"

"Can't get him out of my head. He's with me everywhere." Andy looked down at his trembling hands. "You think maybe he's coming back from the grave? Telling me I forgot something?"

Trace leaned back. "Where'd you get a crazy notion like that? Coming back from the grave?" He frowned. "Hell, Andy, he doesn't even *have* a grave."

That was it. Andy knew. No doubt. He sat bolt upright and swiveled around to face

Trace. "A grave. He's needing a grave. At least a marker. Hell, Trace, we've seen a few out here

on the trail. That's what he wants. A marker." He scrambled to his feet holding out a hand for

Trace. "I'll get right on it."

"Wait, wait." Trace gripped Andy's hand as he stretched to his feet. "You'll what?"

No time to lose. Andy pulled out of his brother's grasp and started off. "Put a cross and

marker on the trail. With his name and date on it. That's what he wants. A grave." He reached

back and dropped the rock into Trace's hand.

First, wood. The right kind for a first-rate cross. Second, a perfect place to erect it. Some place where everyone who passed by would see, stop and think about the person who died. Andy marched to the supply wagon. He rooted around in the boot until he found a sack of tools. Clutching the canvas bag, he climbed down, turned, and ran into Luke.

"What're you doing?" Luke pointed his cigarette at the bag.

Andy held up the canvas sack. "A cross. Building a marker for Perchman. That's what he wants."

"He *wants*?" Luke moved in close and lowered his voice. "Andy... Perchman's dead. He ain't talking. Not to you. Not to anybody."

"He deserves a grave and a cross. A marker. Words said." Andy held the bag between them like a shield.

"Perchman don't deserve anything. He crossed the wrong people at the wrong time. That's all." Luke dangled the cigarette between his lips and puffed on it.

"Well, a cross is what he's getting." Andy shook the bag.

"He won't appreciate the effort." Luke pointed at the tool bag and the wagon behind Andy. Smoke curled from his lips as he spoke. "Put that away and come help with the herd. Besides, it's not like he's coming back or anything. He ain't a ghost."

"He already is." Why did he feel compelled to tell this brother? Luke always made fun of

him. Ridicule him. Endlessly. Tell him it was a stupid idea. Tell him it's all in his head. He's

crazy. Insist he get back to watching the cattle. Andy pulled in air, straightened his body, gazed over his brother's shoulder toward the herd and the other drovers. "He told me."

Laughter. Long and loud. Luke held Andy's shoulder, rocking it back and forth. "You got one helluva imagination, little brother. Always did." He released the grip, walked off shaking his head and chortling. Words trailed behind him. "Oooohhhh. Ghosties and ghoulies.

Ooohhh." More laughter. Andy chose not to listen any longer. He had something much more important to do.

A walk along the stream before it headed underground produced enough big mesquite bushes to provide a few sturdy sticks. Big enough to construct a respectable cross. Wide enough to write on.

Andy spent the rest of the afternoon cutting, carving, wrapping rawhide strings around the sticks to create a cross. As the sun sat on the horizon, he called the others to gather around. He'd chosen a slight hill on which to plant the monument. From this viewpoint, Perchman could see a hundred miles in all directions. And, as if Heaven knew what was happening, the sunset bathed the hill in pinks and golds. A few clouds lingered as if waiting for final words to be said.

At long last with all the men assembled, the herd bedded, Andy let his gaze trail over his brothers, over the hands who'd become his friends, and ultimately over the desert. He cleared his throat, stood up straight, nodded at the cross.

"Zebediah Perchman was a decent man. Maybe not a righteous man. Maybe not always an honest man. But still, he was a man. He helped us get started on this cattle drive. He helped us

find our way. He helped. And we need to thank him for that." He pulled in another big lungful of

air.

"The way he died wasn't right. Wasn't fair. But none of us could of prevented it. His end

was out of everybody's control." Andy caught a single tear rolling down James' cheek. Trace's

mouth turned down, his eyes focused on the ground.

"We can give a proper sendoff to Perchman, who deserved better'n what he ended up with."

"Hear, hear." The words spread across the desert.

Andy gazed upward. "Please, Lord. Take better care of him than we did."

Silence.

"Amen."

More mumbled "amens" raced around the group. Hats were replaced. Other words mumbled at the cross, the men ambled back toward the herd.

James, Trace and Andy remained.

"Thank you for doing this." Trace patted Andy's back and walked away.

"Yeah. Thanks." James ran his sleeved arm under his nose, walked off, his hands smoothing his hair before replacing his hat.

Andy stood, looking down at the marker. He felt better. Much better. Both corners of his mouth turned upward. "You're welcome."

CHAPTER FIFTY

Blistering days, three of them, had passed since Siphon Springs. The cattle bawled for water despite stopping at several small watering holes along the way. If they could survive crossing this scorching Mojave Desert another week or two, finding more ponds and small creeks, they'd be wallowing in the Colorado River, belly deep in water. Andy raised his eyes to the turquoise sky. Were those clouds off to the west? Rain? He calculated days. Should be early June, maybe as late as middle June. Could be rain clouds. Any moisture in the desert, enough to open wildflowers and bring bloom to cactus, would happen during summer with the warm days heating up the sky. Well, hot it was. He wiped his forehead with his sleeve. Had to be well over a hundred this afternoon.

He glanced back at the herd. Still there, still plodding along. All three thousand of them. Today he was riding point. Way out in front. It was the best position—no dust to eat and the first to see what, if anything, was happening. But with the noonday meal sitting in his belly, there was nothing to look forward to except supper and a few hours of sleep. Maybe he'd play cards with Juan Tomás again. Andy enjoyed poker and was learning the finer points of the game. That cowhand had won every hand until yesterday—which was before Trace had given Andy a quick lesson. Last night, he grinned at the memory. He'd won twice.

Movement on the horizon caught his eye. Andy squinted against the sun. Someone appeared over the hill. He squinted harder. Correction. Make that many someones riding over the hill. Six, if his counting was right. He reined up and studied them. Friend or foe?

A quarter mile closer, Andy recognized the blue uniforms of the Union Army.

Absolutely not Confederate. They'd been run out of the Southwest months before, all but

retreating to the safety of the South. In fact, he'd heard the war was winding down. He nodded.

About time. He'd dressed in blue awhile back. Glad to be rid of the uniform, he realized nevertheless, how proud he'd been as a soldier. The scar on his left side tugged. A reminder of his life in the army. Or more accurately, his near death in the army. A Rebel's bullet had left quite a mark on his life.

Soldiers must be out of Fort Yuma. Gigging his horse, he rode to meet them.

The lead soldier called a halt. Andy reined up. "Howdy." He nodded. "You men a long ways from home."

The leader batted at a bead of sweat rolling down his cheek, his dark sideburns plastered

to his face. "Looking for a deserter. Understand he's taken up with a cattle drive out this way.

Seen anybody like that?"

Deserter? Andy ran a quick inventory of the hands. He shook his head. "No, sir. I'm with the herd right behind me and I know everybody. Nobody's a deserter."

"We'll ride on to the herd and ask around." The soldier pointed his chin toward the cattle. "Who's bossing this outfit?"

"That'd be my brothers, James and Trace." Andy pointed behind him. "Trace's over on swing, this side of the herd. And James, way back there, gets to ride drag today." He grinned. "I bet he'd be glad to trade you places for a while. He's eaten so much dirt today, he won't need supper."

Without acknowledgement, the soldier spurred his horse, and the six men rode past Andy. The leader sat tall in the saddle, his dark eyes trained straight ahead.

Deciding he should follow, he thought about Juan Tomás and Carlos. Coozie was too

young to ever have been in the Army. Andy re-thought. He'd been sixteen when he enlisted in

Tucson and nobody had said otherwise. Maybe Coozie had done the same.

He liked Carlos and Juan Tomás, but what did he really know about them? Not much.

Neither seemed like the military type. But, did *he*? Before he could answer any of his thousand questions, he met up with Trace and the soldiers.

Trace and the leader dismounted. Andy followed suit.

"Corporal Ed Harrigan, sir." He shook hands with Trace.

"Trace Colton. Pleased to meet you."

"Colton?"

"Uh huh." Trace frowned, cocked his head. "That a problem?"

"This may not be pleasant, sir. We're after a deserter

we understand is hiding out in a cattle drive in this area." Harrigan's gaze trailed up and down Trace's body, switching over to Andy's. The brown eyes examined everything hat to boots.

"Deserter?" Trace shook his head. "No such person on my payroll."

"Possibly he's with another cattle drive behind you."

"No other drive within a hundred miles."

Harrigan licked his lips. "I think, then, more than likely he's here."

"You have a name?" Trace moved in closer, his hand fisting.

"I'm afraid I do. And a description." Harrigan glanced behind him and within seconds two more soldiers were out of their saddles. "About six foot two. Brown hair, brown eyes. Young. Nineteen, twenty."

Andy stepped back.

Harrigan turned to Andy. "Fits you like a glove." He stared at him. "Name's Andrew

Jackson Colton."

Trace instinctively moved in close to his brother. They stood shoulder to shoulder. Andy

swallowed hard. Cold iron filled his lungs. Deserter? Him? Andy shook his head.

"I'm Andy. And I was in the Union Army, back in '62. But I was honorably discharged.

Ask my brothers. They were there." His mouth went dry as he fought for air.

Harrigan turned to his second in command. "Sergeant."

Andy stepped back while the soldier moved toward him, iron handcuffs dangling in his grip. Trace kept one hand on Andy's arm. "You're not cuffing him. He's no deserter. What he said is true. Discharged in Mesilla in

'62. In fact, it was Captain Homer Greene and General James Carleton himself that discharged him."

"Orders are orders, Mister Colton." Harrigan moved in close and stood nose to nose with Trace. "We'll escort the prisoner back to Fort Yuma where, if it's true what you say, he'll be released in due time."

"Prisoner? Due time?" Trace's face turned red. "He's no deserter!"

"Trace?" Andy turned to his brother. He held his rolling stomach, a sour taste flooding his mouth, covering the ache in the back of this throat. The desert turned gray.

"I won't let them take you. You're innocent." Trace eased his body in front of Andy. "You'll have to climb over me to get to him, Corporal."

Before Andy could blink, a gun stuck in Trace's still-healing chest. Harrigan's words turned frigid. "I don't climb, sir. I shoot."

"What's this?" James slid off his horse and stood next to Trace. "Who're these soldiers?"

"Corporal Harrigan, United States Army." Harrigan nodded, but kept the gun jammed in

Trace's chest. "And you?"

"James Colton. I run this outfit. What's the problem?"

"Your brother here is harboring a fugitive. And if he doesn't stand aside, I'll kill him."

Harrigan glanced at James, returning his stare to Trace.

"Hold on. What fugitive?" James looked at Andy, switched to the soldier. "And who gives you the right to come barging in here, anyway?"

"I have orders to bring in Andrew Colton for desertion. If found guilty, he'll either hang or face a firing squad."

"What?" James stepped closer. "You can't—"

Harrigan cocked the revolver, pushing his gun hard against Trace.

James froze. Trace pulled in air and inched to his left. Harrigan pulled Andy around Trace. The sergeant lifted Andy's revolver from the holster and handed the weapon to his second in command.

"I'll be fine," Andy whispered, his voice quaking. "Take care of the herd."

Andy stumbled, tripping on Trace's boot. Hands gripped his arms. Heavy metal snapped around his wrists. Holding up his manacled hands, he tried to spread his arms. *Clink. Clink.* Shackled like a common criminal. Breaths caught in his chest. His brothers, the desert, his hands swayed. Blackness threatened to close his world.

Harrigan gripped Andy's vest and tugged. "My commanding officer, Lieutenant Rickman, hates deserters. Almost as much as me." His dark eyes and smirk rested on Andy. "You won't be stayin' in the guardhouse long."

Head throbbing, Andy numbly mounted his horse, soldiers' hands pushing him. They sat on both sides, one pointing a gun at Andy's head. He looked down at his brothers, blinked and attempted a smile. "I'll be fine. Don't worry."

CHAPTER FIFTY-ONE

After the first mile, the initial shock of being accused a deserter wore off, turning to worry. And questions. Hundreds of questions. He fought being mad, wouldn't help any. How could they execute him without proper paperwork? He'd been in the army long enough, a little over a year, to understand it functioned on two things—bayonet practice and paperwork.

Bayonet practice consisted of sticking hay bales with bayonets. Lots of jabbing, yelling—like jousting during King Arthur days. If Andy hadn't been so scared as he rode, he would have smiled remembering Ma and Trace reading to him about King Arthur and the Knights of the Round Table. Those evenings around the fireplace were as magical as the tales.

Of all the questions parading through his thoughts, however, one was answered. His

brothers couldn't drop everything and come rescue him. They would have to keep the herd moving, sauntering across the desert, until they came in close to

Arizona City. Would they come visit, travel on up to Tin Town, sell the cattle, and come back?

That would be the smart thing to do. This drive couldn't fall apart simply because of him and some stupid trumped up charge. It was all too important to the family. Andy relaxed. His arrest was all a huge misunderstanding. As soon as he could sit down with the commander, he'd be released. Probably be back to the herd before they could get another few miles.

That evening, after riding due west, the soldiers spoke in quiet conversation near the campfire. Even though he'd asked twice—the asking turning into something close to pleading—Andy's wrists remained tightly cuffed which caused quite a mess when he tried to spoon what passed for supper into his mouth. He wore more on his vest than what sat in his stomach. Andy swallowed stew and anger realizing if he misbehaved in any fashion, he'd be shot. Wouldn't even reach Fort Yuma. Harrigan was keeping a close eye on him. He figured this corporal most likely had taken down more than one "deserter." Yeah, one wrong move on his part...

Despite the day's heat, he shivered. Andy stretched out, resting his head on the saddle.

He jerked at the gun barrel pressed against his ribs. "Try anything tonight, Colton, you won't reach the other side of this fire. Understood?"

Andy nodded. Maybe tomorrow he'd wake up from this nightmare.

CHAPTER FIFTY-TWO

Andy peeked from under his eyelids. What he'd prayed had been a nightmare, remained a nightmare. Corporal Harrigan stood at the fire, swatting an early-morning fly. *No!* fluttered across his brain. Could this truly be happening? A deep breath, a cleansing breath. All right. Face this. Clearly, he'd have to throw back his shoulders, raise his chin, and meet this head-on like a man. Like Ma and Pa had taught him. To be brave and to face things. To *not* run. To make them proud. He vowed he'd all that.

Following a quick breakfast, he mounted his horse, more determined than ever to keep proud the respected Colton family name. Andy rode in the middle of the squad. Behind and to his right, five soldiers trotted along. Stoic faces revealed nothing. To his left, four privates rode within arm's reach of each other. Next to him, a sergeant big enough to carry a horse held Andy's reins in beefy hand. In front, Corporal Harrigan led the parade. Except with this parade, nothing was joyous.

They rode daylight to dusk, taking only one break to

rest and water the horses. Andy's rear couldn't take another mile. How much farther? And how was his horse doing? Being strong, she seemed not much the worse for wear, but he could tell by her slowed trot and drooped head she was tired. He knew how she felt. He was exhausted, and he'd only ridden all day, not trotted.

At last—there—on the horizon. A blue ribbon in the setting sun. Had to be the Colorado River. North of them he'd spotted the meandering Gila River running near their route, taking its time before merging with the Colorado.

Another half mile and the long bridge from Arizona to California popped into view.

Shuddering, he knew he'd ride over that bridge into the fort, walk right into the commander's

hands. And into prison. He swallowed hard.

And then... Fort Yuma. A long row of adobe buildings stood dark brown in the sunset. Off to his right, the houses of Arizona City beckoned. One block over from Main, he remembered, sat Sarah Bowman's house, first one in town, built ten years before by her husband.

While in the Army when their unit camped nearby, he and James had ridden past at every

opportunity, marveling at its white plaster. Quite a fancy house for such a dusty town. But the "Great Westerner," as she was called, named after a massive ship, lived up to her moniker, entertaining men on both sides of the Colorado. And if she didn't personally, her sporting girls did.

Should've stepped inside, Andy thought.

Andy crossed the Colorado, entering Fort Yuma's grounds. Before he could wipe the sweat trickling down his neck, he found himself jerked off his horse, prodded into a building, its adobe walls breathing out cool air.

Sweat snaking down his back, he straightened, relaxing a bit. Had to be twenty degrees cooler.

Surrounded by the corporal and two privates, Andy marched down a long hallway, lit by one lantern, turned to the right, and stopped at a closed door. The corporal knocked, waited for a reply, and opened it. Pushed from behind, Andy stumbled into the room. A man with one silver bar on each shoulder rose to his feet and glared across a paper-laden desk. The golden glow from kerosene lanterns threw eerie shadow patterns across the room.

The officer marched around his desk and stopped nose to nose with Andy. "Excellent work, Corporal." His brown eyes flitted over to the soldier, the gaze returning to Andy. "Give you any trouble?"

"No, sir." Harrigan released Andy's arm.

"Too bad. Shooting a contrary deserter makes the paperwork easier." The officer's lips set a tight line, his eyes narrowed. "Andrew Jackson Colton in the flesh. Well, well, well." He circled Andy like a puma deciding which part to eat first. "I'm Lieutenant Rickman, and I detest people like you."

Andy twisted following the commander's circling. "You have the wrong man. I'm no
deserter."

"Have it on sound authority you are."

"Gotta be a mistake. Somebody has the name wrong or something." Andy's chest constricted. A whisp of terror ran through him.

Rickman picked up a sheet of paper from his desk and read. "Let's see. Andrew Jackson Colton?"

"Yes, sir."

"Served time in the Union Army in sixty-one and sixty-two?"

"Yes, sir."

"Suffered wounds right around here by a Rebel?"

"Yes, sir, but—"

"Recently you were in Nogales having a drink in a saloon?"

"Yes, sir, but—"

"Well, appears I have the right man." He raised both eyebrows.

Andy's anger surfaced much too fast. Try as he might to reel it in, it spurted out too loudly. "Dammit, Lieutenant. Yeah, all that's me, but if you'll listen instead of talking, we can get this cleared up. Hell, send a message to the judge in Mesilla. He'll tell you I'm not—"

A fist to his cheek sent him sprawling sideways, spinning him across the room until he

plowed into a wooden chair. He somersaulted over it and crashed to the packed dirt floor. Blood

filled his mouth. He spat a stream of red, dribbling blood down his shirt. Blue uniforms danced, words echoed off adobe walls. Strong hands lifted him to his feet.

Rickman's face in his. "Let's try this again." He straightened his uniform's gray blouse,

re-tucking the tail into the blue trousers. His fist clenched twice, relaxed. "You're a deserter. The

Army frowns on deserters. They're shot or hanged. Which do you prefer?"

Should he even answer? Andy weighed his options while he worked his jaw back and forth. His face didn't feel broken, only throbbing sore. He considered. If he chose one, did that imply guilt? If he didn't, would he get punched again?

Rickman gripped the front of Andy's vest and tugged.

"Firing squad or noose? I asked you once. You deaf or plain stupid?"

Andy shook his head. "I'm innocent. Was properly discharged." He cringed, waiting for the fist to plunge into his face or stomach. Maybe kicked from behind. A kidney punch. Or knocked on the head.

A snort and Rickman released him, pushing Andy back a few steps. "You're bleeding all over me." He swiped his red-spotted hands down Andy's vest, nodded to the other soldier. "Guardhouse. Keep those cuffs on. No telling what he's liable to do."

Andy wanted to explain again. Wanted to stay right there until this matter was settled.

Instead, he wobbled out of the office, powerful grips on both arms. He limped down a dark hallway, outside across the camp's compound, and into another room where he spotted the iron bars. One door was already open, held so by a soldier he recognized from the squad. A powerful shove, Andy flew forward into the cell.

Clang. The iron door swung shut. A *click*, quiet laughter, silence. Andy stood in the

darkening cell. Shivering.

Alone.

CHAPTER FIFTY-THREE

Lumps in the mattress poked Whid's backside. He wiggled back and forth, dislodging wads of what he hoped were cotton seeds. Satisfied they were squashed, he bounced on the bed. "Damn cheap ass mattress. Oughta be a law against cheap."

Pickett tossed his saddlebag onto his bed. "Sure beats that ol' ground. And I sure as hell don't miss those scorpions and tarantulas a couple nights back." He shuddered. "They was downright *ugly*."

Whid huffed into his beard, grumbling as he examined the room here at the Arizona City Hotel. "Finest amenities this side of the Pacific" the hotel's sign had proclaimed. A longer look. Little blue flowers roared up and down the wallpaper covering all four walls. Everywhere he turned ran a nightmare of blue buds. At least the mirror over the washstand covered half that wall and a window took up a considerable amount of the wall across from it.

"Hell, this ain't a palace, but should be at four bits a night." He bounced again. "Don't hold a candle to the

Great Westerner's." He spit on the rug. "This'll do for a while. Get outta the damn heat."

Whid grunted, struggling to pull off his new boot. Even wiggling toes didn't help ease out the foot. A mighty heave and tug, he sailed back on his bed and held the boot over his head. "Damn fine boot."

"Suppose there's bedbugs, Whid?" Pickett threw back the quilt and peered under the pillow. "I hate bedbugs."

Ejecting his foot from the other boot, Whid padded over to the second-story window

and gazed down on Main Street. Far off across the river sat Fort Yuma and Andrew Colton. He

knew for a fact Andy was there. He and Pickett had followed the procession.

Whid envisioned poor ol' Andy behind bars, begging for mercy, trying to negotiate for his life. "Plead and cry, whine all you want. You ain't never gettin' out." A snigger escaped Whid's chest. This was turning out to be one of his best ideas yet.

"Who're you talking at, Whid?" Pickett glanced out the window. "Andy?"

"Yeah, ain't never gettin' out." Snigger growing into a full-out laugh, Whid's shoulders shook. He wiped his eyes.

Pickett pulled off his boots and sat on his narrow bed. He leaned against the wall, knees drawn up under his chin. "That's a dirty trick you're pulling on that Colton boy. Even for you, it's dirty."

"Workin' out damn well, ain't it?" Whid shuffled over to the bed jammed against a wall. He combed his beard with dirty fingers. "Way I figure, the other Coltons gotta stay with the herd, keep it movin'. Won't be here sooner'n a week from now, ten days. By then... it'll be too late.

Pickett rubbed an eye. "Think they'll hang him before the others get here? That what you talkin' about?"

Whid nodded. Flawless Why hadn't he thought of it sooner? He picked up a glass of whiskey by his bed and held it to the waning light. "Here's to another brilliant plan. And here's to you Andy, for making all this fun possible."

CHAPTER FIFTY-FOUR

Andy stopped pacing, held his ribs, eased onto the cot, and sagged back against the rough adobe wall. He contemplated his life. Five days behind bars. Five days locked up like a damned outlaw. Five days of beatings. Every time Rickman or Harrigan walked by, which was often, they'd ask questions. Questions he had no answers for. Then they'd hit.

He thought back to yesterday when Lieutenant Rickman marched into the cell. Andy remembered the conversation word for word.

"You lying, poor-excuse-for-a-man, deserter. I oughta shoot you and be done."

"Told you a hundred times, sir. I'm no deserter. I'll prove it. Send a message to the judge in Mesilla. He'll tell you!"

"Won't waste any of my men's time on you."

"I have a right—"

"You have no rights, boy."

Rickman kicked him. Again and again, like Andy had seen people do with mutts rooting through trash. He'd been hurting before, but his ribs throbbed incessantly.

Twice he'd woken up on the floor after passing out. More often than not, he slept on the hard-packed dirt floor. It was easier than crawling up into the cot when his ribs and stomach hurt so bad.

Andy sat, eyes closed. Bootsteps stopped in front of his cell. He didn't bother to open his eyes to look. Probably some officer coming by to tell him what a loser he was, how they hoped he'd rot in Hell, what a miserable excuse for a human he was.

"Mister Colton?"

The voice... polite, almost friendly. Sounded like somebody about his age even. Andy

pried open his swollen eyelids. A private waited at the bars, coffee cup in hand.

"Thought you'd like some coffee before the day gets too hot."

If he moved in close enough, the soldier would throw the scalding liquid on him. No doubt. He'd delight in, maybe even dance, watching him burn. Andy frowned. How close should he get? He flopped an arm toward the man. "Thanks. Put it on the floor inside the bars and I'll get to it."

The private did as instructed, stood back and waited. "Coffee ain't too bad, long as it's hot. Tastes tin-like when it cools, though."

Andy eased to his feet, ribs on fire. Gripping his side, he inched toward the bars and the soldier. "Why's Rickman being so generous this morning?" He considered. "They setting up a firing squad?"

The private smiled. "No. No firing squad today. And it ain't Rickman. I seen you sittin' there, black eyes and all, felt sorry for you." The soldier moved in a bit closer. "Name's Private Turner. Ralph Turner. From Kansas."

"Kansas? Me, too." All of a sudden Andy didn't feel so alone. "What part?"

"Up around Lawrence. Folks have a spread over that way." Turner's smile lit up his owlish, indigo eyes. His tanned cheeks pinked. "Have me a girl, too."

"My girl's in Mesilla," Andy said. "But my folks used to farm over by Lawrence. 'Til Quantrill and his men burned it down."

Turner nodded, his eyes searching the floor. "I was there. It was bad. Real bad. Lots of killing, blood, bodies everywhere." He stopped, trained his gaze on Andy. "Your folks all right?"

Andy attempted a grin, but the splits in his lips made him grimace instead. "Fine. Doin' fine. Built a new place closer to town." Was this someone he could trust? Andy knew he had to take a chance. "Turner, listen. I'm no deserter. I was honorably discharged, don't care what Rickman claims." He lowered his voice and looked side to side. "Suppose you could do me a favor?"

"You mean besides bringin' you coffee?" Turner smiled again.

"Would you ask around, see if anybody was with Carlton's Column that fought at Picacho Peak or Apache Pass? That'd be in sixty-two. Maybe they could convince Rickman I'm innocent." Andy prayed this would work. He was out of options.

"Sure, I'll ask. Might take a while, though." Turner pointed outside. "I got duty, but maybe I can come back and visit. I bet we know some of the same people." He stepped back. "Enjoy the coffee."

He'd never tasted better.

CHAPTER FIFTY-FIVE

More visits from Turner and more beatings from Rickman. Andy defended himself by rolling, shielding his face with still-shackled hands. Each session proved harder to fight back, to keep from being pounded into mush. Nine days of gut-punching, head-slamming, pummeling abuse left Andy knowing he would die. With that, a hopeful sense of rescue faded. He grew weaker, and everyone knew. Even Turner sneaked in a cup of whiskey one evening. Grateful, Andy drank without question.

On the tenth day, sunrise streamed through the single window down the hall bathing Andy's cell in rose-silver hues. If he could open his swollen eyes enough, he would struggle to enjoy this day. Energy spent, he sat on the cot and hung his head. Would he sit here all day? No. First things first. A trip to the privy was in order. Soon, a private should be coming by to escort him. At least he was allowed out twice, sometimes three times a day. Even the brief bit of sunshine and air lifted his spirits. That and Turner's coffee and company.

At long last he spotted Corporal Harrigan storming down the hall, headed his way. Andy's chest tightened. This couldn't be right. Corporals didn't take prisoners to the outhouse. Not usually. Maybe today was the firing squad. And Andy the target.

Muttering, Harrigan stopped in front of Andy's cell. "Hell, I have more important things to do. than play nursemaid to this scum-sucking *pendejo*. Rickman says *I* hafta do it right away. *Right away.* Where's those privates? Let them play nursemaid. Hell, they're off marchin' in the desert somewhere. Well, damn Rickman, anyway." He held up a key and glared. "Back against the wall, Colton. Try anything and you'll die right here. Get it?"

A nod was all he chose to give this man.

Andy didn't stay long in the privy. Arizona heat made the trip more of an endurance test

than anything remotely resembling pleasant. He beat his way through swarms of buzzing flies to get out.

They crossed the parade grounds, Harrigan's firm grip on Andy's arm tugging, urging him to hurry. Andy spotted Private Turner. They nodded, and as Andy turned back, he stumbled, exhausted legs unwilling to carry his body.

He took Harrigan down with him.

A fist plowed into Andy's face. "Tried to kill me, Colton." Harrigan kicked. "Tried to escape. Sonuvabitch! I'll teach you!"

Irate fists pummeled his body. One in the stomach. Another in the chest. Vicious ones in his cheeks, his jaw. Kicks, punches, angry curses, threats, accusations, more fists.

Choking on globs of blood running down his throat, Andy curled into a ball and waited for the beating to end. Waited for *him* to end.

Boots to his back kicked him over. He rolled in the dirt, raised his manacled hands, desperate to protect his face. Instead, from this position on his back, he stared up into Harrigan's eyes and ham-sized fist, now zeroed in on his cheek.

CHAPTER FIFTY-SIX

"Andy? Andy?"

Spiraling out of the black fog-blanket covering him, words pirouetted around his head like wobbly angels. They perched on his chest.

"Andy?"

A beacon sliced through the dark fog. Andy recognized the voice behind the words—Pa. Strong, but gentle hands—Pa's hands—shook his shoulders.

"Andy?" More shaking. "Luke, let go! Calm down!"

"Sonuvabitch! I'll kill you. Don't ever touch my little brother again."

"Take your hands off me!"

Boots scuffling. Grunts. Snorts. Strong curse words flew near Andy's ear. Several voices. Angry words, threats, mumbles rang inside the fog. More cursing. *Must be angry. Pa never uses that kinda language.*

Before Andy could retreat to the dark, safe place of unconsciousness, the same strong hands again shook Andy's shoulders. One hand cradled his chin, moving his head back and forth. His head flopped like a rag doll, the kind Ginny's sisters played with. No real life in there.

More words shouted over his body lying on what he guessed was the ground. Whatever supported his body was hard.

"You had no right to beat him like this!"

"Don't let go, James." Pa's voice turned iron hard. "Keep him back!" More softened

words sailed around Andy's head. "You'll be all right. Lie still."

Lie still? I was moving? Determined to figure things out, Andy willed one eye open. That

little bit of effort brought excruciating jabs to his head. They pulsated in rhythm to his heart. Several blinks brought the world into better focus. "Pa?"

"Pa ain't here. I'm Trace."

That didn't make sense. He'd heard Pa, knew his voice, but here, peering down at him, was his oldest brother's face. Worry lines had aged Trace's eyes, tightened his mouth into a line. Worry and panic, anger and outrage, colored his cheeks. Andy took it all in, yet little of it made sense. Even if he wasn't Pa, it was damn terrific to see him.

Trace sat back and looked over his shoulder. "Luke. I said 'back off'. He'll throw you in

here, too."

Many more blinks... Andy spotted iron bars. Bit by bit, his senses grayed into black and white. Voices screeched, echoing against the adobe walls. Part of his memory, the hurting part, revealed where he was.

Trace pointed. "That's it. Move away." He nodded. "James, bring him over here."

Andy blinked again, more pulsating, throbbing in his

head. Maybe if he pressed on both sides, his brains wouldn't leak out. He brought his hands up. Shackled together. Handcuffs still riveted to his wrists. Stomach roiling, he'd throw up if he didn't sit up.

Roaring pain in his head, stomach lurching, Andy grunted over onto his side. Before he could get his elbows under his body to sit, last night's watery oatmeal spurred itself upward, spewing onto the ground. Trace pulled until Andy was up. After another spasm, he felt better. Still shaking, at least his stomach quit boiling.

He leaned back against a knee as a blue neckerchief wiped his face, his sleeve, and the front of his sore chest. "You'll be all right. Want some water?"

Was Pa or Trace talking to him? Before Andy could decide, two other pairs of eyes

watched him, staring. Luke. James. What the hell were they doing here? And before he could put rational thought to the question, a tin cup pressed against his swollen lips. Cool water slid down smooth, soothing raw spots.

"Let's get you on your feet," Pa said. "You'll feel better up."

Strong arms slid under his, eased him to his feet. He groaned. Moans, something resembling a whimper tickled his ears. Were those his? A damp cloth dabbed at his face. While hundreds of words filled his world, Andy stood, waiting for his head to quit hammering. He opened his eyes enough to see through the slits. Here inside the cell, he counted Trace, Luke, James, Corporal Harrigan, and Lieutenant Rickman. All glaring at each other.

He should laugh. They were packed in tight. Like cattle in a slaughter pen. But there was nothing to laugh

about. And why were his brothers here? And where
was Pa?

Words flew back and forth. Over his head. Around his
body. They sailed out through the cell bars. Words.
Simply words. Not one made sense.

Exhausted, Andy closed his eyes, ready to doze off,
ready to let his brothers fight the military. However, a
voice in his face commanded otherwise.

"Hold out your hands."

One eye unglued itself. The corporal gripped the
handcuff key. A turn and *click*, Andy's hands were free
once more.

Red ribbons circled his wrists like sadistic bracelets.
The wrists were sore, but nothing compared to his chest
and legs. How many of his ribs were broken?

Trace elbowed Harrigan out of the way. "Let's get you
out of here, Andy. Think you can walk?"

"Wha?"

"Walk. Think you can?"

"Wha?"

Trace, gripping one of Andy's arms, leaned in close.
"Shoulders back. Head high. You're going out like you
came in." He nudged him forward. "One solid step, then
another."

Luke gripped the other arm, and Andy lurched
forward. He wobbled, but he clenched his jaw, making
his legs take his weight. Keep him upright. Eyes straight
ahead.

At the cell door, Rickman stood in front of Andy. "I'm
letting your brothers take you out of here only because,
one," he ticked off on his fingers, "you need a doctor. A
real one. Two, your brothers have vouched for your
return *when* we verify you are, indeed, a deserter." He

glared at Andy. "I'll be sending a messenger to Mesilla first thing tomorrow. We'll bring your sorry ass back here as soon as I get a reply from the judge."

Andy's legs turned to jelly. Despite his brothers' support, he'd have to sit soon. Their strong hands kept him up.

Rickman's finger poked Andy's chest, harder than necessary. "And when we do, I guarantee you'll *hang* quicker'n you can sneeze."

Luke dropped his hold on Andy and stepped forward. "You lying sack of shit. I oughta

give you what you gave my little brother." He brought his fist shoulder high.

"Stop it!" James wedged himself between Luke and Rickman. "Fighting won't solve anything." He turned to Luke and dropped his voice. "Let it be. We'll get this all cleared up."

Oaths mumbled, Luke relaxed his fist.

Andy, with Trace on one side and Luke on the other, wobbled outside. Bright sunshine attacked his face. He squinted. The euphoria of freedom rose from his chest, crumbling the boulder that had perched there. He looked from brother to brother. He wanted to smile, but his

face—too swollen, too painful—wouldn't allow even a grin.

Trace prodded him.

Andy moved.

"One foot in front of the other." Trace's voice in his ear. "That's it. One foot forward. That's right. Now the other."

The mantra, along with his brothers' support, kept Andy upright and moving ahead. The fort's walls blurred, pulsating in time with his throbbing head, but he kept walking. Before he could bring forth a rational thought, he found himself on his horse, James holding the reins. On his right, Trace gripped his arm and flashed a smile. On his left, brother Luke held his other arm.

Side by side, they rode across the bridge.

CHAPTER FIFTY-SEVEN

Andy stared up at the white plank ceiling. Vague recollections of that ceiling danced through his head. It was familiar, but why? Where was he? Under him, something soft, not the ground, kept his body swaddled in comfort. He blinked and turned his head, realizing a mattress and two fluffy pillows supported him. A bed. He was in a bed.

He let out a soft sigh. A yellow and blue quilt covered his chest which was wrapped tightly with white fabric strips. Luke sat on a wooden chair next to the bed and stirred something steaming in a bowl. Closing his eyes, Andy pulled in heady aromas of chicken soup with some sort of herbs thrown in. *Must be from Coozie's collection.*

Where was he? Andy sighed and studied the room again. A close inspection over the past days, when he could focus, had revealed flowered wallpaper over each wall. Little roses ran up and down in columns, like pink rosebuds in a race. A vanity with a ceramic washbasin and pitcher on top took up one wall next to the door and a clothes rack occupied another. The bed, shoved against one wall, crowded most of the tiny room. Whose room was this? He remembered asking Trace and James, but the answers didn't stick. Luke would know.

His brother concentrated on stirring the soup. A slurp from the spoon, a smile, Luke looked at Andy. "Heaven. Whoever's cooking, must be an angel. It's better than Ma's."

Andy tried to smile, his swollen mouth still uncooperative, but at least his appetite was returning. "Don't let Ma hear you. She'll whack you with that wooden spoon of hers." Memories of swats paraded across his mind. Although the stinging was remembered, the punishment was also deserved.

"Thank goodness Ma's too far away to hear." Luke held up a spoonful. "Open up. If you

don't eat it, I will."

Wagging his head, Andy sighed. "I can feed myself." He held up a trembling hand.

"Look. Rock steady and old enough."

"Hell, if that's rock steady, you shouldn't ever work with explosives!" Luke aimed the spoon at Andy's mouth. "Give me a hard time and I'll get Trace in here. *He'll* feed you."

Still feeling foolish, Andy sat up straighter, opened his mouth realizing Luke was right. His hands shook way too hard to handle a spoon, especially with soup. Maybe tomorrow.

Whatever he'd been eating, it was a miracle. Here after a mere three days, he remembered being told, he was about ready to get out of bed and join the cattle drive. Problem was, his legs wobbled, refusing to hold his weight the two times he attempted to cross the room. Plus, the walls and ceiling spun when he stood.

And at least three, maybe more, ribs were broken. They hurt like Lucifer's fire. Riding would be painful.

Luke offered a second spoonful. "Eat up. Those ladies oughta be stopping by any minute to change bandages and give you another bath." Luke raised both eyebrows. "They're awful smitten with you. They're sure they're the ones nursed you back. They've declared you their... uh... mollycoddle."

Andy glared at Luke. "I ain't nobody's mollycoddle. I'm a *man*." He dropped his voice.

"And I don't need no *coddling*, either." He grabbed his left side and squeezed his eyes. Questions bombarded his thoughts. His eyes flew open. "What ladies? A bath? What bath? Here?" He pulled up the quilt to cover more of his bare chest.

Laughter pushed Luke's mouth into the famous Colton family smile. His shoulders shook and the soup dripped back into the bowl. "You don't recognize where you're at."

That was true, but Andy knew where he wasn't. In jail. But he wasn't where he wanted to

be—either on the trail with the cows and his brothers, or back home in Mesilla with lovely Virginia.

Waving the empty spoon, Luke leaned closer and lowered his voice. "This's the Great Westerner's, Sarah Bowman. And this's Polly's room. She's out for a few days. Doc said Miss Bowman owed him for looking after her girls." His eyebrows shot up. "Lucky stiff. All these women at your beck and call." He glanced over his shoulder toward the door. "And you didn't even know. Hell, you can't even... even... with... with a girl. Hell, Andy, everything on you's busted or bruised."

Everything? Bits and pieces of the last few days glued themselves together—the doctor smearing something over his cuts, stinging stitches here and there, ribs being bound, nothing much until yesterday evening. Even so, it was vague, fuzzy faces—male and female—hovering.

Deciding to discuss what Luke meant by "everything" later, Andy's thoughts turned to his brothers. "Trace? James?"

"Left this morning. We're a few days behind schedule. You were on the mend, according

to Doc, and they knew you were getting excellent care here, so they went ahead." Luke tapped Andy's arm with the spoon. "They're worried you'll like it here too much and never come catch up." He scooped more soup into the spoon.

Pieces of chicken in herb-laced broth cascaded down Andy's throat. It warmed him head to toe. Was it his imagination, or could he actually feel his body healing? More spoonfuls relaxed his aches. This wasn't like Luke to be so nice to him. While he wasn't mean, he wasn't the nurturing type. Not the brother Andy expected to be sitting at his bedside feeding him. Of the three, James would be the one. But here perched Luke, the caustic brother. The one who wanted to chase women even though he was married and father of two. The brother quick to criticize, but slow to praise.

Was Luke trying to change? Trying to be the brother the others were? Thoughtful, caring, family first. However, sporting girls surrounded him here. It hit him. Luke was taking advantage of the situation, their kindness, so to speak. *Doesn't really care about me. How many beds has he*

already been in? Andy's shoulders slumped.

Luke stared into the soup bowl as if it held a secret. A dress whishing past the door caught his attention. He watched the doorway and turned back to Andy. He cocked his head.

"I recognize that look. What's wrong?"

Andy focused on his brother's face, looking for deception, insincerity, anything to explain his kindhearted actions. He held the right side of his head in hopes of keeping his brains from exploding. He spoke over the pain. "Why'd you stay behind?"

"What?"

"You heard me. Why you? Why not James or Trace?" Anger pushed its way into his

words. "You only wanted to see how many sporting girls would take you on for free. You're

using me to—"

"Think they walloped you one too many times." Luke leaned back against the chair.

"Where'd you get such a crazy damn notion?"

"This isn't like you. Feeding me. Being nice." Was Andy wrong about his brother? Part of him wanted to believe he was.

The spoon clanked against the side of the glass bowl. Luke lowered his shoulders and his eyes. He blinked, sighed, blinked again. His chest expanded, but his gaze stayed on his hands. "Truth is, when I saw you in that cell, lying on the floor, busted up like that... thought for sure you were dead. Hell, Andy, you looked dead. Blood, bruises... the way you were so still." His voice trailed off, returning soft. "Don't think I've ever been that upset or sad. Or scared."

As best as his tied ribs and bruised body allowed, Andy rolled onto his side to face his

brother.

Luke brought his eyes up to Andy. "It hit me. You were dead because some jackass soldier had something to prove." Tenderness softened Luke's eyes, something Andy had never

seen before.

"I remember your voice. Yelling."

"Thought we'd lost you. *I'd* lost you. My little brother." Luke put the bowl on the floor

and moved over to ease down onto the side of Andy's bed. "Don't ever tell anybody what I'm gonna say. Promise?"

"Promise."

Luke smoothed his mustache, glanced left and right, down at Andy. "I'm sorry for being mean. My way of funnin' with you."

"I know."

"What would I've done if you'd died?" Luke sniffed. He studied his shaking hands.

Andy let the silence linger. Not only shocked at his brother's words, he was surprised at

how heartfelt they sounded. He hoped Luke wasn't lying.

A smile slid up one side of Andy's face. The cheeks hurt but he didn't care. His eyes met Luke's. A nod. "Love you, too, brother."

CHAPTER FIFTY-EIGHT

Whid shoved his new shirt into the saddlebag. "I'll be go to hell." His mumbles grew louder. "Damn Coltons got here faster'n I figured. What the hell? What'd they do, run those beeves? Got here too damn fast." He huffed into his beard. "Hell, Andy ain't even hanged yet. Or shot."

He jammed socks in on top of the shirt. "And they're here three days. Three damn days. Then two of 'em leave. Only two. Not three. Two. I'll be go to hell."

The Arizona City Hotel room, complete with nauseating blue flowers, stood empty, except for Whid and his saddlebag. Sheets and quilts from both beds lay bunched on the floor—the room had been hot. Not even an open window cooled the summer air. Whid cursed softly, giving the room a final inspection. He wanted nothing left behind that would reveal his true identity. Pickett had been right. Messing with the U.S. army was serious business. He sure as hell didn't want to spend time behind bars like loser Andy Colton. From what he'd seen, that and the real Hell were one and the same.

And the sooner Whid rode out of Arizona City, the better. Purgatory couldn't be hotter. Or dustier. He latched the leather saddlebag and slung it over his shoulder. A step out into the

hallway, another huff, he slammed the door behind him.

Grumbling down the street toward the stable, he recounted his close call. He trotted thoughts out into the open. "Why couldn't they take Andy with 'em? Huh? Why do *I* hafta leave this minute?" More grumbles. "Because if they see me, they'd put two and two together. They ain't stupid. They'd blow the whistle. Hell, *I'd* end up in that stinkin', rotten guardhouse."

Whid didn't bother to acknowledge people stopping, staring as he mumbled his way past.

He didn't care. He'd get the hell outta town and never come back. Not ever.

It was Diamond Lil's fault. Yeah, all her fault. After all, he'd been happy romping in her room at the Great Westerner's, but *no*, she liked the room two doors down with the ridiculous pink flowers. Polly's room, supposed to be empty this week. She said the flowers *inspired* her. Whatever that meant.

Whid cringed. Upon entering the doorway, he and Lil had crashed into each other when they discovered Polly's bed occupied. Fortunately, Andy was asleep, and no brother was sitting by his side like they usually did, around the clock. Why they had to sit and watch poor, helpless, little baby brother sleep was beyond him. For Chrissakes, couldn't Andy do that by himself?

But after scrambling out of Polly's room, they'd returned to Lil's own room to finish

their negotiated affections. Afterward, as Whid strolled out of Lil's, Luke, concentrating on a bowl of soup, walked into Andy's. They'd been feet apart. Close. Too damn close.

His boots clumped down the boardwalk and across the street. Dust spewed up around his

face. He sneezed. "Damn those Coltons." He ran a sleeved arm under his nose and spat. "Who the hell do they think they are? Lousy, worthless..." Curses died under another sneeze.

By the time he met Pickett at the stable, Whid was in a lather. If one of the Colton boys

had been there, he would've killed him with his bare hands. And enjoyed every second of it.

This rage, this retaliation for justice, was kept alive by a deep-buried fire of anger that lingered always under the surface. He'd have time to kill them soon. Real soon. After all,

they were less than ten days from Tin Town.

Ten days. He'd have plenty time to plan. Plenty time to get it exactly right. He thought about his new sheriff clothes. Those would come in handy.

CHAPTER FIFTY-NINE

A long, painful ride lay ahead. Though it'd been four days since his brothers left, Andy still wasn't much healed. He'd gnash his teeth, fight through the pain, and simply ride. He could do that. He *would* do that. No way would he let his brothers down.

Andy stood in the Great Westerner's red-flocked wallpapered lobby filled with a red-quilted fainting couch, two high-backed chairs, and several sporting girls. A quick count revealed ten women. Quite a send-off for a battered and bruised stranger. He nodded at each. Some he recognized from baths and meals brought in, and some he didn't. As fuzzy as his memory was, he'd probably met them all. He leaned back when the Great Westerner herself pushed her way through the crowd and stood in front of him. Her flaming red hair and towering height set her apart from everyone else.

"Be sure to take this three times a day. Doc's orders." Sarah Bowman held out a bottle of
liquid, a brackish concoction, presenting it as if it

were the sure cure to every conceivable ailment. A spoon waved in her hand like a baton. "In no time, you'll be running faster than your horse." She tapped the utensil against his bandaged chest.

Andy took the bottle and spoon, held the elixir up to the light. Bits and pieces of something floated in the brown medicine. Would Coozie approve?

"Thanks to your hospitality, I feel better, Miss Bowman." Andy's cheeks hurt from the

smile, but his chest swelled a bit and his shoulders straightened when he reflected on how kind

these women had been.

"Already gave your brother a bottle of laudanum." She leaned in close. "Go easy on that pain killer. It's full of hops." She winked.

"Yes, ma'am." Had those words come out of his mouth? He worked his stiff jaw.

"You come on back when you're healed proper, Mister Colton." A devilish smile lit up Sarah's green eyes. "My girls're looking forward to seeing you without all those bruises. They say you're quite..." —her gaze trailed below his waist, up again to his face— "... manly."

Cheeks burning, Andy opened his mouth twice. Pointing toward the door, he stammered, "Need horses... to meet. He's... Luke."

Before Andy could rearrange the words, Luke opened the door, heat roiling into the cool lobby.

"There you are." Luke nodded, tipping his hat at the women. He shook Sarah's hand. "Can't thank you and your ladies enough." He glanced at Andy, back to her. "You helped save my brother's life. I'll always be indebted."

"Believe me, it was our pleasure," she said. "Come back soon."

Andy touched the brim of his new hat, the old one lost somewhere in Fort Yuma.

"Thanks again, ma'am." Then to the gathered women. "Ma'ams."

Waves of heat knocked him back as he limped onto the porch. Not a breath of air, not

even a hint of a breeze cooled the parched town, the baked dirt. Even the people on the street appeared wilted, walking slow, slumped, whipped.

Luke pointed across the street, a grin sliding up one side of his mustached face. "Our horses're tied over there." He glanced at the front of the building. "With all these horses lined up on this side, had trouble finding a place to put ours."

Even though it hurt, Andy couldn't help but smile. The Great Westerner was indeed great. He owed her and some day would figure out how to repay the kindness.

"Ready?" Luke pulled his hat down low and squinted into the morning. "If we ride hard

enough, and according to the map Trace left, we'll get to hills where it's cooler. Might even get there by sundown."

"Thank goodness I caught you before you left."

Andy wheeled to his right. Private Ralph Turner. Of Kansas and coffee fame.

"Wanted to come by, see you off." He extended a hand and shook with Andy. "Tried two other times, but you were sleeping."

Andy knew he'd found a friend. Too bad Turner would stay behind to play soldier. Especially under that crazy Rickman and vicious Harrigan. Although painful, Andy gripped his friend's hand. "This'll sound, well..."

"What?" Turner's eyebrows knitted.

"You saved my life. And... thank you." Andy pumped Turner's hand, released it. "If

you're ever in Mesilla, look me up. Or if I'm not there, any of my brothers. We, especially *me*, owe you a lot." Andy meant every word. In the past few days while he'd lay awake listening to the sounds of the house, he'd thought about Turner and how a simple act of bringing coffee meant so much. One goodwill gesture had given him hope, a lifeline of sorts.

"Glad it's all worked out, even though your black eyes are still..."—Turner studied Andy's face "—uh, real *black*. But if you ever get back to Kansas, stop by my folks' farm. I've written 'em and told 'em about you. I suggested they find your folks, stop by and say howdy."

"They'd like that." Luke extended his hand across Andy's chest. "Thanks again for all you did. We appreciate it."

"Glad to help. Oh, stopped by to tell you, also." Turned nodded at Andy. "Found a private, Ed Bartles, said he knew you from that Picacho Pass battle. Said he'd tell Rickman."

"Mentioning my name right now's probably not the best idea." Andy glanced at Luke.

"Tell him thanks, though."

Turner shook a finger at Andy. "Don't give your brothers any more trouble. Hope to see you again some time." A quick salute, he then spun around and marched down the street, disappearing into the blacksmith's.

A nudge on Andy's shoulder, a voice in his ear, brought him back to the present.

"Need to ride. It's gettin' damn hot, and the sun's only been up an hour." Luke gripped Andy's arm. "Sure you're up to this?"

"Let's see. Most stitches are out, drank all the soup,

on my feet. Yeah, I'm up to it." Andy nodded. "Besides, there's cattle to chase."

His body tugged and pulled, complaining, but Andy managed to lift his foot into the stirrup. However, try as he might, his leg and arm muscles refused to help him onto his horse. Luke pushed until Andy settled in the saddle. He held the reins, swung his gaze over to the Westerner's.

"Suppose you'll come back?" Andy knew he'd overstepped the line—asking the obvious. The last thing he wanted was his brother angry at him. "I mean, through town is all. When we're done."

Luke frowned at Andy but changed to a grin. "Brother, I understand and appreciate *exactly* what you're saying." He swung up into his saddle, picked up the reins. "And I might stop by, only to say howdy and thanks." Luke gigged his horse into a walk. One long, last look, he licked his lips. "Unless one of those women has a better idea."

Unable to decide if Luke was serious, Andy concentrated on getting his horse backed out and turned around, heading down the street. He considered. How could he ever repay the kindness? He'd have to think on it as he rode. But for the moment, he'd concentrate on staying in

the saddle.

CHAPTER SIXTY

Rain? James opened his eyes and sniffed. Maybe. He lay on the ground, head cradled by his saddle, and counted stars. What few there were. Like a warm blanket, clouds rolled over the sky, then parted, revealing a canopy of white dots. Pushed by a gentle breeze, the definite scent of rain—dust combined with clean air—wafted under his nose.

Thoughts melted from concerns of weather to the two new men hired to replace Luke and Andy, to Andy's battered body. Anger held inside during daylight surfaced. Memories of his horrifically beaten brother, covered in blood, paraded across his mind, like they'd done every time he closed his eyes. Hands clenched, his stomach knotted. How in hell could an army officer do that? What gave them the right to hurt somebody that way? Hell, he and his brothers should've rescued Andy sooner. They should've known. Damn the officer and damn himself.

On the other hand, they'd done what they thought

best, herding the cattle, figuring Andy would be behind
bars, yes, but certainly not beaten near to death. James
steadied his hands. Nothing he could do about it this
moment. But how was Andy? Doc had promised he
would recover, given enough time.

Time. James counted five days since they'd left
Arizona City. Five more days for Andy to heal up. Would
he be well enough to get to Tin Town and help sell the
cattle in a week? To present them to the buyers? Andy
would want to be a part of the final days.

It was getting close. Time to sell the herd, sell the
wagon, pay off the hands, and head

for home. A tightness grew in James' chest. He
missed Morningstar's tender kisses, her body next to his,
her voice. Everything about her. Quick calculations
showed he'd be back in Mesilla within three weeks. A
week to get the cattle to Tin Town, a day or two to settle
affairs, a day in

Tucson visiting Morningstar's folks, and back to
Mesilla. Yep, three weeks should do it.

Snoring roared from under the blanket near him. Juan
Tomás. That man could sleep anywhere, any time. But he
worked hard and had turned out to be a great drover.
Many times he'd been invaluable.

James would have to be up for his turn at guarding in
about three hours. He willed his eyes closed. Plenty of
time to worry about things later.

Something wet hit his face. And another. Even
though his eyes were closed, a flash of light penetrated
them. He jerked awake and sat. Lightning. The cattle
would stampede without much provocation, and lightning terrified those animals.

No need to wake the others. They were on their feet

already, pulling on black cotton canvas gum blankets, and cursing the weather. Even Coozie, who had already covered the supplies, stood with several reins in hand. Obviously, the horses didn't like lightning either as they pulled against Coozie's grip. But before they could bolt for safety, the men were atop and spurring them toward the herd.

James swung up into his saddle, cinched up the stampede string under his chin, and headed for what he hoped were calm animals.

They weren't.

All were on their feet milling, bellowing, nudging others out of the way, clearing a path to escape their terror. With a faint crackle of lightning, their eyes widened, almost bulging, and their heads swung right and left.

The drovers circled the herd, calling, singing, desperate to keep them from stampeding.

With hills to the west, and here with their bedding ground covered in mesquite, sagebrush and

rabbitbrush, the cattle could get lost for days. Hopefully not permanently. James shook his head.

If they take up into those hills, the drive was done. He thought about earlier in the day when he'd

hoped to ride through there, needing to see tall trees and something besides cows. Now he hoped

he wouldn't.

Another flash of light, he spotted Trace across the herd to his left. Carlos's voice sounded behind him, Juan Tomás's in front. If the cattle ran, these men would be doing their best to get them stopped. Coozie was back at camp, preparing the wagon to move out of the way, if necessary. James hoped the new men they'd hired in

Arizona City, Russell Towers, a freed Negro from Louisiana, and a wide-shouldered, soft-spoken fella named Tex, would do their jobs. They had said they knew cattle, and this was their test.

James rode toward the front of the herd, singing softly, hoping the cattle would remain calm. His horse, ears perking forward and back, told him the cattle would run. She seemed to understand them better than he did.

Lightning sparkled across the desert.

Boom! Thunder rolled off the hills, thudding against his chest.

The cattle bolted.

"Turn 'em. Don't let 'em run!" James yelled over his shoulder, another crack of thunder burying his commands. The lead steers ran hellbent toward the bushes, their hooves tearing across rain-splattered dirt.

Boom! More thunder. Lightning zigzagged through the blackness. Rain pelted James, bouncing off his hat and slicker. The downburst clouded his view. Fuzzy forms up ahead, blurry dark animals running. Lightning, incessant, lit the desert long enough for him to spot the lead steers. He set spurs to his horse.

Wind hurled sand and rain into his face, a tumbleweed against his horse. She bucked,

hopped sideways. James gripped the saddle horn and hung on. "It's all right, girl. All right." Was

his voice calm enough? Memories of a burr under his saddle flashed. Being dragged through the

desert was terrifying. He could've died, and he'd do anything to avoid that kind of ride. He settled his weight in the saddle, reached down and patted Pinetop's neck. "You're fine."

At least he was still on his horse. No telling what would happen if somebody fell in front of these crazed animals. He cringed at campfire stories of trampled men. Deciding to think on that later, James wiped his face and squinted into the dark. A blue bolt revealed Trace less than thirty yards back. Thunder cracked overhead.

Blue devil lightning danced across the sky. And with it, a sulphuric odor—exactly what he figured the devil himself smelled like.

Terrified beeves bolted for safety, each one blindly following the other. Ground rumbled, lightning flared, wind shrieked, and thunder reverberated.

The men rode hard.

Above the din of the cattle's hooves, James yelled over his shoulder. "Turn here! Head 'em off. Bring 'em in a circle!"

"Right!" Russell's baritone voice soared out of the dark.

James, out in front, reached down, and using the end of his gum blanket, smacked one of the lead cows in the nose. The steer turned sideways but ran faster away from the herd. James galloped to keep up and used his raincoat to hit him again. Mesquite clawed at James' chaps.

The steer bolted to his right. James crowded the animal, flicked him again. Again he turned. Leastways he was headed back the way he came. Voices behind him on his left. Trace and Tex had turned the herd. Maybe things would be all right after all. James allowed a sliver of hope.

Was the lightning easing up, too? Mud splattered him as he waved and hollered at more

cattle. From this position on a low hill and with the lightning moving away, he pinpointed two of

his men, both whistling, singing, encouraging the cattle to slow. A lariat swung overhead.

The men would spend the night—a long one, no doubt—coaxing cattle out of the brush and back to the herd. Hopefully, Coozie would be able to boil some coffee.

Rain, pushed by new wind gusts, pelted James' face, stinging his cheeks. Wind howled harder than before, the roaring reminding him of a tornado back home. He dug his chin into his chest, waiting for the wet bullets to ease. Like tumbleweeds, wind propelled mesquite and chamisa branches across his path, raking his chaps.

At long last, wind slowed, and lightning eased. Thunder rumbled farther away. Vision still blurred, James wiped his eyes and surveyed the cattle. Many walked, a few had stopped. He lifted his gaze skyward.

Another crack of lightning revealed a high hill on his right. If his mental map was in place, the cattle had stampeded only a mile. Not bad. Could've been much worse. He turned his horse toward Trace.

They rode side by side in the dark. "Tex took off up in the hills." Trace pointed over his shoulder. "And Juan Tomás went the other way."

James peered into the clear sky, the rain but a memory. He mopped the last of the moisture from his face. "You check on everybody? Anybody hurt?"

"All made it through so far. Those new men seem fit." Trace waved a hand down near a renegade steer. "Turn around. That's it." He smiled over at James. "Wish *women's* minds were that easy to change."

"When Morningstar takes a notion, well... there's no use arguing. Might as well do it."

James smiled, relaxed. He hadn't done so since Andy'd been hurt. Those beatings had done damage to more than his brother. The entire camp was depressed. No jokes, no card games.

They'd slumped through days of herding, eating, sleeping. Like a spark of life had been erased.

Movement in the brush. James wheeled around, yelled at Trace. "I'll catch this one, meet you back at camp later."

CHAPTER SIXTY-ONE

"If we're actually where I think we are," Luke held a burning twig to the end of a cigarette clenched between his lips, "tomorrow night we'll be with the herd." He sucked in air, and the tip flared red. He tossed the twig back into the campfire, puffed on the cigarette until smoke curled out of his mouth. He looked over at Andy, head on the saddle, stretched out near the fire. Bruises on his cheeks glowed green and purple in the fire's light.

His brother's eyes, while closed, were still ringed a deep black and blue. Those bruises would take longer to heal than the rest. He hadn't seen Andy's legs recently, but when he'd helped bind his broken ribs this morning, his brother's back and chest cuts were healing well. Sometime tomorrow, he'd take out the few remaining stitches.

Those ugly bruises, once deep black, were now green and purple. Like the doc said, his brother was healing. Would take longer than either wanted, but at least he was still alive.

"Andy? You awake?" Luke spoke over the dangling cigarette. He resisted the urge to

poke his little brother lying there, blanket tucked around him.

"Should be sleeping." Andy opened one eye. "But somebody keeps talking." He

squirmed, pulling the blanket up higher around his shoulders. More tugging, rolling, Andy groaned as he pushed upright, the blanket laying bunched at his side.

Luke gazed into the fire, flames capturing the end of a stick. Sparks flared blue and settled down to red and yellow. He turned to his brother. "Thought by now you would've asked how we rescued you."

"Figured it was your charm."

"That was most of it, but I feel like we have to keep looking over our shoulders. Maybe

somebody's out there gunning for us."

Andy straightened his shoulders and winced.

Luke poked the fire with another stick. "How'd they know you'd been in the army in the first place? Why'd they decide to come talk to you now? Accuse you of desertion." He frowned into the fire. "Feels like someone tipped them off—"

"With the wrong information." Andy glanced behind him into the dark. "Know anybody who'd make up lies about me? I mean, hell, Luke, who's out here that wants me dead?"

Shrugging, Luke picked up the stick and regarded it. "Trace did manage to get that commander to tell us that a sheriff-marshal from Utah brought in a fella who supposedly seen you in Mexico. That fella said you'd bragged about deserting." Luke drew in the dirt. "You talk to anybody about that?"

"Talked with lots of folks in Nogales. Not about being

the army." Andy examined his healing hand. "Did he say what he looked like?"

"'Bout our height. Older fella, maybe late thirties. A bit on the skinny side. Neatly trimmed bears, but it was long, he said. New clothes. Had a man with him. Rounded, dirty trail clothes. Called him by name, but Rickman couldn't remember. It was a funny one, too." Luke waited while Andy ran a hand through his hair. "Got any clue? It's frustrating. Damn frustrating."

"Perchman's ghost, maybe?"

Luke pointed his cigarette at Andy. "There you go again with your crazy ghoulies. No such thing as ghosts." He blew out smoky *O's*.

Andy peered into the campfire. "Nobody I've seen. But there's parts of my memory still fuzzy."

"I'm sure there's parts you don't *want* to remember."

Andy nodded. "How'd you convince Rickman to let me loose?"

"Wasn't easy." Luke raised both eyebrows. "Took some talking, lots of words, but, after all that, we got through his thick brain, especially since Trace can be rather... persuasive."

Andy knew exactly what Luke was saying. Trace was strong in more ways than just muscle. Finding the words to say what he felt, what he'd been thinking on this ride, came out in starts and stops.

"I'm... I'm sorry, Luke." Andy caught his brother's quizzical stare.

"Sorry about what?"

How to phrase this just right. Andy raised one sore shoulder. "Sorry that I held up the drive and sorry for causing—"

"You're apologizing for what Rickman did to you?" Luke threw his cigarette butt into the fire. He faced Andy and pointed behind them. "You're sorry for being wrongly arrested and accused?"

Andy nodded.

"Hells bells, Andy." Luke scrambled to his feet, paced back and forth. "You did nothing wrong." He knelt by his brother. "Don't ever, *ever*, apologize to me, or anybody. You did nothing wrong." He drew in a breath. "Hell, it should be me apologize to you."

"No."

"Yes." Luke's cheeks burned. "Hell, I shouldn't have let them take you. Shouldn't have let you sit in jail ten days. We should've gone with you." He gripped Andy's shoulder. "Hell, Andy. You almost died. Fact is, you *did* die."

"I did?"

Luke swiped at moisture on his cheek. "After Rickman let you go, we were riding down

the main street, looking for the doc's. I had one of your arms, Trace the other. You slid out of my grip, then out of Trace's and hit the ground." He studied the dirt. "You weren't breathing. You were dead."

"What?"

"Trace shook your shoulders until you took a breath."

Andy leaned away from the fire's heat. "I had no idea."

Luke swiped a hand across his mustache. "See? If I'd gone with you to Fort Yuma, you would've been safe." He lowered his voice. "My fault."

"Don't spur yourself, Luke. It wasn't your fault and guess it wasn't mine." Andy massaged his left cheek and raised his eyes to Luke. "But why'd somebody take all that trouble figuring I'd end up behind bars?"

Luke shrugged. "Guess the better question is—who?"

CHAPTER SIXTY-TWO

"James? Hey James!"

He pulled rein, turned in his saddle, grateful to look at something beside the rear end of cattle, and squinted at two riders headed his way. One held up a hand. Luke. The other rode bent over, holding his ribs. Andy. James breathed out a long exhalation of relief.

Raising his hand in reply, James gigged Pinetop toward his brothers. He galloped, slowing as they met. Andy's pale face reflected the late-afternoon light, and, despite its pallor and bruises, his brown eyes sparkled when he produced a smile.

James reached over giving Andy a heartfelt hand-shake, nodded to Luke. "Damn glad to see you two. 'Bout given you up. Thought you'd turned around, headed for home."

"Hell, we started to," Luke thumbed over his shoulder. "But Andy here's been insisting on having more of Coozie's stew. Can't get enough. And you know Andy when he sets his mind." He shook hands with James.

"The herd pulled a big show last night, what with the lightning and thunder." James wagged his head. "Took 'til mid-morning to get them all pointed the same way. We'll be stopping early, soon as Carlos finds the right bed ground."

Luke swiped at a bead of sweat rolling down his temple, cocked his head toward Andy. "He needs off the horse. Can't ride too far between rests. Gets real bad headaches. Throws up. About used all the laudanum. Hope Coozie's got whiskey." He pointed his chin toward the front of the herd. "How much farther you think?"

Andy straightened. "Told you before, Luke. Don't baby me. I'm fine."

"Never were a respectable liar, Andy." James pointed north. "Another mile or two." He

turned the familial grin on his youngest brother. "Damn glad to see you in one piece. And

awake."

A renegade steer headed into the sagebrush, away from the herd. James tapped spurs against his horse's side and pointed. "Meet you back at camp." He waved at his brothers and turned his attention to the steer. "Why can't you walk with everybody else?"

By the time the herd was bedded for the evening, James had rounded up a total of seventeen steers, two without his road brand. Cattle like that sold just as well, he'd been told. Nobody in this steak-starved country questioned one or two unbranded head. They were simply grateful for the meat. At least that's what people had said. As far as he knew, this cattle drive was the first to trail to California. There'd been talk of driving from Texas north to Kansas where the railroad promised to start building. Already, stockyards had sprung up. But with the War of Southern Rebellion done, Russell had reported, cattle would soon start walking all over the West.

The war. James would have to hear it himself, but both Russell and Tex agreed it was over. The Union had won, and James figured about the time he and his brothers had started this drive in April, General Lee officially surrendered at the Appomattox Courthouse, wherever that was. Russell mentioned even though he'd already been freed at the start of the war, now all Negroes were free. To do what, he had no idea. But presently with war's end, the world was turning on its head. This country had a lot of healing to do.

James tied Pinetop to the lead line at the remuda, brushed mud from his vest and chaps while walking toward the campfire. Coozie greeted him with a cup of coffee and a nod. "Fed some hungry strangers who wandered into camp. Hope you don't mind."

"I'll make sure they work for the food. You can count on that." James sipped the hot coffee and headed for the fire and his brothers.

Although exhausted, James sat up talking with them until past his turn to ride night

guard. When they came in, Tex and Carlos said all was calm with the cattle, no storm on the

horizon. Great news all the way around.

Conversations flew around camp. James thought about injuries. Trace's arm, finally mended, still wasn't in the best working condition. He grimaced and cursed whenever he threw the lasso, pulled calves out of the mud, slept on it wrong. But at least he still had an arm. That's what the doc in Arizona City had said when he examined Trace. The crazy Indian woman had almost cost him dearly. Trace's arm, Luke's shoulder. Doc said both had been lucky. James knew that.

The luckiest, Doc had said while shaking his head, had been Andy. James knew that, too. He regarded his brother sitting cross-legged near the fire. One more beating, one more day with no medical care, he would've died. No doubt. As it was, he had a severe concussion, which was bad. Real bad. Doc said it would take a boot crashing into his head or being slammed against a pole numerous times. Two unbelievably black eyes and ugly bruises cascading down to his chin illustrated that clearly.

James stared into the flames, his body tense, ready to spring. He clenched his jaw until it hurt. Those soldiers. Andy. Regret blanketed his thoughts. A long look at his brothers—both alive and relatively well. He pushed away remorse, saving it for another day, and relaxed. Bootsteps crunched behind him. He turned.

"Thought I'd seen you two come riding in. Wanting free food, place to throw a bedroll."

Trace stood at campfire's edge. "We don't allow freeloading strangers to bed down with us. We do have standards."

Luke scrambled to his feet, extending his hand to Trace. Instead of shaking, Trace

grabbed him into a bear hug, quickly releasing him, patting his shoulders. "Damn sight for sore

eyes. Thought you'd stay in Arizona City till we swung back that way."

"It's Andy." Luke pointed over his shoulder. "Rascal can't get enough of cattle. For some

reason, loves eating their dust."

Andy groaned up to his feet. "Not true, big brother. It was Luke. He likes—"

Trace wrapped Andy in a hug, released him and stood back, his gaze trailing Andy boots to hat. His eyes continued skyward. "Thank you."

CHAPTER SIXTY-THREE

A nod and a snort. Whid leaned over his horse and spat, a trail of brown goo splatting onto the dirt. He ran a sleeve across his mouth while he surveyed the wooden buildings of Tin Town. Such as it was, this place had sprung up in the past few years, the result of gold fever. People from all walks of life dropped everything to scurry to California in search of that metal. And for what? More of the same—killings over worthless claims, worthless dreams.

He spat again.

Rolling hills of green surrounded the valley town standing in stark contrast to the brown of the wooden buildings lining the muddy street. The main street Whid assumed, led through the center of town. Wide enough to send a herd of cattle through—probably six abreast. Too bad. It would be easy for Colton. He wanted everything to be tough for that *pendejo*.

Whid glanced at Pickett on his right. "First thing, you need new clothes. We'll do that before checking into a hotel. Assuming there is one."

"New clothes? Me?" Pickett sat up straighter, his eyes wide. "Why? What's wrong with these?" He looked down at his shirt, scraped dried stew off the front.

Whid reined up and glared at his partner. That man could be plenty ignorant without making a job of it. "Ain't you listened to a word I said last night?" He clenched his jaw and relaxed. He'd be done with Pickett soon enough. He wouldn't have to repeat himself a hundred times. He allowed sarcasm to flavor his words. "My *plan*? Don't you remember?"

Squinting into the noon sky, Pickett nodded at Whid. "Sure, I ain't stupid. Didn't realize I was gettin' all duded up, too."

If he backhanded Pickett, the man would probably leave and maybe even tell the real law

his intentions. Instead, Whid gripped the reins and dug his knees into the sides of his horse. He fought down the urge to pull his gun and end Pickett there. Just as quickly as his last partner.

No, that would bring the law and jail time, or more than likely a noose for him.

He'd wait.

He clenched his hands then relaxed. Whid nodded to Pickett. "Come on. Don't have all day."

CHAPTER SIXTY-FOUR

James and Trace rode into Tin Town, its wide main street beckoning like the promise of warm water on a cold day. It soothed all the nerves. On James' right, the first wooden building in the block sported a sign over the entrance. *Blue Dog Saloon.* Across the street, another saloon. *Lucky Strike.* Two more doors down, *Kate's Emporium.* Enthusiastic banjo music sailed over the batwing doors. "Oh My Darling, Clementine" enlivened the street. James whistled with it.

Farther down stood the sheriff's office. Bars on the window marked its identity. No sign on the front or above the door was needed.

The *Tin Town Mercantile* stood across an alley from the sheriff's. If hustle and bustle were an indication of this store's popularity, it was the best place in town. Customers, mostly women, pushed their way in and out. Women, arms loaded with packages and bundles, eyed James and Trace, eventually turning their gazes back to the street.

As they rode, a woman with two young children navigated the muddy street. The smallest, a boy, jumped in a puddle splashing the girl. A screech and giggles from the kids. James pointed. "Remind you of somebody?"

"Sure does. You. Never seen anybody who liked puddles like you did!" Trace wagged his head. "Unless it was Andy. I swear the two of you could find mud in a dust storm."

James smiled. Pleasant memories.

Trace used his chin to point. "Looks like the mayor's office up ahead on the left."

"Sure will be glad to get money in my pockets instead of sand." James pried his hat off

his forehead and set it back a bit. "Hope his price hasn't changed. What would we'd do with

three thousand animals if he didn't buy them?"

"Said he would." Trace reined up in front of the only brick building on the main street. "Have his letter in my pocket."

Following a quick flick of the reins over the hitchin' rail, James stood on the boardwalk in front of a two-story brick building. He gazed at the brass plaque on the wall next to the front

door. *Samuels and Samuels. Attorneys at Law.*

Same name on the letter Trace had. Carter Samuels, Mayor, Tin Town, California.

James refreshed his mental note to ask about the town's name.

Trace, with James on his heels, pulled open the thick wooden door and stepped in. Wallpapered ceiling and walls greeted them. A large, tightly woven area rug filled most of the room. Its red, green and gold pattern swirled together creating roses. An immense gold framed mirror took up part of one wall. Two high-backed armchairs sat across from each other. In between, a mahogany drum table with a vase of fresh flowers, a variety he didn't recognize, sat in the middle.

Fish out of water, he thought. Never having seen anything so opulent before, James stood in the doorway, mouth open, staring at the furnishings. Blinking like his eyelids were on fire, he turned right, left. Trace mirrored James.

Months of hard trail riding crashed around James. Despite the bath and haircut he'd received in Arizona City, he felt dusty, unshaved, unwashed—dirty. James whipped his hat from his head and raked his hair with his fingers.

Before he could step outside and suggest to Trace they come back in a more presentable condition, like an apparition, a woman materialized in the room.

"Gentlemen? May I help you?"

Her voice. Heavenly. Those dark eyes matching her dark hair seemed to take in every

detail of his body. James squirmed. He twirled his hat in his hands.

She moved in closer. "You looking for a lawyer or the mayor?"

Perfume wafted under James' nose. Lilac. His favorite. A stunning blue dress nipped in at the waist set off her trim figure. Although she wasn't tall—she came to his shoulders—her straight posture emitted confidence and an air of authority. James found himself staring at those eyes, those lips.

"We're here to see the mayor, ma'am." Trace nodded at the woman.

She flashed a smile—lovely, wide, warming. "Wait right here. I'll see if he's available." She started off but stopped. "I'm sorry. I forgot to ask your names."

Names? James couldn't remember.

"Trace and James Colton, ma'am. The mayor's expecting us." Trace gripped his hat in his hand and waited until the woman left the room before speaking. His voice was low. "What's wrong with you? Standing there like a moon-struck calf." He bumped his hat brim against James' chest. "You sick?"

He had to stay focused. Had to stay on task and get those cattle sold. What was he doing thinking about this woman? Hell, he was married. Happily, too. He rethought. There was sure something about that woman...

"James." Trace shook his arm. "You all right?"

A wag of his head to clear the thoughts, James frowned and looked down at his

trembling hands, both clutching his hat. It hadn't been *that* long since he'd seen a woman. At

least one who wasn't a... *professional.* "Yeah. Fine. Reminds me of Star a bit."

"Thought so," Trace said. "Your face is flushed. Fever?" He put his hand on James' forehead.

James swatted at the hand and backed away. "I'm fine." Would *she* come back and see Trace babying him? That would be embarrassment beyond explanation or endurance.

"All right. Sorry." Trace walked the length of the room to an oil painting hanging on the

wall. Two men in formal coats and top hats sat looking serious, stern. "Suppose this is—"

"I'm sorry, gentlemen." The woman appeared in the room again. "The mayor won't be able to see you here."

"I realize we're a few days late. But only two. And we sent a message." James knew he sounded pathetic. Would they cancel the deal for two lousy days?

Her original smile evaporated. She pointed toward

the door. "He said he'd meet you in a quarter hour on the edge of town."

"What?" James' attraction to this woman melted. "What d'you mean? Why won't he see us here?"

Trace stepped in closer. "What's wrong?"

"I'm sorry, sir. Mayor Samuels made it quite clear. You're to wait on the edge of town and he'll meet you there." She pointed west, walking James and Trace to the door. "Good day."

It closed with a bang.

James tugged his hat down on his head. "What the hell? What d'you suppose that was all about?"

Trace pursed his lips and shrugged. "Can't wait to find out." He looked up at the imposing building again. "I got a bad feeling, younger brother. A real bad feeling."

* * *

"Think he's trying to come up with the money?" James paced from the horse to a tree, then scanned the town in the distance. "Knew we were coming. He should've had it ready."

"Hope he's not welching on our agreement." Trace, reins in hand. "Probably wants to inspect the stock before handing over the cash. That's what I would do."

Although Trace's tone sounded hopeful, James wasn't so sure. But, then again, maybe there wasn't a problem. Maybe he and Trace had imagined one. Surely, that was the answer.

James squinted toward town. Was that a black buggy coming their way? There's been plenty time for the mayor to collect the money and come calling.

Trace pointed. "Looks like the mayor's paying us a visit. 'Bout time."

Did he dare hope? "Can almost feel the coin jingling in my pockets." James raised his brows while one corner of his mouth tugged upward.

A man, resembling the person in the painting, drove up in a buggy, pulled to a stop, and sat, staring.

When he didn't get down, James, with Trace at his side, started toward the buggy. "Mayor Samuels?" James stuck out a hand.

"Don't come any closer." Samuels held up a black whip. "I'll use this if necessary."

"What?" Trace stopped.

"Why?" James cocked his head. "What's wrong?"

"What's wrong? What's wrong you ask?" Samuels leaned as far back in his buggy as possible without falling out the other side. "You a buggerty dunderhead?"

"No, sir." James stepped closer.

"An inch more and I'll use this on you." Samuels held the whip higher.

James glanced back at Trace. Confusion corkscrewed his eyebrows.

"No need for the whip, Mayor." James held up his hands. Memories of three months of Apache abuse chilled him. Heart pounding, he touched the wide scar on his cheek. Scars on his back pulled and tugged as reminders. Fighting the past, he returned to the present. "We truly don't understand. What's the problem?"

Samuels dropped his voice. "Anthrax." His eyes opened wide, narrowed. "How dare you bring it here. How dare you!"

"Mayor, we don't have anthrax. The cattle're healthy. Real healthy. Come see for
yourself." Trace stood straighter. "Who told you that?"

"Doesn't matter who told me. It's all over town."

Samuels lowered the whip. "Peddle your diseased live-stock elsewhere."

"What?" Trace and James spoke in unison as they moved in toward the buggy.

"You heard me. When I advertised for cattle, I expected healthy stock. Not some...

some... half-starved, disease-riddled farm animals." Samuels' round face turned red. "Get out of my town. Out of my county. Out of my state. You're not welcome here."

Trace pulled the letter from his vest pocket. He waved it at the mayor. "Have your letter right here saying you'll buy our cattle. We held up our end of the bargain. You taking back your word?"

Samuels's face flushed an even darker red. A vein throbbed on his forehead. The hand gripping the reins fisted. Samuels brought the whip up over his head and cracked it down next to Trace. Both brothers jumped.

"What the hell was that for?" Trace threw his arms out to his sides.

"We trailed those steers a thousand miles and now you're backing out?" James struggled to contain his anger, but confusion, outrage surfaced anyway. He pointed at the mayor and marched toward him. "Our cattle are fi—"

Crack.

James grabbed his left forearm, spun around and bent over. The excruciating pain—remembered from before. Sharp. Gut wrenching.

Trace charged the mayor. Before Samuels could strike again, Trace grabbed his shirtfront, wrenching him out of the buggy. A fist to his face sent him reeling back against the buggy.

"Don't ever touch my little brother! Ever!" Trace raised his fist again, but lowered

the anger. "You had no right. No right!"

Samuels scrambled back into the buggy, rubbed his cheek, and brought himself upright.

He wagged the whip at the brothers. "I said leave. And mean it. You'll be hearing from the sheriff." He flicked the reins over the horse, turned the buggy, roared off.

"Get back here!" Trace ran after him. "Come back coward!" He slid to a stop and turned to James. "You all right?"

James raised his trembling hand from his forearm. Both brothers inspected the wound. Underneath his ripped blood-soaked sleeve, a long red line already puffed. Skin split.

"Sonovabitch!" Trace clenched both fists. He wrapped his neckerchief around his brother's arm and stared down the street. "What the hell?"

James winced, chiding himself for shaking so violently. Painful memories, fearful images, terrifying nightmares flooded his mind. Cochise's face. He shook harder. Tribal drums beat in rhythm to his heart. The pounding grew louder. Louder.

"It's all right." An arm slid around James' tensed shoulders. "It'll be all right. Wasn't Indians." Trace squeezed. "No Apache around here. You're safe."

A nod. He waited. The drums faded. Cochise vanished.

Trace nudged James toward his horse. "Let's get you back to camp. Try to figure all this

out."

James wagged his head. "Not quite the reception I was expecting."

CHAPTER SIXTY-FIVE

"Sheriff? Sheriff Sam Cooper?" Whid hoped he had the name right. After all, he'd read it moments ago on the sign outside. He waited for the man to look up. "I'm Marshal Smith—*Amos* Smith—and this here's my deputy, Pick... Pickman. We're all the way down from Utah Territory." He extended his hand as Tin Town's sheriff stood.

The hand was firm, callused. Obviously this sheriff was a man of action—and hard work. A glance behind the desk revealed a wall of wanted posters, pictures or pencil sketches standing out on each one. Was his or Pickett's still there? He hoped not. After all, he'd done his time. They both had. But Pickett had spent only six months in county jail. Easy time. Whid, however... Three long, rotten years. Three years of hard labor. Three years of plotting and planning. And now? The time was at hand. It would be over in a matter of days. Maybe even hours.

The conversation in his ear turned his attention back to the office.

"... nasty hombres, Sheriff Cooper. That's why the territory sent us down here." Pointing to the tin star on his new leather vest, Pickett narrowed his eyes and nodded at the sheriff. He used one hand to straighten the front of his vest.

Whid had to guess at the first part of the conversation. But he'd rehearsed Pickett about what to say until his partner had mumbled it in his sleep. With Pickett, however, nothing was ever a sure bet. No matter how simple, he always managed to blow to hell whatever it was.

"Marshal?" The sheriff stared at Whid and cocked his head. His blue eyes bore into Whid's face.

Whid rubbed his beard. "Sorry. Must be tired from riding so far."

"Understand." Sheriff Cooper pointed to wooden chairs in front of his desk. "Take a load off. Tell me more about these men. I sure as hell don't want them lurking around my town. Especially not with the big doings tomorrow."

Whid pulled the chair farther from the desk and dropped into it. "'Big doings'?"

"Fourth of July doings." Cooper's eyes widened. "Always big around here. Especially so, what with that danged war over." He leaned over his desk. "Don't you folks celebrate the Fourth up in Utah?"

Pickett tugged his new black hat down low on his forehead. "Course we do, Sheriff. 'Course we do. Fireworks, bands, barbecues, speeches, eatin' contests, horse races. The whole shebang."

Whid glared at his partner. He's laying it on a bit thick. Pickett ain't never celebrated anything. "We're as much American pie as California, Sheriff." He pulled in air, began his practiced spiel.

"Reason we're here, like my deputy said, is we're huntin' four men. Ruthless, cutthroat, murdering, stop-at-nothing horde of degenerates." Whid nodded to Pickett, who nodded back.

Whid continued. "Four brothers. All look alike... ugly. So ugly their pa made 'em sleep in the barn. But if you've seen one, no cause to wonder what the other fellas look like."

Pickett held his hand up over his head. "Six one, two. Brown hair and tiny, beady eyes.

Oldest is mid- to late twenties. Youngest, nineteen." He opened his mouth to continue, but Whid shot him a silencing glare.

"He's right, Sheriff." Whid leaned closer for emphasis. "They're bad hombres. Downright mean." He fished into his vest and pulled out folded papers, glanced at them. "Fact is,

judge's determined to find 'em. Sent us to bring 'em back. Alive preferably." He glanced at

Pickett. "But dead would be good, too."

Stretching across the desk, he offered the pages he'd worked hard on, copied from a legal notice in the newspaper.

Cooper nodded, swatted his hand at the papers, picked up a pencil and located a clean sheet of paper. "How can I help?"

He had him. And right where he wanted this lawman. On his side. Not on the Colton's. "Their last name is Colton. C-O-L-..." How did they spell it? He waited for the sheriff to finish writing. "I need you to lock up the oldest and the two youngest. The second one is mine."

Laying down his pencil, Cooper frowned up at Whid. "Why's that, Marshal?"

Because his wife shoulda been mine. Because I spent my life

*behind bars when it shoulda been him. Because I hate everything
about him.*

Whid tucked the papers back into his vest, pulled his
shoulders back, inhaled a long pull, and explained. "The
second one, *James* Colton, is a cold-blooded killer. Shot
and killed a sheriff in Mesilla a few years back."

"No!" Cooper's eyes grew wide. "Heard about that!
Sheriff Fuente?"

Whid nodded.

"It was *him?*"

"Sure was," Whid said. "If that's not bad enough,
hell, even involved with Quantrill's Raiders, he was. That
hombre'll stop at nothing to get what he wants. I'd
rather handle him myself since I've been on his tail for a
while. Understand him well. Understand his pattern.
And I'd hate for anyone else to cross his path."

Before Cooper could ask, Whid pushed on. "And
Trace, the oldest, well... he's a

fighter. Trace is mean. Real mean. Had a run-in with
Cochise a while back. Tends to think and

act more like a red heathen than a white man. You
best arrest him right away before he shreds your town
bit by bit."

"And, Sheriff," Pickett said. "Trace thinks he's a
sheriff down in Mesilla. Has a pretend

badge and everything... some people wear pretend
badges."

Whid kicked Pickett with the side of his foot. Pickett
jumped.

"But don't you pay no nevermind to all that badge
business." Pickett's mouth formed a

pout, but it reversed and turned up. "Well, Trace
Colton... he's... acts like he's smoked too much of that
loco weed."

Cooper nodded, continued scribbling. He mumbled more to himself than to Whid. "Dangerous." He underlined the word twice.

Whid hadn't had this much fun in years. "But third brother, Luke."

Cooper looked up, scribbled faster.

Whid continued. "Well, even though he's homely, Luke's a womanizer. Best lock up your wives and daughters."

"That ain't an arresting crime, Marshal Smith."

"It is when he marries three or four of 'em."

Pickett threw his shoulders back. "At the same time."

"That's right. At the same time. He gets them... gets them..." Whid cupped his hands over an imagined extended stomach. "In a delicate condition, you understand. Then he skips town." He turned to Pickett. "Remember poor Miss O'Toole? And that widow... what was her name?"

"Simmons, I think it was." Pickett nodded. "Luke's a fella with no morals, Sheriff."

"Certainly don't want him around." Cooper dotted part of his writing, scanned it. "Damn odd a whole family turn that bad." He looked up at Whid. "You said there were four?"

"Four. Right. The youngest is Andy. Andrew Jackson Colton." Whid tapped his finger on the sheriff's sheet of paper and waited for him to write the name. "You'd think with a name like that, named after one of our finest presidents, he'd be a pillar of the community. But no." Whid wagged his head. "He's an Army deserter. Yes, sir. Fact is, why recently he was arrested down in Fort Yuma for desertion. But he escaped. You can write them and ask. It's a fact. His brothers, the Colton Gang, busted him out."

Cooper drew in a sharp breath. "From Yuma Prison? You don't say?"

"Sure do." Whid had no doubt this law dog would find and arrest the entire brotherhood of Colton. He couldn't wait. "Andy was arrested, the gang broke him out, slick as a whistle. There was scuffling and such. Andy was beat pretty bad but managed to get away. More 'n likely he's still sporting black eyes."

Pickett pointed south. "And soon as the army can regroup, they'll be sending out troops to bring him in."

"Not unless I get him first." Cooper straightened his shoulders, added more notes.

"So, Marshal. Any idea where these outlaws are at?"

Victory was sweet. Warmth flushed over Whid's body, flowing from his feet up to his

head. It was, indeed, turning into a glorious Fourth. Whid fought a smile. "Sure do, Sheriff. Sure do."

CHAPTER SIXTY-SIX

Luke sat on his horse while the herd munched stirrup-high grass. The cattle, longhorns mostly, stood, basking in the mid-afternoon sun, seeming to enjoy not walking anywhere. Luke grinned at simply sitting, not worrying about Andy and catching up to the herd. He swung his right leg over the saddle, hooking it around the horn. He took his time rolling a cigarette, struck a match against his chaps, shielding the flame, always careful not to startle the docile creatures. They'd stampede at cowboys lighting up, and he sure as hell didn't want to spend his last day on the trail chasing cattle.

Luke puffed, spotted Andy riding in, who reined up next to him.

"Think James and Trace have the money yet?" Andy glanced into the sky shielding his eyes from the glare. "They've been gone a while."

"These things take time, I guess." Luke eyed the valley stretching before him. Fields of white flowers smothered a low hill, reminding him of a white carpet. Soft. Thoughts of lying there floated through his head.

"Wish I could've rode in with them," Andy looked toward town sitting two ridges over. "Sure would like to see what they're planning for the Fourth."

Fourth of July. Luke thought back to his childhood. Always his favorite time of year. Ma fixing pies and cobblers. Especially chokecherry with the flakey crust. Plenty of fireworks. Everyone coming into town from the surrounding farms. He would play with other boys he hadn't seen since school. Work for the day stopped while everyone celebrated. Especially the adults. Yep, Fourth of July. His favorite.

Andy pried off his hat. "Hope James gets as much money as he bargained for. Hope *we*

do. The Four C Square." He fanned his face. "Kinda warm today."

Luke drew in another lungful of tobacco and looked over at his brother. Those bruises

were fading, but the eyes remained ringed in black. One coal-colored strand zigzagged down his left cheek. Luke cocked his head. "What're you gonna do when this is over?"

"Meaning what?" Andy ran his hand through his shoulder length hair.

"Meaning what are you planning to do? Ride back and marry that little gal? Open that saloon you and Trace talked about? Stay here in California? What?" Luke blew a stream of smokey *O's* into the air.

Andy turned his eyes on Luke. A shrug. His words turned soft. "Hadn't much thought on it." His healing lips pursed. He winced as he moved. "Guess I'll head for home. Sure as hell not riding near Arizona City again."

"Don't blame you there." Luke blew out more smoke and studied his cigarette. "Looking forward to buying cigars in town. These are poor substitutes."

"Guess when I get home, I'll court Ginny some more," Andy said. "A lot more. And I'd like to marry her. Real soon."

Luke wagged his head. "Don't do it."

"What?" Andy sat up straight. "What gives you the right to tell me how to run my life? Just 'cause you're older—"

"'Cause I'm sure of what I'm sayin'. Hell, Andy. Look at me. I'm twenty-one, twenty-two in September."

"So?"

"So. I already have a wife and two kids. *Two* kids." Luke frowned into the field. "Hell, if I'd been smart, Sally and me wouldn't be married. I wasn't ready to settle down. That wasn't the

life I wanted."

"But—"

"I realize I ain't the best husband around." Luke let out a stream of smoke and ground

out his cigarette on his chaps. "But I'm tied down. Like a damn prisoner. Like *you* were." A fist formed in his chest. "How *did* you like having your hands tied? All cinched up. Hell, you couldn't even scratch your own damn butt."

"Hated it." Andy spoke in a low voice reserved for dreaded things. "Truth is, scared the hell outta me."

Luke fought rage and glanced over at Andy. "I'm like you were. Only this time, my brothers can't come rescue me. They can't fix it."

"You didn't have to get married."

"Like hell I didn't. Everybody knew me and Sally were sweethearts. Everybody knew we didn't dance when we went to that party." Luke slid his eyes sideways at Andy. "Least not the kind of dancing you do in front of other people."

Andy finished the thought for him. "And everybody knows the Burroughs are fine,

upstanding people, what with Mister Burroughs being a reverend and all. They wouldn't allow their daughter and family to be shamed."

Memories flew around Luke's brain. Highs and lows. Sunny times, gloomy times. "We married before she showed."

"Yep," Andy said. "I was there. Remember?"

Luke let the afternoon breeze float around his sweat-drenched body. Those memories were still real, still hard to deal with. He loved Sally, no doubt. But he loved his freedom, too.

How could he put into words what he wanted to tell Andy before it was too late? Before

he married and ruined his life, too. The words spurted out.

"Please wait. You're young. Hell, you ain't even twenty yet." Luke fished another

cigarette out of his vest pocket. He'd made several and kept them around for times like this.

Times he didn't want to trouble himself by rolling. "You might find somebody else. Then what?"

"Won't be anybody like Ginny."

He'd have to work harder to get Andy to understand. "Maybe. Maybe not. Ask James. That's what he thought about Lila. But who'd he marry?"

"Morningstar." Andy cocked his head. "But things were different for him than for me."

"Yeah. But point is, he loved them *both*." Luke reached over and patted Andy's shoulder.

"Truth is, there could be somebody else out there—in a few years—waiting for you. Even more perfect than Virginia. Hell, please give yourself time to grow up."

"But—"

"Luke. Andy." Carlos rode up. He pointed over his shoulder. "Your brothers are back at camp. They say come right away. I'll take your place here."

Luke flashed a wide grin at Andy. "Looks like we're in the money, my little baby brother." His smile faded as he studied Carlos's frowning face, eyebrows bunched. "What's wrong?"

"You need to ride back." Carlos cocked his head toward the front of the herd. "James is hurt."

"What the hell?" Luke swung his leg over the saddle horn and spurred his horse. Andy followed right behind.

Within minutes Luke and Andy stood in camp watching Coozie tend James' whip cut.

James, shirtsleeve bunched above his elbow, leaned against the side of the wagon, Coozie

pouring an acidic-smelling liquid concoction over his arm. Luke moved in close. Black horsehair stitches laced the swollen, red skin closed. "What happened?"

Trace wagged his head and shrugged. "The mayor. Thinks the herd's infected with

anthrax."

"So he took it out on James?" Andy peered over Coozie's shoulder.

"Damnation!" Luke bunched his fist. What else could go wrong? He turned to Trace. "I'm guessing you didn't sell the herd."

Andy frowned at all three brothers. "Who told them about anthrax?"

Wincing, James brought his brown eyes up to meet Luke's stare. "Sure as hell *we* didn't."

"Somehow, they found out what we did back on the trail." Trace ran his hand across his face. "Or took a wild guess."

Luke stepped back and gazed into the distance. "Hell, somebody doesn't want us selling those damn beeves."

"Question is who?" Andy cocked his head at Trace. "And why?"

"Hell, I'm not sitting around here waiting." Luke started toward his horse, but Trace's strong grip on his arm pulled him to a stop.

"Where're you going?" Trace held tight.

"Talk to that mayor. Try to reason with him." Luke glared at his brother's hand still on his arm.

"Calm down," Trace said. "You head off half-cocked, mad as you are, you're apt to wind up in jail. Or worse." He released Luke's arm. "Let's think this through."

Coozie tied white gauze strips around James' arm, knotted the ends. James rolled down his sleeve and nodded to Trace. "Hate to say this, but Luke might be right. Maybe if one or two

of us rides in, checks out the place, gets some information, we can figure it out."

Luke stood straighter. At last, a brother valued his idea. He fought a grin.

James continued. "They're already on the lookout for Trace and me. But they haven't seen Luke or even Andy." He looked over at Trace. "What d'you think?"

A bird cawed overhead. Coozie set down a bowl.

Trace let out a stream of air and raised his eyebrows. "The two of you be damn careful." He turned to Andy. "You up for this? Your ribs? Headaches?"

"Fit as a fiddle."

Trace tilted his head, wagging it. He turned to Luke. "You're older. Watch out for him."

"Always." Luke tapped Trace's shoulder. "We'll be home early, Ma. Don't wait up."

CHAPTER SIXTY-SEVEN

Tin Town sported more buildings and people than Luke had imagined. People squeezed in and out of stores, wagons and buggies trotted up and down the streets, children and dogs played on the boardwalks. Anticipation and excitement tingled the air.

"This burg's sure jumpin'." Luke tipped his hat to a woman he spotted on the boardwalk.

Andy stretched his arms wide. "This's what I'm talking about." A smile blossomed. "Look at all those banners, those flags, the decorations." He turned in his saddle, pointing to each red, white, and blue streamer, his head swinging in a dizzying sweep, left and right.

Luke's patriotic pride straightened his shoulders. "Big doings, I'm thinking."

"Extra big! No more war." A wider smile brought a long-lost sparkle to Andy's eyes. "Suppose they'll be lots of fireworks and such?"

"Maybe some tonight, but for sure tomorrow." Luke soaked in the fervor. Men toting various musical instruments stood on a makeshift bandstand, each selecting an appropriate spot for a rehearsal. The *thud thud thud* of pounding hammers echoed against the wooden buildings. The entire town was one big party.

"I can't wait," said Andy. "Suppose there'll be pie eating contests and such? I'm skilled at pie eating."

Luke nodded. "Sure are. You won what... three, four contests back home?"

"Only two. But I'm starving hungry thinking on it." Andy licked his lips. "Cherry, apple, blueberry. I'd take any pie long about now."

"Me, too. But we need to stay focused. The mayor whipped James, and I aim to see him pay for it." Luke gigged his horse into a faster walk.

Andy rode beside him. "I agree. At least find out what he's thinking."

They covered another half block. "Look over there." Andy pointed to a row of shanties hidden behind main street buildings. Men in white pants and shirts shuffled about, their long pigtails flapping behind them. "Who do you think they are? Never seen anything like them before."

Luke reined up and stared. "Chinamen. Look there." He pointed up an alley. "That's laundry they're doing. Those shacks are where they live."

"They're sure short," Andy said. "I've heard they work in the mines, too."

"Uh huh." Luke shrugged, nudged his horse. "Maybe we'll get to talk to one today. Wonder what they sound like."

"Bet it's nothing like Spanish." Andy grinned. "Maybe I'll get some clothes washed so I can hear them talk."

"Getting *your* clothes washed for any reason's an

excellent idea." *Clothes*. Like a fist to his gut, recent memories assaulted Luke. His brother wore all new clothes thanks to those incessant beatings at Fort Yuma. No one could get all the blood out. Too many rips and tears. He eyed Andy, sitting a saddle, holding his ribs, but his groans were subdued. Reluctantly, Luke let the bitterness subside. There would be time for a reckoning later.

He stopped in front of the Tin Town Mercantile. "Let's start here."

Nothing inside the Mercantile was a surprise. The usual mining and farming equipment, baking and sewing goods, even the jars of licorice whips, gumballs, dried apples, and other items displayed on the counter were usual. And the many customers inside were usual also. No one stood out. No one seemed to be lurking in the corners spreading gossip. Simply women chatting with other women, children snitching candy, men admiring pickaxes and shovels. Nothing out

of the ordinary.

Andy and Luke stepped back into the late-afternoon heat and peered down the dirt street. Even though Trace had warned them about the mayor's office, still Luke wasn't convinced it was a bad idea. He turned to Andy.

"I'll take a quick trip to see the mayor. See what I can find out."

Andy shook his head. "Don't do it. Trace said not to."

"It'll be all right." Luke started down the boardwalk and stopped. "Tell you what. I'll

meet you there." He pointed across the street at the Main Claim Saloon. Piano music, accompanied by banjo, sailed over the batwing doors. "Half an hour. I promise."

"Watch yourself." Andy let out a long sigh. "Still don't like you doing that."

Luke waved over his shoulder as he strode away.

The brick building was impressive, but Luke shrugged it off as a grand gesture of wealth and self-importance. No big-shot loudmouth would hurt his brother again. What gave him the right to whip James? And to renege on a business deal? Luke gripped the doorknob, harder than necessary. One hand fisted while the other turned the knob and pushed open the door.

Through his anger, Luke noted the expensive furnishings, the grandeur of the lobby. The more he inspected, the tighter his chest constricted. Before he could take in more, a feminine voice spun him around.

"May I help you, sir?"

Those eyes. Dark. Mesmerizing. Those lips. Parted a bit, they curved sensuously on both ends. Luke could taste her lips. Like honey. Sweet, like honey.

He tossed his Colton family grin at her. It disarmed women and he used it when

necessary. She smiled back.

"Ma'am." Luke tipped his hat, removed it. "Fine weather for this time of year. Don't you think?"

"Yes, it is." She moved in closer. "What can I do for you?"

Plenty of ideas raced through his mind, but none he should voice. Instead, he held her gaze and eased close. "I'm passing through town and have questions. Hoped you could answer them for me."

Luke fought to keep his mind on business. But something about this woman, this heavenly creature...

"I'll try." Her long arm swept toward two armchairs set on either side of a small drum table. "If you'd like a seat, maybe I can answer. If not, I'm sure the mayor or his brother could help you."

Luke followed her to a chair. The way she held her

head high, her shoulders back, her hips... He sat on the edge of one after she sat. He leaned closer. "I'm starting a ranch west of here, over in the San Fernando Valley, and I'm needing to buy a herd. Mainly cows with a bull or two. Would you be aware of any for sale?"

The woman's smile, showing a delicate dimension of sensitivity, turned downward. She cocked her head. "I'm sorry. I didn't catch your name."

Name? Luke hadn't thought that far ahead. He sure as hell couldn't use Colton. So far she hadn't connected Trace and James with him. So far. Ideas flew through his mind. He settled on one. "Burroughs, ma'am. Franklin Burroughs. Out of Kansas." His father-in-law wouldn't mind

sharing his name.

She extended a dainty hand. "Pleased to meet you Mister Burroughs." The smile reappeared. "I'm Brigid Hennessey. From here in California."

"Brigid?" Luke sat back. "That's my mother's name."

A nod and laugh. "She must be Irish, too."

"That she is." Luke remembered the lilt of grandpa's brogue. So many words sounding

more like music than speech. Many words his ma spoke—exactly like Grandpa's. Damn, he missed that man.

"... cattle ranch, Mister Burroughs?"

Luke fought to pull himself back into the present. This woman—her smile, her nearness, her smell, brought warmth to his body. "Would you like to have coffee with me, Miss Hennessey? I noticed a café down the street."

Brigid turned in her chair. "I guess that would be all right. Both brothers are out until after the holiday. And it's almost closing time, anyway." She stood. "I'll be only a minute."

While she tidied up, Luke took in the lobby. Paintings, plush furnishings, the grand rug, wallpaper—all reeked of wealth.

A stroll down the boardwalk gave Luke time to plot and plan better. He'd have to be careful as to how he asked questions. Brigid struck him as a smart woman. Beautiful and smart.

She stopped at the doors to the Golden Nugget Café and Restaurant. "They have great coffee and it's quiet. We won't have to shout to be heard."

They located a table near the back, ordered coffee and rolls. Between sips, they spoke of family, weather and California. Luke steered the conversation toward cattle.

"As I said earlier, I'm looking to start a cattle ranch. Need some decent stock. You heard of any?"

Those big eyes glanced at him over the cup's rim. She sipped, lowered the cup to the
saucer. Luke followed every move.

"Mayor Samuels bought a herd from New Mexico, but they're..." She dropped her
voice to a whisper. "They're sick."

"What d'you mean?" Luke's stomach twisted. And it wasn't because Brigid leaned closer.

"Anthrax." The word came out as a whisper.

"Really? Says who?" With more gentlemanly persuasion, maybe Luke could get her to give him a name. He'd find that *pendejo* and beat him senseless.

Brigid's slim shoulders shrugged. "Mister Samuels says it was a marshal from Utah Territory that first told him. But I've heard it all over town."

What the hell? Luke didn't know any marshal—from Utah or anywhere else. Could it be somebody Trace knew? He frowned into his coffee cup, up at Brigid. A plan. Yes, indeed, he had a plan. "I'm walking down to the sheriff's office. Maybe he can tell us what's going on." Luke scooted back his chair. "Would you like to come with me?"

CHAPTER SIXTY-EIGHT

Andy leaned back in the chair in the Main Claim. Cowboys, miners, businessmen, and ordinary townsmen rambled in, ordered drinks, sat and chewed the fat. The place was filling up fast. He visited with several cowboys, but nobody had heard anything about a herd of cattle, healthy or otherwise. A barmaid in a low-cut green satin dress tried to sit on his lap, but he'd eased her over to another chair. He bought her a drink and after she'd sipped the first inch, she moved on to another table.

He checked the sunlight cutting through the saloon. Lower since he'd first got here. Way past time for Luke to show. Late, as usual. Probably found a woman to sweet talk, one of his many talents. Andy stood and stretched, careful to twist his back without hurting his ribs too badly. The wooden chair wasn't even close to as comfortable as his saddle. His back complained. Another twist and for sure another beer would help heal the aches.

No hurry. Andy ambled over to the bar. Having another drink would help pass the time. Maybe he could meet someone else who knew something about this cattle misunderstanding.

After ordering, he leaned against the bar, his back to the bartender, and sipped lukewarm beer. At least this beer wasn't as warm as the ones he'd had in Mexico. While that beer quenched his thirst, it wasn't half the flavor of this one. Luke would like this brew. And his brother was picky about beer.

Andy surveyed the inside of the Main Claim again.

Nobody unusual. Nobody whispering to another and pointing. Nobody dressed like a cattle baron ready to buy the herd at a steal. Nobody but men looking for a first-rate time. A place to celebrate.

Whooping and hollering from outside rolled over the doors and swirled inside the saloon. Behind the noise, five men, a few sporting blue Union soldier jackets and kepis, stumbled in and lurched across the room to the bar.

"Beers for everyone, Barkeep," one of them yelled. His long, thin arms waved toward the

center of the room.

Cheers erupted. Andy, caught up in the revelry, hollered loud, like everyone else.

"Need to see money first." The bartender raised both eyebrows and stuck out his hand.

One of the new patrons leaned his belly against the bar, stretching his body halfway over

the top. "What's wrong? Don't you trust us?" His eyes trailed over the men at the bar. He pointed to his hat. "Why, sir. We're true blue American soldiers. Back from fighting."

Another man, also sporting a blue kepi, leaned across the bar, too. "You know... the *war*. That war 'tween the states." His words slurred. "Yessiree. The Brothers' War.

War of Southern Rebellion. Why, I done shot me a passel of Rebs, I did. Them no good, no account, sons of—"

"Show me your coins." The bartender pointed again to his outstretched hand.

If Andy had had enough money, he would've bought the round simply to watch the fun. But this far into the cattle drive, he was close to broke. Correction. He was broke. Buying the barmaid a drink had reduced his cash down to allowing him one more beer. Hopefully Luke had money.

Maybe when they had their drinks and found a seat, Andy would saunter over and sit with these men. After all, he was a Union soldier, too. *Former* Union soldier.

A man from the far side of the room pushed his way forward. "What'd you say about Rebels? You blowhard Yank!"

"I said they're cowards. Ever' single one of 'em damn Graybacks." The man's hands

fisted while his voice grew louder.

Before Andy could say anything or even edge outside, a clot of men stood on the far side of the bar and bowled their way toward him. One of them growled. "What'd you say, Yank?"

Another blue-capped soldier elbowed his friend. "Looky there, O'Niell. A passel of Sunday Soldiers." He stared directly at the cowboy in the lead. "What's wrong, Johnny? Can't take a lickin'? Admit when you're beat?"

A third man who had remained silent, stepped in close. "Hells, bells, Winston. Them

Parlor Soldiers ain't whinin' 'cause they lost that piddly little scuffle."

"They ain't?"

"No siree. They whinin' 'cause they miss their ma!!"

A fist flew out and connected with the third man's face.

Andy pushed away from the bar and stepped between the men. He held up his hands. "No need for fighting. War's over. We're all family again."

Whack. A fist plowed into Andy's face, right where the last big bruise had recently turned green. He reeled back crashing into the bar, spun, slumped to the floor. Bright lights and legs danced around his face. Realizing he'd be stepped on or fallen over, he had to get out of the way. Andy muscled himself up to his feet.

A body plowed into him. The impact sent both reeling back, slamming into a knot of men. Angry words battered Andy's ears.

"Call me a Sunday So—"

"Worthless Yankee scum."

"You don't talk like no real 'merican."

"This one's for Vicksburg."

A boot to his leg dropped Andy to his knees. Another boot crashed into his stomach.

He doubled over ready to lose dinner.

Somebody fell on top of him. Both men crumpled to the floor.

Shouting.

Yelling. Cursing.

Andy wriggled out from under the body who groaned, lying sprawled like a rag doll. Rolling to his right, Andy spotted boots under the batwing doors. They charged into the saloon.

Bang! Andy's ears range from the .45's massive load.

"That's it! Break it up!"

Bang! Smoke stung his eyes.

"I said, 'break it up'!"

Andy lay on the sawdust floor, waiting for sanity to

reign again. The crowd grew silent. His gaze trailed over to the boots, up to the man with a badge. The man held two .45s chest level. The scowl on his face meant business.

"Let's have us a peaceful celebration, men," the badge said. "That don't include bustin' up this bar."

One man Andy recognized stepped forward and pointed behind him. "Hell, Sheriff. We was only discussin' politics."

Still on the floor, Andy worked his jaw. Stiff and roaring sore. Was it broken? Fire throbbed in his ribs and face, but his leg and stomach hurt worse. *Some discussion.*

The sheriff holstered one revolver but kept the other pointed. He looked left and right. "Who started this mess?" His eyes traveled over each and every man.

"He did."

"Yeah, Sheriff. It was him."

More voices bombarded Andy's ears. "All his fault."

"He started it."

Andy used his one unswollen eye to see who the fellas were pointing at. Red, bruised faces stared right at him, fingers pointing.

An iron grip on his arm pulled Andy to his feet. The sheriff's face, inches from his, scowled. "You drunk?"

"No sir. Waitin' on my brother." Did Andy's words come out like he wanted? With his jaw hurt, no telling what the sheriff heard.

"He's a lousy Secesh, Sheriff." A tall, muscled cowboy moved in closer. "Bet he rode with Sherman—killing, looting, raping."

"No!" Andy shook his head. "Carleton. I rode with the California Column."

"Like hell you did." The same cowboy jabbed a finger in Andy's sore chest.

The sheriff elbowed the cowboy away, squeezing Andy's arm harder than necessary. "Give me your gun. Butt first. Nice and gentle."

Hating to relinquish his only weapon, Andy used thumb and forefinger to remove his Colt and hand it over. The sheriff stuck it under his own gunbelt.

"Atta boy." He shoved Andy toward the door. "Move." He shoved harder. "Now."

"What?" Andy massaged his jaw, hoping the words came out clear. "Why?"

"Jail." The sheriff pushed harder. "We don't take kindly to people coming in here, busting up our town. A day or two sobering up oughta do it."

Andy halted inside the batwing doors, pulled his arm out of the sheriff's grip. His voice

rose above the crowd. "I didn't do anything."

"Shut up." He shoved Andy outside. They stood on the boardwalk while men poured out

from the saloon, their jeers and farewells filling the air. Many raised a beer glass to the spectacle.

Andy scowled over his shoulder.

CHAPTER SIXTY-NINE

The sheriff heaved Andy off the boardwalk and into the street. They stopped, standing nose to nose. "Got a helluva red fist mark glowing on your cheek there. Eyes're lookin' a bit black, too. Yep. Looks like you're a helluva rabble rouser." His gaze roved over Andy. "What's your name, boy?"

As much as Andy didn't want to give his name, didn't want to get arrested, didn't want to spend the Fourth of July in jail, he had no choice. "Colton."

"You're mumbling, boy. What'd you say?" The sheriff frowned.

Andy worked his jaw around until he thought words would form. "Colton."

The sheriff stood back, cocked his head. His eyes widened. "Andrew Jackson Colton?"

How the hell did this sheriff know his name? His full name? Before Andy could think any further, the sheriff shoved the gun in Andy's chest. He pulled back the hammer. Metal grating on metal echoed in Andy's ears.

"One wrong breath, Mister Colton, and you'll have a hole the size of Texas in your

belly."

"But—"

"Ah." The sheriff shook his head. "No talking. Hands up. Way up."

Andy reached for the sky despite the burning of his healing ribs.

"Turn around. Start walking."

Do not to argue with this man. For whatever reason, the sheriff figured he had a

real *desperado* in his clutches. Andy sighed. He'd reason with this fella later. When things calmed down. *After* all the Fourth of July festivities.

The trek down the center of the street, past several buildings, took days. At least it felt

that way. Leg aching, stomach roiling, head thumping, he limped through throngs of people, everyone turning to stare. He couldn't get to jail soon enough.

At the sheriff's office, Andy waited for the door to swing open and stepped in before putting his hands down. Numb, they tingled as the blood returned. A survey of the room revealed the usual pile of paperwork on the desk, notices and various wanted posters tacked on the wall, potbelly stove, desk and chairs crowded the wooden room. On his right, two cells, iron bars gleaming in afternoon sun, stood empty.

A hardy shove on his shoulder and Andy stumbled into the closest cell.

Slam. Click.

The sheriff held up the keys. "Thought I'd have trouble finding you, Colton. Never dreamed you'd walk right in, so to speak." His brown eyes grew wide, flashing. From under a manicured mustache, his lips rose on each end. "Make yourself comfortable. You'll be here a while." Snickers rose from the sheriff's chest. "Circuit judge don't come 'til August."

Since the cells were in the same room with the sheriff, no wall keeping the prisoners hidden from view, Andy hoped he'd have a chance to reason with this lawman. If he could get his jaw working right, his head to quit pounding, maybe he could figure out this mess. Maybe when Luke discovered he wasn't at the saloon, he'd come looking. Maybe when Luke did, he'd explain the mix up and get the sheriff to release him. Maybe.

Andy slunk down to the lumpy cot and put his head in his hands. He stared at the wooden floor. In jail again. Eyes closed, he let his mind drift off to happier days. Days with Ginny. Days back home in Kansas. Days—

The office door squeaked open. Andy glanced up expecting to see a deputy or at least

townsmen come to gawk at the new prisoner. A prisoner who didn't deserve to be here. Blurred images, a man and a woman, stepped in and shut the door. Andy pressed his hands against his throbbing temples, squeezed his eyes, opened them again.

The sheriff jumped up from behind his desk and dashed to the woman. "Well, howdy Miss Hennessey." He tipped his hat. "What a pleasant surprise." A grin stretched his clean- shaven cheeks.

Andy stared at the man with her. Luke. Relief brought his puffy lips to a curve. But his brother, obviously enamored by the woman, hadn't spotted him yet. From what Andy could tell, she was a looker. No wonder Luke had been late meeting him for a beer.

"Sheriff Cooper," the woman said, "This is Mister Franklin Burroughs. From Kansas."

Her eyes sparkled as they softened on the sheriff's face.

Franklin Burroughs? Andy frowned. Luke's father-in-law?

Sheriff Cooper extended a hand. "Mister Burroughs." His eyes flashed on Luke and returned to the woman. "Please, have a seat." He pointed to an empty chair.

Not wanting to miss a chance to get released, Andy pushed up to his feet and called to

Luke. "Mister Burroughs? Think I recognize you. I'm from Kansas, too." He stretched out one of his arms and waved it between the iron bars.

Andy smiled when Luke turned and jumped. His eyes widened, narrowed as he stepped over to Andy. The woman and sheriff followed.

Cooper held the woman's arm keeping her from getting too close. "He's a scoundrel. Nothing but pure trouble." He pulled her against his chest. "Don't get any closer, Brigid. Don't want you in harm's way."

A smile transforming her face into pure sunshine, she turned to the sheriff. "I'm

perfectly safe with you, and Mister Burroughs here. I'm not worried at all."

Luke frowned at the sheriff and cocked his head toward Andy. "What's he in for?"

"Let's see." Cooper held up fingers as he counted. "Disorderly conduct, as you can tell by the shiner. Drunk, no less."

"What?" Andy grabbed the bars.

"Resisting arrest."

"What?" Andy hollered at the sheriff. "Resisting? Hell, Sheriff, I came peaceful."

"Army desertion."

Luke turned to Cooper. "He told you that?"

"Yep. Sure did. Told me himself. Deserted from Carleton's California Column."

Cooper's shoulders straightened. "Seemed mighty proud of it, too."

"Liar!" Andy shoved his entire body against the cell bars. "Liar! I'm no deserter. Who told you that?" Anger surfaced before he could contain it. "I wasn't causing trouble either. I wasn't drunk." He reached through the bars, the hardness pressing into his chest. Could he grab the lawman and shake sense into his head? "Dammit, Sheriff, I didn't desert."

"Yes, you did, boy." Cooper moved within inches of Andy. Too close. Andy grabbed the sheriff's shirt, pulling him against the cell bars. Before Andy could get a tighter hold, the sheriff whipped out his .45 and brought the walnut butt down over Andy's head. Andy crumpled to his knees, gripping the iron bars simply to stay upright.

Silver streaks raced across his eyes. As much as he fought to stay upright, his strength faded. He released his grip on the bars and slumped to the floor. Luke's boots ran at the sheriff.

"Dammit! You can't treat him like that." Luke's voice bounced off the wooden walls. "Get a doctor. He's hurt." Luke squatted down by Andy and reached through the bars.

"Why should you care, Mister Burroughs?" A long pause, his tone turned flat, ice cold.

"Well, I'll be sent to hell. You two look alike, talk alike. Ain't no doubt you're brothers."

Images pulsated, growing large, tiny. Andy grabbed his head and rocked back and forth on the wood floor. Movement only made things worse. Luke's voice floated over his head.

"Brothers? What gave you that notion, Sheriff?"

"Hand over your gun Mister *Colton*." Cooper's voice. Frigid. Decisive. "Nice and easy. Butt first." He snapped his fingers. "That's it."

Was that a gun jammed in Luke's chest? Andy strained to see but black and white stripes danced across the cell instead.

"Brigid, get me those keys. Ones to the cells." Cooper's words reflected a smirk. "Get in there."

Luke's boots shuffled to the adjoining cell.

Clang. Click.

"Andy?" Luke knelt close to the bars. "You all right?"

Using every inch of strength left, Andy rolled onto his side and looked at his brother. "No."

Luke stood and pressed against the iron bars. "Get a doctor. He's hurt bad. You had no

call to buffalo him like that. No call!"

"Shut up! Don't order me around." Cooper straightened his shirt and glared down at Andy. "You attempted murder on a peace officer, boy. You'll hang for that."

"What?" Luke stared at his brother.

Andy groaned.

"Besides," Cooper shrugged. "Doc's out of town 'til the fifth. Hates all the noise." He

slid an arm around Brigid's shoulder. "Miss Hennessey, I've captured half the notorious Colton

gang. Yep. Right here in Tin Town. Quite a feather in my cap, even if I do say so myself. The other gang members are more'n likely close by." He faced her. "Once I get the reward for these yahoos, it'll be enough to buy you that house you've been wanting. We can get married, and you won't have to work for old Samuels anymore."

Brigid melted in his arms. "Tom, are you asking me to marry you?"

"I was saving it for tomorrow, along with the big fireworks. But guess this's as right a time as any. Will you?"

"Yes." Brigid cuddled into the sheriff's chest.

Andy eased across the wooden floor, struggled to sit, his back against the bars. Every inch on his body hurt. Even his hair. He fingered the rising knot on his head and swiped at blood trickling down his forehead.

The sheriff released Brigid, pointed a finger at Luke's face. "And you. You must be brother number three. Luke. I was warned about your womanizing. Looks like they were right."

"What?" Luke gripped the bars.

"You were trying to steal my girl."

"What?" Luke raised his palms. "I wasn't trying to steal anybody. Who told you?"

Cooper wagged his head. "He sure was right. Description's near perfect."

"What description?" Luke frowned down at Andy and up at the sheriff. "Who told you?"

Luke looked at Cooper.

Andy looked at Cooper.

Brigid looked at Cooper.

Sheriff Cooper straightened his shoulders. "The man who's been trailing you for weeks."

He jerked his thumb over his shoulder. "That marshal from Utah. That's who."

CHAPTER SEVENTY

Nothing was soft about the ground, no matter how many coats and blankets James lay on. They could never replace even a lumpy, straw-filled mattress. He'd be glad to sleep in a bed for a change. He stretched as he yawned. Despite what the mayor had said, maybe today they'd get the herd sold, and then the entire Colton clan could spend tonight in a hotel, on real mattresses.

Another stretch, *pop-pop-pop*, vertebrae snapped into place. A bigger yawn, he rolled up to his knees. A long look around the campsite revealed grayed outlines of horses, trees and Coozie at the campfire pouring coffee. James grunted to his feet, arching his back. A rub, he hunched his shoulders. How did men do this year in and year out?

Coozie greeted him with a cup of coffee. *"Buenos dias, Señor James."*

"Morning, Coozie." The aroma, bitter but refreshing, wafted under his nose. A sip. Coffee slid down his throat, hot. James sipped again, surveyed the camp with more awake eyes. No signs of his younger brothers. Their bedrolls were still rolled up, right where they'd left them the day before. A familiar knot thudded in his chest. Something had to be wrong. This wasn't like them. "You seen my brothers?"

Coozie nodded, his shaggy hair brushing against his shoulders. "*Si*. Trace is out with the

herd. Left almost an hour ago."

When he didn't continue, James pressed further. "Luke and Andy? They were supposed to have this watch."

"*No se.*" Shrugging, Coozie stirred batter for flapjacks, a real treat out on the trail. "Trace, he took their place this morning. Carlos and Juan Tomás are sleeping, but maybe the new men... they were up most of the night."

"Thanks. I'll check with them." James handed the empty cup to Coozie and headed for

his horse.

The answers weren't what he wanted. Shrugs and shaking heads didn't fit with his

hopes. James reined up next to Trace. If dark circles under the eyes and slumped shoulders were an indication of exhaustion, Trace had a full-blown case.

"No Luke or Andy?" James let his gaze wander over the backs of the steers, cows and

calves, their legs folded under them, waiting to be somebody's supper.

"I'm gonna wring their necks," Trace said. "Promised they'd be back. On time."

"Think they're in trouble?"

Trace eyed James. "Maybe. I sure as hell hope not. Part of me's worried, the other's disappointed. Thought they'd behave themselves."

"Me, too." James wasn't sure which of his emotions was stronger, fear or anger. "You

think they had a few too many? You know Andy and Luke. They love the Fourth. More than likely they started celebrating early."

"You're probably right. They haven't had a real chance to unwind in months." Trace turned his full attention on James. "What d'you want to do?"

James rubbed his chin; a shave was in order this morning. Rays of sun cut through wispy clouds hanging on the horizon. Within moments, the sun would be full up. He pulled in air and cut his eyes toward Trace. "Better ride into town."

Trace wagged his head, his shoulder-length hair sweeping his collar. He studied the horizon, returned his gaze to James. "What say we have some grub, then go in, keep a low profile? Too early in the morning to meet up with that mayor."

* * *

Riding straight down Main Street, out in the open for all to see, was not an option. A quarter mile

from town, James and Trace tied their horses in a thicket of trees, and walked in. Side streets offered limited protection, but even so, James cringed every time somebody shouted. Which was often.

They walked two streets north of Main and, from the look of things, Chinamen had erected canvas tents and one wooden building. Smoke twirled out from the back of most shanties. Laundries, James guessed. He and Trace walked the street peering into various tents. Sure enough, in one, a small man in Chinese clothing, hair pulled back into a long pigtail, stared back, a dirty shirt in hand, piles of laundry behind him.

"Any reason they'd be here?" James knew the answer.

"Luke likes to be clean, but I'm thinking not today." Trace shook his head. "We're both thinking where he's liable to be at. And I'm not wanting to walk inside and ask."

"Me neither. Wouldn't tell us, anyway." James peered down the street. Two more shanties and nothing. End of town. He pried off his hat and used it as a fan. The heat from all the fires, bubbling pots of water and fetid odors of dirty clothes at the Chinese laundries, added to the anvil pressing on James' chest. Here they'd made it clear across the desert, a thousand miles from home, pushing all those cows... and now this.

Where the hell were his brothers? Something was wrong. Absolutely wrong.

Trace turned in a half circle and wagged his head. "They're not here. We're wasting time looking." He pulled in air, pointed. "I'll head over to the sheriff's. See if he's heard anything."

"That's a dumb idea." James reset his hat and frowned. "That mayor sure as hell went crying to the sheriff yesterday. Probably has an arrest warrant out on both of us." He shielded his eyes from mid-morning sun. Band music, mostly trumpets, started up a few blocks away. "Let's keep looking."

Every house they passed, every store they dared enter held no clues. Another half hour of searching, Trace stopped on Main Street's boardwalk and wiped a bead of sweat off his temple. "Tired of this. I'm talking to the sheriff."

"But—"

"If I tell him I'm a lawman, too, show him my badge from Mesilla, he'll be reasonable." Trace fished around in his vest pocket and pulled out his badge, pinned it to his shirt. "See? It'll be fine."

James sighed, wanted to argue, but there would be no more discussing, no dissuading, no changing his brother's mind. Locked up tight. He raised both hands, palm up. "Still think it's a dumb, no... *really* dumb idea."

"You check the saloons," Trace said. "And the bawdy houses."

James raised his eyebrows. "Can't imagine Andy being in one of those."

Trace used two fingers to rub his chin and put a light hand on James' shoulder. "Thought the same thing about you 'til Mexico."

"Never can tell about brothers." Trace stared down the street. "They're full of surprises."

Not completely sure who his brother was referring to, but he bet it had to with a woman in Mexico who... James focused his attention elsewhere and backed away from his brother's reach. "Meet you down at the saloon across from the jail. The Red Garter, I think." He pointed. "And stay away from that mayor."

"That's the plan." A grin pushed up one side of Trace's face. "See you there. I'll let you

buy me a beer." He pushed through a crowd lining up for a horserace down Main, waved over his shoulder as he disappeared into the mob.

CHAPTER SEVENTY-ONE

James hadn't seen this many people in a long time. Elbowed, pushed, and stumbled into, he looked forward to being out in the desert again—alone. The cheering people, squealing kids, even the raucous band, set him on edge. Too many people. Too loud. Even so, he scrutinized every face, hoping to recognize one or two. None looked familiar. Panic crowding in, he pushed aside alarm.

An hour dragged by while he ducked into each and every mercantile, dry goods, saloon, and brothel on Main. He asked every bartender and patron along the way. Nobody remembered seeing them.

By the time he paused in front of the Red Garter Saloon, his legs groaned and complained, too heavy to take another step. A long, low sigh, James stared down at his feet. Could he simply give up? Never. He edged into the saloon, scanned the patrons. No Trace. Or Andy or Luke. He took a chair at a table near the front and leaned back. He sipped his beer then downed the rest in a few gulps. The second glass he enjoyed more than the first.

Sipping slower, at last he was able to appreciate the taste. Not bad. And, the liquid was almost cold.

This close to the front, he was afforded a view of each man who stepped through the doors. So far, every shape, size, temperament and clothing style strolled in, but no one resembled any of his brothers.

Even with all the commotion outside and the number of men shoving aside those swinging doors, James jumped at a voice in his ear.

"Mister Colton? I'm the marshal from Utah Territory. I'm afraid I have bad news about your brothers."

Hard fingers of fear clutched James' throat. He stared at the man leaning toward him, inches away. The man's badge reflected the outside light. James stammered. "They all right?"

The lawman shook his head. "You need to come. One of 'em's hurt bad, the others... Well, they're askin' for you." He pointed outside. "Follow me. I'll lead you right to 'em."

James jumped to his feet, his chair falling over behind him. He bolted for the door, the marshal following on his heels. On the boardwalk, James stopped and pointed across the street. "Sheriff?" He took a step.

A jerk on his arm stopped him.

"Empty. Just came from there. Empty. Sheriff's out doin' whatever he does. You know, the Fourth and all?" The marshal tugged James' arm in the opposite direction. "This way's fastest."

Bumping into people as he trotted down the street, James ignored the dirty looks and mumbled curses tossed his way. With every step, his jaw clenched harder, his muscles tightened, his heart thudded.

They wound down the street, through an alley, past two more streets, crossed behind Chinatown into the hills. Pine trees, flanked by junipers, crowded together forming a brushy wall. A few yards into the thicket, James froze.

In a small clearing sat Andy, Luke, and Trace, all ratcheted against trees, hands behind them, mouths gagged with bandanas. Ropes wrapped around their outstretched legs at the ankles. Three wide pairs of eyes stared back at James.

A stocky man, one James thought looked vaguely familiar, stood behind his brothers, gun in hand.

Words, questions, disbelief flew around James' head. None came out clear. "What?" He

turned to the badge. "What's going on?"

The marshal pointed a gun at James' chest, its barrel pressing hard against his shirt "Your gun. Nice and easy."

Confused, James hesitated.

Whack! The marshal backhanded James, the gun and fist crashing into his mouth. James staggered back, spun, managing somehow to stay upright. He rubbed the welt on his cheek. Pulling James' gun out of the holster, the lawman shoved it into his own waistband.

The marshal gripped James' arm—tight. His own gun in hand, he waved it toward the

brothers. "We'll have us a little celebration all our own. A celebration of the end." He turned the gun on James. "*Your* end."

Heart pounding so hard he fought to hear words, James held up his hands. "What're you talking about?" Something about the marshal was familiar. The eyes, the mouth, the beard. "I'm thinking we've met."

A long, low rumble welled from the man's chest. He rubbed his beard. "We met." He nodded to his deputy. "Train your shooter on the youngest there. He's next."

"What?" James fought to understand.

"On your knees, James Colton." The marshal once again shoved the gun barrel into James' chest. "Hands behind your head."

James eased to the ground, his hands cradling the back of his neck. A peek at his brothers. Trace, red welt bulging on his cheek, squirmed against the bindings. Luke glanced side to side. Andy squeezed his swollen eyes shut. With the deputy's gun pointed at Andy's head, one twitch of the man's finger and his brother would die. Andy sat deathly still, black eyes and new bruises glowing against pale skin.

The marshal circled James, keeping the gun pressed against his head. "Remember

Nogales?"

How could he forget?

"That special *mescal*?" The marshal snickered.

The man at the bar. And his partner. These were no lawmen from Utah. These were the men who plied them with bad tequila.

James met the black-eyed gaze of the man holding the gun. "I remember." His hands shook and his stomach roiled. "What kind of sick game're you playing?" He cocked his head sideways toward his brothers. "Tying them up. Holding a gun on me. What d'you want?"

"Already told you." The marshal squinted at James. "You. I wanted you, and now I have

you." He tipped his hat. "Whid Amos MacGilvray. And that there's Pickett."

"Why?"

"Been following you since before you left Mesilla," Whid said. "Hell, I'm the one put a

burr under your saddle way back when." He turned to

Pickett. "If that horse had done her job, this here fella'd be long dead. Right?"

Pickett nodded.

"I put poison in that waterin' hole, too. Almost killed ol' Trace over there." Whid wagged his weapon at Trace then trained it on James. "And," he pointed to his own chest. "Even bought you that fallen angel in Nogales what gave you a tumble. Spent five whole pesos on her." He chuckled. "By the way, I'll tell Morningstar all about your little fling. Serafina spilled every tiny detail. Said you..."

"Shut up!" Still on his knees, James glared up at Whid.

"Your fine little wife'll be mighty interested, seein' as how you bedded—"

"You sonuvabitch!"

"... a plain, Mexican whore." Whid's snicker grew into a laugh. "Her legs wrapped 'round you, you—"

"Shut the hell up!" James scrambled to his feet and lunged. "We didn't do anything!"

Fisted hand gripping the gun, Whid swung.

Whack! James flew sideways, hit the dirt, his face throbbing. He scrambled back up to his knees.

Whid looked down at James, behind him at the brothers. "There's more. Lots more.

I shot that Indian, put an arrow in your brother's shoulder." He pointed his finger like an

arrow toward Luke. "First time I shot a bow and arrow. Right fine aimin', I'm thinkin'."

Whid blurred. James gritted his teeth. "You're a murderer. A low-down stinkin' murderer. You killed Perchman. You—"

"Ah!" Whid waved the gun in James' face. "It wasn't

us what killed Perchman. Those Indians did *that*. All on their own." He grinned at Pickett who nodded back.

James clenched his fists. "Sonuvabitch!"

"And don't forget the anthrax scare you gave this entire town." Whid snickered. "Why,

James Colton, you and your brothers near sold an entire herd of diseased animals to this quiet,

unsuspectin' little town. Couldn't let that happen now, could I?"

"Sonuvabitch!" James glanced at his brothers. Trace gave a reassuring nod.

Whid waved his gun again toward the brothers. "But what I'm most proud of, besides this... this... little family reunion... is gettin' Andy's army records set straight." His words turned sympathetic. "Why it's such a shame, a pity really, a family with a fine name such as yourselves, has a army deserter among the members. You all deserve so much better than him."

He glanced over at his partner. "Don't they Pickett?"

"Sure do. A real tragedy."

"Tragedy?" Whid sneered. "Hell, Pickett, your vocabulary's improvin'. You sound almost smart."

James knew to keep his tongue, but with his head throbbing, he couldn't contain anything. "Why us? Why're you harassing us? We didn't do anything to you!"

Whid grabbed James' arm, tugging him to his feet. He moved in close, his words turning deadly. "Like hell you didn't. You stole Morningstar."

Garlicky stale beer breath in James' face made his eyes water. What the hell was this madman talking about? What did Morningstar have to do with him?

Before James could ask another question, Whid snarled. "I was supposed to marry her.

Me. Whid. Not *you*. You... sniveling, pathetic excuse for a human. Look at your scars. Hell, you turn my stomach lookin' at you. And what does Morningstar see? How can you let her be so repulsed every day? Probably takes one look at you and wants to throw up. You ain't no *man*. You're a monster."

How could he voice all the things James had already considered? All his insecurities? Who *was* this man?

Whid lowered his voice. "She was supposed to marry me back in Tucson. We courted for months. But I ended up arrested, sent to prison. By you! 'Member that little tussle in a saloon? That fella got killed and you... you, stinkin', lousy James Colton... testified against me!"

That's where he'd seen him. Now he had a beard. James pulled old memories.

Whid continued his rant. "While she was pinin' away for me, you come in and took her away. Snatched her up like a stolen prize watermelon." Gun in one hand, he gripped James' vest front with the other, squeezing until his knuckles turned white. "After today, she ain't married to you no more, James Colton. After today, when you're dead, I'm ridin' back and make that poor widow woman mine. Yessiree, she'll love me this time. And if she don't, I'll..."

"Touch her and I'll kill you!"

Whid moved within inches of James' ear. "I'll show her how a *real* man makes love. She'll wonder what she ever saw in you."

"Sonuvabitch!" James knocked the gun out of Whid's hand. It flew into the dirt near Luke's feet. "She could never love you! Never!"

A fist to his stomach doubled James over. He came up with a roundhouse to Whid's jaw. The rattle of teeth knocking together only fueled his fury.

"You all right, Whid?" Pickett's voice came out of a fog.

"Andy! Shoot Andy!" Whid grabbed James' throat.

"No!" James kicked Whid's shin hard enough he lost his balance. Buckling, Whid crashed into James taking both men to the ground. They somersaulted toward the brothers. Fists

pummeled James' face, his shoulders, stomach.

Body on fire, James rolled out of Whid's grip. James turned his shadowy vision on the gun. One, two yards, he could reach it. He scrambled to his feet, diving toward the weapon. Whid's huffing pounded James' ears. Right behind him. Close.

James threw himself on the gun, the weapon digging into his chest, rolled over onto his

back, cocked and aimed up. He pulled the trigger.

Bang!

Whid staggered backward, clutching his stomach. He crumpled to the ground, blood

spreading across his shirt. His entire body shook.

James scrambled onto his knees and crawled to Whid, hoisting him up by his shirt. "Don't die yet, you sonuvabitch. Tell the sheriff you lied. You *lied.*" James shook him hard. "All of it. Tell him... the desertion, the anthrax... you lied!"

Whid narrowed his eyes and wheezed. "See *you* in Hell."

CHAPTER SEVENTY-TWO

"What the hell were you thinking?" James gripped the iron bars, part of him glad he couldn't reach Pickett cowering in the cell's corner. No matter how far he stretched his arm, the other part wished he could reach far enough to squeeze the man's thick neck. "Why didn't you stop him? What the hell?" He jerked his arm out of the cell. "How can you ride with a man like that? What were you thinking?"

All five men crowded in front of the cell. James stood shoulder to shoulder with Trace on his right, Cooper, Luke, and Andy on his left. James shook his pointed finger. "Why?"

"I always told Whid I couldn't shoot nobody." Pickett eased forward, still out of arm's reach and shrugged. "And I sure wasn't shootin' Andy."

"Like hell you weren't!" Trace moved in closer, his fists opening and closing. "You even cocked the gun."

James jabbed his pointed finger at Pickett. "You lyin' piece of—"

"But you would let him shoot Mister Colton, isn't that right?" Sheriff Cooper frowned at Pickett.

"Didn't want him to. Told him, lots of times." Pickett gazed down at his feet, as if those new boots would bring him the peace of mind he sought. "But he don't listen to me."

Cooper turned to James. "Shouldn't have left him alone with your brothers. Didn't realize he was all horns and rattle. He took them when I was out." He glanced left and right down the row of men. "Still don't understand how he managed to parade you all through town and into the woods without bein' seen."

Pickett shrugged. "Hell, Sheriff. That was easy. What with the bands and doin's and all,

nobody paid no attention." He looked down at his boots, then back up. "And with two of 'em

knocked sideways, they staggered like they was drunk. Like most folks."

Luke spit words between clenched teeth. "Your gun in my back didn't alert anybody." He shrugged. "Hell, I even bumped into as many people as I could."

"But nobody said anything." Andy rubbed his left temple.

"Glad I was close by when I heard gunfire." Sheriff Cooper sighed. "Ran fast as I could." He eyed James. "Got there before somebody else got shot. No doubt Marshal Smith, excuse me, *Mister MacGilvray* was guilty. He would've killed you all if Mister Colton hadn't shot first."

Throbbing on James' cheek pounded in his head. He pressed the folded, wet bandana against his face. The coolness didn't help much.

Pickett looked at James. "What Whid did was wrong. Harassin' you, trailin' you. And I told him so."

James pictured his arm threading between the iron bars again, this time reaching Pickett, decking that sonuvabitch with all the energy he had left. Damn, that would feel good. "Why didn't you stop him? Hell, he almost killed us all." He eyed each of his brothers. Andy's new bruises stood out against his too-pale skin. "Trace was sick for days, Andy beaten nearly to death. Luke's shoulder kept him out of the saddle for a week."

Cooper nodded at James and turned his eyes on Pickett. "Mister Colton has a fair enough question, Pickett. Why *didn't* you stop Mister MacGilvray?"

Pickett ran his hand through his straggly brown hair, then draped one strand behind an ear. "I owed him." He looked at the sheriff. "Up in Utah... that's where he put together the idea to be the marshal from... I was on the losin' end of a bar fight. Had five men on top of me poundin' away. Said I took their money, but I didn't."

Flashes of a pounding James had taken in Santa Rita, New Mexico, a few years back

charged through his mind. He'd been on the wrong end of angry fists. They took his poker

winnings and nearly his life. James glanced at Trace who nodded.

Pickett sighed, letting his gaze sail out past the cell bars. "Yeah, I would've died, but Whid, well, he took pity and pulled those fellas off. All by himself. When it was over, and I'd healed up enough, I figured I owed him. Been with him ever since."

That still didn't excuse his or Whid's actions, but with Whid Amos MacGilvray dead,

James knew he'd never have all the answers. But maybe Pickett would know about Morningstar, where she fit into all this. Was that a secret she was keeping from him?

Wanting to find out, but dreading the answer, James asked anyway. "Pickett, Whid says he courted Morningstar. But she's never mentioned him."

Pickett let out a snicker followed with a laugh. "That Whid. All the courtin' was done in his head. He'd come into Doc's office, saw her, since she was the doc's assistant, and decided she was the one. Morningstar never gave him nothing but a smile, like she did with everybody else when they come in." Pickett leaned close and lowered his voice. "Your wife turned him down every time he asked her out, which was all of once. She was real nice to him, that's all. But what made him true mad was her pa tellin' Whid to skedaddle. Her refusal and Doc's threat didn't set well on him."

Should he believe this man? James considered. Why not? He would talk to his father-in-

law about Whid when he visited him in Tucson next week on his way home. Maybe Dr. Martelli

had other details, could fill in the missing parts.

Before James could think any more, the office door squeaked open. He recoiled recognizing the figure bowling his way in. Mayor Samuels. Another man with him had to be his

brother. Sure looked alike.

All turned to stare at the man... the mayor who'd welched on the deal.

Cooper stepped over and shook hands with both men. "Thanks for coming on such short notice. Especially on a holiday." He held out his arm toward James. "James Colton, I don't think you've had a *proper* introduction."

Mayor Samuels stepped over to James, extended a hand.

No way would he take that man's hand. Such a crook.

Instead, James rubbed his bandaged arm. The skin, swollen and raw, split from the whipping yesterday, still throbbed. He glared. "We already met."

Samuels held his gaze on James. "I apologize. To both of you." He looked back at his brother. "Guess I rather over-reacted."

He'd accept the apology but still wouldn't like, nor trust, the mayor. James took the mayor's hand. It was soft, like the man had never gripped anything rougher than money. "Guess you did what you thought was best. But my arm still pains me, though."

Something came up into the mayor's eyes. Real regret or hiding true feelings? James took a step back.

"I'm sorry about that. I had no right to hit you." Samuels hung his head, then looked back up at James. "Tell you what. You see Doc tomorrow, have him take a look, fix you up. Send the bill to me. I'll take care of it." He surveyed the other brothers. "Look like they could use Doc, too. On me."

Throbbing arm and face put James in no mood for pleasantries. "That deal solid as the last one?"

Samuels raised one well-groomed eyebrow. "Guess I deserve that." His straight shoulders sagged. "You have my word... in front of the sheriff."

A piece of James' anger crumbled. Maybe this man wasn't so deadly after all.

Trace jerked his thumb back toward the hills. "What about the herd? You buying those cattle like you promised?"

The other Samuels brother stepped in closer. "Yes, we are." He held out a hand.

"Clemson Samuels, Carter's brother."

James and Trace shook his hand. Luke and Andy shook hands with both Samuels men.

"In fact," Clemson said, "we'll offer you top dollar for your beeves. I have no doubt they're anthrax free."

"Yes sir, they're nice and healthy." Andy stood straighter. "Plenty of solid meat on 'em, too. We didn't run 'em or anything. Purely let 'em mosey."

"Glad to hear it." Mayor Samuels turned to the sheriff. "Thanks for sending your deputy to find us and explain. I appreciate learning it was a misunderstanding."

CHAPTER SEVENTY-THREE

The little valley that until noon had been crammed with cattle now stood empty. All that remained was trampled meadow flowers, grass, and spindly shrubs. If James listened hard, he thought he could still hear cattle bawling as they were herded away.

It'd been a mere hour or so since the last of the ranchers' cowhands had driven off their share, but James grew wistful. Those animals had been part of him for the last three months. His gaze traveled over every small hill, then to Trace standing, chatting with Coozie.

Of all the trailhands, only Coozie was left, reins in hand, ready to take off. The two new men had already found employment at a nearby ranch, helping wrangle cattle toward their new home. Carlos and Juan Tomás had said good-bye half an hour ago. The cousins were headed west to the Pacific, both stating they wanted to "splash in salt water" before riding back to the ranch.

Andy and Luke knelt by the campfire, now nothing but glowing embers. Narrow spirals of smoke snaked from the center. Trace stood with Coozie, both nodding, both pointing in different directions. James smiled. They'd made good friends on this adventure, and the brothers' bond had become tighter than ever imagined. He'd miss the teamwork, friendship, camaraderie associated with a cattle drive. Hell, he'd learned so much about cattle, people, and life in general, he couldn't begin to count.

But, it was time to go home. To Morningstar. Was she yet with child? How could he wait three more weeks to find out? With the money safely tucked in his boots, between the sale of the cattle, the wagon, and spare horses, he had enough to buy Star a bigger, better home. He'd give her everything she wanted.

Reins in hand, James wandered over to join Trace and Coozie in their spirited

conversation. What could possibly hold their attention for so long? They stood near the smoldering campfire, both men still gesturing, pointing east, west, then south.

"You settle it." Trace gripped James' shoulder, the hold tight.

"Fine. Settle what?" He shrugged under the grip.

Coozie and Trace spoke at the same time. "Stagecoach is faster."

"Horses are faster."

James held up a hand, easing out of his brother's grip. Andy, Luke on his heels, joined the group. James frowned at the men. "What's the question?"

Trace dropped his voice as if explaining to a three-year-old for the fifth time. "Coozie says we should ride our horses back to Mesilla. I'm thinking stage would be easier, faster." He spread his arms, palms up. "Not being in the saddle, not worrying about coyotes, rabbits, watering holes, burrs under the saddle." He pointed to

James. "Just sitting there in the coach, sleeping, letting somebody else be in charge."

"But riding a *caballo,* you stop when you want. Camp where you want." Coozie raised one shoulder. "Too, it's *muy* cheaper."

"Hell, Coozie, we got jingle in our pockets now." Luke took a drag on his cigar. "We deserve to go home in style."

"What'd we do with the horses if we take the stage?" Andy glanced behind him at his horse, head down, pulling at grass.

"Sell 'em." James kicked at a rock. "Plenty of ranchers looking to buy." Both ways getting home sounded all right, just as long as they got home. He looked from Trace to Coozie to Luke, his gaze resting on Andy. Black streaks still ran down both cheeks that were now green and ugly yellow. He held his ribs most of the time, didn't complain or say much, but he winced often.

James held up a hand. "Here's what I'm thinking." He waited until four pairs of eyes turned to him. "Let's get a couple rooms at the hotel tonight. Have us a fine steak dinner, a beer or two. Then tomorrow, take the first stage that'll get us closer to Tucson." He cocked his head toward Andy. Someday, he would be all right. James had to believe. "I want my father-in-law to take a look at little brother here. From there, we take the next stage to Mesilla."

James raised one shoulder, expecting everyone to agree. The logic was unquestionable.

Silence spread into fifteen seconds before everyone spoke.

"Stage is too bumpy and dusty."

"My horse runs faster than those stage ponies."

"Sit back and enjoy the ride. Stages are safer than just horses."

"Maybe we should go to the ocean first."

"Nah. I wanna get home."

"What's it cost to take the stage?"

James let the conversations wash over him. They'd figure it out, eventually. Words flew on the late afternoon breeze. He regarded his brothers. Each making his case, voice loud, then soft. Each still healthy and in one piece.

His smile reached into his heart and warmed him.

A LOOK AT: LADY OF THE LAW

Women in the 1870s have little control over their lives and the women of Dry Creek, California, look to Sheriff Maud Overstreet, a thirty-something spinster, as an example of women's progress. Following a disastrous fire that leveled the school, Maud appoints a woman as fire chief.

Inspired, several women step forward to run their own businesses—a bakery, charm school, and newspaper—much to the consternation of the male town councilors.

While searching for the school arsonist, Maud witnesses a shooting which left a man dead, questions the new concept of insurance, and assumes the salesman was the arsonist. She also takes on the role of campaign manager for two of her friends, both vying to be Mayor. Toss in more fires, a wild romance, a rowdy town dance, establishing a school for Chinese girls, and mysterious threatening notes, Sheriff Overstreet faces each new challenge with determination.

She is, after all, a Lady of the Law.

AVAILABLE MARCH 2023

ABOUT THE AUTHOR

Growing up in southern New Mexico, my mind raced with characters from the Old West–gunfighters were my favorite. My novels reflect my fascination–and ties–with that era. As a New Mexico Gunfighter re-enactor, I entertain visitors at Albuquerque's Old Town, allowing them a glimpse into earlier times. My books reflect my passion for rodeo and appreciation of historic wooden bars. Yes, bars–the front and back wooden structures. They are amazing--just like the rodeo performers. I rode bulls a few times and it's not easy. But riding provokes a feeling like no other–adrenaline at its finest. So, come with me on an amazing adventure.

Made in the USA
Las Vegas, NV
21 July 2023

75061465R00225